MICE AND MEN BOX SET 2

SHATTERED THRONE & MENDED CROWN (THE WAR OF ROSES UNIVERSE)

LANA SKY

ACKNOWLEDGMENTS

Thanks so much to everyone who supported this draft along the way, including the many beta readers who provided encouragement! Please keep in mind that this story includes dark, graphic, and explicit content matter that is not suitable for readers under the age of 18—or for readers who are uncomfortable with the following subject matter: age gap relationships, explicit sex, mentions of sexual abuse, and graphic depictions of violence.

SHATTERED THRONE

Shattered Thorne

Shattered Thorne By Lana Sky

Copyright © 2021 by Lana Sky
All rights reserved.

No part of this publication may be reproduced, distributed, or transmitted in any form or by any means, including photocopying, recording, or other electronic or mechanical methods, without the prior written permission of the author.

This is a work of fiction. Names, characters, businesses, places, events and incidents are either the products of the author's imagination or used in a fictitious manner. Any resemblance to actual persons, living or dead, or actual events is purely coincidental.

Cover Design and Interior Formatting by Charity Chimni
Editing by Charity Chimni

EVGENI

I used to fear the dark above all else. Almost every night, I'd wake up screaming, convinced that any variety of monsters lurked within the shadows. To comfort me, my mother repeated the same bit of wisdom—*Stay strong. This fear? It's nothing.*

As she saw it, the real horrors worth battling couldn't be found on earth in physical form. No beast, or criminal, or illness around was more terrifying than what lurked within the human soul.

"The dark," she said, *"is constant. It can be fought against with light. You know what can't be banished so easily? Sin. The things you do, the lies you tell. One day, they will be what you see in the shadows."*

She was right, of course. Monsters can be fought; beasts outrun. Neither foe is comparable to what a man learns to truly fear—himself. His past is a beast of his own making, relentless in its pursuit.

The sad part is for all her wisdom, my mother couldn't even fathom the cruelty of men. The sins that some can easily sow with no remorse. The chilling past that lurks in their wake. She chose to see the good in anyone she met, and that kindness blinded her. So much so that she fell in love with a monster of her very own.

To her dying day, she never regretted any second of that life spent with him. I carried that burden for her, saddled with the weight of my father's sins and her blind devotion. Once, I was naïve to think I could ignore the baggage. Face that beast and say no more.

Now? I can admit that I've never stopped running from it.

I still am.

"I was wrong," a woman's purr intrudes on my inner monologue, and I nearly swerve off the road.

Briar Winthorp. I'd forgotten she was here or maybe my brain feels driven to ignore her. Her presence is a thorn piercing through my otherwise logical thought process. Mischa fucked up and took his frustration out on me. I had every right to leave.

When he decides to listen to reason, I'll go back and make amends.

Allowing us both enough space to process our anger is a fitting courtesy.

But I should have tossed her out of the car ten miles back, Briar Winthorp, one of the three women at the forefront of my mind. Willow Stepanova is the other, followed by a newer name. As of yet, I have no idea just where she fits within this mess regarding Mischa and Vanici, just that she's related somehow.

Safiya Mangenello.

Suffice to say, I'd prefer the company of the latter two than the woman accompanying me now.

"I thought you were boringly predictable," she says dryly. "A man I could trust to always do what he perceived to be 'the right thing' no matter the cost. But now? I see that you are just as stubborn and reckless as any other man. I should have taken my chances with the other lackey you work with."

She sounds genuinely disappointed, and I have to scoff. "So now you drop the coy, mysterious act?"

A damn shame. I prefer her silent and smirking.

She barks out a callous laugh. "Why shouldn't I? Given the way you stormed out of there and the fact that Mischa hasn't joined us, I'm assuming that you reneged on our agreement to have me meet with him. You're of no use to me now."

Her uncanny ability to see to the core of the situation aside, I marvel at the dismissiveness in her tone.

"Is that all people are to you? Useful peons?" If so, I'm not surprised. Given her upbringing, I'm sure that Briar

Winthorp excelled at living up to every last stereotype of a selfish socialite. *Selfish* being foremost.

"I feel it's better to be pragmatic than emotional," she replies with an iciness that I suspect isn't an act. The cold gleam in her eye I spy when I glance in her direction reinforces that suspicion. "Though, I should have guessed that someone who deigns to work for my sister would be of the latter quality. Don't forget that I did my research on you, Evgeni Volkov. A quiet, dutiful man prone to sadistic outbursts of rage." She sounds like a student reciting her notes. Maybe she is. "I assume you and that brute Mischa had a tiff, and you stormed out. I hope it wasn't over little old me—"

"You're wrong," I lie, irritated by the fact that she's not. Beneath those coy expressions and superficiality is a shrewdness I better not underestimate. That doesn't mean I can't use those same traits to my advantage. "For all you know, Mischa wants you dead. I could be on my way to kill you."

The way she sucks in her breath…

It shouldn't trigger a pang through my cock, but it does. I risk taking my eyes from the road to catch the way hers widen in the rearview mirror. Another twinge through my abdomen has me gritting my teeth. Fear does more for her appeal than makeup. In an instant, the cold, bitchy exterior is stripped for a stark, honest mask that almost makes her seem human.

Until she blinks, boldly meeting my gaze over the mirror's surface. "Coming from any other lackey, I might believe that," she admits. "But you? No. You strike me as the noble type too proud to get his hands dirty."

"Oh?" I adjust my grip over the steering wheel, scanning the road ahead. "Then you didn't do nearly enough research on me as you should have."

Her mask falters a second time, and she doesn't recover as quickly. Her mouth betrays her where her words don't. I watch her tongue flit across her lower lip, and I mentally file the reaction for later inspection.

"Where are you taking me?" she demands, overlooking my statement entirely.

I don't respond. I'm too busy trying to figure out the answer for myself. I've left the countryside, heading in the direction of the city. Not toward the hospital, I decide. Another location comes to mind, less frequented than most would ever admit.

Bringing her there could be another miscalculation, but hell, it's not like I can let her go.

And she knows that. A grim understanding dawns across her features, hardening them. She stiffens in her seat, and I don't doubt that she has a weapon or two hidden within that red dress.

"You're angry," she points out, catching me off guard once again. "Tell me why."

"You sound nervous."

"For you," she points out. "I'm not the sort of woman you want to kidnap."

"Is that a reference to your friends in low places?" I ask, though internally, I'm forced to reconcile the possibility that she's not bluffing. Whoever attacked the Stepanovs had the resources to do so. I glance at the rearview mirror again, this time checking the road. A black sedan lurking a few yards back wasn't there before. A tail?

Or, perhaps, her backup.

If so, I just brought her right to the manor's front door.

The tires squeal as I slam on the brakes, swerving toward the side of the road. This section borders the forest just beyond the city limits, and it's pretty much deserted this time of day, at least for another hour.

It's a good thing I've learned to excel under a time limit. Once, my entire life was to the tune of a stopwatch. How fast I could eat. Shit. Kill…

A minute and six seconds via strangulation was my best record. The fastest way to achieve that? Crushing a windpipe with my bare hands. Her throat looks thin enough to break that record.

"What are you doing?" The tremor in her voice feeds the part of me I've long thought dormant. It stirs to life as I wrench open the door on my end and climb out. Three strides bring me around to her end of the van before she can even attempt to lock it. Her hand flies to the door handle, but I have it open before her fingers can even make contact.

I grab her wrist, yanking her out, and I barely manage to miss the knife she swipes at my face. My body reacts on autopilot—I pivot, knocking the weapon from her hand with a ferocity she doesn't expect. Hell, I don't either.

My hand is already around her neck. It's like riding a bike, these instincts. How to move. How to anticipate a human response. How to feed off the fear of another and use it to my advantage.

She doesn't expect the pressure I apply to her windpipe. Subtle. Nowhere near enough to break my record, but I'm not inclined to try.

Yet.

"What are you doing, Evgeni Volkov?" Her tone is almost level enough to disguise her fear, but those eyes can't lie. They widen, and it's like staring into reflective pools. Endless and yet shallow at the same damn time, showing more of myself than the depths they might contain.

But the man I see? He's not the loyal mercenary under the employ of Mischa Stepanov. He's a creature I thought I left behind a decade ago, unpredictable. Ruthless. A monster.

But she's no victim. I tell myself that as I steer her backward, manually hauling her off the road and into the underbrush. She moves woodenly, her eyes on mine. Despite her fear, the fact that she maintains her composure at all betrays a familiarity with violence I don't expect.

"What the hell are you doing?" she demands, her voice an octave higher.

"I think it's my turn to ask questions," I point out, tightening my grip by a fraction. "Who are you working for?"

She doesn't answer.

"Did I forget to mention that I'm asking you nicely? I won't do so for very long." To demonstrate, I slam her against the nearest tree, ignoring the gasp that rips from her throat. It isn't faked. I'm not holding back, but for the time being, I don't give a damn if I do hurt her. My focus is singular, fixated on one goal.

"Tell me, or I'll kill you."

Her lips flit into a shadow of her coy smile. "You won't—"

It's comical how little pressure it actually takes to silence her. A flick of the thumb and a crook of my index finger results in beautiful, instantaneous silence. Just as quickly, I loosen the pressure.

Damn. My heart is pounding. It's been so damn long since I've thought like this.

I refuse to give in now.

"Speak," I demand, my breathing heavy. "I suggest you don't play any more games. The truth. Now. Who are you working for? Why are you here?"

And why do I relish the soft feel of her throat more than the sound of her voice…?

"Alexander," she croaks, prompting me to loosen my grip further. I blink, regaining control over my senses, as she gulps at the air, brushing her fingers across her neck. "*He's* why I'm here."

Her voice contained a suspicious note. Fear? "Your employer."

Her eyes narrow, and it's clearer than ever to track her thought process. To lie or not?

I flex my fingers, and she gulps. "The truth. Now. Who is Alexander?"

"He is my son," she says. "And the man who has him is a big enough threat that I would crawl to Mischa Stepanov for help on my hands and knees. Does *that* answer your question?"

I school my expression to disguise my reaction. A son. It could be a lie. She's presumably in her early thirties, certainly old enough, though she doesn't strike me as the maternal type. She's too guarded, revealing none of the softness Ellen Stepanova possesses.

However, being a selfish cunt doesn't mean she could never birth a child.

"Who are you running from?"

"That doesn't matter," she spits. "You wouldn't be able to track him down even if I gave you his identification card and birth certificate. He is a shadow. On paper, he doesn't exist."

The tremor in her voice catches my notice.

"You're afraid of him." Or so I assume that emotion is what lurks behind her eyes, quickening her breathing. Fear.

"Afraid?" She scoffs at the suggestion, jutting her chin proudly into the air. "You would have the sense to be if you knew what he was capable of. Given your ignorance, I'll ignore your vain attempt to intimidate me."

"A man so powerful, and yet you can't even give me a name?"

"How about Jonathan?" she snipes. "Though that name won't lead you anywhere."

It could be a lie. One name, however, wasn't.

"Alexander," I say, circling back. "Your son. How old is he?"

She looks away, disguising her reaction. "Three," she says.

"This Jonathan… Why did he take him?"

"That's for Mischa to learn," she says coldly. "Not you. Don't forget your role in this, Evgeni Volkov—a mere cog in the wheel."

"Correction. I'm your only chance of getting to Mischa."

She raises an eyebrow. "You're so sure of that? I think I could easily find another lackey and grease his palms."

Her voice radiates more confidence than I'd like. A bluff? If so, I decide to call it out.

"Do that, then," I suggest, turning back to the car. "Don't let me stop you—"

"Wait! Wait…"

Her mask cracks. I can smell the desperation coming off her. See the loathing in her eyes as I turn to face her. She keeps her chin high with defiance, but I can see right through the feigned bravado to the pure terror lurking beneath.

She really is afraid. But why. Or of who?

Parsing her previous answer, it doesn't take much to pinpoint the main suspect.

"Tell me more about this Jonathan."

Her breathing hitches almost imperceptibly, disguised behind a cocky laugh. "He's dangerous, more powerful than you can imagine, and even your Mischa can't counter him so easily."

"So why come here? Is your son's life in danger? You don't seem particularly worried—"

"He won't hurt Ali," she says absently. "As long as he's useful to him."

"Which means that *you* aren't."

She doesn't deny it. If anything, the rage flashing in her eyes reveals that she's well aware of that fact as well.

"How did you meet him? Why take your son if not to use him against you?"

"Ali is special," she says cryptically. "I'm sure if you think really, really hard about it, you might discover why."

I let the barb pass, seeing beyond the insults to what she isn't saying.

"So, this man has your son. Has no need for you, and you're desperate enough to come to Mischa. He wants you dead?"

She smirks. "A lot of people want me 'dead.' Few have the balls or the resources to follow through—"

"But I'm assuming this Jonathan does. You're on the run from him."

"Run is such a very strong word," she retorts. "And if he wanted me dead, I would be."

"Unless you have something he wants. Something you aim to use to curry favor with Mischa."

Her smile widens. "You do catch on quick."

"That I do. You're desperate with a sworn enemy being the first person you run to. Whatever you have, it must be good —but not definitive enough for Mischa to trust it outright, meaning you needed a patsy to vouch for you to get close."

"Don't be a showoff," she scolds, waggling a pale finger. "Cockiness doesn't suit you."

"You know what does suit me? A drink—"

"What?" I sense her on my heels as I return to the road. "You need to go back!"

"I will—" I wrench open the door to the driver's seat and turn to see her lurking by the tree line. "Once you give me a damn good reason to. Something more than a name and a cryptic warning. I want something concrete; otherwise, you can find another fool to manipulate."

I climb in without looking back and start the van. My next destination should be Stepanov manor to make amends with Mischa and see if he knows anything to corroborate the woman's story. If she really has a son, for instance.

The sound of the passenger's side door opening catches me off guard. I turn, genuinely surprised to find her standing there, eyeing the vehicle in disgust.

"Don't look so smug," she warns as she climbs in beside me. "Whether I tell you a damn thing, he won't know the difference. He'll kill you too. Congratulations, Evgeni Volkov. You've just signed your death warrant."

WILLOW

J was ten when I witnessed the ruthless cunning of Donatello Vanici up close. Looking back, I should have known then what I do now—he never loved me. Tragedy didn't change him, either—the man was always a monster.

From the very start, he only saw me as a tool.

"Business" was the reason he gave for summoning my father to his headquarters an hour's drive from the city. Typically, Gino went alone, but that morning he shoved me into the back of our battered station wagon as well.

Little did I know that Donatello himself requested I come along.

"You be on your best fucking behavior," my father warned from over the steering wheel. "You even look at him the wrong way, and I'll beat the shit out of you. Don won't put up with you like I do. Just stay the fuck out of his way."

I fully intended to. Up until that point, I'd only caught a brief glimpse of my father's elusive boss. A man who wore a gray dress shirt and addressed me with a directness so different from the way most adults spoke to me.

Would this second meeting be similar? As our destination appeared on the horizon, a tendril of unease shot through my belly, compounding my dread. It was a fitting day to meet with a monster, in retrospect. A web of clouds obscured the sun, and everything looked an ominous gray, wilting in punishing heat.

The second we left the car, sweat dripped down my neck, soaking through the stuffy dress I'd been forced to wear. Gino had boasted with pride at being able to afford it—purely because of the generosity of his powerful new boss.

I couldn't understand the allure one man could command so easily. *Donatello Vanici.* Gino uttered that name with the reverence usually reserved for a king.

Or a God.

The location of his office seemed anticlimactic in comparison. Just a squat series of buildings strewn across a desolate field, enclosed by an ugly metal fence. The main building featured an equally colorless interior with plain walls and linoleum flooring.

Unimpressed, I'd counted the ceiling tiles above as I followed in Gino's wake. When he entered through a doorway, I thoughtlessly did the same...

And I froze mid-step. A new flavor tinged the air, reminiscent of cigarette smoke, cologne, and musk. Breathing it in, I knew instantly that it was the scent of a new creature, more than just a man.

He was a predator.

I shivered before I even saw him, feeling every hair on the back of my neck stand on end. It was the same way I'd felt on a school trip to the zoo a week prior. *"Don't look the animals in the eye,"* my teacher had warned. *"They may be in enclosures, but you don't want to trigger their natural urge to hunt..."*

As we neared the lion's enclosure that day, I understood exactly what she meant. The animal's glinting eyes tracked my every move. If it truly wanted to pounce, a thin sheet of glass couldn't protect me.

The same instinctive warning haunted me in Donatello's office. *He's different,* it claimed, *a creature best inspected from afar.*

His size was the first detail I noted, swallowing nervously as I did so. Massive, like a wall of muscle, he sat behind a desk almost as tall as I was, staring down the world with a calculating focus. A rich navy, his tailored suit—overall, a much better outfit than our first meeting—enhanced the color of his eyes, a hue so dark, it touched on black.

Beautiful, I remember remarking in awe. It was the first time I realized someone could embody two opposing things at once. Donatello Vanici had beautifully dangerous eyes.

"Glad you could come," he said in crisp Italian. The rough cadence of his voice bolstered my predatory comparison—as nuanced as the most ferocious roar. He didn't utilize Gino's brash method of curses paired with shouting. His authority went beyond swagger.

"It's nice to meet you again, Safiya," he declared next, seeking me out despite my hiding place behind Gino. I froze beneath the scrutiny, more confused than afraid. Most adults treated me as though I were a part of the furniture, equating my silence with stupidity. Usually, I had to wave and pantomime to get any attention.

Not with him. *His* gaze lingered over me, much like that lion's, proving that our first meeting was not a fluke. He was different, more perceptive than anyone I'd ever met.

"Do you know why I invited you here?" he asked.

I shook my head instinctively, but I wasn't his focus.

My father shuffled closer to the desk, his head bowed in deference. "No sir," he said, but it was a tone vastly different from how he spoke to me. Groveling. "I thought it might be take your brat to work day, or something." He choked out a harsh laugh that his employer didn't return.

"Not quite." Donatello folded his hands before him, and I suspect he deliberately let the seconds tick by before stating, "Optics. The Hortega have been like fucking vultures. Apologies for the language—" he cut his eyes toward me, though Gino scoffed.

"The brat's mute. She can't repeat shit, if that's what you're worried about."

At that point in my life, I'd heard every curse word under the sun from him. Still, something inside me had swelled with a strange mixture of awe and alarm at the way Donatello Vanici uttered just one. *Fucking.* In *his* world, curses were lapses in judgment meant to be apologized for. Every word had a purpose to him. A place. A meaning. Conversation was his very own game of chess, played expertly with a skill most took for granted.

"Hortega?" Gino sounded sloppy in comparison, mangling the pronunciation. "You mean the Cartel."

"Yes, the cartel."

Anger was another aspect where this man differed from my norm. In Donatello, rage was a slow-moving storm. He never even had to raise his voice to convey it. His eyes darkened first, much like rain clouds, as his lips flattened into a stern line.

"Their raids have been more targeted than usual," he continued in a voice as sharp as lightning. "They've been attacking nearly every shipment. Almost as if they know exactly when and where they're coming in."

A strange emotion colored his voice. Suspicion? My mother sounded similar when she asked if I'd made a mess, despite being well aware of the answer.

Picking up on the same mood, Gino shifted in place, running a hand down the front of his cheap suit. "You think there's a mole?" His voice sounded even enough, but his fingers shook.

Donatello nodded. "They've been covering their tracks fairly well. However—" He inspected a gold watch on his wrist. "The next shipment comes in tonight. Few men know that, and yet the Hortega have been staked out along the road for days. Whoever their mole is, he's feeding them their info in real time."

"Son of a bitch!" Gino scoffed, clenching his fists. "Do you know who it is?"

"I have my suspicions," Donatello said. His upper lip quirked in a chilling imitation of a smile. "For one, I know the Hortegas have been hitting up the Saleris' properties as well, looking for an opening—" suddenly, his smirk spread into a genuine, chilling smile. "But today? I plan to stop my leak for good."

Gino frowned. "How?"

"The Hortegas and their rat have been looking for an opening. And, you, my friend, just gave them one."

Gino whirled around to follow the line of his gaze.

To me.

My heart stopped; my mind went blank. Words can't describe the fear I felt in that moment. I don't know what I might have done—peed myself? Maybe, if the man who so effortlessly incriminated me didn't meet my gaze the next second. I can't recall exactly what he conveyed. A wink? A nod? A slight tilt of his jaw?

It happened too quickly to pinpoint, and yet I sensed his message instantly—*Trust me.*

Gino, however, sputtered with confusion. "W-What?"

I'd never seen him like that—struck dumb, his face twisted in concentration as he wracked his mind for whatever scheme or lie he might have accidentally revealed. In a way, I pitied him. Almost. It was the same disorienting fear he loved rousing in other people.

His torture, however, lasted the space of a heartbeat before a guttural burst of laughter erupted from his employer. "Relax, Gino," Donatello said, still chuckling. Despite the jolting cadence, it wasn't a happy sound. More crazed than anything else. "You've done me a favor. Do you remember what Giovanni used to say when it came to dealing with sons of bitches like the Hortega?"

Gino shrugged halfheartedly. "I... I don't follow—"

"You play dirty." Donatello flattened his hands against the desk and stood. Any resemblance he had to a zoo lion vanished. He wasn't a caged beast, but a monster on the prowl. "What your enemy perceives as a weakness becomes your weapon. Think of it this way..."

He crossed the room to a window overlooking a lonely expanse of field. From this angle, the grayish daylight illuminated the softness of his features. He appeared regal, like some benevolent king from one of the fantasy books I'd read—but when he spoke, it was with the ruthless cunning of a general at war.

"They see the men come in and out of this complex, and they have no idea when to strike," he mused, glaring at the horizon. Where I only saw gray sky and trees, I imagine he viewed a territory ripe for conquering. "They have no idea what our defenses are, and it's a risk to attack while blind. But if you bring in a child… Suddenly, an opening presents itself—a weakness. If I were the mole, I would run straight to the Hortegas and urge them to hit me now. Good old Donatello would easily fold rather than risk a child being injured on his watch. Juan probably expects that he can pin me down until the shipment arrives and take it without so much as a fight. I plan to use that arrogance to my advantage."

"What do you mean?"

His next smile resembled a snarl, more befitting of the lion than a man. "I mean that if I were a soulless son of a bitch like Juan Hortega, I'd make my move now, even if it risked exposing my mole. There aren't many suspects capable of feeding him that kind of knowledge. If you want to know the truth, it's that I've suspected everyone—" He turned, leveling the full brunt of his gaze toward Gino. "Even you."

I can honestly say it was the only time I ever saw Gino truly afraid. Terrified. Such fear transformed him, shrinking him to nothing despite his bulk.

All he could do was stammer his innocence. "You…you know you can trust me—" he pointed to me as if my mere presence meant something. "I brought my fucking kid here. You know that I wouldn't—"

"I do," Donatello said, and Gino nearly collapsed with relief. "But, it's time for you to earn my trust. If you want to stay in the *famiglia*—my *family*—then prove you're willing to die for it."

"What about the girl? You want to use her as bait or something?"

Donatello's eyes narrowed as if the idea of putting me at risk insulted him. "In a family, everyone shares the risks, even me." He raised his voice. "You can come in, Liv."

On cue, a woman appeared in the doorway, and lovely was the only word I could think of to describe her. She looked delicate amid such an industrial space, her upturned eyes a shade in between green and brown, her sun-kissed skin glowing. Even Gino seemed caught off guard, clearing his throat in respect. The way he deferred to her was shocking in itself, but Donatello's expression was what resonated with me. Despite my sparse experience with love, I knew that *this* had to be the utter epitome of it—this man, his head inclined, his eyes blazing with undeniable passion.

Never had I ever witnessed something more beautiful.

Or terrifying.

"This is my wife, Olivia," he explained, cradling the woman's cheek against his palm. "Only a handful of men know that she's here. If one of them is the mole, they'll squeal that information directly to Hortega. The bastard wouldn't miss the chance to attack if he thought he had me pinned. Olivia will stay with Safiya. They won't be in any real danger," he added, returning his attention to Gino. "By coming here, you've already displayed your loyalty. That makes us family in my book, and I always protect my family."

It was a reckless move in hindsight, using your own wife and a child to draw out an enemy. Looking back, I can admit that I never felt truly afraid, hidden in a back office with Olivia while only God knew what took place. Why?

Thus was the confidence of Donatello Vanici. He said it himself—we were family. For two years, I cherished the safety that came with being *his*.

But I was naïve.

The truth is, Donatello Vanici never loved me.

I was only a tool—and now? I'm his weapon.

"I'm going to bend you to my will, little bird," he swore just days ago. *"I'll erase any identity you've had before me. As long as you're here. You're mine…"*

Though, when all is said and done, I'm the one who agreed to marry him—and if he believes he holds the upper hand, he's wrong.

He may have taught me my first lesson in betrayal, but Mischa instilled his own teachings in me—how to turn vengeance into an art form. The only way to defeat someone like Donatello Vanici is to play by his rules. To view the world as a game with a checkmate being the only goal.

Last night the rules changed. He may have set this war into motion, but I won *that* battle, using the one virtue that he sees as my weakness against him.

My body. My innocence. *His* lust…

Lying beneath him, I held the power for once—he admitted it himself, his voice raspy against my ear. *"You like to exert control over me?"*

Control is a strange way to describe it. What it felt like to have him watch me explore myself in a way I never have—and never before someone else. It should have felt wrong, the exact opposite of control.

Instead…

Flesh transformed beneath his scrutiny, becoming electrified against my touch. Raw. Alive. My throat constricts at the memory, and I have to fight to steady my breathing.

But you enjoyed it, some sinister voice in my head whispers. *You enjoyed every minute of it…*

I shrug aside any shame that threatens to descend. Maybe I had every right to enjoy it. After all, I utilized the same war tactic he himself praised all those years ago—*What your enemy perceives as a weakness becomes your weapon.*

Or, in this case, a double-edged sword. Because, for a second, I glimpsed something more elusive than his hate, and it haunts me. It's easy to despise the caricature of him I've created in my skull. But the real man?

He's a walking contradiction. Laughing menacingly one moment, moaning in agony amid the throes of a nightmare the next. I'm never prepared for the vulnerability he shields behind that mask.

He claims Safiya Mangenello meant nothing to him, but her name is carved into his chest—and yet he won't even tell me why he sold her.

Sold me.

The answer shouldn't matter. *Damn him.*

Crack! I stumble over something, forced to brace a hand against the wall to stay upright. The motion snaps me from my thoughts, and I'm back among the grim reality of this old pink room. *This* is who Donatello Vanici is—a monster who turned my childhood home into a prison.

It shouldn't be possible to hate him any more than I already do—but my body hums with the force of it, as though I could explode.

When I look down and spy the cause of my near fall, though, all thoughts of him vanish.

Objectively, the box lying in the middle of the floor is nothing special. It's stained in places, coated in a layer of dust that betrays how long it must have languished in the corners of this house. The only clue as to what it contains is a mass of colorful fabric peeking beyond the partially closed flaps, and the faint scent of feminine perfume tinging the air.

Olivia's, to be exact, Donatello's wife. Apart from one blue dress—the same one I'm wearing now—I haven't scrounged any more clothing from that small collection.

I can barely bring myself to look at it.

Though, if I truly wanted to twist the knife and beat Donatello at his own game, I'd use anything to get a reaction from him. I'd prance around in Liv's old dresses and dare him to say a damn thing in protest.

But the memories starring her feel different from the others tainted by his betrayal. Sacred. They belong to innocent days when this house was alive with laughter and warmth— a time that seems so distant from the present, it might as well have been a dream.

The current reality is a nightmare. The warmth is gone, replaced by a persistent, bone-numbing chill. My teeth chatter, every cell in my body tense with discomfort.

Without thinking, I stoop and gingerly pry apart the lid of the box. Maybe it's my mind playing tricks, but remnants of heat ghost my skin, emanating from the clothing within. Even the remnants of Olivia feel like an antidote to Donatello's frigid presence. The first item I find is coincidentally a cream sweater, neatly folded. I reach for it, pressing the soft fabric against my cheek.

Liv... I remember her calming voice. Her gentle smile. Her grace, paired with Donatello's brashness, was the epitome of beauty and beast, and I used to admire that contrast.

Years later, having witnessed the aftermath of that affection firsthand, I now know differently. Love is brutal. Mischa's devotion to his family spurred him to kill, and Olivia's death destroyed what remained of Donatello's soul long before he betrayed me. Though could such a man truly love anyone? I picture the way he looked at her that day in his office, and I'm inclined to think so.

Though it could have been an act from the start.

Of course, that cruel inner voice whispers. *Why else would he lie with you in that bed if he loved her so much?*

My cheeks flame, and I hunt for any distraction from the memory. I can't think about last night anymore. Getting dressed is as good a stall tactic as any, but as I withdraw the sweater, a glint of silver catches my eye. The source is too bright to be fabric, cool to the touch, easily fitting in the palm of my hand.

It's a container, square in shape and decorated with engraved vines that sparkle as I hold it up to the light. A jewelry box?

I flick a clasp along the side to open it, only to find a stack of neatly folded papers filling the space. As I stroke the top page, two distinct smells pepper the dust-choked air. The first is lighter, floral? But the second… My nostrils tingle as I inhale it, a deeper, richer scent.

I'd forgotten that he used to smell like this. Like masculine cologne and cigar smoke and the hint of peppermint-scented aftershave. I used to drink in the stench, sitting at his feet while he pored over documents in his study. This handwriting might even be his, but these missives don't look like they correspond to business.

A floorboard creaks from the direction of the hall, and I stiffen, running through the likely suspects. Luciano? The little girl? Donatello?

The latter is the most likely. He'll be chomping at the bit to taunt me, I assume. Throw last night in my face.

Are you so eager to be corrupted, little wife?

I cringe at his imagined voice, shaking my head to clear it. Still crouched, I wait for the door to fly open, revealing him behind it.

Another step breaks the silence. *Thud.*

Another. *Thunk…*

That one was further away. Several more steps confirm my suspicion, and I sigh in relief—whoever the culprit is, they've retreated down the hall.

But I'm not naïve enough to think he won't come back.

Whatever these letters might contain, examining them within Donatello's orbit feels too dangerous. The air is too thick in here. Too heavy.

I find my gaze drawn to the window, feeling reckless enough to jump from it. Anything just to breathe without inhaling him too.

Instead, I tuck the box beneath the bed frame, removing the topmost letter. Then I approach the door, pressing my ear to the wood before easing it open. Luckily, the hall is empty, and I slip out before the lurker returns.

It's too early for the dawn light to have penetrated the house's interior. Everything is quiet, bathed in shadow, like some twisted version of purgatory.

Once I reach the first floor, the itching need to be outdoors feels even stronger—but I know better than to risk leaving through the front door. Turning on my heel, I navigate the hallway to the kitchen. Here, a battered screen door bars the access to the yard, easily unlocked.

I ease it open, my lungs swelling with the crisp morning air. Despite my aching muscles and bare feet, I sense I could still run if I wanted. Take off through the close-set trees and never look back.

I only let the fantasy dwell for a minute before turning my attention to the letter.

In the end, I don't go far, staying on the porch. My toes flex against the peeling wood as I scan the lonely yard beyond it.

This section of the house is just as aged as the rest, the lawn overgrown and empty. A pale bit of sunlight pierces the cloud cover, and the fresh air displaces some of the tense atmosphere. Leaning against the siding, I lift the letter, straining to read in the overcast light.

You have no idea how much I love you, do you? The author wrote, their passion evident in every stroke of ink. My cheeks heat, sensing the intimacy before I even read on. *How much I crave being inside you, every goddamn minute of the day. It's the only time I ever feel peace...*

I rip my gaze up to the sky, feeling my heart hammer against my ribcage.

He wrote this to Olivia. His unique touch is evident from the strokes of ink to the deliberate way it was folded. The care recalls a thoughtfulness so different from the man he is now. A man who prides himself in always maintaining his control. Who denies his own lust merely to prove a point.

He didn't always. He used to confess his desire on paper for anyone to read...

Because he loved her, that cruel inner voice insists. *Just like he loved the idea of sweet, little Safiya—not you. Never you...*

"She's not in the room." The present-day Donatello's voice booms like thunder, startling a flock of birds from a nearby tree. "Where the hell is she?"

I whip around, expecting him to barge through the back door, but the kitchen is empty. The next second, a series of distant thuds betray his location—storming through the upstairs—and he isn't alone. A familiar voice rings out, the tone soothing. *Fabio?*

That's right. We're to meet with Mischa to discuss our sham of a marriage today. On its face, the idea would seem comical if it weren't so tragic. Or strategic. When all is said and done, Donatello stands to gain more than revenge. Namely, leverage and power—two tools I've come to find that all men cherish.

On the other hand, I'll have lost the most.

"Where the hell did she go?" He sounds closer, downstairs now, probably in the hall right beyond the kitchen. "Get a van ready. She fucking ran."

His murderous inflection sends a thrill through me. *She ran.* Just what might he do to this figurative Willow who dared to escape him? I almost wish that I had run. That I was out racing through the woods like hell, heading back to my family.

Anywhere but here.

This house holds only misery and confrontation. If I stay, I'll have to face more than our "engagement." I'll have to see him for the first time since last night, but I'm nowhere near prepared for that moment.

Will he ignore it?

Pretend it never happened?

Or will he give Fabio and everyone within earshot a verbal play-by-play…

"I knew this was a stupid fucking plan," Donatello continues to gripe, sounding clearer than ever. I swallow hard. If I had to guess, he's only paces away. "And *you* thought we should reason with her."

He says it with so much derision. *Reason.* How dare anyone try. I'm merely an avatar for his hate, or lust, incapable of any rational thought. My primary purpose in life is to thwart him.

Not this time. I won't let him play the victim.

Cautiously, I reenter the kitchen and find it empty, but my hunch wasn't wrong. He is close. Commotion comes from the main hall, and I creep there to find Donatello throwing open the front door as if he plans on running out after me, his eyes blazing.

For a heartbeat, the rest of the world mutes as I take in the sight of him.

He changed into a black suit, but it hangs loosely on his bulky frame, the collar unbuttoned, shirt untucked. In contrast, a figure standing by the steps cuts a stunning silhouette in a crisp navy suit. Fabio. The only item distracting from his ensemble is a cream-colored shopping bag hanging off his left wrist.

"I suggest we organize a more thorough search," he says. "I'm sure she couldn't have gone far. Have you looked everywhere—" he turns his head, spotting me. "Speak of the devil. She's right here."

"What?" Donatello whips around, and the force of his attention hits like a physical blow.

Somehow, facing him in the harsh light of day is worlds apart from the creature he can seem in the dark. There's no vulnerability. No shadows to hide the worry lines etched around his mouth or dampen the intensity of his eyes. Narrowed to slits, they rake over me with none of the lingering interest he displayed just hours ago.

"Where the hell were you?" His voice penetrates my skin, infecting the muscle underneath. I jump instinctively, and yet I have enough sense of mind to tuck the letter behind my back, out of his view. Or so I think. His head cocks, following the movement of my arm. "What do you—"

"That doesn't matter!" Beaming, Fabio advances down the hall, blocking me from view. Before I can react, he slips an arm around my shoulders, angling my body toward him. I stiffen, but he's too busy steering me past Donatello to notice my discomfort. "What matters is she's safe and sound. Though, apparently you weren't the only one who forgot to get dressed this morning—" He casts my clothing a wary glance. I'm still wearing the dress I wore last night. Olivia's, to be exact.

"Luckily, the meeting with Mischa has been canceled," Fabio adds.

He sounds cheerful almost—nowhere near as panicked as he should be. I am. My brain jumps to the most likely reason why Mischa would refuse to meet—because he's planning something far more thrilling than afternoon tea.

"We've rescheduled for tomorrow," Fabio explains, picking up on my unease. "Though, I did manage a different arrangement for Willow in particular, at the hospital later this afternoon—"

"You didn't." Donatello's tone is so cold I half-expect ice to form over my skin.

I don't understand why he's so hostile at first. Then I remember—he's not the only one with family at the hospital.

"Of course, I did," Fabio says, an eyebrow raised. "What better way to test both yours and Mischa's commitment to this bogus engagement?" To me, he flashes the faintest hint of a smile. "Your mother is awake, my dear. Would you like to see her?"

A wave of emotions washes over me, countered only by the glare Donatello shoots our way. But even he can't detract from a rare bit of good news. Ellen is awake. Though, who knows what Mischa has told her...

"Willow?"

Meeting Fabio's gaze, I nod.

"Good. Then it's settled," he says, guiding me to the stairs. I get the sense that he's positioning himself strategically behind me as a barrier against anyone who might approach from below. "I'll make all of the arrangements," Fabio says, raising his voice. "It will have to be a short visit, and contingent on your mother's condition, of course, but it will give you at least some time."

"And plenty of time for Mischa to mount an attack while she's gone," Donatello snaps.

His steps resonate through the floor, and I risk looking over my shoulder to find him mounting the bottom rung of the staircase. I make the mistake of meeting his gaze—and the house, Fabio, and the entire world vanish.

If I hoped that he wouldn't remember last night, one look at his eyes proves the opposite. He has.

"Did you think I wouldn't notice?" he demands now, in a tone reminiscent of crackling hellfire. "In all of your scheduling, you left out me visiting Vincenzo."

Fabio. He's talking to Fabio—a fact that doesn't sink in until the other man turns to face him. "Don... I don't think that would be a good idea."

"Bullshit."

"No—" Fabio nearly trips while mounting the next step. "He's still recovering from surgery, but as soon as there is a marked improvement in his situation, I'll escort you there myself."

Donatello's eyes flit in my direction, and I feel a sudden urge to shield myself in any way I can. With my hands. By running. Hiding. In his gaze, every inch of myself is on display. Nothing is hidden.

Nothing.

"Did you draw up the papers?" he asks, still speaking to Fabio. "Even if Mischa gets a reprieve today, I don't think we should allow him to forget the terms. *No one* should forget them. I want every fucking detail in writing."

"And you'll get that," Fabio insists. "In fact, wait for me in your office, and we can go over the terms one on one."

"Terms," Donatello hisses, his nostrils flaring. "I think it's about time I devise a few of my own."

He storms off, barreling in the direction of his study. I sense that the last part of his statement was directed solely at me.

"Willow?" Fabio taps my shoulder. "Are you alright?"

I'm shivering. Forcing a nod, I mount the rest of the stairs on trembling legs. That pink room is a haven I practically race for, fumbling to get the door open.

"I brought you some clothes," Fabio says, following in my wake. "It's not much, but it should last you for a few days. At least until we can arrange a shopping trip or have your things brought over from Stepanov Manor…"

I look over my shoulder as he falls silent, and shame heats my cheeks—the mess I've made of Olivia's belongings stands out in stark contrast to the overall barren room.

I race to grab the clothing I'd left in piles on the floor, returning them as neatly as I can.

Fabio enters the room after me. "Jesus, Mary and Joseph," he croaks. The pain in his voice shouldn't catch me so off guard, but I fumble with the silver box of letters, dropping it. He knew Olivia, from what I remember. She was his sister.

Of course, seeing her things would affect him.

"I… They shouldn't have brought you all this—" he clears his throat, gesturing helplessly. Then he reaches for the nearest articles of clothing, shoving them into the box. When he sees the silver container, he pales. "Why the hell would he—"

He snatches it, and I can tell from his horrified expression that he knows exactly what it contains. For the longest time, he eyes the silver lid, his hand shaking. Then he starts to tuck it into the pocket of his suit.

I don't know what comes over me. I grab for it.

Those letters are all I have of the past. Of Donatello.

"I think I should take care of these," Fabio says softly. "It's just an old trinket—"

"Fabio?" Donatello calls from what sounds like the base of the stairs. "What the hell is taking so long?"

"N-Nothing!" Fabio starts toward the door, trying to shove the box into his pocket. He winds up dropping it instead, though I don't think he notices, already lurching into the hall.

Before leaving the room entirely, he hesitates, his gaze flitting in my direction. "He shouldn't use her… He has no right to torture you like that. No right."

Torture me. The remnants of Olivia take on a newer significance—until I remember that Donatello wasn't the one to bring me these items. Fabio himself saw me wear one of her dresses—the same one I'm still wearing now—but for whatever reason, this strikes him differently. He's angry, his cheeks scarlet, his hazel eyes ablaze as he inspects me one final time. With a sigh, he retreats, his voice reaching back to me, "When you're ready, we can set out."

I stare after him, more unnerved than I think I should be. I know he disagrees with Donatello's insistence we stay here, but the thought of his sister's memory being used as a cudgel enrages him more. It makes sense. No one would stand for that.

But it was the way he looked at her belongings, the letters in particular. Like whatever memories they conjured weren't merely painful…

They scared him.

The reason why might lurk in the very paper still clutched in my grasp, but I release it as if burned. Maybe it's far better to avoid learning the secrets that lurk within Donatello Vanici.

Whatever happened last night was merely another round in this twisted game. A test. A new attempt for him to manipulate me and reinforce whatever hold he thinks he has.

Dwelling on it is precisely what he wants me to do.

So instead, I turn my attention to the one topic he doesn't want me to focus on—my family. Hope flutters in my chest at the thought of seeing Ellen and Eli again. Then I remember the circumstances I've brought upon them, and the excitement turns to dread.

Everything has been ruined because of me.

Because of Donatello Vanici.

DON

*H*er smell lingers in my nose hours later, potent enough to taste. *Roses*—though I know for a fact she hasn't come near the damn flower. She smelled like sweat, too, and sweet... A scent my brain avoids identifying though the pulse shooting through my cock has no trouble —arousal.

Irrefutable evidence that last night wasn't a dream.

As if I could ever imagine a scene so twisted. So fucking wrong. So goddamn intoxicating I can't get it out of my head. Remnants of her heat sear my skin even now. I've never felt a body like hers. Soft enough to crush in places. Firm enough to grip in others...

She's a walking contradiction, playing the role of a stoic *mafiya* princess one minute. Transforming into a writhing little hellcat the next. Even inside my own skull, it sounds insane to spell out exactly what she did.

The little minx climbed into my bed and slid those delicate

fingers of hers into a place no heiress should want to be defiled by a monster.

I grit my teeth at the mental image, catching my bottom lip between them. The harder I bite, the sharper those images become. I taste copper by the time I finally relent to the mental assault. Fabio be damned, I should have dragged her here by her hair and demanded an explanation.

Waking up to find her gone was a godsend, prolonging the moment I have to face the aftermath. Hell, I wish she had escaped—it would be easier to write off last night as nothing more than a nightmare.

Some sick part of my soul craves to rewrite the narrative, anyway. I'm the aggressor in this new version. I pinned her down and forced her to perform for me. I held all the cards.

Not her.

I might have believed that until she crept from the shadows this morning—still wearing that blue fucking dress— playing the innocent victim at my expense once again. I could almost hear her laughing; she won that round.

She got my attention. What was her aim? To taunt me? Toy with my head? Test how much I really meant my vow to never fuck her?

Stubborn as always, she showed me what I'd be missing in excruciating detail.

If only she resembled Gino—may the bastard rot in hell, right alongside Antonio Salvatore. It would be easier to hate her, then. As pathetic as it is to admit, if she had his eyes, I could look at her and see him staring back.

It would be even better if she had Stepanova branded across her fucking forehead. Though, hell, I could always do it for her. Get a knife and carve that name into her pretty flesh, letter by letter. My fingers twitch against my desk, and I picture the dagger I left somewhere upstairs. *Her* blade, the perfect tool to do it with. A bloody brand would ensure there is no forgetting who or what she is.

A toy.

A distraction.

An albatross around my fucking neck.

Instead of branding her, I could always just kill her. Wrap my hands around that pretty throat and squeeze. Mischa no doubt has a trust set aside in her name. As her husband, I could stand to collect it all.

Though what use would I have for a fucking fortune? The only reasonable answer is a name, just one. Vincenzo. At the end of the day, marrying her is a distraction. My only goal is to give my heir the life he deserves.

No matter the cost.

I lean back into the leather seat as my attention rightfully turns to him. *Vinny.* As I see it, two factors dictate his future—money, and security. The second should be the easiest to accomplish. Once I marry Willow, I'll propose an out to Mischa—a divorce in exchange for a promise. The fucker will have no choice but to uphold his word. I play my cards right, and Vincenzo will have his balls in a vice for the rest of his life.

As for the money…

Killing the girl could garner him more than enough, but it's too risky. There's another way, though. Another time, I might have shied away from it, but not anymore.

I already owe Vincenzo my life. Why not let him profit from it?

"I wouldn't be so concerned about the Stepanovs as I would be about yourself," Fabio scolds from the doorway of my office. He's smiling, but it's strained at the edges. I recognize the look.

"Am I in for a scolding?" I raise an eyebrow. "Or is that your idea of a *threat*, Fab?"

"You know what? I would threaten you to take care of yourself if I thought you'd listen. You look like hell, Don."

I use his change of subject to ignore the suspicion eating away at the back of my skull. He was upstairs for a few minutes, at least. With *her*. Scheming?

I wouldn't put it past him in his quest for peace and harmony.

"We can't all spend our days shopping," I counter, noticing the bag he had before is gone.

"Even the finest tailor can't help you if you don't brush your hair and shave, at least." Laughing, he enters the room, but I never trust Fab's brand of charm. He's better than anyone at concealing his true feelings. You have to hunt for the truth in what he doesn't say.

"I've been sober for too damn long," I counter, playing along. "We could always move your little rendezvous to the bar?"

"And while I'm glad that you've laid off the drink," he adds as if I never spoke, "there is the matter of withdrawal…"

And there it is, the truth he's been dancing around—he's worried. Perhaps for a good reason. A dull ache throbs behind my temples despite my best attempts to ignore it. Still, I shrug.

"I'll try to find time to check into a rehab in between this insane wedding stunt and making sure that Mischa doesn't try to finish off Vincenzo. Or that his daughter doesn't lead his personal army to our door—"

"Rehab would be a good start after everything you've been through," Fabio interjects, suddenly serious. "For now, we can start with this—" he withdraws a small brown vial from his pocket, rattling the contents within.

Given its size, I take a wild guess. "Pills? I thought drugs weren't your thing."

"*Unprescribed* pharmaceuticals are not." He crosses to the desk setting the vial within my reach. "These, however, were suggested by a doctor whose opinion I trust. Librium. It's a taper, just for a few days to keep you from seizing on your path to sobriety. You're a tough son of a bitch, but no one can quit cold turkey. I wasn't kidding before—you look like utter hell."

"I think I'm more of an expert on that dominion than you," I say, picturing the fiery abyss awaiting the end of this long, fucking life.

If all goes to plan, I'll be there soon enough. What's a seizure from withdrawal compared to a bullet to the brain?

"Don't be a masochist," Fabio snaps, slamming his hand against the desk. "You've got that look about you. I don't like it. Take a damn pill."

I snatch the vial and tap out a green capsule onto my palm. "Happy?"

"Don't thank me yet," he warns. "I specifically told him to put you on the smallest dose possible. You won't be getting high on my watch."

"Thanks, Mama Fab." I salute him before choking down the capsule.

"Good. Now we can discuss the real reason why I'm here, apart from mothering you."

I sigh at his tone. Dramatics aside, I'm not in the mood. My head is throbbing like a motherfucker, my tongue buzzing. I could chalk the discomfort up to withdrawal, but the true cause is deeper than that. I still taste her. Feel her. Smell her.

She's the only substance infecting my blood, turning my own body against me.

I can't remember the last time I've been this hard for this long. Hell, I should just get myself off, if only to smother the lust. Drive her out of my skull some way.

Because I'll never experience that body in person. Those slender thighs and whatever lurks between them will forever remain a mystery—because I won't fuck her.

I staked our engagement on it.

"Don?"

I look over to find Fabio staring, his smile replaced by a frown.

"You going to gape at me all day or get to the point?" I snap.

He tugs on his collar. "To get the trivial matters out of the way first, I don't want you staying here. Not in this—" he glances around with a look of disgust. "Goddamn house."

I croak out a laugh, dragging a hand through my hair. Part of my reflection is visible in the metal base of a nearby lamp, proving Fabio's initial assessment accurate; I look like shit. "If you're cursing, it must be serious."

"You're damn right I am. It isn't good for you. And Willow? What do you think must be going through her mind to be back here?"

Oh, but I know exactly what's on "Willow's" mind, and it has nothing to do with the past. Just revenge. The little witch aims to torment me. Punish me. Drive me fucking insane.

And after last night? I think she succeeded.

My eyes drift to the bottle nearby, and I curl a fist to keep from grabbing it. Though, hell, why shouldn't I take more? I'd down every last pill just to wipe that moment from my memory.

Fabio snatches the pills first, returning them to his pocket. "Don't tell me I'm going to regret giving you these," he grumbles. "The last thing we need is to have you relapse in any shape or form."

"Speak for yourself." I'd kill for a sip of liquor right about now. I'd go out and find one too, if it weren't for Vincenzo. I should be by his bedside as he recovers, not playing house with some *mafiya* witch.

"Maybe I *should* overdose," I suggest coldly. "At least then you couldn't bar me from the fucking hospital—"

"And now," Fabio says gently, "we cut to the heavy stuff. There's a reason why I didn't want you to see Vin. Do you want to hear it, or do you want to be angry?"

I'm not ready for the fear that slams into me like a gut punch, and I grapple for the edge of the desk. "Is he okay?"

"He's fine." Fabio's smile is tired but authentic. "Better than fine, actually. He hasn't opened his eyes yet, but the nurses have already noted a marked improvement. Far better progress than even the most optimistic predictions."

I feel a corner of my mouth twitch upward. My Vin was always a fighter. Yet, Fabio's own actions undermine the good news.

"He's doing better," I rasp. "So why keep that from me?"

"Because I don't want you barging in there and camping out by his bedside, that's why." I've known him long enough to guess what he's too classy to say out loud—*You'll fuck it all up.*

He thinks I'll do more than visit Vin—perhaps take a detour and pay Mischa's family the same respect he's shown toward mine.

Is he wrong? I scoff rather than dwell upon an answer. "Glad to see you have so much faith in me, Fab."

"I do," he counters, "and I want you to keep a clear head and squash this mess between you and Mischa. *That* will keep Vincenzo safe. You can't help him by scowling around his wing, intimidating the nurses—"

"Bullshit." I recognize the significant dip in his inflection. Fab rarely lies to me outright. Primarily because he's piss poor at it. "You learned something," I say, a suspicion confirmed by the way he's averting his eyes. "What?"

"First, I need to know how well you trust what little fragments of the *famiglia* remain—" he jerks his chin toward the doorway. From deeper in the house, a series of footsteps betray the movements of someone else. I'd almost forgotten we aren't alone. At least four *famiglia* men patrol the property, scavenged from the ranks of Antonio Salvatore.

"You know Antonio was potentially working with whoever wanted you dead," Fabio points out. "What about them?"

A damn good question. Luciano, Antonio's second, is the only one who seems to hold any real sway. He denied knowing about the attack and, for what it's worth, I believe him. He's already had more than enough chances to kill me outright.

Though I don't believe that he's stuck around out of the goodness of his heart, either.

"I'll vouch for them," I say finally. "For now."

"Alright, then." Fabio braces his hands against my desk and takes a deep breath. "I did some digging into the financial records of Paulie Vanetti. Whoever bankrolled his little operation definitely wasn't Antonio Salvatore. They're smart. Very, very clever. Hid the transaction behind a million different fucking hidey-holes. Even the best sleuth couldn't track the original bank account for a few years at least."

"Anyone but you," I point out, crossing my arms. "So where did it lead?"

He frowns. "Nowhere definitive yet. There were a few offshore accounts thrown into the mix. The kind'd deeply embedded in several European nations that can't be easily accessed by just anyone."

"Anyone like Antonio Salvatore," I admit. That bastard didn't have that kind of political pull. Though I can think of someone who does. "That kind of intel isn't out of the realm for someone like Mischa Stepanov."

"Exactly. I will give you that." Fabio strokes his chin, his brows drawn in concentration. "It doesn't seem likely that he would accidentally mastermind an attack on his own family—"

"But it's in his wheelhouse," I say, sitting straighter. Renewed hunger for retaliation surges through my blood, banishing any discomfort. Fuck withdrawal. I feel better than ever. If Fabio himself can deem Mischa a threat, he couldn't stand in my way. "Foreign influence. Dark money. It has his hallmarks."

"It does," Fabio admits. He would know. "I didn't want to feed your paranoia, but remember his interest in your harbor? Well, it seems several listings on the city's west end have suddenly been bought up. In cash. Even after the accident that happened at your port office—"

"You mean Mischa Stepanov setting it on fire?"

Fabio winces. "It's still prime real estate. I bet whoever wants it, still does. Especially when they've spent over ten million to secure a bunch of rundown warehouses and random businesses."

"Ten million?" My eyes widen. It's an impressive sum. "That's a lot of dark money."

If not Mischa's, then whose? The city's west end is known only for abandoned warehouses from the steel mill days. Nothing worth developing.

"What about that bitch, Vanetti? He mentioned a J.W.," I say, picturing the bastard I tortured. That name was the one bit of information I managed to get from him. "Does that mean anything?"

Fabio shrugs. "Whoever this puppet master is, he went through a lot of lengths to cover his tracks. Meaning that he has not only the resources, but the intelligence with which to do so. I found another alarming clue, though. Something unexpected."

"What?" It takes more than the usual gambit to surprise Fab.

"I got curious and had my informant run a search across the international database for anything that caught his eye. It might be unrelated, but—" He starts to pace, still stroking his chin.

"If you're mentioning it, I'm guessing it might not be so *unrelated* after all."

"Perhaps. A rash of sudden deaths at a firm overseas has rattled the corporate world. A plane crash, it seems, killed the entire board, leaving a slew of new investors in charge. The company isn't major, mind you. It only controls a small fleet of cargo shippers—far too small to matter in the international trade, but—"

"I don't believe in coincidence."

"Exactly," Fabio agrees. "If that hunch pans out, then something big is afoot, which is why I want you to stay focused. And to stay *clean*—" he pats the pocket where the pills reside. "Let Vin heal and find whoever did this so we can end the threat permanently."

"You sound like me," I say. "Usually, you'd be prattling on about peace and love and healing."

"I preached peace and love once," he says softly. "And it didn't turn out so well in the end, did it?"

He's referring to an event well beyond the shitstorm with Mischa Stepanov. Back when I, to put it nicely, went off the fucking deep end, leaving him to pick up the pieces. Did I ever thank him for that? Acknowledge it out loud? Knowing Fab, he wouldn't even want to hear it if I did.

"Who knows where the hell I'd be without your peace and love," I tell him.

He scoffs, lightening the mood again. "Don't get sappy on me, Don."

"Sappy or withdrawal, who can tell the difference?"

"Let's try to avoid both then, shall we?" Fabio continues to pace, nearing the window by the time he finally looks my way again. "I need to ask you something."

I stiffen. He's serious. "About what?"

The way he's staring has me on edge. I can't even begin to name the expression on his face.

"Have I grown three fucking heads or something?"

"Why would you give her that stuff?" he demands hoarsely. "What did you even tell her? I know it wasn't the truth, or she would have burned it all—"

"Tell her what?" *Her*, being the girl. At least one hunch is proven correct—something happened between them. "What are you talking about?"

"Damn it, Don…" He sinks onto a nearby chair, but the lack of usual poise ages him decades.

"Whatever I've done, spit it out—"

"*Olivia*." His knuckles white as he grips the hand rests. "Those clothes. I didn't realize you gave her those clothes. Why would you give her those—"

"I didn't give her shit." It's the only thing I can think to say, but it's the truth. Luciano was the one who dredged up that box from only God knows where. "I'm sorry if you—"

"It's not me I'm worried about," Fabio counters, his gaze on the floor. "I just don't understand why you would… Never mind—" He stands, composed again. "Anyway, I'll escort the girl to the hospital."

"Alone? Hell no. Take Luciano and—"

"Yes, alone. I think it will be a better show of faith than marching in there armed to the teeth. I also took the liberty of bringing her some more suitable clothing. While I'm there, I'll check on Vincenzo and update you on his progress. In the meantime, you will?" He phrases it like a fucking pop quiz question.

I offer him another mocking salute. "I'll stay out of trouble."

"Stay *focused,* Donatello." His sharp tone heralds yet another damn scolding. "I know you've been reformed, but I wouldn't mind a new, improved, sober Donatello Vanici, the *famiglia* leader for a few days. At least until this mess is sorted."

I have to chuckle. "Shit must be worse than you're saying if you want Il Mostro back."

"Not the monster you became," he corrects. "The *real* you. Confident, cocky Donatello, full of life who loved his line of work. Remember him?"

He makes it sound like something out of a goddamn fairy tale. Maybe it was. A perfect man with a perfect life who just so happened to run an organized crime syndicate on the side. What a goddamn aspiration.

"Yeah, I remember..." I'm on my feet, approaching the window on autopilot. I used to spend hours in this spot, eyeing the overgrown yard beyond it. Once, two children played tag beneath that old oak tree. They were cocky and confident, too, trusting that their uncle Don would always protect them...

And he failed them both.

"Fuck!" I pivot, smashing my fist against the nearest section of the wall. Again. Again. Specks of white paint chip off, joining the dust coating the floor.

"Don!" Fabio rushes toward me, but I wave him off.

"It's fine." A look at my hand contradicts that statement. My knuckles are bloodied, scraped by the plaster, but I don't feel any pain.

For seven years, I've felt nothing.

Liar. Last night, lying in bed with a writhing blond beneath me, I felt something alright. A wrenching pang in my gut as I watched her suck in air, her throat quivering. Pure, fucking misery—but I wasn't suffering; I relished in it.

Goddamn it. I slam my bloodied hand against my temple as if that could drive her from my skull. It doesn't work. She's still there, taunting me with those eyes, her lips trapped between her teeth, an elusive emotion lurking behind that gaze. Anger? Hate? Disgust?

In that moment, I would have given her anything just to reveal what the hell it was…

"Are you okay?" Fabio's shouting, his hand on my shoulder.

"No," I admit. Being here is fucking with my head, blurring reality with the past. Fab's right. I should go back to the villa at least. Or, better yet, somewhere far away from Hell's Gambit.

I head for the door, but a figure appears there as if conjured from thin air to stop me.

Watching her is like being torn in half. My body reacts as any man's would, my cock stiffening, blood pumping, while the beast in my skull stirs with the anger only she arouses.

Fabio, the bastard, went out of his way to portray the sweet heiress image the Stepanovs have projected to the world. The frothy yellow dress he gave her swallows her curves, bathing her in false innocence. My little *principessa*.

I almost prefer Liv's dress on her. At least then she embodied exactly what she is—a thief, stealing from me whatever she can take. Grief, rage, Vincenzo, my sanity. She'll claw it all away.

Dressed like this, she's untouchable, holding her head high, gazing past me like I don't fucking exist—and to someone like her, I normally wouldn't. But she wasn't always Willow Stepanova.

The walls of this house alone prove that. Every decrepit, rotting inch is an anchor to the past, giving me an advantage I wouldn't have anywhere else. We leave, and it's easier for her to ignore me and play the role of a *mafiya* princess, above it all.

To forget.

Here, we're both in hell, burning amid the flames.

"We're staying," I say, looking straight at her. "We'll fill the place with marital bliss."

"Jesus, Donatello," Fabio exclaims. This place is hell for him too.

But he doesn't have to dance toe to toe with a ghost from his past every day. He doesn't have to breathe her in every fucking second, knowing that she alone is proof of what he truly is at his core.

A monster.

Usually, she looks at me like I am one—until *now*. Her gaze flits over me for a heartbeat that lasts an eternity. Like she's hunting for something beneath the outer shell she loathes. She sported the same look earlier when she came from the kitchen.

A memory rises up—her as a little girl, trying to pretend she didn't have a water gun hidden behind her back. That was her favorite plan of attack—to lure me in close and then strike with the advantage.

We're well past the stage of water guns. Considering that I have her knife, what the hell is her weapon now?

"Right…" Clearing his throat, Fabio chooses that second to brush her arm, guiding her toward the door. "Well, we'll be off. In the meantime?" His eyes beg me to play along. Be a good boy. Heed his plan.

"I'll stay out of trouble," I snap, turning my back to them. "Which reminds me, I have some errands of my own for you."

Fabio hesitates for a second before replying. "Such as?"

"Let's say that I've found a new lease on life—" I have to laugh at how it sounds. "Anyway, I want to go over my life insurance policy. The one you had notarized for me. You still have it?" I run my hand across the surface of my desk to disguise the hitch in my voice. Not that Fabio would ever miss a damn thing.

"The one we drew up years ago?"

I nod. Over seven years ago, to be exact.

"Is there anything, in particular, you want to change?"

"No," I lie. "That a problem?"

"Of course not. In fact, I'm glad you mentioned paperwork. I'll leave some files here for you to look over. I'm especially interested in the waterfront property listings, and I'm curious to get your perspective."

Knowing him, there's more to it than that. First, a mysterious overseas business. Now local property listings.

"And?"

"*And,* I'm curious if you get the same suspicion I do," he says. "Finding the answer might be a little like searching for a needle in a haystack, but it's not like you don't have the time. And, you can feed your paranoia regarding Mischa. While you're at it, see if you can spot a pattern."

"Fine."

When he finally leaves, property listings aren't at the forefront of my mind. A pair of limpid eyes are, and I tear into the hall, heading for the stairs without fully understanding why. Then it hits me—she saw something.

Information worthy of coloring those dark fucking irises with an emotion in addition to the pity or hatred I'm used to seeing there.

A weapon?

Those clothes, Fabio said. *I didn't realize you gave her…*

Gave her what, exactly? I reach her room, but the second I grip the doorknob, a fiery sensation explodes beneath my ribcage, so unexpected I grunt. Is this withdrawal? Or guilt?

Or both.

Gradually, the pain subsides, but I'm paralyzed. The past has me by the balls, but it's my own damn fault for inviting this particular bit of nostalgia. How many times did I pass by this door, knowing Safiya was safe beyond it? How many times did I reassure her that I was here and would always protect her?

Too damn many—and yet every single time turned out to be a lie.

Get a grip. I fight to get my breathing under control, gulping at the thickened air. There's too much dust in here. I'm suffocating. Before I know it, I'm racing downstairs, finding myself in the kitchen, aiming for the yard. More memories live in this room, though, and I don't even make it to the door.

Olivia. Fabio rarely even mentions her, his own sister murdered in cold blood. Murdered in this very house.

In an ideal world, we would have never met. Born to a wealthy family, Olivia Botelli had been destined for a life far better than the one she got. I'll never understand why she chose me.

"You were my fairy tale prince," she murmured every time I asked. *"Come to save me from a boring life. I'd always pictured he'd be blond, but you're decent enough."*

Decent enough to marry, but when it came down to it, I couldn't protect her.

Of all the places to die, it had to be here. In the house she loved, not far from this very spot. It's crazy how I can look around this room one second and just see the emptiness. The dust. The decay.

Then I blink, and it's full of life, the halls echoing with laughter. Liv's... I can see her, standing at that counter over there, her hair loose, hips swaying. Barefoot, she'd be wearing a brightly colored dress that popped against the beige walls. *"The brighter, the better,"* she used to tease. *"I need some way of getting your attention, old man."*

God, it's like she's here, her back to me, her neck bare. I reach for her...

And she vanishes. I eye my hands, startled by the calluses and scars that weren't there in the past. The ravages of time have spared Liv, but they've hammered me.

Even her face is getting harder to recall. The same one I once spent hours memorizing every inch of, tracing every last freckle. On the other hand, her death is etched into my fucking skull—her body, lying limp, the puddles of her blood dotting the floor—but the good times are just fleeting snippets…

I only have myself to blame. I've spent damn near a decade drowning myself in alcohol just to forget her. The fact that I succeeded shouldn't come as a shock.

"You okay?"

I shake my head to make sure the figure standing in the doorway is really here. Luciano. When I blink, the bastard doesn't disappear. Going off his raised eyebrow, I suspect he's been standing there for a while.

"Yeah. I'm fine. What are you doing here, anyway?"

"Food," he replies, crossing to the fridge. "For your other *guest*, or did you forget?" He inclines his head toward the doorway, but a glimpse of black curls is all I get of the tiny figure lurking just out of sight.

Kisa Salvatore.

If I weren't set on sobriety, she would be another figure I'd want to wash from my skull.

"What do you plan on doing with her?" Luciano asks, lowering his voice. "Sell her to the Saleris?"

I haven't thought about it. I could always let her go. Dealing with the Saleris would be more trouble than it's worth.

Though, I didn't exactly think through taking her in the first place. *Damn.* Fabio's been selective in his choosing which battles to fight. He complains about the fucking house but not the shit I've brought *inside* it. A new wife. A stolen child.

History repeating itself.

Who knows, tomorrow I might return to find blood splattered on the walls and bodies lying in the foyer. I can almost smell the salt. Around me, the cupboards distort, dripping red…

"What the hell is wrong with you?" Luciano snaps. His eyes are on my hands, grasping for the nearest wall.

"Nothing," I snap. When I look up, the blood has vanished. "I'm fine."

Leaving the kitchen, I enter the hall.

Fabio was right. Finding the man who set me up and staying one step ahead of Mischa is all that matters. The best method to achieve both goals is to fall back into my old role. Run the *famiglia*. Hunt for clues. Come up with a plan and make my glorious return to the city's criminal stage.

Donatello is back, and he's not afraid of anyone.

Least of all, Mischa Stepanov.

"Where are you going?" Luciano asks.

"To read about a waterfront property listing," I call back. "It's time to find a needle in a fucking haystack."

abio and his hunches are never wrong, but he can be prone to a paranoid streak every now and again, which isn't surprising, given his line of work. Money is the root of all evil, and he makes a living laundering it clean.

If Mischa or anyone else has their sights set on the city's west waterfront, I can't see the appeal. Developing a port from scratch would cost more money than it's worth. Why pick Hell's Gambit in the first place?

I can't focus. Rather than ruminate over property listings, my attention keeps returning to the same damn subject.

The same woman.

Fuck! It was stupid to let her go with Fabio. Mischa will be there, hovering over his wife. If the bastard is smart—and he is—he'll grab her, our "engagement" be damned. The second they enter Mercy, the *mafiya* will be waiting. My eyes narrow at the thought, and I plant my fist against the desk, scattering the documents lying there.

But would she go willingly?

Trying to predict her is dangerous. Almost as risky as letting her climb into my bed in the first place. I close my eyes and still see her. That haunting gaze. Those wet lips parted, eyes widening with an enticing fucking mixture of curiosity and alarm. Like she didn't even know what pleasure was…

"You don't know the first damn thing about what really happens between a man and a woman," I told her. *"You've*

never fucked…and I'm assuming you've never touched yourself, either."

I'm still sure of that. Just like I know, *this* was her aim all along. To get inside my head and infect my lungs with her smell. Distract me to the point of such carelessness that I'll let her skip right out of my reach.

Though, is she ready to quit playing with me?

I could always get there and find out for myself. I should do that. Grab her. Make her choose.

Mischa or me?

My vengeful fantasy goes murky before I have a clear answer as to who she'd pick. If I had to guess, no one could force "Willow" to do a damn thing.

Again, I recall those eyes heavy lidded, glittering in the dark. They bore into mine fearlessly, like she had every right to be there. To see into my damn soul.

She thinks she owns it.

It's wrong to compare her to Liv. Fuck my brain for even going there, turning from the *mafiya* princess only to dredge up an old memory.

"I never know what you're thinking," she told me. The context is murky, but she looked sad. Damn, I hated the way her eyes could get like that, a cloudy shade in between brown and green. With one look, she could reduce me to a piece of shit, unworthy of her.

"You never let me in. I try so hard to think like you, but I never can. Are you even listening to me? Can you hear me? Donatello? Donatello!"

A scream cuts the air, and I'm on my feet, lunging into the hall.

"Liv?" My body reacts on autopilot, urging me toward the stairs, but the figure descending them isn't Olivia. She's too small, her eyes wide, and another name slips out of me before I can choke it back, "S-Safiya?"

"It hurts…" The fact that she's speaking at all shatters the illusion. This girl isn't Safiya Mangenello. Already, my brain is tallying up more clues that prove it—her eyes are blue, her hair dark and curling, but that shirt…

I remember picking it out in the store myself, wracking my damn brain to consider what a little girl might like. Something pink, I decided. Little did I know it was her favorite color.

"Kisa!" Luciano races past me, and I finally recognize the child before me. Antonio Salvatore's little girl. "What the hell happened?"

Blood spills down her left arm, dripping onto the floor in rivulets. I blink, but it's no hallucination. She's been cut— and it doesn't take long to find the weapon.

Luciano snatches it from her, hissing in disgust. "Where did you even get this?"

A grunt of recognition rips from my chest as he lifts the weapon high. The dagger is a distinct silver, with a dark handle, engraved with the word *Mouse*. I know where she got it from—my room.

I say nothing, but when Luciano sets the blade down, I grab it, slipping it into my pocket.

"Kisa, honey." He spins her to face him, but she stares blankly ahead, unresponsive. "What the hell is wrong with her?"

"She's in shock," I surmise.

When he reaches for her injured arm, she blinks, finally meeting his gaze. "It hurts," she says.

An understatement. The wound looks deep, slicing across her forearm. Judging from the amount of blood, the blade nicked a vein.

"We need to apply pressure to it." I shrug off my jacket and wad up an edge of the sleeve around the slender limb.

"It's deep." Already I can feel the warmth seeping through the fabric. Standing, I throw the jacket aside and lift the girl into my arms.

"What are you doing?" Luciano is hot on my heels.

"I'm taking her to the hospital," I say. "She needs stitches."

The irony isn't lost on me. I got my wish. Though who knows, Willow Stepanova could already be safely ensconced in her fucking mansion, forever beyond my reach.

Or I could get there in time to ruin this little family reunion.

"I'm coming with you," Luciano warns, and I realize I'm already heading for the door.

"Good. You can cover me."

The girl doesn't react as I carry her outside, her wide blue eyes fixated on mine. That look… Someone else used to stare at me like this. Boldly. Like nothing on earth scared her, least of all Donatello Vanici.

Though that little girl had been taught more than enough fear in her life. Gino Mangenello was my second in command, but I didn't know the extent of the brutality he showed his wife and child behind closed doors. The day we met comes back to me so clearly; it's like I'm there in my office, watching her peek from around his bulk.

Taking her in wasn't my choice, but I never once doubted it. Not once.

"Are you sure you're okay?" Luciano calls from behind.

I look down and realize I'm standing just before the driveway with a trail of the girl's blood in my wake. Teeth clenched, I keep walking. "I'm fine."

"I don't think you are, and I damn sure don't think you should be driving."

"I said I'm fine." The further I move from that house, the better I feel. When I finally wrench open the door of one of

Antonio's cars—a flashy black sedan—and shove the girl onto the back seat, I feel even clearer.

"I'll be right behind you," Luciano warns as I settle into the driver's seat. "Keep pressure on your arm, Kisa!"

I don't think she hears him. By the time I start the car, she's gaping into space again, her arm resting limply on her lap.

"You're bleeding," I warn. My voice isn't naturally soothing like Fabio's, and she jumps. "Keep pressure on it until we get it checked out."

She clutches her hand to her chest at least. As her eyes stoically scan the road, I can't resist the comparison—she's nothing like Safiya—a girl so bubbly, despite her silence, it felt as though an entire chorus of people were battling to speak all at once. You only had to listen.

Antonio's girl is an entirely different creature. She's like her father, how he was back in the day at least. Like ice, an impenetrable wall from which you only ever got a glimpse of genuine emotion.

But Antonio was never innocent.

"Are you a bad man?" The small, crisp voice comes as such a shock I nearly veer off the driveway. As I wrench on the wheel to right it, a horn sounds from behind me. Luciano.

Ignoring him, I eye the girl in the rearview mirror as she turns the full brunt of those eyes on me. They aren't a reflective brown, but piercing, her tiny lips quivering. "Are you a bad man?" she repeats.

"Yes," I reply without a shred of hesitation.

The answer doesn't surprise her. "Why?"

She makes evil sound synonymous with a pair of shoes someone decides to put on in the morning.

Maybe it is that simple. I joined the *famiglia* and served Giovanni because I wanted to, but I can't pinpoint the exact moment I stopped giving a fuck.

When did Donatello turn "bad"?

As pathetic as it feels to admit, only one answer comes to mind. "I don't know."

4

EVGENI

"This is it?" the woman remarks as our destination comes into view. "After how long you've been driving, I'd assume we'd be in China by now, at least."

I bristle at her haughty tone, but she's not exaggerating. For hours, I've traced the backroads sprawling around the city, trying to come up with some semblance of a plan. The day is damn near over, but this is the best course of action I could decide on. Keeping her in Hell's Gambit.

For now.

"This is it," I say coldly.

"You live in a slum." Her apparent disgust betrays her knowledge of the area. Though, in all fairness, the place looks the part, complete with public housing and streets strewn with garbage. "Why am I not surprised?" she adds, her lip curled in disdain. "I suppose being a hired hand doesn't pay much."

I don't correct her. Bringing her out in public at all is a risk, but one I'd rather take by coming here—an apartment intermittently used by the *mafiya*—than my main base. She could still run either way, but if she's truly afraid of this man, she'll prove it.

"You must have a death wish," she declares as I park. "I tell you, the man I'm running from is a monster. You parade me in public."

I frown. One point proven, at least.

"Move," I tell her, shoving open the door on my end. "If you're really on the run, the last thing you should want is to be alone."

I forge ahead without looking back—not that I have to. She's noisy in her haste to keep pace, her heels clacking, breaths heavy. Her desperation has a musical quality.

I look over my shoulder, hoping I'm the only one privy to it. The unease I felt earlier grows more potent as we enter the building.

The apartment is on the top floor, but it's a hell of an ascent. The elevator has been out of order for as long as I can remember, leaving a rickety staircase as the only way up. The woman pants, sweat dripping down her forehead by the time we reach the flat.

I fish the spare key from beneath a ratty welcome mat before the door. When I unlock it, the woman scoffs, unimpressed.

"Don't take offense to this, soldier," she says, eyeing the barren entryway and the worn couch serving as the sole piece of furniture. "You could really use a woman's touch."

"Like Safiya Mangenello's?" I say, taking a shot in the dark.

If she recognizes the name, however, she's damn good at hiding it.

"Is that a lover of yours?" Her tone is sweetly hostile as she inclines her head to inspect me. "Charming. Though, I think you need someone with a bit higher standards when it comes to cleanliness."

"I'll tell you what I *need*—" I whirl on her, grabbing her arm. She's quick, reflexively kicking between my legs, but brute strength is the one thing she can't easily counteract. I pin her to the wall and kick the door shut. Leveraging my weight, I apply pressure to her shoulder joint, just hard enough to make her wince. "I need answers."

She fights to suck in enough air, her voice a hiss. "You won't get them if I'm dead."

"No, but I can think of a variety of ways I could take advantage of your last moments. If you've done the 'research' on me that you claim, then you should know what I mean."

I feel her shudder.

"You certainly talk the talk," she says, feigning confidence. "But trust me, if you ask nicely, you won't need force."

"Fine." I let her go, stepping back. "I'm asking nicely. Speak."

She faces me, pressing her back to the wall, her hand rubbing her shoulder. "He wants the Winthorp fortune," she says finally. "But that's merely a side note. His real aim is to turn this city into his stepping-stone. I don't know his full intentions, but I can assure you they aren't pleasant."

She pauses deliberately, forcing me to ask.

"How so?"

Her smile is sly. "Use that imagination of yours. I'll give you a hint—he needs allies and equity. Fast."

"What's his name?"

Her lips twitch. I suspect she hesitates before saying, "I know him as Jonathan Harmon, but it's just an alias. He's smart, shielding his true identity between several dummy accounts. You won't be able to find his real name; I can promise you that."

I feel my eyes narrow. "And he wants your son to claim the Winthorp fortune."

She nods.

"But he's a child. Three, you said. Which means even if he did miraculously come into the fortune, he wouldn't be able to touch a dime."

But presumably, his mother could.

"Now you're thinking," she taunts as if reading my mind. "I knew you had it in you."

Though I doubt she realizes the full extent of what she's revealed.

"If anyone has a motive to want the fortune," I say, advancing toward her a step. "It's you."

"Yes," she says dryly. "I want to take on Mischa Stepanov all by my lonesome and skip merrily into the distance with his gun pointed at my skull."

"Not if he were dead," I counter, crossing my arms. "You hate him."

"I do. But if I really wanted to go along with the plan, would I be begging *you* for an audience and staying in some piece of shit motel?"

The frustration in her voice rings true—as much as I loathe to admit it. She strikes me as the kind who doesn't spook easily. And yet, she's quivering despite that poised mask.

Her nerves are contagious. I swear I see a shadow flicker beyond the room's sole window. A bird? Or something more ominous?

Ripping my gaze back to the woman, I decide to stop beating around the bush. "What are you afraid of?"

She sucks in a breath, her eyes darting from me to the doorway and back. Sensing her motive, I move to block the exit.

"You want to know?" Her eyelids lower, disguising her intentions behind thick lashes. "I'm afraid that your Mischa has no idea as to the deck stacked against him. Frankly? I don't want to be caught in the crossfire."

Audible once more, that truthful note in her voice is hard to deny. I step forward, intrigued despite myself.

"I'm listening."

Her lips part, but another flicker of movement beyond the window draws my notice. There. A warehouse lurks across the street, but my gaze hones in on a broken window in time to catch a flash of shadow. That is no bird.

"Shit!"

Relying on pure instinct, I move, shoving the woman aside. She cries out a split-second before glass shatters.

I land on my knees, tasting blood as my ears ring. She's in my grasp, her body curled beside mine. One look at her eyes, and I know she didn't plan this. Formlessly, her lips part, but she doesn't scream.

"Run!"

Another buzzing sound cuts the air, this time easily identified. A gunshot.

This bullet shatters what remains of the window, ripping plaster from the wall behind me.

One attacker, I deduce, aiming from the west, most likely from a high vantage point.

"Stay low to the ground," I demand, grabbing the woman by the arm.

Pivoting, I kick open the door and drag her with me, staying out of range.

Another shot whips past, shattering the edge of the door as I slam it shut.

A lone window illuminates this section of the hall. A glance from it reveals the next building over and the empty street below. There are no windows, at least. A sniper can't cover this angle.

We were followed here. If I were managing a hit on one lone woman, I'd send two men. One shooter, and a backup to cover the bases in case of an escape.

"They'll be watching the exits," I say, approaching the window. It's a single pane, opened easily by lifting from the bottom. Below, a rusty fire escape provides a bridge between the height and the street.

The woman balks.

"We need to jump," I say, pulling her closer.

She shakes her head, gripping the sill with trembling fingers. "Are you insane?"

"That doesn't matter. It's the only way out."

And I suspect we have seconds to move before the shooter takes aim from a different angle.

There isn't time for permission. I grab her waist and shove her forward.

"Go!"

She grapples for the wall, trying to steady her descent, but her foot loses traction too soon, and she plummets onto the base of the fire escape with a sound loud enough to alert the entire damn city.

Her pained groan stirs a semblance of guilt as I follow, landing in a crouch beside her. Already, she's lurching to her knees, grasping at my shoulder as I head for the ladder leading to the street.

She moves cautiously, and I consider it a miracle when we make it to the street level without drawing an audience.

Yet.

Footsteps advance in our direction, and I grab her wrist, heading for a nearby alley. Hand on my holster, I scan the street, hunting for movement.

This is a sloppy hit, I decide as we reach the other end of the block without crossing anyone suspicious. Sloppy and reckless.

If her attacker didn't want her dead, he wanted to prove a point.

Perhaps her cryptic speech wasn't entirely for show.

This man is dangerous.

Taking a chance, I haul her toward the van and shove her onto the back seat.

"Stay down," I warn.

Then I drive, unsure of where the hell to even go next.

5

WILLOW

I can't put into words what it felt like to be accepted by Mischa Stepanov and his family. If someone held a gun to my head, the closest comparison I could make is coming inside to a warm fire after ages spent lost in a blizzard. *Finally*, I had shelter again. Everything Donatello Vanici ripped from my life, Mischa offered me tenfold. Safety. Security. Love.

How have I repaid his generosity?

With tragedy and pain.

In hindsight, it's not that much of a shocking outcome. The events of the past few days have only proved what I've known in my soul—as much as I love the Stepanovs, I never truly *belonged*. I was a weed, plucked from a wayward field to grow amongst a cultivated bed of roses. They've shielded me within their beautiful, protected world, but no amount of love can change what I am—a suffocating, creeping outsider.

In a twisted way, I should thank Donatello Vanici for helping me to realize that. Never again can I simply exist as Willow, or even Safiya.

I am a piece on a chessboard, a prize to be won.

"I'm worried about him."

The cautious tone snaps me back to the present. I blink, struggling to recognize my surroundings. White walls and polished floors abound. That's right, we're at the hospital, navigating a clinical floor. Or at least *Fabio* is while I trail in his wake. I increase my pace to draw even with him, not that he seems to notice.

"He has his *issues,* yes," he continues obliviously. His tone leaves no doubt as to who he's referring to. "I've never seen him like this. Never... I'm sure you see it, too?"

I just stare. His attempt at conversation is a drastic role reversal from Donatello's insistence on maintaining the captor and captive dynamic, but I sense he's speaking to himself more than me. Concern contorts his expression, his gaze turned inward.

"It's that goddamn house," he says under his breath, heading for an upcoming corridor. "Trust me, it wasn't my idea for him to bring you there. I'm sorry. Those letters..."

He meets my gaze, lowering his voice. "Do you still have them?"

I weigh the option of lying, feeling selfishly protective of that dusty silver box for reasons I can't explain. In the end, I nod.

"Thank god," Fabio exclaims, pressing a hand to his chest. "I don't think he's read them—and he shouldn't. Never. Do you understand? Please give them to me."

My confusion must show on my face because he looks over his shoulder warily before leaning in even closer to me. "Please. Some memories… Some memories are better left buried. Those letters are just old trash, better off discarded. I need you to give them to me—please. And keep them away from Donatello. Can you do that? I know it's offensive of me to even ask you this, but please… Try to understand what it's been like for him."

I recoil as if he slapped me. I wish he *had*. It would be easier to fathom than his request—try to understand poor, poor Donatello—the man who destroyed my life and left me for dead.

"I didn't mean it like that," Fabio insists. Maybe he didn't. The sudden hoarseness of his voice reminds me of one of my professors during a lecture on musical complexity. *Ignore the background,* he warned us. *Focus only on the notes. See beyond the superficial noise to the pain beneath. That kind of emotion can't be studied, only felt…*

But there is a marked difference between music and madness.

"It's like he doesn't even remember. In his right mind, he'd never—" For several seconds, he seems lost, until a doctor brushes past him and he startles. Shaking his head, he continues walking. "It's like he blocked it out or something. But at other times, he's back there, reliving it over and over... No man could suffer what he's been through without losing some sanity, but to go back to that goddamn house. Those letters. If he really has forgotten, he can't read them. He can't—" He breaks off, and I get the sense that he said more than he meant to. Clearing his throat, he gestures toward something up ahead. "Anyway, here we are."

I follow the line of his gaze to a door presumably leading to another ward. A stoic man in black fatigues stands guard beside it, his face vaguely familiar. A Stepanov soldier?

Disappointment stings. I have no right to wish for anything, but I almost pray Evgeni is inside as part of Mischa's personal retinue. He'd be angry with me, but at least I'd have someone familiar to guard against the guilt. Not that I deserve a lifeline.

The thought of facing Ellen and Mischa—let alone Ellen's reaction to what I've done—is a harrowing possibility I didn't have the sense to dread until now. My throat goes dry, my stomach in knots.

"I know your mother is awake," Fabio explains, smoothing his hand down his suit jacket as the guard spots us. "I think your brother may even be in the same wing—though, I didn't exactly call ahead for obvious reasons. Allow me." Motioning for me to stay back, he approaches the man alone.

As I watch him, what little resolve I felt vanishes. I almost consider retreating somewhere—anywhere—to give myself more time to think. Come up with some way of explaining what I've done.

The guard, however, seems unmoved by Fabio's words. It's only when he points to me that the man stiffens with recognition. Heeding my cue, I step forward, but by the time I reach them, I only catch the tail end of what the guard says.

"Yes…yes sir—" He's speaking into a headset affixed to his ear. Nodding, he opens the door and steps aside. "This way, Ms. Stepanova. Your father is expecting you."

I swallow hard. Donatello's mocking remarks run through my mind with every step I take—though he might have been right to worry. Mischa is the last person aiming to uphold this twisted bargain. I doubt Fabio alone is any match for the Stepanov retinue. There is nothing to prevent me from running now if I wanted to.

In fact, it's probably the one way to fix the mess I've made. Go home. Return to that safe bed of roses and never dare to leave again.

As if reading my mind, Fabio looks at me and winks. "Let's hope for the best, yes?"

Rather than respond, I turn my attention to our surroundings. My initial suspicion was correct regarding this being a private wing. Few medical staff populate the spacious hall. Only a few rooms appear to be in use—the occupants of one are in the middle of a conversation, their voices barely audible. A woman's gentle hum rises above the others, as lilting as a bell chime. "You look so serious…"

Ellen. For a second, the sterile surroundings fall away, and the day of the attack unfolds like a never-ending nightmare. I keep seeing her face, pale from blood loss, her body limp…

"You should get some rest." The deeper voice responding to her yanks me back to the present, and I wince as fresh guilt rips through me. *Mischa.* Do I even have it in me to face him again?

Before I can decide, yet another figure pitches in. "We've gotten a lot of rest already," a boy declares. My heart clenches at that familiar tone, still as cheerful as ever. "When can we go home? I'm so sick of the gross pudding they serve here. It tastes like barf."

"I'll let you take the lead," Fabio says softly, placing his hand on my shoulder. He inclines his chin in the direction of the voices. "Take all the time you need."

Even from here, I can tell that the room is slightly larger than Vincenzo's, with a wide window displaying the city's waterfront. The jagged mass of skyscrapers forms an unexpectedly beautiful backdrop against the white walls.

"So stern," Ellen says as I round the doorway. She's sitting upright, her lips in a strained half smile—but her skin is still so pale only her hair gives her any definition against the white sheets. That, and the shadow cast by Mischa, dutifully standing over her.

Perched on the end of her bed, dressed in bright blue pajamas, sits a smaller figure, his attention consumed by the book lying open on his lap. His hair hangs wildly and unkempt, but his blue eyes sparkle with their usual mischief.

So much relief hits me at once as tears well in my eyes, threatening to fall.

But then I notice the bruise marring Eli's lip, and the beige cast covering his right arm. The injury is severe enough that he manipulates the pages as he reads with his left hand.

"I hope you were this way with the girls while I've been gone," Ellen taunts Mischa without noticing me. "They won't dare disobey you then."

"Is that so?" A wrinkle alongside his mouth softens the otherwise austere expression. Until he sees me, and his lips flatten entirely.

I choke on his silence, though it lasts barely a second before a smaller figure bounds in my direction.

"Will!" The force of his hug nearly takes me off my feet. His good arm wraps around my waist, and I'm reminded of just how tall he is now. "Where have you been? We've been asking and asking—"

"Willow!" Ellen extends her hands, her entire face alight with a smile.

I step forward, suppressing a shudder at her touch. She's as fragile as porcelain, liable to break if I apply enough pressure. An IV snakes from her wrist, feeding clear liquid into her veins. Bandages encircle nearly the length of her right forearm, and the glaring bruises hammered beneath her eyes look ghoulish in the overcast daylight.

As if to distract from the physical reminders of her recovery, her faint smile widens. "You look so pale, darling." She smooths her hand along my cheek.

"You look tired," Eli chimes in.

I glance at him, wondering if Mischa has told either of them the truth.

No. I decide. Eli would be furious if he had.

"Easy," Mischa says, placing a hand on Ellen's shoulder as she tries to sit upright.

Ignoring him, she pulls me closer. "Look at you," she croons, running her fingers through my hair. "You look exhausted, sweetheart. Both of you. Don't tell me you were worrying yourselves sick over me—"

"Why wouldn't we?" Mischa spins on his heel, lumbering toward the window. His long hair hangs down his shoulders, wild and unbrushed. From this angle, the shadows dwelling in the divots and lines of his sharp features are deeper than ever.

Ellen releases her own quiet sigh. "Did something happen? You've been acting odd all day. Are the girls okay? Ivan?"

"I can go home if you need help," Eli suggests. "I can. The doctor says my good arm is—"

"Everything is fine," Mischa insists in a softer tone. "*Everything*." This time, his eyes find mine, conveying an unspoken warning.

And now I know for sure—he hasn't told them. Not about Donatello. The engagement. None of it.

My hand falls from Ellen's, and I step back, feeling dirty in this clean room. My breathing quickens, my throat even drier. That childish sentiment rings truer than ever—*I don't belong here.*

"You need to rest," Mischa insists, returning to his wife's side. "Both of you. Once you're well enough, we can bore you with every detail."

When he eyes me again, I don't see the judgment I expect to find. There isn't room for anger. He looks so old. So worn. So tired.

Because of me.

Shame spreads through my body like fire, eating away what little doubt I might have left. I've been so damn selfish. First by leaving, and then again by playing Donatello's game. What is the cost of peace when it comes with so many caveats attached?

And why protect Donatello Vanici when time after time he's proven that he doesn't give a damn about me—because that's what I've been doing, whether I want to admit it or not.

By going along with his insane plan, I've been protecting him from himself.

And tormenting my own family in the process.

"We should go." Mischa heads for the door. "I'll be back later tonight."

"With Ivan and the girls?" The hope in Ellen's voice is so palpable I flinch, but another rare smile tugs on Mischa's mouth.

"Of course. I'm sure they can't wait to bombard you with all their complaints about my bedtime stories in comparison to yours." His voice is too deep, his gaze distant as he turns away; I sense he's holding something back. Ellen doesn't miss it, either.

"Are you sure?" She grasps for a handful of the sheets, threatening to rise. "Is something wrong—"

"No," Mischa replies, returning to her. With gentle pressure, he eases her back against the pillows.

"And Elena? I'd like to see her before she goes home." Her lips part in a genuine smile. "I assume Willow will help you with her until I'm released. And Anna, of course—"

"I'll have her brought over soon. Sleep," Mischa insists. "Come, Willow."

"It's not fair," Eli grouses, an uncharacteristic whine in his voice. "The baby gets to go home tomorrow. Why can't Aunt Ellen and I go, too?"

I sympathize with the longing glance he casts toward the window. Days of bedrest must be torture when he's used to spending his free time roaming the Stepanov property.

"You know the doctors suggested a few more nights of observation," Mischa says. His gruff tone betrays that he isn't necessarily happy with that prognosis. Still, concern for his family supersedes all. "The second you both are cleared, I'll bring you home myself."

"It's because of my stupid arm—" Eli eyes his cast with disgust. "But it's getting better. I swear. They just wanna poke and prod and—"

"Not now," Mischa says, heading for the door. "Let me get Willow home, first."

I flinch at the insinuation as I follow him into the hall. Perhaps Donatello wasn't paranoid after all…

Defiant, soft steps pad in our wake. Eli. "Can I walk out to the car at least?"

"Not this time. Go back to your room," Mischa commands in a sterner tone.

"Aww!" With an exaggerated sigh, Eli marches into a room across from Ellen's. Fabio suspected correctly—they share the suite.

I wish I could stay longer. Stay hidden in this little sliver of their universe and pretend the rest of the world doesn't exist. Shielded by these walls, Donatello Vanici is just a memory…

"Willow." Mischa's already nearing the exit, his back to me.

I swallow hard, increasing my pace to keep up. Every step feels weighed by enough shame I fear I'll go through the floor as Mischa finally turns to face me.

My eyes burn with the tears I've kept at bay all this time. Finally, they threaten to fall as I look up to face him.

But he's already lunging toward me. His heat slams into me with the force of a train, contrasting the relative gentleness with which his arms crush me to his chest. It's an earnest embrace, so tight I can't breathe, and I'd stay here forever if I could. For a brief moment, Donatello Vanici is just a bad memory…

Just as quickly, Mischa lets me go.

"What the hell is this?" he demands, whirling to face a figure I didn't realize was still standing here, out of view from any of the rooms. Fabio. "The bastard's way of taunting me? I know that's the trick he likes to play—"

"No trick," Fabio insists, his hands raised. "Merely a gesture of good faith."

"Faith?" Mischa's voice resonates like thunder, so loud I'm sure he can be heard from the lobby. Belatedly, he seems to realize that as well. With one last glance at Ellen's room, he storms ahead, barging from the private suite with Fabio and me on his heels.

Cocking his head, he poses another question from over his shoulder. "I assume your *faith* is the only thing stopping me from taking my daughter home?"

Fabio frowns, confused. "I don't—"

In a blur of motion, Mischa pivots, grabbing my arm without warning. The force with which he yanks me to him nearly takes me off my feet. From the corner of my eye, I see the guard at the door step forward to bolster the unspoken threat.

To his credit, Fabio doesn't even flinch. "You and I both know that were any harm to befall me, your little spat with Donatello would escalate."

"You think Vanici is in the position to threaten me?" Mischa replies, his voice low.

"Perhaps not." Fabio shrugs. "You have ten times the men and resources—but Donatello can wreak more damage than you can imagine, even alone."

"I've heard of the kind of 'damage' he likes to cause," Mischa snarls. "So have you. After what he did to your sister—"

"Olivia's death was an accident," Fabio says smoothly. "A terrible tragedy."

His voice remains level enough, but I catch the subtle wince he suppresses behind that blank expression.

"An *accident*." Mischa raises an eyebrow. "Has he even told her the truth? Have you?" His eyes narrow with a sudden realization. "He hasn't, has he? The fucking coward. And you. I would have thought you would be above this sick little game—"

"I don't think we should discuss the past here," Fabio insists, his tone soft.

Mischa's fingers tremble, biting into my skin with a strength I don't think he's aware of. It hurts, compressing muscle and bone, but I don't resist. This pain is only a fraction of what I've already caused him. If he ripped my arm off, it wouldn't be punishment enough.

"You've known all along, haven't you?" he harshly accuses. "What he did. I thought maybe you were in denial or believed his lies—but you don't even have the decency to tell her the truth. What *really* happened to your sister. Why he sold her like chattel—"

"Trust me, you don't even know the half of it," Fabio warns, but the words lack bravado. He's not boasting. He's begging.

For silence?

What really happened to your sister...

Is Mischa implying there was more to her death than senseless violence?

"The past is in the past," Fabio continues. "I love Donatello like a brother, but I wouldn't wish his wrath on even my worst enemy. I can't predict him. Given that the *mishap* between you two nearly resulted in the death of his nephew, I'll be honest—the fact that we're both unscathed is a blessing. For now, at least, there is a path to peace, however ridiculous it may be. I suggest we take it."

Mischa scoffs, releasing me—but not as a gesture of good faith. Using his weight as a barrier, he blocks me from view, instead. "You do have a way with words. If the past is so inconsequential, then why don't you tell her now, what he did?"

I crane my head enough to see Fabio, still unfazed. "There is no point in dwelling on the past," he repeats. "Allowing your daughter to come here was a display of goodwill on Donatello's part. I hope that you can match that courtesy by attending our meeting tomorrow. Rather than bring up old grievances, our time might be better spent tracking down the man who caused this mess in the first place."

"J.W.," Mischa says, his accent thick.

I can't suppress my body's reaction—revulsion. Bile threatens to crawl up my throat as I remember the brutality Donatello utilized to glean that bit of information from a man he tortured. Then killed.

"According to my best men, no one by that name exists," Mischa adds.

"He's clever," Fabio admits. "As we speak, Donatello is tracking down leads as to the culprit's identity. We can discuss this further tomorrow."

"Tomorrow."

I can't see Mischa's face from this position. Every second that passes without a response from him makes my breathing hitch. Finally, his fingers capture my chin, forcing me to meet his gaze.

"You insist on this?" I suspect he doesn't want an answer. Whatever he sees in my expression makes him turn away, releasing me. "Of course, you would… You've always been so damn stubborn. The only way to make you see the truth is to prove it to you."

Without another word, he storms off, leaving his guard by the door. A wary glance is the only acknowledgment the man sends my way before he returns his attention to the hall in general.

"Well…" Fabio sighs, tugging at his collar. "That was intense, wasn't it?" He forces a faint smile, and I have a new appreciation for his quiet authority. Few men could keep their composure in such a situation.

Though, fewer men could tolerate the varying moods of Donatello Vanici. The latter proudly sports his title of a monster—with selling a child being one crime among many —but what does that make a man who so faithfully stands beside him?

Surprisingly, Fabio's expressions are more nuanced than even Donatello's. "I hope the visit went well?"

I look away, trying to process the tumult of emotions battling to shape my mood. Foremost, I'm relieved to have seen Ellen. Though, the next time we meet, will she grace me with that same loving smile? Mischa hasn't told her what happened yet, though how could he? How do you even begin to explain something so insane?

Fabio, I suspect, would have trouble despite his charm.

"I see," he says softly. "Well, these things do take time to adjust to, even in the best of times. And I can admit that this isn't the most tactful of times to mention it, but I would really like that box of my sister's. In exchange, I will personally ensure that Donatello allows you regular visits. Deal?"

When I look at him again, a wide smile obscures anything he might be thinking beneath the mask. He's an expert at shrouding his emotions. Is he truly concerned for Donatello?

Or does his wariness of what that box contains go beyond that?

"We'll worry about that later. Come with me," he says, extending his arm. A warm smile heralds the abrupt change in subject, but I doubt he'll let the topic rest for long. "We'll head back, though we need to make one last detour, if you don't mind."

Minutes later, we arrive before a familiar hallway on the fourth floor. It's changed since the last time we were here, but I recognize it instantly. Vincenzo's wing. Now a hive of activity, medical professionals dressed in white congregate across from the lone occupied room.

"You can wait here if you'd like. I only need a few minutes," Fabio says before approaching them.

Someone I assume to be a doctor stands to greet him, but I'm too far back to hear their conversation. What few words I do catch make my stomach constrict. *Coma. Brain waves. Uncertainty.*

I've had enough of death and suffering, but for whatever reason, an invisible hook seems to catch my spine, compelling me into Vin's room, regardless. Crossing the threshold, I feel like an intruder, unwelcome in this neat, quiet place.

Not that the sole occupant can voice a complaint. Vincenzo. His bed is in the same place, but the machinery around it has drastically changed, and an unexpected pang of relief makes me sway. Gone are most of the tubes and heavy equipment. He seems to be breathing on his own, though even more bandages cover his head than I remember.

That's right, Fabio mentioned a surgery.

Frozen in place, I press a hand to my chest in response to how fast my heart is beating, every pulse resonating like a blow. I have no right to ache for him. It's my fault he's here…

He doesn't react as I approach, and the steady rise and fall of his chest is the only sign of life. When I press my hand to his cheek, however, it's warm.

It's surreal seeing his boyish features matured, enhancing his resemblance to his uncle. Some things never change, though, and I brush my thumb against his mouth, remembering his impish grin. No matter how serious the moment, one joke from Vincenzo could erupt the world in laughter.

I'm sorry. I wish I could say those words out loud, but I trace them against his lips instead. I'm sorry for everything. For the past. For never getting the chance to say goodbye…

What did Donatello even tell him? The truth? That he left me. Sold me. Betrayed me?

My finger freezes as another possibility comes to mind. What if Vin knew all along? Could I stomach knowing that?

I haven't come up with an answer when a flicker of movement draws my attention to his face, and every other thought leaves my mind. I know what I'm seeing must be a trick of the light—or a hallucination—but when I blink, nothing changes. I swipe my hand over my eyes, expecting reality to shift.

It doesn't.

Vin's eyes are open, partially hidden behind thick lashes. Dark and rich, they fixate on me, so much like Donatello's, it's chilling.

But instead of hate, another emotion takes shape, ten times more painful to witness. It glimmers faintly, giving life to his otherwise gaunt, sunken features. An answering flutter flickers in my chest, impossible to mistake for anything else. *Hope.*

His lips part, his voice nearly drowned out by the squeals of nearby machinery. "Saf…"

I strain my ears to listen, leaning closer. It's as if he's fighting with everything in him to stay lucid. Even if he can't trust what he's seeing…

By his sides, his hands twitch over the sheets, too heavy for him to lift. Finally, his eyes drift shut. "Am I dead?"

His gravelly sigh sounds resigned. He's dead. He has to be.

Because he thinks I am too.

No! I grip his hand tighter, willing him to understand what I can't put into words. I'm here. I'm alive.

His lashes flutter as his eyes re-open, but this time, they're distorted by a sheen of moisture. Tears. "Safy—"

A piercing alarm blares from one of the monitors connected to him, triggering a symphony of chaos. Almost instantly, a flood of people come rushing into the room, all of them speaking at once, jostling for proximity to the bed.

I find myself shoved aside, forced to observe, unable to help. A woman in white pushes past me, racing to adjust the various tubes and lines snaking from Vin's body.

"Vincenzo!" That shout rings out, louder than the rest. Confused, I whirl toward the door, expecting Fabio. Another man stands there instead, his dark eyes ablaze.

"What the hell is happening? Is he okay? Vincenzo!" He starts forward, but a burly doctor rushes to block his path.

"Can everyone clear the room, please?" someone else insists.

The next thing I know, I'm in the hallway as the door to Vin's room is shut, muffling the noise beyond it.

I turn in the direction I last saw Fabio, but someone snags my forearm in a vice grip, locking me in place. Considering the fact that Fabio is racing toward me now, he isn't the culprit.

"He spoke to you," my captor breathes against my ear. Donatello. Am I surprised he ignored Fabio's plea? No. Nothing is sacred to him, certainly not a promise. "What... What did he say?"

I bite my tongue so hard I taste blood. The raw hope in his voice shouldn't affect me. Especially not now.

Unmoved, Donatello's grip bites deeper. "What did he say?"

As if I could forget. Those four words circle my brain in a mocking loop. *Safy...am I dead?*

The tears I kept at bay around Mischa descend at full force, blurring my vision. Deep down, I think I always knew Donatello lied about the truth of what happened to his precious Safy. I just never thought I'd have to face it. Face him.

His betrayal was one thing, but this...

His rejection is a living creature clawing through my chest, ripping open the wounds I'd hoped were healed. I'm left bleeding without a mark to show for it, once again forced to grapple with the depths of how little Donatello Vanici cared about me.

When he lets me go, I inspect the ragged planes of his face, trying to imagine how I could ever see warmth in them or seek solace in that deceitful grin. He wasn't happy with just destroying Safiya. Only a heartless monster could sell a little girl—but it takes true evil to lie.

He told anyone who might care that I was dead. He told *Vincenzo* I was dead.

I want him to gloat over that fact now. I want him to laugh. Chuckle. Spit.

As my vision blurs, I glare at him, daring him to do so. Isn't this what he wanted?

He won. He hurt me.

He swallows hard instead, his lips parting wordlessly. The shock lasts only for a second before the hardness returns, steeling his gaze. "What did he say—"

"Donatello!" Fabio appears by his side, strategically drawing him away from me. "What are you doing here?"

For a second, I doubt he even knows where "here" is. Helpless, his eyes fixate on Vincenzo's door. He takes a step toward it only to stop when Fabio grabs his arm.

"Donatello, what are you doing here? Jesus, Christ are you okay?"

Only now do I notice the absence of his suit jacket, and the red liquid staining the hem of his shirt.

"The girl…" He jerks his chin toward the ward's entrance, but it's empty. "She cut herself. I brought her in to get it treated."

"The hospital for a papercut?" Fabio asks, an eyebrow raised. When Donatello says nothing, he places a hand on his shoulder. "Let's go."

"Vincenzo—"

"He'll be fine," Fabio says, flashing an unexpected grin. "Better than fine, actually. The doctors have been astounded by his progress. The lead surgeon assures me that he's improving better than he could have ever hoped for. Let them work and let him rest—" His eyes cut in my direction, conveying more alarm than his voice reveals. "I'll bring you back myself as soon as he's stabilized."

For a second, I swear Donatello will shrug him off and barge into the room regardless. Abruptly, he turns on his heel instead and starts down the opposite hallway.

"You've been making a lot of guarantees lately, Fab," he calls back. "Let's hope you can come through on them all."

To his credit, Fabio laughs. "I haven't failed you yet, have I? One day you'll learn that, of all people, I always have your best interest in mind. Why? Because as long as you're around, your fearsome reputation intact, I have nothing to fear from anyone. I lose you, I lose my bulletproof shield, and we can't have that, can we?"

Donatello grunts in a way that betrays he isn't sure if the boast was entirely in jest or not. I suspect it's more of the latter. Fabio is every bit as invested in Donatello's well-being as he is in his own. So much so that he helped him spin a lie for everyone, from himself to Vincenzo, to live under.

So much so that he's terrified by whatever the past might reveal.

If I give him Olivia's letters, I might lose the chance to discover the truth for myself. Safiya might have been susceptible to his manipulation, and recently I've been inclined to give him the benefit of the doubt—but no more.

He stood by as Donatello threw me away, and he helped him maintain the lie that I was dead.

As far as my own well-being goes, I know one thing for sure—I can't trust either of them.

6

EVGENI

The outskirts of the city seem like the safest bet. Already early evening, the district is decently populated, with enough traffic to deter any shooter worth his pay.

Though I get the sense that whoever I'm dealing with is no skittish amateur. A few potential witnesses wouldn't be enough to dissuade them if they really wanted their target dead.

I eye the woman in the rearview mirror. So far, she has far more pros in her column to support her story than cons.

"Someone tried to kill you," I say once we're far beyond the building.

She laughs from the back seat, her hair tussled, smile manic. "You seem surprised, soldier. Aren't you used to danger?"

"No," I admit. A fact I don't regret one damn bit. "Certainly not from someone this sloppy. They didn't care who the hell saw."

Which means one of two things—the would-be killer is a goddamn rookie. Or…

"Still don't believe me?" she taunts, still cackling. Another glance at her betrays her bravado for what it is. She's in shock. "Perhaps if I caught that bullet between my teeth, you'd grow bored of accusing me of lying—"

"Enough."

I pull onto the side of the road.

"What the hell are you doing?" Real fear rattles her voice as I turn to face her directly.

"Damn." This angle reveals what I couldn't see from the front—blood painting a steady trail down her forehead. I lurch toward her and grab her chin, tilting it for a better look. It's a cut, alarmingly deep. "Were you hit?"

She attempts to shrug me off. "You sound so concerned."

A few more seconds of inspection, and I have my answer anyway. She must have struck her head sometime during our retreat. A glance at her pupils reveals no worrying dilation, but I wouldn't put a concussion out of the realm of possibility.

"I suggest you trade in that motel for a hospital room," I tell her, letting her wrench out of my reach.

The words must strike a chord. She stops laughing. "You wanted to know why I would come begging to Mischa? I have nowhere left to go."

Vulnerability on her is disarming. Her voice loses its characteristic purr, her eyes an icier blue than ever. I'm not completely fooled. Manipulation is her one last trick, and I sense she's an expert at utilizing it.

I try to focus only on the logistics. The man didn't want her dead. He wanted her shaken.

"You said he needed your son," I point out.

"But not me." She presses herself against the door, averting her gaze. "In case that wasn't already obvious. I know too much. I'm too dangerous to leave alive."

"What do you know?"

Her eyes flicker, flashing a shade of blue I've come to correlate with her lies.

"Tell me the truth or here—" I reach past her and wrench on the door handle. As it opens, her eyes widen. "Get out and take your chances."

"Not much of a knight in shining armor, are you?" she spits. Then, very deliberately, she grabs the handle and pulls the door shut. "It's complex," she warns, crossing her arms, her head cocked to appraise me. The blood dripping down her cheek melds with her dress. Given her lack of visible pain, the garish liquid might as well be part of her outfit. "Your brute-like brain might not be able to handle it."

Now I'm the one laughing. Though going off her startled grimace, maybe I growled.

"Try me. You said he needed equity."

"Let's just say that his business ventures require a lot of discretion and a close proximity to the port."

Going off the disgust in her tone, I take a wild guess.

"Trafficking? Of drugs? Sex?"

She shrugs. "I'm not exactly sure. He took pains to hide most of his plots from me, but I have my methods. He's planning something big. Something dealing with the harbor, but I don't know when or what."

It's more than she meant to say. She bites her lip as if irritated by the admission.

This time, I doubt she's lying.

"You sure love to play with hypotheticals—"

"You know what isn't a hypothetical? Getting a bullet in my brain! I've told you what I know."

"So where do the Stepanovs come in?"

She sighs, leaning back against the seat. "He wants the boy," she says. "My sister's."

"Eli," I clarify. "The last Winthorp heir. Without him, your son would be next in line to inherit, if his bloodline was proven, that is."

She smirks. "I can see your suspicions forming, Mr. Soldier. Let's hope that you won't need to see a bullet whiz past his head next to believe me."

"Let's suppose I do believe you. You decided to come to Mischa with scattered bits of information and a bunch of 'what ifs'? No. You're smarter than that."

She looks away rather than meet my gaze, and I have my answer.

"He wouldn't want you dead unless you knew something important. I suggest you tell me."

"I don't know what he's planning exactly. But—" she raises a finger as I scoff in annoyance. "I think I know something. He's been working with local associates to gain a foothold in the city's infrastructure."

"Who?"

She shrugs. "Something, something, Saleri. And a sneaky bastard named Antonio Salvatore."

I sit forward, my interest piqued. *Son of a bitch.*

"*Gregori* Saleri?" I clarify.

She nods, but I'm not surprised.

A Saleri, and Antonio Salvatore. Two men with influence in the city who might have a reason to want Mischa Stepanov gone.

"I think I have your interest now, soldier," the woman says quietly. "Now, if you don't mind, get me the hell out of here."

Her eyes are on the rear window where a black car appears in the distance.

"Fuck."

I whip around, and sure enough, it's gaining ground, and I'd rather not take a chance of it being another visitor.

"Hold on," I tell her.

"Where are we going?"

I try not to give away what I'm thinking. Honestly? I don't fucking know.

"I saw the way you sneered at my motel," she remarks with a watery laugh. "You didn't stop to ask yourself why?"

She doesn't need to explain. A shitty motel with even the barest level of security would be safer against an attack than anywhere else.

Except…

"I suggest a hotel," she says. "A very nice one in the heart of the city. On *your* dime, of course."

I put the van back into drive, irritated more by the fact that she's right.

Meeting her gaze in the rearview mirror, I say, "And I suggest you keep talking."

7

WILLOW

Kisa's "cut" turns out to be more severe than Fabio's skepticism warranted. When we finally reunite, she has ten stitches to show for her ordeal, as well as her entire left arm in bandages. As for the cause of her injury, neither Donatello, nor—the man with him—Luciano, give an adequate explanation other than "it happened." Fabio raises an eyebrow at that but doesn't argue. Always more practical than emotional, he vows to get the girl new clothes instead.

Her little pink shirt and jeans are ruined, stained red. As we exit through the main lobby, the scarlet hue blazes, and she looks more morbid ghost than girl. Falling into step beside her, I can't resist straining my neck for any hint of Mischa or his men as we navigate the darkened parking garage.

I'm not the only one on edge.

"I should take Kisa," Luciano suggests, placing his hand on the girl's shoulder. "If there's any trouble, I can cover you from afar—"

"They'll both come with me," Donatello declares, circling around to a black car. "You take up the rear," he tells Luciano. "I'll lead."

"I'll ride with you Don," Fab cuts in. "I'll arrange to have my car brought back."

Donatello nods to Fab, but doesn't even look at me, though he grabs Kisa's good arm to steady her as she climbs into the back seat.

I'm more surprised by the action than I should be—along with the fact that he brought her to the hospital at all. Considering his detour to Vincenzo's wing, her injury turned out to be more of a convenience than anything.

Or an intentional ploy. Would he really harm a child to suit his own motives?

Of course, he would. *He* was the one who took Kisa from her home in the first place, according to Luciano. He killed her father and threw her in the trunk of a car as though she were a piece of luggage. Cutting her would be par for the course for him.

And yet this sick, pathetic voice in my head keeps whispering that he wouldn't.

I inspect him from the back seat as he drives, Fabio beside him. The reddish glow of passing headlights illuminates his features, enhancing the deep amber of his eyes and the stubble on his chin. If Kisa resembles a ghost, then he is the devil holding her soul captive, every bit the callous crime lord he claims to be—and these past few days have given me more than enough proof to support that image.

I should hate him. I *do.*

And yet… The little girl I used to be is harder to smother than I thought. She still can't pair that reality of who he is with the figure in my memories. I close my eyes, and I still see him—the charming Donny who played with me. Who read me bedtime stories until I fell asleep. Who swore to protect me.

The very same man who wrote passionate letters to his wife in explicit detail.

Then I open my eyes and see the monster who stripped me naked and turned my misery into his game. Jerking my chin, I stare from the window, watching darkness paint the city black. My heart pounds at the thought of returning to Havienna. Fabio won't stick around forever, and I'll have to face Donatello Vanici again.

I'm not fooled by his silence. He's going out of his way to ignore me now, but I sense an invisible timer ticking the seconds down.

The question he asked near Vincenzo's room still echoes clearly in my mind. *What did he say?* Sooner or later, he'll demand an answer.

And Vincenzo's words alone should cement the cruelty of who Donatello Vanici is at his core. He told him I was dead. All this time, he let him believe that. It's beyond malicious. It's cruel.

"Finally," Fabio exclaims.

Sick with dread, I follow his gaze, and my heart sinks when I spy the house looming on the horizon.

When we pull into the driveway, Donatello exits the vehicle without saying a word, his body bathed in shadow, eyes blazing like hellfire.

"Well, today was eventful." Fabio appears before me, extending a hand to help me from the car. "You should try to get some sleep," he continues. "By the way, Donatello, I made some calls and had my assistant find the documents you wanted. I'll come by tomorrow before the meeting. I expect to find you here, having fully rested, okay?"

The other man is already storming up the front steps, barging into the house without a response.

"He's not too talkative, is he?" someone remarks, stepping forward. Luciano. He drove the van behind us, though I suspect not by choice. Moving quickly, he approaches the door on my end, ushering out a small figure. "Come on, Kisa."

Together, Fabio and I follow them, the last to enter the house.

"That box," he murmurs to me, scanning the hall warily for Donatello. "Bring it to me now. I'll wait here."

Only now does the amusing nature of my predicament truly sink in. From captive to unwanted house guest. It's obvious which iteration of those roles Donatello would prefer I keep.

Fabio's talk of "equal terms" is just that in the eyes of Donatello Vanici—talk. He prefers I be locked away, a foe he can rail against, rather than an equal he has to face on even ground.

Ironically, the foundation of this old house seems to conspire with his wishes. The floorboards creak beneath my weight, and I half expect them to crack as I mount the staircase.

From here, Donatello is visible as a shadow, marching toward his study. Up ahead, Luciano is herding Kisa down the hall into her room.

I'm ignored for the time being—time that a smart woman would use to plot some way of turning the tables again. Proving to Mischa that I don't aim to humiliate him. He is my family.

Donatello will always be the enemy.

Being here reinforces that divide. My throat itches with every dust-choked breath I take. I miss the quiet beauty of Stepanov manor, and my old room. Thoughts of it haunt me as I ascend the rest of the steps and enter that pink hell, shutting the door behind me. The back of my neck prickles with the awareness of Donatello lurking below as I tiptoe past the box of Olivia's belongings. Hidden beside the bed, I find the silver container untouched.

Though his motives are unclear, I doubt Fabio is a liar. He meant what he said—in exchange for the letters, he'll arrange for me to see Ellen and Eli. It's an offer that should easily outweigh the allure of any secrets I could uncover. There is no real choice to make.

But…

Olivia's scent teases the air, and the truth feels far more complicated. Curiosity is a dangerous temptation—but it might be my only way to gain some leverage. Insight. To learn more of the man who wrote of his wife as though she were the driving force of his entire world.

In theory, I should only need a night to read them all. No more. Then I can give everything to Fabio without regret.

I don't let myself overthink the action as I return the box to its hiding place. When I find Fabio, still at the base of the steps, I shrug with what I hope is a helpless expression.

"You couldn't find it? Damn!" He strokes his chin, pacing the length of the foyer. "I know it couldn't have gone far. Maybe I dropped it on my way to the car…"

He's so caught up in retracing his steps, that he doesn't even say goodbye.

And I'm left alone to pore over Donatello Vanici's secrets in peace.

Even as I reenter the pink room, doubt has me second-guessing everything. It's selfish to lie to a man about his own sister. Selfish to read the words of a dead woman.

Reading them in this house feels wrong. I wish I could sneak onto the porch, but gauging Donatello's reaction this morning, leaving would only give him an excuse to rage. I consider locking the door, but I wind up crouching on the edge of the bed without doing so.

Let him rage. The sting of the lie he told Vincenzo aches badly enough to blind me to any caution. He's controlled the narrative for so damn long…

It's about time I glean some knowledge of my own.

As quietly as possible, I open the box, hunching over the contents. In the harsh glow of the ceiling light, the letters look pristine, as if stolen from Donatello's desk this morning.

Some of my favorite moments were spent curled at his feet, watching him work through my lashes. Nothing in the world could compare to his face when he forgot to maintain that hard, stern frown. His lips would droop, and some of the intensity would leave his gaze. Not much, but just enough. I could see into his head, then, or so I thought. See every concern and woe to trouble his mind…

But as I scan the first letter, I realize that it's a good thing my child-self couldn't actually do so.

I woke up with the taste of you on my lips, and I finally knew what peace was. He wrote. I stiffen as the page slips from my grasp, landing face-up on the floor. All I can do is stare at it.

I didn't need the confirmation, but now I know for sure how hollow his sexual taunts to me really were. None of them packed the same punch as the ones he penned years ago.

I need you, Liv. Every day like fucking air to breathe, I need you. Don't forget that. I know it hasn't been easy. I love you more for sticking it out. I love you.

If I didn't know his handwriting so well, I'd assume I found someone else's stash of love letters. Not Donatello Vanici's.

Heart racing, I set the first letter aside and grab another. This one isn't quite so intimate, and the handwriting is different from his. Lighter.

Don. I miss you. I miss you.

I never knew Olivia well, but I can sense the pain she must have writing this. Missing a man whose smile could light up a room. Someone so caught up in his work at times it could seem like he was in another world.

I never feel better than when I'm inside you, he replied in his next letter. *When your body is the only thing tethering me to this fucking planet, your moans in my ear. I live for that, Liv. All I want is to give you what you deserve. I'll make it up to you for all the nights you've been alone…*

The next page is in my hands before I realize it. Soon, I lose track of how many I devour.

It's an addictive feeling as much as it is repulsive. For once, I'm truly inside the head of Donatello Vanici. The man he used to be, anyway. Someone so driven he'd do whatever it took to succeed—and yet so blinded by ambition he didn't notice the changes taking place in his own wife, evident on the pages.

I had been far too young to grasp her emotions, then. With this newer perspective, so many old memories have greater context—the wistful way she used to stare from the window during the long days Donatello was gone. I missed him too, but I couldn't imagine the sheer depth of her loneliness. Her aching, desperate loneliness.

You stay with me for one night every ten, and it's heaven, baby. And it is hell to wake up knowing you're going to leave me again. I love you so much. I'll never doubt that you believe you're doing this for us—but sometimes I just need you. I need you to be with me.

It's strange how you can feel so connected to someone merely by the words they leave behind. The connection between Olivia and Donatello is as palpable as the paper in my grasp.

Their love should seem as inspiring as it did when I was younger. Beautiful. But I feel an ominous sensation gnawing through my gut the more I read. Because of Donatello's innuendo? Or the fact that Olivia's missives become shorter the deeper into the stack I go…

So I fucked up, Donatello wrote one day, a blunt admission when compared to the previous romantic exchanges. It's the echo of the monster he would eventually reveal himself to be—always enraged. *We're in the same damn house, and you can't talk to me? Talk to me. Write me a fucking letter if you have to. Talk to me.*

Sometimes it feels like this is the only way we actually understand each other, Olivia replied. *I miss you.*

When I reach for the next folded note, I realize that it's one of the final few remaining. Donatello's writing is stark across the page as if he pored over every letter, pressing against the paper until it tore in places.

You can't even look at me, he wrote. *Even when I'm inside you, you're miles away. I know I did this. You have the right to be pissed. But I need you to talk to me, Olivia. Tell me what I can do to fix us. I love you too much to let you slip away.*

Was their marriage in more trouble than I realized? Olivia's response isn't on the next page—but the slashed handwriting conveys the author's anger even before I read his words. *You don't want me. You don't seem to want this baby. What the fuck do you want, Liv?*

I read those lines over and over, gripping the page so tightly a rip appears in the middle. Safiya never witnessed this tension, so brutally spelled out. Wracking my memory, I can't recall a single fight between them.

For the first time, I'm wary of what else I might discover. The past feels as fragile as a house of cards—and as much as I loathe Donatello, I don't want everything from those days tainted. Still, I grapple for the next letter…

And a shadow falls over me. At the same time, my nostrils flare with a scent that has become engrained on my subconscious—a potent, lethal musk, fresher than the traces embedded in these pages.

I finally look up, already resigned to what I'll find—Donatello Vanici himself standing in the doorway. He could be a figment of my imagination if he weren't so drastically different from the man I remember, the same passionate figure forever immortalized in his own letters.

This man has aged decades in seven years, his hair unkempt, his eyes narrowed to slits. Behind him, the door sways, and I wonder if he threw it open, letting it slam.

If so, I'd been too engrossed in the past to notice. The ink beneath my fingertips seems to prove what I felt in the car —I wasn't wrong. He wasn't always like this. An irrational impulse to preserve the evidence has me shoving the box behind me.

But it's too late. He's already spotted the haphazard stack of read letters on my lap, and recognition flits across his face. I hate shock on him. It's brief but jarring, undercutting his rage with a dangerous glimpse of what lurks beneath—*pain*. Unimaginable in quality, comparable only to a stab wound.

Straight through the heart.

A grunt rips from his chest, and he staggers, his hand grasping for the doorknob. The color drains from his expression, humanizing him for a heartbeat.

Before rage swiftly sets in.

I tense, expecting him to lunge. Instead, his eyes flit up to mine, ice-cold. "Where the hell did you—"

"No!" A tiny voice pierces the thin wall, loud enough to drown out his growl.

"What the hell?" Donatello stiffens, bouncing on the balls of his feet as if torn between lurching at me or investigating the sound.

Then several more shrieks pierce the air. "No! No!"

Alarm washes over me as I recognize that high-pitched cry. *Kisa.*

"Fuck." Donatello turns, racing into the hall. I'm already on my feet, following him despite every instinct warning me not to.

As we advance down the hall, a masculine voice rings out. "I have to, honey. Just let me—"

"No! I said no!"

The door to Vin's old room is already ajar, and inside, Luciano stands over a crying Kisa.

"She took her bandage off," he explains.

Sure enough, she's clutching her injured arm to her chest, sitting amid a pile of bloodstained bandages. The fact that she's still wearing her bloody clothes adds a ghoulish quality to her vacant expression. She's a broken doll, her dark curls astray, those big blue eyes utterly lifeless.

"I'm trying to help her redo it," Luciano explains. "But she won't let me—"

"No!" Kisa screams, coming to life to bat away his attempts, her arms flailing. "You can't cover it."

"We need to," Luciano insists, crouching to her level. He grabs a nearby metal box that has *First Aid* written across it. "Let me fix it. You might open the stitches—"

"No! No, you can't! If you cover it up, I'll get sick and die like Mama! You can't."

I take a step toward her—and the color drains from her face. As a gust of warm air grazes the back of my neck, I realize why.

"You're making a lot of noise for someone who is in danger of getting sick and dying," a man declares from behind me.

As he stalks forward, I do a double take. The strange dichotomy of the two Donatellos is on display once again. The only change? His voice. Underlying warmth softens the guttural baritone just enough to differentiate from the customary growl he uses with me.

Regardless, Kisa whimpers. My heart flinches at the sight of him towering over her like the monster from a fairy tale. She's so tiny. Helpless.

I don't think. I just react, reaching for the hand he extends toward her. His eyes cut to mine, and I freeze. I can't name what passes between us. Understanding? After days of torment and animosity, the fleeting hint of clarity strikes me to my core. *He won't hurt her.*

Do I truly believe that? I don't have the chance to decide; he's already crouching down on one knee, much like Luciano had.

"Let me see it." He extends his hand out to her.

"No." Her tone wavers, but far softer than the one she took with Luciano. "I'll die. I'll get sick and die."

"You ever been shot?"

Kisa blinks while Luciano curses under his breath. "She's just a kid—"

"Have you?" Donatello presses, but a softer inflection betrays he isn't trying to scare her. Yet. "Because I have."

He tugs aside the collar of his shirt, revealing a wealth of scars marring the tanned flesh. My breathing feathers with recognition. Less than twenty-four hours ago, I felt each one up close, sensing the varying textures beneath my fingertips. Every scrape. Every scratch. Every scar.

Kisa's eyes widen at the sight of one wound in particular—a silvery circle along his right shoulder.

"You know what saved my life?" Donatello asks, readjusting his collar. Then he reaches for the first aid kit. "Bandages."

"No," Kisa whines as he fishes out a clean length of gauze. "Mama hurt her arms, and then she wore bandages, and then she went away!"

My brain takes that statement, translating it from the childish phrasing to a darker reality. *Mama hurt her arms. Then she went away.* Could she really be alluding to the worst-case scenario?

Luciano winces, his expression pained. "Kisa—"

"I knew someone who hurt her arms too," Donatello says while arranging various utensils on the floor before him. "She didn't die because of the bandages. I think your mama had the same sickness, and I can tell you for a fact that you don't have it."

The sad part is I don't know if he's lying or not. His tone straddles the boundary between gruff and unemotional. If he isn't bluffing, then it's yet another example of how little I really know about him.

Kisa observes him cautiously. "How?"

"Because I said so," he declares. "And I know everything."

Despite the curt tone, Kisa seems to mull over that line of logic. "Is that why you hurt my daddy?"

"Honey, you're bleeding." Luciano hisses through his teeth, noting the bright scarlet streaking across the front of her already filthy pink shirt. "You need to let us fix it. Now."

She eyes both men for another tense few seconds before finally, extending her wounded hand toward Donatello.

He's efficient in his movements, briskly cleaning her wound with antiseptic and testing the integrity of the stitches. Apparently satisfied with their state, he rebandages her arm with a familiarity that makes me suspect this isn't the first time he's bound a wound.

Given his line of work, it probably won't be the last.

"Keep them on," he warns once finished. "Take them off again, and you risk that cut getting infected. It might not kill you, but it definitely could wind up in you needing your hand amputated. That means cut off. Understand?"

She nods, inching closer to Luciano, who places a hand protectively on her shoulder.

Donatello stands, turning for the door. His eyes meet mine a second time as he passes me, but I can't decipher the emotion they convey. Something that makes me shiver even as he finally leaves the room. Perhaps the look contained a dare.

Or a warning.

I banish the unease in favor of turning my sole focus to Kisa. I help Luciano wipe the blood from the floor and her skin, but he hisses in disgust at the sight of her shirt.

"Could you grab a new one?" He nods to indicate a box in the corner of the room, and my blood runs cold.

It's dented, aged with time, but I recognize the contents as I approach. My old clothes—*Safiya's* clothes—all bought on Donatello Vanici's dime. He even picked them out for me…

No. I disconnect from the assorted garments, searching through them as I would any random clothing. Eventually, I resurface with a fresh light blue shirt and jeans, handing them both to Luciano.

"What the fuck is up with him?" he asks, cutting his eyes toward the doorway. Then he seems to remember the child within earshot, and he clears his throat. "Time for bed, Kisa."

I watch her obediently take the clothing and scramble into the closet to change. The question she asked Donatello keeps echoing in my brain. *Is that why you hurt my daddy?*

After he claimed to know everything.

What could—at least in her mind—warrant her own father worthy of death? The possibilities are chilling. I don't want to know the answer.

Though…would I have wished the same on Gino Mangenello? Looking back, I never mourned him the way I have the man who betrayed me.

But Gino wasn't the person I expected to tuck me in at night. His voice isn't the one I remember murmuring bedtime stories to me as I drifted off. As it stands, I barely even knew him.

I didn't know Donatello either, apparently. The man from my past and the current iteration might as well be two different people—but at least now I have proof. I wasn't wrong, and I wasn't a fool for trusting him, at least not then.

Something changed in him—and I think it went beyond Olivia's death. Fabio's reaction to the silver box all but cements that.

Some memories are better left buried...

What did he mean? Renewed curiosity spurs me into the hall, my fingers flexing impatiently at my sides. I know Donatello saw me with the letters—I'm taking a risk by even returning to that room.

But they alone provide insight into a side of him I'd been blind to as a child. Perhaps they contain the answer as to why he did it. Why he left?

I can only hope he assumed they were nothing of importance. Just trash.

When I round the doorway of that pink room, I don't know if I'm surprised or relieved to discover the silver box lying on the end of the bed. As I come closer, though, I realize the letters I left behind are gone. A tendril of dread runs down the back of my neck before I even open the box. Only one slip of folded paper remains inside it, but it's stark white.

New.

When I unfold it, the message is simple, penned in fresh ink that smears as I run my finger across it.

You want to nose into the past? You come ask me directly.

8

DON

All those letters I wrote to Liv… I don't even know where the witch found them; I just know they're real. To make sure, I bring them beneath my nose and inhale the crisp scent they still carry.

Lilacs and honey. Closing my eyes, I see her clearly for the first time in so damn long, still beautiful. Still mine. That upturned nose and hazel eyes. *Liv…*

I continue to breathe her in—but another, fresher smell doesn't belong, itching my nostrils. *Roses.* It's an insidious stench, overpowering Olivia's until she vanishes completely.

I wonder how many letters the little witch read.

Writing them was Liv's idea. *"Come on! It's silly, but it's also romantic,"* she explained, flashing her crinkled smile. Silly or not, I would have carved the notes into my skin if she asked me to. So, I settled for scribbling a piece of my soul down on paper every damn day. For her, only her. Like lovestruck teenagers, we traded the notes back and forth, leaving them under the pillows on our bed.

After all this time, I can't even remember what they say. Not a damn one. Anyone else might crave the chance to re-explore these snippets of the past, but I toss them aside. For what it's worth, little Willow can win this battle. I'm not brave enough to unearth these memories. Hell no.

The past is dead.

For good measure, I shove the letters in a desk drawer and turn my focus toward the one thing I have any damn control over—the future. Once I adjust my insurance policy, Vin will be protected, and my little wife will finally get to see her revenge enacted…

Everyone wins.

I smile at the thought, but the satisfaction doesn't last long. A familiar scent catches my nostrils, fresher than the stench infecting the letters. *Roses.* The source appears in the doorway the second I identify it, her hair loose, a new slip of paper in her grasp.

I blink to see if she vanishes like Olivia.

She doesn't; my imagination isn't wild enough to conjure that haughty fucking expression. She and Fab project a similar smugness. Like they know something I don't, while they conspire together, visiting Vincenzo without me. Did he give her those letters in the first place?

I wouldn't put it past him in some misguided attempt at "peace."

"What do you want?" I flatten my hand against the desk, noting its width in comparison to that pretty, pale neck. I could curl a fist around that throat and have my fingers meet. One hard twist would snap it.

I should do far worse than that.

"What did he say to you?" Fresh irritation roughens my voice. I should have confronted her the second I saw her in his room.

Hell, maybe *that* was my karmic punishment—watching her stand over Vin's lifeless body after I tried my damn hardest to destroy her. God is a cruel son of a bitch.

So is she. Her eyes reflect nothing but my own staring back. She has no trouble reading me, but it's rare when I can't read her.

I slam my hand against the desk hard, and she jumps, not so stoic after all. "Tell me."

She doesn't have to. Her cheeks flush pink with rage, and it's confirmation enough. Despite his weakened state, Vin told her the truth—he thought Safiya was dead.

Fuck. I sit back, caught off guard by the guilt rising in my gut.

Do I regret the lie? No. If Vin knew what I actually did, that I left her...

He would never forgive me for that.

Never.

She's smart enough to have already guessed that. It's why she's here, even if she can't state as much out loud —blackmail.

Well, she can get in line. As I lift my hand, a streak of blood draws my notice—the Salvatore girl's. She's another future hellcat with an ax to grind, not to mention the Saleris, and Mischa, and whoever set this all into motion…

In the grand scheme, Willow Stepanova is one in a long line of many.

"You think you have leverage over me now?" I say, cutting to the chase. A chuckle slips from me before I can help it, but the little witch isn't playing along.

Her eyes widen as if she's confused by the statement. *Bullshit.* I'm not falling for the innocent act.

"Fine," I admit. "You got your wish. I'll play. Keep your mouth shut. Or…"

Once again, those eyes convey her response without her having to utter a word. *Or what?*

"If he knew… It would kill him," I say coldly. Though, I can't keep the truth from him forever. "Give me time to tell him myself."

She purses her lips. *Why?*

"You seem to be in the habit of making ultimatums," I point out. "Keep your mouth shut, and you set the terms."

I expect her to pretend she's above blackmail, but she seems to enjoy proving me wrong.

Rather than leave, she approaches the desk. Shock roots me to the spot, and she's close enough to touch before I know it, that frothy yellow dress swishing around her. The thin fabric conforms to those softly curving breasts and slender hips, falling just above her knees. By her side, a pale hand flinches, and I suspect what she's after even before she flattens her palm against the wood's surface.

Let me speak.

I tug open a drawer—the same one I shoved the letters into —and withdraw a fresh sheet of paper and a pen, sliding both toward her. She takes them in her delicate hands, manipulating each one the way I assume she would piano keys.

Mischa turned her into a musician, but at her core, she's an assassin—whether it's a knife, or a pen, she wields both weapons against me without hesitation. The cut she left on my cheek still stings, but I must be addicted to her brand of pain. Here I am, letting her take yet another shot. I shouldn't indulge her. Her words shouldn't matter.

I'm staring anyway, feeling the front of my pants tighten. Watching her write is way more enthralling than it should be. As sick as it sounds, there's something sensual in how she grips that pen. Her thumb strokes the barrel as she takes her time forming each word.

The end result is blunt as hell—*You lied to him. You are a coward.*

I grit my teeth. Surprisingly, I don't feel the anger I'd expect. She's right. I lied to Vincenzo, and I'd do so again.

"I am a coward," I admit, leveling her with a searching look. "But no different from your Mischa."

Her eyes cut to slits. *Don't you turn this on him.*

But it's the only weapon I have—deflection.

"He knew my identity," I add, sitting forward.

She bites her lip and *goddamn*. The sight of that pink flesh between her teeth is hell. Aware of my attention, her eyes narrow, her cheeks reddening—but she can't deny she's pissed. Good.

"Mischa," I continue, fighting to stay focused on the topic at hand. "He let me live all this time in proximity to you without breathing a word. He denied you your revenge. Does that count as a lie?"

Her nostrils flare as she retracts her teeth, leaving her lip blood-red. It's the closest I figure she'll come to an outright snarl, and it's a look that requires no interpretation—*You are a monster.*

"I thought we already established that I *am* a monster," I point out.

She doesn't look satisfied by the admission. Her eyes trace mine in that searching way I noticed last night, and it takes everything in me to hold still.

I last only a heartbeat before turning away. My gaze is on the drawer again, and I have to wonder. What the hell did she read in those damn letters? Something to dampen her anger with more goddamn curiosity.

I consider ripping one open to find out. But why should I? If intimidation doesn't sway her, I know what will.

"How many of those letters did you read?"

Her pink lips quirk downward.

"Not all of them," I say, my suspicion confirmed. "You want to poke inside my brain, little wife? Nose into the past? Be my guest. I'll let you."

The witch might as well be made of glass. Nothing can disguise the flicker of interest crossing her face.

"Keep your mouth shut, and I'll give you what you want. I'll give you the letters. Read to your fucking heart's content, I don't care."

Slowly, though, I don't mention that part. I'll give her pieces one at a time to stave off the inevitable.

But she's not so easy to manipulate. Skepticism is written all across that pouty little mouth.

"Here." I wrench open the drawer and eye the letters. She already had them sorted between the bed and the box. I'm assuming the ones she hadn't read were still inside it. Maybe ten, if that. I grab the topmost one and present it to her on the flat of my palm. "I'm a man of my word."

Too late, do I realize the irony of that. She doesn't take the letter, lifting the pen instead. Her words come faster.

Why did you lie to him?

I frown, caught off guard by yet another direct question.

"Why?" I lean back in my chair, eyeing the ceiling. "You know the answer to that, little wife."

The only one that makes sense, anyway. Nonetheless, I give her what she wants and utter the line with all the bravado it deserves. "I couldn't face the shame."

I look over, expecting to find her smug. Instead, she grabs that pen again.

You're lying.

A surprised grunt rips from my throat. "Why would I lie?"

That pen remains in her grasp, her gaze turned inward as if she's mulling it over.

Damn her.

Curiosity is unnerving on that pretty face. Alarming. If I had to guess what those letters contain, personal shit I could only say to Liv. Thoughts of her. Descriptions of her. Of us.

Maybe the little witch has a voyeur streak?

"Do you want it or not?" I raise the letter, fingering the end as though I mean to rip it in half—and I should.

I don't realize she moves until the page starts to slip from my grasp. She wants it. So badly she forgets to disguise the desperate, hungry gleam in her eye.

Right when she almost has it freed, I snatch the letter back.

"I've changed my mind. Let's talk first, before we discuss business. Get a few things squared away. Unless you want to leave?"

I expect her to run. She surprises me again by perching herself on the edge of the nearest chair. The tight line of her jaw warns she's well aware of what I'll ask before I even voice it.

That doesn't mean I don't take pleasure in doing so. "Fine. Let's talk about last night, and why you came into my room —" Damn. The genuine curiosity leeching into my tone shouldn't be there. "What was your intent? To seduce me in the hopes of derailing our little engagement? Did you really think it would be so easy?"

WILLOW

Did you think it would be so easy?

Smug cruelty lurks within his tone, bordering on obscene. Why did I "come" into his room last night? The obvious response is innocent on its face. I heard him having a nightmare and went to investigate.

The real answer lurks deep within that nest of emotions he alone arouses in me. Hateful fascination is one way to describe it. A need to prod. To poke. To hate everything there is to hate about Donatello Vanici and push him to his breaking point.

Lies... The voice is faint, easy to ignore at first—but ruthlessly persistent. *You love proving him wrong. You crave his attention. It's why you're here. It's why you've stayed...*

My initial impulse is to deny. I don't want a damn thing from him, though if I did...

I've gotten my wish. His eyes are riveted to me, piercing through flesh and bone. I have his *undivided* attention.

"Did you think I would ignore it?" His tone is genuinely puzzled, once again steering the conversation toward a topic I've spent all day suppressing. "Pretend it never happened. Live in shame? No, little *principessa*. My cock may react to you, but that's as far as any attraction goes."

His words hit their bullseye. I'm blushing; I can't help it. Even Mischa's guards never spoke vulgarly within earshot of the family.

Not that anyone would dare talk to me the way he does. It's his only method of turning the tables—insulting me. Scaring me.

But he's not the only one capable of analyzing that moment. My eyes drift shut, and I'm in his room again, on that bed…

A disorienting sensation makes me sway, like that anxious few seconds before a live performance. Still, I push through, hunting each recollection for something to use against him. Perhaps his size. My breath escapes in a rush as I recall the way his weight pinned me down. Never in my life had I felt as small as I did beneath him. So exposed. In fact, I remember feeling a distinct hardness graze my hip…

His cock reacted to me, all right.

When I open my eyes again, the pen is still in my grasp. I level it against the page before I even process what I'm writing.

Voice rasping, he recites the words as I go, switching the pronouns. "What makes me think that you could want me?"

I can almost hear the statement strike true. *Bullseye.* I hit my target, but at what cost?

That particular wording proposes a dangerous hypothetical. Why would the daughter of a man who could offer her the world want someone like him? A washed-up crime lord with little to his name, forced to play mind games to stay afloat. A creature with no warmth. No soul.

The logical cons add up, but I make the mistake of meeting his searching stare, and all thoughts derail.

"I think you should elaborate, little wife," he prods, his voice dangerously low.

I ignore the bait, responding only to the direct challenge. Elaborate? I'll put it bluntly.

I am a Stepanov. What could you possibly offer me?

I've always refused to embody such a haughty mindset—the arrogance of an heiress with her nose in the air. In this moment, pride is my armor, and I wear it proudly.

My opponent, however, isn't so easily deterred. He stands, circling to my side of the desk.

As his steps draw nearer, warmth teases my cheek, and I face the wall rather than give him the satisfaction of looking his way. I don't have to—I've memorized his touch by feel. His *thumb* is the source of the slight pressure, grazing the space beneath my lip.

Then lower, down my throat.

Lower still.

Only when he nears the flowy neckline of my dress does he pause, stroking the fabric in a way that dares me to react—but I'm frozen. Every nerve in my skin paralyzes with awareness of him.

He feels so different from how he should. Not repulsive. Just ragged. Rugged. Years of pain and toil have shaped the grating texture of his callouses and the harshness of each gnarled scar…

Hands brutal enough to ruthlessly kill a man. Soft enough to bandage an injured child.

I'm so distracted by the conflicting sensations that I nearly miss the second he lets his hand drift downward, over my breast. Not because he truly desires to touch me.

This is just to prove he *can*. When he wants to. How he wants to.

Time slows to a crawl as his fingers deliberately trace that mound of flesh, grazing over my nipple with each pass. With light pressure at first. Then harder, sowing a burst of electrifying heat.

My reaction is automatic—I bat his hand away, and he chuckles in triumph.

"Don't be shy now, *principessa...*" His mouth finds my ear. "What could I offer you? Nothing. Nothing that would appeal to a sheltered little girl." Irritation roughens his voice, and I know my words hit their mark. I've won this round.

Not that I have long to savor my victory. I don't see defeat in his expression as he moves to stand before me. Instead, his upper lip quirks in a disarming smirk.

"The real question you should be asking is, if I'm so beneath you, why do you keep coming back for more?" He cradles my chin against his palm, letting his fingers rest against my fluttering pulse point. "I guess even an heiress can be a glutton for punishment."

I don't think. I just write. From the corner of my eye, I see the end of the pen dance across the page, guided by my hand, and I draw strength from my ability to finally counter him on a level playing field. I won't be silenced again.

Though, he craves nothing more than to ignore me. His brows furrow as he mulls whether or not to break eye contact first—then he does, reading aloud. "Then why strip you naked?"

It's a damn good question, and I'm surprised by just how much I crave an answer. Why does he enjoy lording his sex over me, if corruption isn't his end goal? If I don't appeal to him, why look at me like I do? Why groan in torment that I was beautiful before he knew who I really was?

As if the same thought is on his mind, his eyelashes flicker, obscuring his intentions.

"Why?" Without warning, he reaches out, fingering a lock of my hair. "Because it unnerves you. You hate being out of control."

His grated tone unlocks a memory I've tried to suppress.

Touching myself, knowing he was watching. Letting him stare. Knowing that he couldn't stop me even if he wanted to...

"Use that brain of yours, *principessa*," he scolds, and the memory fades. "Your body isn't what I'm after."

Liar. The other night wasn't the first time we neared some unspoken boundary, that moment in the shower, for instance. How his eyes raked me over while he bit his lip —the same way I'm doing now, biting hard enough to sting.

"You do this when you're angry," he declares, stroking my chin.

I wrench away from him, but it's a second before I realize what he means.

"Bite your lip like that—" his eyes fixate on my mouth. "You do it when you're angry, even when you're aroused. You don't believe me?"

I'm doing it now. Defiant, I pry my jaw apart, exposing my wet lips to him, teeth bared—but this is exactly what he wants. My rage. My anger. My hate. He feeds off every emotion, seeming to grow larger and more dominating until I'm drowning in his shadow. He wants me seething and helpless.

It's the only way he knows how to operate.

I may bite my lip, but he has his own tells. The way his eyes flash, for one, when I kissed him. Or when I met his gaze without flinching the other night. When I prove I'm not afraid of him.

I stand, and, almost instantaneously, he steps back.

"I suggest you run off to bed. Get some sleep," he taunts. "Though, maybe you should practice what little skill you showed off with those fingers. You'll be a lonely wife on our wedding night—"

He falls silent mid-word as I reach for the pen. A muscle in his jaw flexes, the same way it did the other day in the elevator when I dared to challenge him. If I had to decipher its meaning, I'd guess alarm mixed with a hint of amusement.

Writing to him is an unnecessary gimmick, but it turns the tables. With a few strokes of ink, he's beside me, craning his neck over my shoulder to devour every word.

"I've seen you naked," he recites, providing his growled version of narration. It's unsettling how aggressive he makes me sound. Bold. "I've violated you, seen you, touched you… What do I define as sex?" His tone deepens with a rare hint of unease. I wish I could savor it, but my heart is racing. Especially when he utters gruffly, "You want to codify your virginity?"

I drop the pen, letting the thud as it meets the desk speak for me. *Why not?*

I face him, allowing him to see the dare I know lurks in my expression. What does Donatello Vanici deem corruption? Something more than kissing. Touching. More than looming over someone as they experience a twisted sense of intimacy.

I want him to flinch. Cringe. Admit his shame.

He laughs in my face.

"Oh, *principessa*. If I wanted you…" He strokes my cheek again, this time letting his nail graze the tender skin. "You'd know it. I'd have my cock inside of you, for one. You'd feel my seed against your womb, and you wouldn't need to ask what corruption feels like. Don't be fooled by our little games. Your worth to me has only ever extended to who your father is, and the role you play. Willow Stepanova."

A lie. I know it is. Confident of that, I withstand his mocking laughter without flinching. I don't turn away.

Instead, I grapple for the pen and write.

So kissing isn't corruption?

Or seeing me naked or telling me to touch myself. The list goes on and on, but in the world of Donatello Vanici, those count merely as a game—one he thinks I'm too bashful to play. But he's wrong.

In all other ways, he's stripped my identity, but *he* can't break this one last boundary. The same reckless impulse that infected me in the elevator strikes again. I step away from the desk, dropping the pen. Using that same hand, I grip the neckline of my dress, tugging on the fabric the way he exposed his scars to Kisa.

My display isn't quite so dramatic. This body doesn't contain nearly the same number of secrets his does. The cool air tickles my exposed skin, rousing a reaction I can't suppress. He notices, his eyes darting from my face, to my body and back.

I've made my point but, breathing heavily, I keep going, dragging the fabric down as far as I can. My breasts creep beneath the modest neckline first. Then one nipple. Another.

Narrowed to slits, his eyes rebel, raking over my body to snatch glimpses of what he claims to not desire.

The attention is proof enough—he's a liar.

I can read it so clearly in his gaze; it's laughable. How his eyes narrow over my bared breasts, tracing a path down my stomach as if he can't help himself.

"Enough," he hisses, his voice so detached I stiffen. "Don't embarrass yourself."

Shame nibbles away at my resolve. Maybe I'm wrong? Or not. He's always been like this, able to easily turn the tables.

The only way to ever defeat him has been via one method, and one method only.

Play dirty.

Slowly, I raise my hand, dragging my fingers sloppily over my own skin. Why exactly? I don't have a clear aim in mind —not until I see his eyes widen. The tip of my index finger is nearing the swell of my breast. Closer…

I've never explored myself like this. Not even that night in his bed did I feel this exposed. On display. Doubt creeps in. I almost give in to the overwhelming impulse urging me to stop. Hide.

Somehow, the sight of a muscle lurching in his jaw gives me the strength needed to keep going, grazing the peak entirely. A jolt shoots through me as his eyes cut to slits.

So, I do it again.

The strange sensation continues to build as I swipe over the tip of a nipple a third time. I hate the feeling. But I repeat the action, watching him all the while.

Again.

Again.

I barely see him move before his fingers latch over my wrist, ripping my hand away. "Don't—"

He breaks off, releasing me, but the reaction is proof enough. After all this time, he can't bring himself to tarnish his precious little Safy.

How noble of him.

Tears sting my eyes, and for a second, I almost can't swallow down the wave of bile that rises up my throat. It's sick to think this way. Objectively I know it's insane. Disgusting. Wrong.

But I'm not that girl anymore. No one can ever use that past against me, least of all him.

He taunts me with corruption.

I'll give him something far better than that. My head is throbbing with the weight of the twisted, insane need for revenge—but it feels better than wallowing in hate.

I'll make him sully the part of me he's left untouched. I'll make him destroy me.

He takes a step back as if reading my intentions. So, I move forward, clinging to this newfound power. Step by step, I invade his personal space.

He lets me come close. Close enough to feel his breath. To choke on his scent and be reminded in vivid detail of the other night. As his eyes darken, I even get a glimpse of the fleeting look I saw in him then. Fear.

Then he blinks, and he's ice. "You think you can seduce me?" His breath is hot against my exposed throat. "Stick to the boys around your little manor. You have some appeal as a captive toy to dangle over Mischa's head, but apart from that? You aren't woman enough."

I almost falter. Almost. Any other time, I'd retreat to lick my wounds. He's anticipating as much, lowering his gaze to my mouth as if waiting for my so-called tell to appear.

Instead, I lift my hand to his jaw, pressing my fingers against the hard plane of it. His frown is an electric twitch of muscle, but I keep going, copying the way he stroked my mouth, tracing the seam of his lips with my thumb. His are larger than mine, alarmingly soft. I'm nearing the middle when they part, his breath like fire.

I don't remember inching closer. Maybe he's the one that closes the gap first, bringing our chests within a hair's width of distance? The front of my dress feels tighter, the fabric sandpaper against parts of me that tense involuntarily. My breasts. My nipples.

Alarm is a living thing I have to choke down. Once I do, I try to ignore everything but the need to keep touching him. To prove…

What?

That I affect him. He's forced to cock his head to maintain eye contact, and when his nostrils flare, I know it's not a normal breath. He's inhaling me and me alone.

The longer I extend the contact, the more unstable he becomes. In a flash of white, he bares his teeth as if to bite. Then his lips spread further apart, mouthing the pad of my finger.

I've yanked my hand back before I even realize it. "Don't play with fire, little Stepanova—" that same tongue traces the rim of his mouth. "This is a game you should *want* to lose."

But I've always been a sore loser. He is, too—and we both were prone to cheating just to avoid defeat.

I don't think. I just move, sliding the same finger I had at his mouth into my own. I can't explain why. To see his reaction, or so I tell myself. Not to taste him. Regardless, the mingled flavors of salt and musk explode over my tongue, and my thoughts scatter.

I've tasted him before, but never like this—a carefully controlled dose of Donatello Vanici. He is all the things fairy tales warn their readers to avoid—the same stories he used to read to me years ago. Vile nuance. Bitter aftertaste.

A flavor that goes on and on, igniting a trail down my throat, through my spine, pooling between my legs…

I despise my body's reaction, how my belly quivers, heart pounds. I should choke. I start to rip the digit out, but then I see his expression, and my brain spirals all over again.

In a violent tandem, his nostrils flare and deflate. Flare and deflate.

Then he moves. Two broad strides bring him closer, and there is no escape. My jaw is in his grasp, helpless against the force he applies to wrench it back. Before I can move, his thumb nudges my lips apart, demanding entry to steal his own taste.

I bite down automatically, catching the meaty pad between my teeth, but he doesn't move. He doesn't even flinch.

I don't relent, applying more pressure. More. More.

His eyes glint almost as if daring me to keep going. Hurt him. Harder. *More!*

My jaw aches with the pressure. Eventually, hot liquid floods my tongue, tasting like salt and copper. Disgust rips through me, but I don't pull away. I can't.

Not until he does, dragging his thumb against my cheek as he retreats. My heart hammers as he turns away, putting his back to me. I swipe my hand across my face, choking down the mysterious liquid. When I look at my fingers, they're streaked with scarlet.

"Let's talk about why you're here—Vincenzo," he says, distracting from my building horror. I watch him, fighting to get my breathing under control. In and Out. Out and In...

His composure is enviable. He's stone again, and doubt gnaws away at the back of my skull. Was it all an act? Maybe I don't affect him.

"You get to pry into my past," he says, his voice level once more. "In return, you keep your mouth shut."

My mind struggles to keep up. *Pry.* It's a grudging offer, but I can see through it to the unspoken dare underneath. Play my role. Stay within the box he's set for me. Uphold his lie. Remain a martyr.

And most importantly? Don't test him.

I remember the way he relished unnerving me back at his warehouse. His initial tactic? Strip me down to nothing and watch me squirm. He mocks me for interpreting that as desire, but would he feel the same if the tables were turned?

The thought is so dangerous I can't seriously consider it. So, I don't think at all. My knees bend, dropping me to the floor. With my eyes on his hips, I can't discern his reaction —my only clue is his sharp, startled intake of air.

With single-minded focus, I reach for the waistband of his pants, and he seems to levitate. Before I can even touch the zipper of his fly, he snags my wrist in his fist.

"Don't." His voice is a roll of thunder, perilously deep.

Despite every nerve in my body warning me not to, I risk looking up. Viewed through my lashes, he's more predatory than ever. A beast caught in a trap, fighting for survival. Does he submit?

Or does he chew his own leg off to escape?

He's considering the latter. With every passing second, his grip tightens, the nails slicing into the meat of my wrist.

I don't expect him to *tug*, forcing my hand against his waistband. To test me, I realize. He wants me to feel the risk up close. How the fabric is stretched taut over the muscles of his hips…

When my finger strikes the polished surface of the clasp at the cusp of his fly, a jolt runs down my arm. I start to pull away—but that's what he wants.

So, I prod that clasp instead. His harsh exhale scrapes the air, urging my focus outward to a million other sounds I didn't notice until now. Murmured voices. Creaking wood. The wind lashing at the exterior of this old house. Each faint noise forms a cocoon around us, as if we're separate from the rest of this world in this single, twisted moment.

"You'd suck my cock to prove a point?" he grates, and I shiver in response.

I'm not afraid—or so I tell myself.

I've seen his cock before, an image I've tried so hard to suppress. A dangerous length of flesh and muscle, shrouded by a thatch of dark curls. A weapon young women are warned about from the earliest age and taught to fear. Revere.

Up close, would that organ truly hold such power?

He's seen all I am. He's ripped my clothing, stripped me bare, and shoved his own finger inside me. How cruel is it that exploring him isn't nearly so simple?

It's a journey through silken fabric that doesn't want to conform to my touch and a metal zipper that resists when I tug it.

The biggest barrier in my way is the man himself, exhaling so harshly each breath resembles a growl.

"Stop."

I don't. I can't. I keep tugging. Ruthlessly, persistently pulling until the material finally gives way, revealing darker cotton beneath. Boxers. A bulge shapes the front of them, and I balk, my face heating.

"Enough." Donatello's hand returns to my shoulder, gripping hard enough to sting. "Don't embarrass yourself, little Stepanova," he warns, yanking me to my feet. In the same motion, he refastens his pants and turns away. "You want to play blackmail? Well, then you win. I suggest you enjoy your spoils of war while you can."

My body resonates with the threat, but I don't give him the satisfaction of letting him know that. Swaying on my feet, I turn to the desk. The only way to put distance between us is to circle around to the other end of the table, utilizing the wood as a barrier.

I win, he said?

Aware of his gaze, I open the drawer he kept the letters in. I'm tempted to grab them all and run—anything to get another glimpse into the man he used to be.

Instead, I withdraw only the one he initially offered, denting the page with how tightly I hold it.

It feels like a live wire, unnaturally hot as I press it to my chest. Before I move from the desk completely, I grab the pen and a fresh sheet of paper as well.

Wordlessly, he watches me leave, my spoils in tow.

And we both retreat, aware that yet another round of this war has ended in a draw.

10

DON

She isn't the reason why I fall asleep at my desk. I'm not afraid of her sneaking into my bed again, determined to suck my cock for real. *No.* I'm merely waiting for our next round to commence.

The parting look she sent my way all but guaranteed our game isn't over yet—but therein lies the real mystery. What the hell is she playing at?

Does she even know… One minute she's coming at me with a knife. The next, she's on her knees. Touching me. Flashing those angry eyes when I deny her.

My cock throbs, threatening to burst through my damn zipper. Not because of her. Any woman with her mouth at the ready would trigger the same reaction. A pulse shoots through my abdomen as if to call me out—*liar*. My cock pulses in agreement. Only one woman is on my mind now. I still see her, those pouty lips glistening wet, her hands reaching for me…

Fuck. A cold shower is in my near future if I plan on meeting Mischa with my dignity intact. I always could use my hand to get myself off, but that's what she wants. To get inside my head and play with fire.

Maybe I should let the little Stepanova burn?

I toy with the thought of dragging her beneath me, forcing her to put that mouth to work.

And, as if on cue, soft footsteps echo from the hall, and my head shoots up, my gaze on the open door. Before she can even show her face, I preempt her, "Back for more, little—"

"More what?"

Fabio appears in the doorway in lieu of a sly blond. He looks bright-eyed and bushy-tailed, his hair slicked back, his designer suit perfectly tailored, another shopping bag in tow. In fact, he seems *too* polished.

Not to mention, he's eyeing the wall behind me rather than meeting my gaze. He's hiding something.

"You look ready to get this shitshow started," I remark without calling him out.

"I hope you're ready," he says, finally glancing me over. His eyes linger over my hands as if he's making sure that nothing sharp or dangerous is within my reach. All he finds is blood and scabbed knuckles.

His eyebrow shoots up. "What the hell happened to you?"

I flex my fingers one by one. The Salvatore girl's blood is still smeared across them. "I played nursemaid."

Later, I'll dissect the girl's actions. Not only did she sneak into my room and steal the knife, but the nurse who treated her wound implied it was self-inflicted.

"Do I even want to know? Anyway, here—" Fabio withdraws the Librium from his suit pocket and fishes out a capsule. As I choke it down, he adds, "According to your outfit, you aren't ready, as usual. Take this and then go get dressed. We're meeting with Mischa in an hour and—"

"Cut to the chase, Fab." I rise to my feet as color floods his cheeks. "Spit it out. If your eyes dart anymore, they'll fly out of your head. What's wrong?"

He grits his teeth. Then he sighs. "Mischa has returned to the table with a…request."

"Oh?"

I don't like his tone. I don't like the way he keeps eyeing the doorway, either.

I'm surprised Mischa didn't take the girl from the hospital. Either he's had a change of heart, or he's found another way to derail our "engagement."

"And?"

Fabio exhales, grasping for an edge of the desk. "I wasn't even going to tell you," he admits. "Frankly, it's something I could arrange without your consent via my contacts, though it would be violating several medical privacy laws—"

"What, Fabio?"

"He wants a blood test."

I frown. "Of Willow? Let him have one. I can assure you that I am not the father."

Perhaps this is Mischa's way of reminding me of that boundary? The sick fuck. I wasn't her father, but I took her in when she had no one else.

And in the end, I hurt her worse than Gino ever did.

"On *both* of you," Fabio clarifies, now facing the wall. "Says it's to…clear the air as to the nature of your relationship."

I ignore that obvious bait, paying closer attention to the fact that he still can't look at me. "What aren't you saying?"

"He…"

"Fabio!"

"Okay, okay." Finally, he mutters, "He wants the testing extended to Olivia… And Nico."

"What?"

I see red. I taste the rage, welling over my tongue like blood. I black out. Go numb. The next thing I know, I'm barging into the hallway, unable to contain the restless energy that demands I do something. Punch something. Stab. Fight.

"I want you to think rationally, Donatello," I hear Fabio warn, but he's smart enough to keep his distance.

Think rationally.

How the hell can I? All I see is Olivia's beautiful face, Nico in her arms. Their blood all over this fucking floor…

I close my eyes, leaning against the wall as the world around me spins like a fucking merry-go-round. When I re-open them, it's still spinning, an endless, dizzying blur.

"Donatello," Fabio says softly. "Hear me out—"

"You were going to do it anyway." I'm surprised to find the guilt openly expressed on his face. "Son of a bitch! You were going to let that fucker toy with your own damn sister's body. Why?"

"Why?" With a shift of his stance, he transforms into the stoic accountant, only concerned with the fucking logistics. "Because I loved Olivia more than you will ever know, but she's gone. *Vincenzo,* on the other hand? He's still here, and I would give my own soul to ensure that fact remains true."

"You…" I take a step toward him, my hand clenching.

"D-Don?" Fabio stiffens, raising his arm in defense. I don't think I've ever seen him afraid.

Could I hit him?

My knuckles crack as I raise my fist, eyeing his unblemished jaw. I pivot instead, striking the wall. Pain rips up my arm, but it's not painful enough. So, I hit it again.

Again.

"Donatello!"

"Mischa started this," I bellow over him. "If anyone should be kowtowing to ridiculous demands, it's him. Why the fuck are you making me play like this is an even fight? It's not. I have every right to kill him if I wanted."

"No," Fabio says so quietly I have to strain to hear him above my panting breaths. "I watched you destroy your life over revenge once. I refuse to let that happen again. You hear that, Donatello?"

He steps directly into my line of sight. "I refuse to. You went through hell, I get it, but have you ever stopped—just once—to wonder what that was like for me? For Vincenzo?"

His words have the effect of a punch to the gut. I go limp, watching the shredded flesh around my knuckles drip droplets of red.

"We had to watch you *die* without having the benefit of a funeral to mourn you. Do you think that was easy?" I've never heard him like this, and he clears his throat, fighting to return to his usual tone. "It wasn't. So, fuck Mischa Stepanov. He could ask for the moon, and I'd grant it. Why? I'm not afraid of him. He isn't the one I give a damn about."

"Mischa wants my blood. Fine—" I lift my bloodied hand. "Have him come here and prick me his damn self. But not Olivia. Not Nico."

"They're gone, Don," Fabio says gently. "They're gone. No one else can ever hurt them. Do you want to know why Mischa really asked for this asinine request? It's because he thinks it will tip you over and that he has the upper hand. He wants you to drop the charade first, giving him the opening to go for your throat. I've spent longer with the man than you have, and I have no delusions as to his merciful side. I'll let you in on a secret—he doesn't have one."

As the words leave his mouth, the scent of roses hits me full in the face. *Fuck.* I don't even have to turn around to see her lurking there, watching from the bottom step. For how long? Long enough.

"He doesn't care for anyone outside of his family, that is," Fabio corrects, spotting her as well. "Do you want to give him the satisfaction of turning you into the villain after he nearly killed Vin? I haven't forgotten that, and you better not either. The only way to win is to keep your head. Stay focused. Have I ever steered you wrong before?"

He waits, letting my silence serve as his answer.

"If you want my advice, you go in there with your head held high and your willing bride on your arm. You acquiesce to any asinine request, and you gather the evidence necessary to find the real culprit behind this 'misunderstanding.' You didn't get to the top by using your fists. You used your head."

"Giovanni could have used a recruit like you," I admit, but it's no compliment. "You're damn good at manipulation."

He shrugs. "I didn't have the stomach for it. Speaking of 'stomach,' I got you a suit that hopefully fits you properly, so you don't look in danger of busting out of it—" I hear a papery rustle as if he set his shopping bag down. "Put it on, clean yourself up, and meet me in the car in twenty minutes."

When I don't argue, he finally turns to the girl. "I've already made it clear that you have made your voice heard in these negotiations."

Finally, I look at her. From her blank expression, she interprets the statement the same way I do—not as a respectful olive branch, but as a bone thrown to keep the beasts satisfied for the time being. In the grand scheme, Fabio doesn't give a damn about her "voice." He's made it clear that he has his own motives for wanting this sham to go on. I suspect they all aren't as selfless as he would lead me to believe.

Maybe he's been the puppet master all along. I honestly wouldn't be surprised. He's nothing if not resourceful. While my life went to shit, Fabio thrived despite the stigma of being attached to the Vanici name. While achieved on his own merits, Vin's success was also a direct result of Fabio's quiet influence. Someone had to help him into the best schools by providing the stability and references I couldn't.

He said it himself; whoever is behind the scheme with the harbor is smart. Too smart. Fabio could have grown bored of having to clean up my messes…

The doubt doesn't even have a chance to resonate before I flick it aside. Even in anger, I can admit that if Fabio is anything, it's loyal. I also know that he's right—he's never steered me wrong yet. Though, no one could fault me for wanting to grab the damn wheel for a change.

"Since you seem to be so accommodating, I would like to make a request of my own during this meeting."

"Donatello…" When he faces me, I note the strain around his mouth. He's fighting to keep from frowning.

"It's only fair, isn't it?"

"Fine. What request would that be?"

I incline my head, mulling over the options. Mischa aims to humiliate me, and his daughter to dominate. What arbitrary demand could prove to them both that I am no one's whipping boy?

"I'll voice it at the meeting," I decide. I even flash a smile to broadcast my good intentions.

Unconvinced, Fabio sucks his teeth. "Donatello—"

"I'll play by your rules," I say, heading toward the end of the hall. As I pass him, I place my hand on his shoulder. "Don't worry. I'll keep my cool—but on *my* terms."

He sighs, but his reaction isn't the one I'm watching for. *There.* A flit of emotion appears in the dark eyes of the woman nearby. Was it fear? Satisfaction? Smug anticipation of what might happen next?

Either way, I'll take pleasure in once again having her on her knees before me—figuratively this time.

That mood spurs me upstairs and into the master bedroom. I strip my shirt and throw it on the bed, reaching for the new suit Fabio left. Only then do I see it.

A strip of folded paper placed over the pillow, left for me to find.

11

WILLOW

I've found that writing a letter to a madman is a lot like playing the piano. You require the right rhythm, and the confidence to execute the piece the way it's meant to be performed—or in this case, lay down a challenge of my own.

Did he read it? I catch myself observing him as we file into the car. He's fully dressed, his hair slicked back. The clean suit and grooming set him apart from the ruthless figure who cornered me in his study. Instantly I'm on edge, my belly tensing.

I look from the back seat window instead, but my reflection is a mocking specter, obscuring a view of the trees beyond. Fabio chose my outfit with *his* in mind, I think. Wearing this cream-colored frock, my hair loose, I appear innocent in comparison.

The perfect willing fiancée in a sham engagement.

In a way, our outfits are a chilling callback to when we first met, the day I discovered what a predator smells like. Thick cologne obscures his scent now, but hints of it buzz within my lungs, threatening to shatter what little resolve I have left.

What the hell are we doing? From the outside looking in, we could be on our way to some lavish party.

Not a parlay.

Even the chirping of nearby birds and the yellow sunlight create a harsh contrast to the overall heavy mood. It's all wrong. A moment like this requires a fitting soundtrack—one even the best composer in the world would have trouble devising. An unorthodox piece, bending the rules of music. Something with a slow tempo, followed by a series of off-key piano notes. Their glaring noise would herald the unnerving presence of one figure dominating the scene.

Donatello.

He is the catalyst upon which the entire impromptu symphony hinges. His breath alone plays a lethal cadence, infecting the mood of whatever domain he chooses to claim. Whether it be the house, or the car, or the small, quaint café we arrive at, driven by Fabio.

I can't help wondering if he knows just what "condition" Donatello will announce. Something devious, I'm sure. Malicious. Cruel.

As I watch the tight line of my captor's jaw from this angle, another, more terrifying, idea comes to mind. That his aim extends beyond getting revenge on Mischa. I'm his target.

Whatever stunt he'll pull today will be done with one goal in mind—reinforce the boundaries between us as he desires them.

Captor and prey.

"Here we are," Fabio says as the van comes to a stop. He exits first and races to open the door on my end before Donatello can move—by design, I suspect. With a deft twist of his body, he keeps himself between us, guiding me to the curb.

The position provides him enough cover to whisper near my ear without Donatello seeing him. "Those letters. Have you found them, yet?"

I look away in the hopes of disguising the truth. I found them, alright. Curiosity is a desperate itch that grows stronger the more I try to imagine just what those notes might contain. Oddly enough, Donatello doesn't seem inclined to read them.

Fabio, on the other hand, sighs when I shake my head. "Damn. Please. We must recover them—"

"Are you giving my fiancée words of encouragement?" Donatello remarks coldly. He inspects my face with a piercing gaze. Whatever he sees makes his brows furrow.

"Let's head in, shall we?" Fabio says with a nervous laugh.

The building across the street is our supposed destination, but not one I would picture for a meeting of this nature. It's too cheerful, sporting a bright red awning that shields the glass front where white lettering spells out the establishment's name: *Donna's Café.*

"A strange choice," Donatello remarks. Something in his tone draws my attention, different from his usual rasp. *Pain?* His frown, however, reveals nothing.

"I know the owner," Fabio admits. "It's a nice place, serves a vanilla biscotti, and it's semipublic with a clear view of the city park—" He nods to an emerald plot of land across the street. "The perfect venue to host two men as liable to punch each other as they are to peacefully enjoy said biscotti and some thrilling conversation. Shall we?"

He extends his arm toward me, his smile dazzling, but I'm nowhere near as confident. Unease floods my veins, infecting every muscle.

As Fabio insisted, the café sports a cozy interior with beige walls and hardwood floors. A smiling woman greets us in the entryway. Fabio's friend, I presume. She shows us to a private room near the back of the venue, which just so happens to sport a better view of the park. A stream of people flocks past, crowding the sidewalk beyond. Innocent bystanders.

Or potential witnesses.

Now it makes sense why Fabio chose this place—he's left nothing to chance. A wooden table in the middle of the space is already set for four. Conveniently, the chairs are arranged so that Fabio and I sit directly in between

Donatello and whoever happens to claim the spot across from him.

Considering the purpose of this meeting, everything down to the presence of butter knives in place of a sharper utensil, seems carefully choreographed.

"He's late," Donatello remarks coldly. Pale sunlight washes over him, and I don't expect the thrill shooting through my belly. His black suit hugs his frame, deceptively softening the hard planes of muscle lurking beneath. At least until he raises a fist, propping it beneath his chin—the sleeve bulges. "I hope you have one of your scolding speeches ready."

"One isn't necessary," Fabio quips while reaching for a pitcher of water. Gracefully, he fills each of the four glasses, his hand steady. "He isn't the one I'm trusting my reputation to."

Donatello scoffs, flicking his napkin into the air. "And yet, you seem willing to entrust all of our lives to him. A true display of your priorities, Fab."

"You and Vincenzo are my priorities," the man remarks while spreading his own napkin over his lap. I notice the calculating way he scrutinizes Donatello.

"So… Have you thought about whatever 'condition' you wanted to set?" he asks, cutting to the chase. Apparently, he hasn't guessed this mysterious demand either. "It will need to be added to our predetermined paperwork, of course." He lifts his leather briefcase and withdraws a black folder which he sets in the center of the table.

"Paperwork." Donatello's laugh inspires goosebumps. "I don't think this request needs to be written down. In fact, I think it's so small, we can uphold it in name only."

His gaze cuts to mine as I try to decipher his tone. A threat? *Yes,* warns the ominous sensation running down my spine.

"You know what? This just gives us the time to rehearse how this meeting should go. I present the documents," Fabio suggests. "Everyone agrees to the terms, and then we all go about our merry way. No surprises. Understood?"

Donatello grabs the nearest glass of water and takes a sip, his head at a skeptical angle. "There isn't very much 'merry' to find in the situation, is there? Having to play tea party with the man who tried to kill my son—"

"A fact that we all are very much aware of, and one you shouldn't attempt to bring up during said tea party." Abruptly, Fabio breaks off, craning his neck for a view of the doorway. Whatever he sees makes him sit straighter, tugging at his collar. "Speak of the devil."

I turn just in time to witness the entrance of said devil. As shame sears my cheeks, I figure it's a fitting taste of hell. *Mischa.* He enters the room, scanning the surroundings with a predatory focus. Clothed in dark fatigues, he's flanked by a guard I don't recognize.

My heart pangs. I don't have the right to crave a friendly face. Still, I can't resist the thought. *Where is Evgeni?*

"Welcome." Fabio stands, the picture of poise—at least until Donatello pushes back from the table and stands as well. He's rough, jolting the silverware and causing the water jug to skid toward the edge.

I hold my breath as he approaches the door, entering Mischa's path, coming dangerously close to a set of silverware lying just beyond his reach. Rather than lunge for them, he extends his hand.

"It's good for you to come here."

My ears ring. I don't recognize his baritone. Or perhaps I *do* —the speaker is just haggard with age and unrecognizable without his trademark grin. Only his old letters preserve him in this way—Donatello before life destroyed him. Seeing a glimpse of him now is anything but comforting.

Ignoring him, Mischa claims the empty seat while his guard stands near the door. He looks at me directly, his gaze piercing. In that expression, I see all of his pain and irritation reflected. My fingers twitch, and I find myself grappling for my napkin. Using the excuse of unfolding it, I stare down at my lap.

Because I'm a coward.

"Forget your *terms*," he hisses, his accent thick. "I'm here to bring my daughter home."

"Strange," Donatello says. An unmistakable shift in baritone transforms his tone, and I wince in anticipation. Rather than rant, he moves. His steps echo, followed by a shudder running through the table as he returns to his seat. I imagine him bracing his hands over the surface, prepared to lunge at the slightest provocation.

"I can't bring my nephew 'home,'" he says. "If you wanted to protect your daughter, Mischa, then you should have thought of that before you put a bullet through his brain."

"And you know all about putting bullets into skulls," Mischa counters.

My head shoots up, my gaze darting between them both. Mischa is stoic, but genuine confusion flits across Donatello's face. "I don't think you're in the position to trade body counts—"

"I've killed *men*," Mischa says, baring his teeth in a grim imitation of a smile. He looks directly at me as he speaks. "Only men. Can you say the same?"

Donatello blinks. "What the hell are you getting at—"

"Enough." Fabio somehow manages to straddle the delicate line between cordial and authoritative, effortlessly regaining control of the room. "Let's get down to business, shall we? Our terms."

He lifts his folder and opens it, displaying the documents within.

"Both have been agreed upon by each party prior to this meeting, and while it may seem 'foolish,' I think we shouldn't hunt for blame in a rush to point fingers—" His charming grin erases the sting from the insult. "I suggest we move past old slights and focus on the future. Speaking of which—"

"Yes, let's focus on the future," Donatello says over him, "rather than dig up the body of a dead woman and her child."

Color floods Fabio's cheeks. "I don't think now is the time to—"

"Is there a reason you wouldn't want a routine test done?"

I cringe at Mischa's tone. It's cruel. His words from the other day were uttered with the same harshness. *"Do you even know why the bastard sold you?"*

"Don't fuck around," Donatello bellows, lurching to his feet. "Though playing with the blood of innocents is nothing new for you. Your wife still sports the scars, doesn't she?"

"My wife is alive," Mischa says, matching his icy, level tone. "But what about yours?"

"Oh, dear." Fabio's quiet utterance punctuates the tension.

It's as if a storm rolls in across Donatello's face. Recognition shoots through me—the same instinctive warning I felt the very first day I entered his office.

"First, you want to toy with her dead body," he snarls. "Now you want to slander her memory?"

Mischa shrugs. "I may have hurt my wife. I never killed her—"

"Enough!" A fist connects with the table hard enough to jolt it, but I'm surprised to realize Fabio is the culprit. "Olivia was my sister," he says hoarsely. "My sister. I won't hear any sick rumors implied. Understood?"

He glances angrily from Donatello to Mischa. When no one interjects, he snatches a handful of documents and shuffles them.

"Out of the three of us seated at this table, I am quite confident in assuming that I am the only one who can claim without a doubt that he hasn't killed or maimed anyone. So, can Vincenzo. It is time to stop this game. In fact, have you stopped to wonder who might prefer that two of the most powerful men in the city be at each other's throats rather than focused on the impending threat?"

He withdraws a page from his stack and shoves it to the center of the table.

"There is a new venture taking root in the city's Western harbor front. Its origins are shrouded in mystery and so many layers of paperwork that even I have yet to unravel them all—but the primary investor's aim is clear—to infiltrate the political system and forge contact with the biggest players of the underground networks. Our dear friends, the Saleris have been contacted, a fact I doubt either of you will find comforting. Well?"

He waits for confirmation.

Donatello remains hunched over the table while Mischa finally shifts his gaze away from me—but their silence serves as the closest they might ever come to an agreement.

"Go at each other's throats if you want," Fabio warns. "But I don't think whoever was smart enough to pull off this attack will lurk in the shadows much longer."

"So why this sham alliance? It's better if we each turn our resources to finding the snake," Mischa suggests.

Fabio's smile betrays a chilling edge that robs all warmth from it. Instantly, I get a hint of the man who managed to rise to such a position, able to command two crime lords as though they were naughty children.

"That would be a decent plan, if I trusted either of you. You want to know my motive in forging this 'alliance'? Self-preservation. I'm a peace-loving man, but I'm also shrewd," he says. "Shrewd enough to know that nothing gets two beasts to work in unison better than being tethered to the same cart."

"Those are bold words," Mischa warns.

"Very bold." Fabio's grin returns, dazzling and full. "But if my opinion meant nothing, I assume you both wouldn't be sitting at this table right now. So, if you would rather squabble and fight, by all means. I won't waste my resources on a solution that is doomed to fail."

Mischa stands. "Business and family are two separate notions. You want to discuss business? Let's do it without my daughter being held captive—"

"Captive," Donatello counters in that eerily calm tone. "I didn't drag her here, Mischa. I never have. In fact, you should ask *her* why the hell does she keep coming back?"

"Watch yourself."

Donatello laughs. "Or what? You'll kill me? Do it, like you should have done day one, rather than aim at Vincenzo. I'm the monster? I don't cloak my actions under the guise of being a protective father."

"So, what would you describe your 'actions' in selling a child to a known trafficker?" Mischa counters. "Or are you still pretending that she died?"

Silence falls with a startling impact. Donatello holds Mischa's gaze for so long my lower back begins to throb; I've been sitting so stiffly. Finally, he inclines his head, gazing from the window. "I never hid who I am. I can admit what I've done."

"All of it?" Mischa prods. "Like your uncanny luck with wives."

More confusion flits across Donatello's face, drawing an irritated scoff from Mischa. He's hinting heavily at something—something to deal with Olivia—but for whatever reason, Donatello doesn't seem to be in on the joke.

Or he's refusing to be.

"If we are done with the schoolyard tactics, I'd like to discuss business," Fabio says. He opens his folder again, withdrawing two sets of documents. He hands one to Donatello and the other to Mischa. "Our terms, as agreed upon. Unless anyone would like to make any last-minute adjustments..."

We both look at Donatello, who says nothing.

"Then are we agreed?" Fabio asks. "Peace, in exchange for coordination on pinpointing the threat?"

Mischa remains silent, turning his gaze on me. "Is this what you want?" It's the tone he used when we first spoke about Donatello, heavy and restrained. As though there is so much he wants to say.

For whatever reason, he doesn't.

"I suggest we take her silence as an affirmative," Donatello snidely suggests. "Or is she your property, too?"

"She is family," Mischa corrects, cutting his eyes to him. "That term means something to me. But it also means that she needs to learn the truth for herself—not all men believe the same."

"Then it's settled," Donatello says, shifting the subject. He extends his hand toward Fabio, prompting the other man to fish two pens from his briefcase. Donatello accepts one, signing the stack before him. Cocking his head, he observes Mischa. "Do you agree?"

Mischa rises from the table and heads for the door. "I'm not going to play this game—"

"This has never been a game," Fabio says, his tone harder than ever. "You claim to care about your daughter? Then think of her—" He withdraws another page from his briefcase and places it on the table. "These are her demands.

She's made her voice heard, whether or not either of you want to hear it."

Mischa pauses, his body rigid. Swiftly, he turns on his heel and snatches the other pen. He signs on the stack nearest him and slams the pen down.

"I guess we're in agreement," he says coldly.

"It seems we are." Fabio accepts the documents in stride, tucking both into his briefcase. "As promised, here is the information I've gathered so far on the as of yet unnamed threat."

Mischa returns to the table, accepting the document, as does Donatello. While they read, their frowns deepen eerily in unison.

"Son a bitch!" Donatello looks up at Fabio. "Why didn't you say anything about this before?"

"That whoever masterminded this rift between you two has quietly bought out a third of the harbor's waterfront property? I thought that would be best discussed once the more volatile topics were squared away."

"But you don't have an identity yet?" Mischa demands.

Fabio shakes his head. "They're clever, but with the combined resources of the *mafiya* and *famiglia*, we might be able to better pinpoint a name at least."

"If he's as 'clever' as you say, then why haven't we heard of him until now?" Mischa argues. "The Saleris or anyone else wouldn't have the tact to cover their tracks. But we're supposed to believe that someone new has come out of the blue? Bullshit."

"I'm working on it," Fabio says. "My suggestion is that Mischa, you use your territory in the waterfront to your advantage. Start leveraging your position against the owners who have sold and see if you can squeeze out a name. And there is one more thing..." He tugs at his collar, his expression suddenly grim. "I think that, given the intelligence of this particular individual, we should be aware that there may be moles embedded where we least expect them. He has to be getting his information from somewhere."

"I will vouch for my men," Mischa says, eyeing Donatello.

Surprisingly, the other man doesn't take the bait. He stares off into space as if he's too lost in thought to notice.

"Money can sway anyone," Fabio says. "In the meantime, Donatello and I will work our contacts to find out where the money is coming from."

"Like one happy family," Donatello snarls nastily.

Mischa says nothing, rising from the table again. With one last glance at me, he heads for the door, his guard following dutifully in his wake.

"Just one last thing," Donatello adds. His faked nonchalance sets off alarm bells in my mind. Instantly, I'm on guard. "We didn't discuss the wedding details."

"We can agree upon those later," Fabio says quickly, gathering his briefcase. "Let's—"

"There's no need," Donatello suggests. "In fact, I insist on it."

"On what?"

His smile is a chilling display of white teeth. "On planning every detail of the ceremony. I'll let Fabio pick the place and make the security arrangements, of course, but everything down to the gown of my beautiful bride will be at *my* discretion."

My breath catches. For a harrowing heartbeat, the rest of the world fades to a murmur, drowned out by my surging pulse. The bright, cheery café falls away. All I see is him, staring back with a look that heralds only danger.

It feels like an eternity before other noises break through. In reality, it's been just seconds.

Mischa's eyes flash as he snarls a reply.

Fabio beats him to it. "I thought your fiancée made her opinion clear on that front?"

"She said she wants to pick her own clothing," Donatello says, still holding my gaze. "But I'll make an exception for the wedding dress."

Fabio frowns, seemingly puzzled by that point of contention.

But I'm not. Again, it only cements the suspicion I've had from the start. I'm the only one he truly perceives as his enemy. Mischa is just a distraction, a respected opponent in war.

Me? I am a thorn in his side.

DON

"*B*ravo," Fabio snarls, clapping. "That was a marvelous performance."

We're in my study, but already the place feels different. Dustier. Dimmer. By the day, this old structure seems to get even older, further removed from the past. Soon these walls will split and collapse in on themselves, swallowing anything left between them.

"You made your point, Don. At least you kept it PG, so I guess I can't complain. Here—" Pausing mid-rant, Fabio draws a different set of documents from his briefcase. "The insurance forms," he says. "Should I ask why you wanted them now?"

"No reason." I take them, setting them on my desk. I feel Fab's eyes on the back of my neck, and I'm careful not to give away too much interest.

But those papers contain Vin's future.

"You reverted control of the port back to me, correct? What's left of it, anyway." How could I forget? Mischa Stepanov decided to set it on fire. In all the chaos since, I haven't had the time to survey the damage.

Regardless, the land itself is still worth something.

"Yes," Fabio says warily. "I haven't gotten to finalize the finer details amid our recent eventful schedule, though."

"I want it all listed," I say, raking my eyes over the language of the insurance document. "All of it goes to Vin."

"Don't tell me you're this worried about our troublesome newcomer?"

I shrug off the thinly veiled concern. "Don't read too much into it, Fab. Just do this for me, okay?"

"Okay." He reaches past me, gathering the documents. "But I think I'll hold onto these at my office. And I shouldn't have to say this… I don't *want* to say this, but—" He meets my gaze, and for once, he doesn't put on the poised, unshaken mask I'm used to. He openly wears his fear, his face constricted, eyes wide. "There is a clause that suicide would render the policy null and void. Vin would get your assets, but not your very hefty payout. Not that you would even consider doing something like that to him."

He waits, daring me to fill the silence that falls. Lie. Make an excuse. Anything he can use to solidify whatever suspicion is growing in his skull.

"Goodnight, Fab," I say, claiming my chair.

He deliberately lingers in the doorway before retreating into the hall with a sigh. "Goodnight, Donatello."

I sense the moment he leaves the house, but I lose track of time after that. Without the insurance documents to distract me, my brain turns to its current chosen vice—her.

The letter she left me burns a hole in my pocket. I felt it, searing away during the meeting with Mischa. And now? It's hellfire-hot against my thigh, distracting me from reviewing the numbers Fabio presented.

Like always, he's right. The threat of a new player should be my sole concern. Not her. For all I know, she left me a blank piece of paper.

And if she did…

Fuck it, I'd see it as a sign—I got inside her head. I got her to back down. I won.

Why prolong the inevitable? Triumph can trump business, just this once.

Eagerly, I fish out the page, flicking it open with my thumb. A grunt rips from my throat. Shock? Or amusement. The little witch wrote to me, all right, the firm handwriting undermining her innocent *mafiya* princess image. No princess writes like this.

You took those letters because you are a coward.

I laugh out loud, but I keep reading, feeling my eyes narrow to slits.

You pretend that you don't give a damn, when in reality, you are the child now, hiding from the horrors you don't want to face. What are you afraid of? That I'll see the truth? I am not afraid. I want to know.

Why did you do it?

I crush the note in my fist, rising to my feet. It's already later in the day than I feel it should be—as if thinking of her eats up more time than I realize. My study is nearly pitch dark. Beyond the window, the sun is below the tree level, painting the horizon blood red.

The walls reflect the scarlet hue, embodying Mischa's taunt —*My wife isn't dead.*

Again, Fabio is right. This fucking house is a prison—all along, I've convinced myself that being here hurts her more, but it's a lie. Masochism might be the real answer. What else could explain wandering these halls, stepping over the bloodstains still visible if you squint hard enough? The past battles for supremacy every fucking moment. I swear I hear laughter one minute. Footsteps the next. A voice...

"We need to talk."

That voice isn't Liv's. Still, I take my time looking over my shoulder to find Luciano behind me, someone real at least —and relevant to the topic that should be my sole concern. If Antonio was a puppet, then his closest disciples had to know something.

"We do need to talk," I say, returning to my desk.

"I need to know your plan," he says. "With Kisa. With the boys and me. If you keep us on, then we deserve a cut of whatever the hell you're planning. No more secrets. No more orders. I'm not your fucking babysitter, either—"

"Have a seat." I gesture to the nearest chair. After a second's pause, he sits. "I need to know who Antonio was talking to," I say before he can reply. "If he were taking his marching orders from someone, you had to see something. A regular visitor. Something. Tell me what I want to know, and we can discuss fair compensation for your efforts."

He rakes his hand through his hair, cutting his gaze to the wall behind me. "Define visitor," he says finally. "He only took business at his office. Those appointments were the Saleris, and a few associates."

"No one out of the usual?" Following Fab's line of logic, this culprit is a newcomer, highly intelligent with wads of cash to throw around. Someone who couldn't fly under the radar for too long.

"Not that I recall. He didn't do business with very many people. Now, who he had at the *house*? That's a different matter."

I'm not surprised. Antonio had always been a hotshot, even in the days of old Giovanni. It was a rare thing to see him without a new whore on his arm—before and *after* his marriage.

"He liked his parties," Luciano adds. "Men. Women. Lions, tigers, bears. He's had all manner of shit in and out of that place, and I couldn't even begin to keep track. But there was one woman I saw more than the others. Older than his usual type. Blond. But I couldn't tell you more."

I file away the description for later.

"What about Kisa? Did you keep *track* of her?" I don't know why she's on the forefront of my tongue now. It could just be a sloppy segue to the real question on my mind when it comes to Salvatore.

You have an alliance with one of the most powerful families in Hell's Gambit, and a cushy position as the *famiglia* head. Why risk it all to take orders from an outsider?

What the hell did he have to gain?

"What about her?" Luciano says, his tone colder.

"You've been with Tony since he took over, haven't you? Did you know her mother?"

He grits his teeth. So that's a yes. I can't understand his defensiveness, though. Unless, like me, he remembers what Kisa let slip.

"She used to hurt herself?" I ask, recalling how the girl put it. *Mama hurt her arms, and then she wore bandages, and then she went away.*

"You don't know a damn thing about her," Luciano warns. Apparently, this woman is a touchy subject. "Kisa's just a kid. She doesn't know what she's saying half the time. I agreed to help you fix Tony's fuck up. Elisa wasn't part of that."

"Elisa. Was that her name?" I doubt I ever met her. Antonio must have married her not long after Liv died, going off his daughter's age.

The bastard. He took my life away and forged his own on the ashes.

"Speaking of Kisa, it isn't right for her to be cooped up here. If you want to dangle her over the Saleris' heads, then fine. But she should be in her own bed, with her toys and her clothes. Don't make her suffer because of her father's fuck up."

"You heard the nurse's judgment when it came to her wounds," I say. "She's what? Six? Seven? Not many children know how to slice open their arms with a dagger—"

"It's not her fault *you* leave weapons lying out in the fucking open, is it?" he counters.

"She's part Saleri," I point out. "And yet Mateo hasn't come barging through my door to get her back. Why do you think that is?"

One reason could be that I put the fear of God into him and Gregori—another is that they're too distracted to give a fuck, even about their own blood. My gut is leaning toward the latter option.

Especially when Luciano stiffens, his expression hard. "Don't bring her into this. She's just a kid."

Just a kid. But the way he says her name draws notice. Hoarse. Similar to the same way I say Vin's.

Full of guilt.

"You spend a lot of time with her," I add, stroking my chin. "You could have taken her at any moment and sold her back to them. Hell, maybe that's been your aim all along? I'm guessing Antonio wasn't much of a doting father."

"You could say that." His tone is careful, his expression blank.

"You didn't cry too much about Antonio." Something that didn't stick out until now. I remember the day he saw me on the steps of the Salvatore Mansion. Tony's death didn't enrage him the way seeing me with Kisa did. "Did he hurt her?"

The girl isn't right. I can look at her thousand-mile stare and know she's been through her own personal hell. My mind doesn't want to go there. But fuck it.

"Or maybe *you* hurt her?"

"Hell no!" He lurches to his feet, his face flushing red. "I would never hurt her!"

The reaction is the only answer I need. I've seen enough men on the defensive to spot the difference between indignant rage and protective anger.

"Fine," I say softly. "Forget the girl, let's talk business. I want you to secure Antonio's mansion for me. All of his business docs. Everything else, you pack up for Fabio."

He blinks, swallowing hard as he switches from anger to business. "I'll need at least two of the others for backup," he says. "That is, if the Saleris haven't already tried to reclaim it, in which case we're all fucked."

I wave him off. "Take them." Fewer men leaves me open to an attack, but I'll have the chance to pump another potential informant for information. She's been so fucking talkative all of a sudden. What more might she reveal?

That's my only reason for indulging her. Information and nothing else.

"Oh, one last thing," Luciano calls from the door. "The docks. He obsessed with them, always down at the marina."

"The marina?" I remember that the bastard had a yacht he liked to show off. "He had a boat?"

"He kept two docked there, I think—but he wasn't so fixated on it before about a month ago. He talked about the port like it was life or death."

Which explains why the bastard tried to threaten me into selling my property to him.

"Tell me if you learn anything else," I say.

When he leaves, I return to my desk, poring over the previous documents Fabio left. Within minutes, I'm too distracted to focus on the details.

She left me a note, after all. It's only polite to send a timely reply.

On autopilot, I head upstairs, approaching a closed door. Her smell acts as a beacon, broadcasting her presence. Sure enough, I push the door open and find her seated on the bed as if she's been waiting for me.

And she was. Her head is cocked, those eyes focused on me with a fearless gleam. Her lips part, and I figure any other woman would take this chance to issue some kind of verbal challenge. A threat? A boast?

Not her. She merely lifts a sliver of paper resting beside her and offers it to me. Another note, another game. But her first message still demands a reply.

"You think I'm the one who is afraid?" Closing the door behind me, I take a step, expecting her to flinch. To her credit, she merely lifts those eyes to mine, her hand still outstretched.

"Because I'm not," I tell her, advancing another step. "I'm not the one who's been coddled for the past seven years. I'm not the one who can't accept the truth when it's told to her outright."

The idea that I sold her for pennies on the dime isn't good enough for her. Neither is my insistence that the act meant nothing. *Nothing.*

As if to counter that, I feel my own hand brush my chest. Her name is tattooed there for a reason. I ripped the skin open myself with a blunt knife, for a reason…

Insanity could explain it. Or the fact that I have no soul. I'm a goddamn monster. Her eyes tell me that and more. She's mocking me again, drunk on whatever secrets she read in those letters.

I may have given her one, but it might as well be a bullet she's eagerly loaded into her chamber with the barrel pointed right at me.

"What's this?" I snatch the page from her, lifting it to my eye level. "Another little note?"

Not one written by her, anyway.

Liv's delicate scrawl blares from the page, and recognition hits like a lightning strike. God, I can smell her again, the faint scent of her perfume tinging the air. I see her—those wide hazel eyes, that sexy half-smile when she was excited or content.

And the devastating frown when she wasn't…

When I blink, she disappears. All I'm left with are the remnants of whatever she wrote years ago.

I feel invisible around you, baby. Sometimes it's like I'm a ghost. You're already a brilliant father, but as your wife, I'm just an afterthought. I miss you, but I have to wonder if you feel the same?

I don't remember this, not even the context of what might have been happening when she wrote it. I was busy—I was always busy—but when I look back, I always see Liv smiling from the doorway of my study, or smiling from the porch as I came home after being out all night on behalf of the *famiglia*. Always fucking smiling.

"What the hell do you want, huh?" I crush the letter in my fist. Mischa or his fucking daughter won't destroy Olivia's memory. Over my dead body. "Did you want to earn tips from my first wife? I'll give you a hint—stay out of my way."

She flinches. Not because of the threat, but that word and all the connotation it carries. *Wife.*

I eye the letter again. Why show me this? To gloat, most likely. Prove that I was always a fuck up—but her cruelty isn't what sets my nerves on edge. What else might she have gleaned from the other letters?

Why the hell can't I remember?

"Don't move." The words are out of my mouth the second she stands.

I expect her to run, push past me for the door. Instead, she turns to the window, putting her back to me as if I'm as inconsequential to her as Liv thought she was to me.

"You're so talkative all of a sudden," I snap. "But you were silent when Mischa threatened to end your little game before it could start. What are you playing at?"

She doesn't react, but I know she's processing every word. As I approach, I can see myself reflected in the glass. She already has that fucking lip between her teeth, her eyes blazing—but her knuckles whiten over the windowsill when I finally come close enough to touch her.

"Did you enjoy prying into what a happy marriage was like?" I ask her, raking my gaze along that pale, slender neck. A slight quiver betrays the way she swallows. "Poring over my relationship? I'm sure your father would get a kick out of that. You should have been a good girl today and gone back to him."

She whirls to face me, her hand outstretched, and a part of me stirs…excited? Either that or fucking relieved. It's about time she fought back. Hated me. Seethed. Raged.

When her fingers land against my chest with no force behind them, I just assume I've overestimated her strength. She's lost that hellcat spark.

But those eyes pack enough of a punch to make up for the softness, doggedly riveted to mine, blazing like hellfire. One by one, she fans out each finger, grasping my pec. Damn. I know what she's doing—tracing the letters carved into the flesh beneath the cotton of my shirt—proof of my lie.

Olivia's name isn't here. *Hers* is.

I snatch her wrist, wrenching her around so that her back is to me.

"Was it the fucking you liked reading about?" I ask against her ear, taking a shot in the dark. I'm sure I wrote about the sex; we both did. Private, intimate shit that I should be pissed at her seeing. I'm not. Maybe because I know the truth, she won't admit to herself. "Were you jealous? You should be, because you'll never feel that."

I'm not referring to fucking me, either.

"What it's like to have a man crave you from the inside out. To have him in your skin. Your soul—"

I break off the second her lips twitch. Silence was never a hindrance to her. God, it's like I can hear her voice in my head, sly and taunting. *But you were. You tried. You watched me.*

"I'm not talking about having someone watch you get off, either. You don't even know what love is, do you?"

Her eyes flit away from mine, and *bullseye.* I've got her.

"You don't. You have no idea what could drive a man to go to any lengths for you—and I'm not talking about Mischa," I add, slipping my hand around her throat, letting my thumb play with her windpipe. It doesn't feel as good as I imagined—it's even better.

This way, I can feel the slight quiver as she swallows, that involuntary hitch in her breathing. Her fear.

"I'm talking about someone so dedicated to you they'd blow their own brains out if you asked them to," I say, startled by the rasp in my voice. "They'd give anything. Do anything. The sex isn't the why—no. It's the how. You let them into your body, into your soul, and you hook them for life. You want to know what love is? It's finding the one person who sees the shit in your soul—who you really are—and they don't even flinch. Can you understand that? No, you can't."

I scoff at her ignorance, but inside I'm reeling at my own fucking words. The insanity of it. The truth…

That's the shit I felt for Liv. Constant need. Constant pain. When she hurt, I ached. When she died, a part of me died right along with her. Her absence left a black hole inside me. Fuck, maybe it's where my heart should be.

"You have no idea what it's like to mourn for someone day fucking in and day fucking out, hating yourself for being the reason they're gone—"

She rotates so quickly I don't even see the slap coming. Her palm packs the full force she held back just seconds ago, knocking me off balance. Impulsively, I reach for her, snagging a fistful of golden hair. I pull until she's forced to face me, her head back, chin in the air.

Despite the awkward position, she continues to fight, kicking, punching any part of me she can reach. Anger in her is always easy to read, but that term doesn't even begin to describe the emotion ripping through her now. She's not insulted, oh no…

I've hurt her again. More specifically, she thinks I'm *wrong*.

"You didn't love me. You didn't."

Her eyes flash, challenging that point, but this is a battle she won't win.

"Real love is like nothing you've ever felt."

Though it's not her fault. Mischa's kept her sheltered tight. And I…

I broke her trust in the worst way.

"You know, I wish you could shout at me." I tighten my grip to keep her eyes on mine. "Every word, every curse. I'd let you air it all out. Maybe then…"

What? All would be forgotten? No. My motive is far more selfish than that. I need to hear it—everything she went through so I can tally it up like a cowardly bitch and wring some kind of salvation from the list of grievances. Mischa saved her. She wasn't raped. She wasn't beaten. She lived. Therefore…

What I did couldn't be nearly cruel enough to feed the rage harbored behind these pretty eyes.

"Sorry wouldn't be enough, would it?" I ask, not expecting a response. Her flared nostrils give me one regardless—*Hell no*. Still…

A real man would say it and mean it. He'd get on his knees and rip his heart out with his bare hands just to atone, despite knowing that he never could.

"I won't," I tell her, stroking that pretty cheek. "I won't ever say it, and I'll tell you why. It would never be enough, never."

I think of Mischa and the hate boiling beneath my skin for what he did to Vincenzo. That fucker won't get to walk away scot-free. Not if I have any say in it—and she's the best final word I could ever hope to have. Vengeance triumphs over any guilt.

It has to.

"I say it, and what?" I demand. "You won't forgive me. You can't. So, I say it, and all I'd do would be giving you a piece of me. A small, fragile fucking piece. You take that; I've got nothing left." My thumb stills against her artery, registering every frantic beat of her heart. "Would it help if I gave you more reasons to hate me? If I cut you. Scarred you. Abused this body to match the mental toll. Would that fucking be enough?" I can't stop myself from touching her anyway, grazing the top of that quivering shoulder, then down the length of one arm.

She's so damn soft, her skin a beautiful canvas ripe for abuse. A million different ways flash through my mind, all of them twisted.

"I could hurt you, *principessa*," I say against her skull, pressing her body against mine. Slight and warm, she shudders at my touch, her breaths growing more frantic by the second. "Rip you open. Make you bleed. Is that what you want?"

My fingers crawl down her spine with a mind of their own, finding the divot of her lower back. Then lower to graze the round curve of her ass and the slender valley between both cheeks.

She stiffens, the air escaping her lips in a startled breath. If she's never had a man in her cunt, then she's most definitely never had a man back there.

I withdraw far enough to see her face, expecting terror. *Damn.* Instead, that lip is between her teeth again, a bitten shade of red.

"You *would* want that," I deduce, my voice guttural. I swipe my thumb across her cheek, relishing the silky feel. "And that's all I'm fucking good for. Hurting you."

To her credit, she doesn't cringe. Doesn't fight.

Her response is ten times worse—liquid glistens at the corners of her eyes, spilling down her cheeks without warning.

"I just can't win," I rasp more to myself than to her. "I don't want to. To win would be to admit there's something here worth claiming, but there isn't. You mean nothing to me. I mean nothing to you. That's all there is."

She grits her teeth, and I assume that's her unspoken answer —*Yes*. We're nothing. Nothing…

Her fist comes for my head, so swiftly I can't dodge it. The blow lands with a flurry of stars. Then another. She throws herself at me next, and I snatch her waist, pulling her with me as I stagger back against the wall. For a moment, I let her fight—and she does viciously. Punching. Kicking. The thud of every impact serves as the only audible sound she can make. But, for the life of me, I can't feel a damn thing.

Not until I see her face. The pain there. The raw, pulsing frustration—a feeling few in the world can understand. Internal pressure like a bull in a pen, pacing, and pacing, hunting for a way out. But there isn't one. All it can do is just charge the barrier keeping it contained with a reckless hunger for freedom.

I grit my teeth, feeling something in me give way for just a second…

But long enough for her to witness whatever it is. She goes rigid, her fists still balled. When she lunges a second time, I throw my hands out—but not in defense.

She goes limp, and I'm the only surface keeping her upright. Not by choice. It's pain. The kind of pain you feel so deeply you go numb in the face of it. There's no putting into words how it feels or what you need. You just scream beneath the onslaught.

But she can't. For once, I'm not eager to look at her. *Fuck.* I stave off the inevitable until I have no choice. Craning my neck, I see her, cheeks red, painted wet with tears, her mouth open and gaping at the air.

A part of me tries to shrug the reaction off—she saw I'd told her the truth, that's all. She believed me. She meant nothing. Not a damn thing.

The only problem is I think she *wanted* to see that indifference emblazoned on my fucking face.

I couldn't even give her that much.

"I don't remember," I croak, staring blankly at the wall as if it contains the answer. What was I feeling as I did what I did? When I left her.

I should have felt *something*. The same shit I tried to rub in her face at least—smug, remorseless pride. Why else would a sick, twisted motherfucker do something so fucking cruel without a damn good reason? All along, I've been telling myself the answer was simple masochism—selling her hurt me more than Gino's betrayal.

But for the first time since seeing her again...I can finally admit it out loud. "I don't know why I did it."

What drove me there, with her hand in mine? Looking back, those memories are shrouded in a web of hate that obscures everything beyond it in a red haze. It's an inferno, burning too brightly to even see what lurks beneath the flames.

Not that the reasons matter. Her father deceived me, and I sold her in return. On its face, that's more than enough of a reason for a sick monster to betray one of the few people foolish enough to put her faith in him.

"I don't remember, is that what you wanted to hear?" I demand to silence. My fingers are in her hair without permission from my brain, creeping through the tresses shrouding her skull as if it alone contains the answers. All I'd have to do is break it open...

I curl each finger, feeling my nails graze the delicate skin. I could hurt her with no effort at all. It takes more energy to hold still. "Tell me why. Tell me what you remember."

Her own nails bite into my wrist, her face against my chest. I can guess what she would say—*You left me. You left....*

I did—but when I inspect those memories, it's like watching a stranger's unfurl. I'm blocked from the bastard's mind, blind to his motives. Why did he do it?

Not that it matters.

"I'm glad you hate me," I tell her, withdrawing my hands from her scalp. Finally, she moves, inclining her head to face me. One swipe of her hand across her cheek banishes any tears. She's stone again.

For whatever reason, my thumb drifts down, catching the edge of that pouty mouth before she can smother all emotion completely. I apply just enough pressure to make her lips part, imagining the words she'd say. *I'll always hate you.*

"You should," I reply. "At least that means I taught you one damn thing worth remembering."

Something beyond how to play hide-and-seek or swim.

"I taught you to never trust anyone—" I shove her back and head for the doorway. "You got that? No matter how much they claim to love you, it doesn't matter. They'll leave."

Just like how I did when it came to her. Just like how Liv left me. Intent doesn't matter; it's fate. There is no such thing as a happily ever after.

Leaving now is one final shred of mercy I can give her.

But she won't let me. Her scent is a drug, dulling my better judgment, weighing down each step I take as though I'm wading through quicksand. Then I stop. She's pressed against the wall, her expression frozen, those eyes so endless; one look, and I'm drowning in them.

When I finally move, it's in the wrong direction—advancing on her corner, watching her shrink in on herself. My heart pangs, and I tell myself that this is what I want—her afraid and shivering.

Her hand flies out without warning, pressing against my chest. I grip her reflexively, dragging her closer, inhaling that fucking scent in stereo. I groan, telling myself a million different lies. This means nothing. It's not capitulation if I don't penetrate her. Holding her means nothing. Nothing.

The fact that she relents is irrelevant, her hands on my forearms, her face against the name etched into my skin.

"I'd give you anything to make it right…" The promise escapes my mouth, unbidden. Do I even mean it?

I look down at the sliver of her face exposed to me. The soft bone structure. A dark eye squeezed shut, cheek glistening with tears.

She's beautiful.

She's hell, my personal devil here to ensure my soul burns eternally for what I did. I have no right to touch her, stroking the bridge of her nose with the tip of a finger.

I feel driven to keep talking to her, "You won't have to endure me for long."

Her head jerks up, her gaze cutting to mine, demanding an answer. Do I mean it as a warning? A mercy?

"You'll be free in due time, little *principessa*. Free to marry your prince and live the sheltered life promised to you."

This is mercy, I decide. The truth, even if it's not exactly what she's after. She'll be freed from her monster soon enough—both her and Vincenzo.

She should take comfort in that.

Instead, her eyes blaze, body stiffening with indignation. Her answer is almost too easy to guess—because I'm seeing only what I *want* to see.

No, she says, my selfish little witch. *You belong to me.*

She sinks her nails into my flesh, and I figure it's just a proxy for what she really wants—to dig her claws into my soul.

"I've changed my mind," I rasp. Suddenly exhausted, I stop resisting, bringing my mouth near her ear, forcing her back to bow beneath my height. "I'll teach you one more thing— to know when to fold. Some battles aren't worth winning."

She's always been a greedy fucking thing, though.

She doesn't let go, even as I lean back against the wall, allowing the rickety structure to support our combined weight.

She stays, her eyes seeking out mine in the dark.

I will win, they say. *You owe me this.*

13

EVGENI

"How does an heiress wind up beholden to a trafficker?" I ask of Briar Winthorp. After hours of driving to ensure any tracker lost our trail, it's the first time I've spoken to her directly.

Though, a better question would be, how in the hell have I become beholden to *her*?

Somehow, she wound up picking our latest destination. Far from any "slum," the Norfolk hotel is a venue well beyond my typical price range. I suspect her insistence on it specifically isn't pure coincidence, either. She's planning something.

When we first entered the suite, she went directly to the window to "enjoy the view." Not exactly the behavior of a woman just targeted by a sniper. Unless that attack was all for show.

Or, she's fixated on something enough to ignore the risks.

When I come up behind her to inspect the view for myself, all I see is the city's center, the harbor in the background.

"You can start talking now," I warn her. "I specifically requested a room with no neighbors."

"And here I was, assuming you just valued your privacy." To her credit, she's damn good at obscuring her fear. And her motives. I find neither in her gaze as she turns to face me.

"After sitting on my ass while you played chauffeur for the better part of two days, I need a bath, soldier. You can wait to interrogate me after or join me." Her sly smile doesn't fool me. She's aiming to stall.

When I don't respond, she strolls across the room, entering the bathroom.

"You could have sprung for the penthouse suite," she remarks in disgust from inside it. "But this will do."

She starts to close the door and jumps when I spring forward, blocking its closure with the flat of my hand.

"I think I will join you." I ignore the rasp in my voice. It's not eagerness. It's impatience. With force, I shove the door open, making her stagger back in alarm.

"No more stalling. No more games."

Her throat jerks around a hard swallow. She's unnerved but recovers well enough. As she slinks toward the enclosed glass shower, her sly grin returns in full.

"If you wanted to see me naked, you could have asked." She fingers the straps of her dress before sliding them down her arms and shimmying from the material.

My eyes track the garment's descent. I'd be a fool not to watch her in case of a concealed weapon—but as her ass comes into view, a potential ambush is the least of my concerns.

Apparently, she views underwear the same way she does morals—unnecessary. Bare skin forms a healthier shape than I'd expect, given how thin she is.

Damn near perfect…

Minus one glaring flaw.

"Here." I snatch a rag from the counter and approach her, reaching for her hip.

She jumps, whirling around. "Don't you dare touch me—"

"You're hurt." I nod to her lower back.

She contorts her hip to follow my gaze. Her lips purse together, her eyes narrowed over the bruise taking shape there. Dried blood streaks the skin, stemming from a vicious scrape marring the flesh along her left upper thigh.

"You must have landed on it when you fell," I say.

It looks painful. The rush of adrenaline must have kept her from feeling it—and the injury alone might be proof that our dramatic escape wasn't entirely faked.

Someone so vain would never willingly undertake the risk of bodily harm.

"It's just a scratch." She snatches the rag and swipes at the wound before dropping it and stepping into the shower. "Faux concern doesn't look right on you, by the way," she quips. "I much prefer your aggressive side. When you have your hands around my throat. I do like it rough, after all."

I ignore the part of me that reacts to her words. My cock jolts, but celibacy is the reason, not her in particular—it's been a while since I've fucked anything, be it a woman or my hand. Approaching the counter, I run the water cold and wet my fingers—all while watching her in the mirror.

"You never answered my original question."

She sneers. "Why didn't I stay with my sister and enjoy the secondhand benefits of her perfect, happily ever after, you mean?" She whips that curtain of hair around her shoulder and turns on the faucet. With an exaggerated moan, she puts her back to the spray, bearing her front to me. This part of her is unmarred, her nipples hardening as the droplets of water make contact.

"In case you haven't noticed, I'm not cut out for peace and tranquility." She winks. "I much prefer chaos and danger."

"Chaos," I echo. "Like supposedly leaving your son in the hands of a monster?"

She stiffens, glancing away. "You can ogle my ass all you'd like, soldier, but don't make the mistake of thinking you intimidate me. I left my son. You killed a young girl. In the grand scheme of evil deeds, one seems to outweigh the other."

I shut off the water, and she grins in triumph. Her aim is to rile me. All to distract from that topic.

"Your son," I say, not taking the bait. "Do you even care about him, or are you just worried about protecting your own neck?"

She strikes the glass barrier of the shower with the flat of her hand. "How dare you!" Anger paints her cheeks red, her body tense.

I almost believe she's truly insulted.

Then she drops the act with a mocking laugh and leisurely arches her back beneath the water.

"I left my son," she says as though it were an act equivalent to forgetting a toothbrush. "Don't expect maternal theatrics from me. I am not my sister. You won't be able to use Ali to play on my heartstrings."

"Ali," I echo, recalling the last time she mentioned the nickname. Short for Alexander. "You don't give a damn about him?"

She raises an eyebrow. "Do you give a damn about the things you leave in the past? Like Amina… Wasn't that her name?"

Damn it. I flatten my palm against the counter, and she giggles.

"This isn't about me," I snap.

"Then I suggest you carefully weigh where you want this conversation to lead, soldier." Despite her playful tone, I recognize a warning when I hear one.

"Don't tell me that you don't enjoy probing, personal questions—" She grabs a bar of soap and drags it across her breasts. "Though, I don't blame you. I prefer *probing* things of a much different variety."

Her nipple hardens further with the contact, repelling the droplets of water that baste it.

I look down at the counter, watching my fingers flex against the polished surface.

"Antonio Salvatore," I say, steering the conversation to a different topic. "You knew his name but not one of the Saleris. Did you work with him personally?"

She laughs. "*Work* is a loaded word. I much prefer 'play' to describe my relationship with dear Tony."

It's a deliberate nod toward the one subject she seems to prefer—sex. So, I'll play.

I turn to face her, keeping my hands at the ready in case she tries to run. "You fucked him, I'm assuming. Did this Jonathan use you as a whore to further his aims?"

Her smirk falls.

"No," she admits, turning around to wet her hair. "I was to keep an eye on him. Make sure he was scouting the properties he was supposed to—"

"Properties?" I take a step forward, noting the shiver that wracks her spine in response.

So much for her haughty demeanor.

"He wanted him to buy them. One in particular, but the seller was proving difficult—"

"Donatello Vanici?" That certainly rings a bell. Even Mischa had his eyes on the section of the port Vanici had gotten ahold of.

Despite the offices having been burned to the ground, it seems the interest in that particular piece of land hasn't abated any.

She shrugs. "Perhaps. I was to convince Tony to keep his attention on the end goal."

"How. If not through sex… Blackmail?"

She presses a hand to her chest in mock horror. "Do I look like the sort to do something so heinous?"

No. She looks like the sort to use her body as a weapon and toy with her nipple to distract me. It works.

Objectively, her body is a work of art—and as soon as I think the thought, I cringe from it. Shaking my head, I refocus.

"I'm assuming your man had something on him. What?"

For minutes she doesn't respond, humming contently as she washes herself. Finally, she shuts the water off.

"Could you hand me a towel, please? I'd rather not catch my death."

I snatch one from a hook on the door and throw it at her.

Laughing, she catches it, but drapes it around her hips, leaving her breasts bare. At the same time, she inclines her head to meet my gaze with sudden seriousness.

"Tony liked girls, and he liked them young. Young and... Not necessarily willing."

Her words land bluntly, but I know instantly it's the truth.

That sick son of a bitch.

"The Saleris supplied them," she continues, running her fingers through her damp hair. "Regularly. They also disposed of them, but they kept the records. Detailed, meticulous records. My role was to periodically...remind him of those records."

"So you worked for the Saleris?"

She shakes her head. "I never met them. Not directly, anyway. I only ever interacted with Tony and...him."

"You don't like to say his name," I point out, curious as to her reasoning. Is the hesitation part of some sly little game? Or true fear.

She whips her hair back, obscuring her face, and I can't decipher her reaction.

"Fine. So, the Saleris were the ones putting the pressure on Tony," I reiterate. "But couldn't that backfire? All he'd have to do is blow the whistle, and they'd both go down."

She laughs, and her gaze returns to mine, glittering with amusement.

"I may not know the Saleris personally, but I do know that name. I'm assuming you do as well. Tony would have no sooner walked into a police station than found himself mysteriously hung in a holding cell with no witnesses, all records misplaced. You know how this city is run, soldier."

I do.

It's a shithole where the rats are in charge, the Saleris paramount among them.

"Well, you got your wish." I start for the door. "I'll call Mischa. If Tony and the Saleris were working together—"

"Wait!" Her hand latches onto my forearm, still wet. "Are you that much of a fool? You can't."

I raise an eyebrow, inspecting her from over my shoulder. Her mask has slipped again, those eyes wide with genuine fear.

"Isn't that what you wanted?"

"I wanted to see him in *person*," she clarifies. "But now it's too late. They've already tracked me, and I wouldn't be surprised if they know where we are. I don't have long to make a move. You try to reach Mischa—"

"And what? You lose your little game of leverage?"

"No," she replies softly. "We'll all be dead. If he knows I'm out, he'll rush to enact his plans. You tell Mischa, and he'll already have one of his spies whispering in his ear. Then he'll kill Mischa's pretty little daughter. Willow. Does *that* name ring a bell?"

I snatch her arm, unfazed by her startled gasp. "What the hell do you mean?"

"I mean, he'll kill her next and frame the man she's with. All to distract Mischa as he merrily goes about his final plan. After we're both killed, of course."

"Talk then! What is his plan?"

She sucks in a breath and releases it in a rush, "He's on a tight timeline, so he can't wait for permits and follow zoning laws like a normal businessman would. He also needs to make a splash in the city so that the people who matter know outright to fear him. He needs *fireworks*, you see—"

"Enough games." I drag her closer, watching that throat quiver as she swallows. "Talk. What is he planning?"

"To blow up the city," she says. "And kill several birds with a very large stone. How is that for 'fireworks'?"

14

DON

We don't sleep. We just endure minutes of each other, painfully close. When dawn finally creeps in to displace the shadows, she disentangles her limbs from mine, turning her back to me.

I enter the hall like a man possessed, feeling so damn old. I'd kill for Fabio's bottle of Librium. Cyanide. Anything to dull the confusion muddling my head, turning every thought on its head.

First Liv's letters. Now the memories of what I did to Safiya.

Maybe I'm too much of a coward to remember. To face what I've done and dwell in it. The blond little waif haunting me now with her watchful dark eyes is merely my punishment. She'll make me pay for my sins one way or another.

But for the moment, I'm not thinking of her.

I'm thinking of Liv. She's here, back from the dead, enraged by the way I've let another desecrate her memory. Blazing with judgment, her eyes watch me from the bottom of the staircase. It's so real…

When I blink, she doesn't vanish. *What the hell?* I take another step and realize why—the same eyes are staring at me in real life, just in a very different face.

"Fabio," I say, aware of the woman in my wake. How long has he been here? "Come to dispense with more mothering?"

"No," he says, but the sternness of his tone sets me on edge. Only one of three things could ever draw this level of seriousness from him. Death, money, and Vin.

"He's awake, Don," he croaks. "Vincenzo is awake, and he's lucid."

I grab the banister, gripping it tight as a million different emotions barrel into me all at once. Relief. Guilt. Dread. "You mean he's speaking?"

He nods slowly. "He wants to see you—" His eyes move to someone behind me. "Both of you."

In the grand scheme, I never deserved Vincenzo. Hell, after how badly I've failed him, I have no right to even stand in his presence.

Fabio, and his insistence on "timing," got it wrong this time. The best thing for Vincenzo would be to let him come to terms with the piece of shit his uncle is and secure him a future without me. I have the insurance papers finalized.

All that's left is to ensure he can collect.

The second I cross the threshold of his room, one look at him dispels every other thought in my head. He's still pale as a ghost, but his eyes are open, that signature shade of brown.

"Vinny…"

"He's sedated," Fabio warns, coming up beside me. "But—"

"You look like hell, Uncle Don," Vin says tiredly, his words slurred but still delivered with his trademark grin. It's weak and strained with pain, but it's there.

Crossing to the bed, I grab one of his hands and suppress a shiver. He's still so damn cold. "You're not looking too hot yourself," I croak, noting the bandages on his head. Still, I force a smile of my own. "We need you back on your feet and at that fancy university."

"Same old Don," he rasps, squeezing my hand with what little strength he has. "Always the hard-ass…"

He trails off the exact second I register the scent of roses. She always had a certain presence about her, louder than any fucking sound. It's her stare. That subtle sensation of being watched—*really* watched by someone noting every detail. Every twitch. Every flaw.

Looking at her, it hits me how fucking blind I was not to see her true identity before. I'd referred to her only as *tigre*. Maybe Vin knew the truth all along; he just didn't trust his own eyes.

He didn't doubt what his uncle Don told him. How sick is it that I never truly stopped to think what her loss might have done to him? Sure, I've seen his pain when her name was mentioned—because he was usually the only one brave enough to ever bring her up. Perhaps I was selfish enough to hope he'd forgotten.

Of course, he wouldn't. And I'd give anything in the world —my own goddamn life—to erase the pain twisting his mouth. His eyes widen and what little color remains in his skin drains away.

"Saf...Safy?" He tries to sit up, triggering a series of alarms from the machines connected to him.

"Easy, Vinny! Easy!" Fabio appears at his other side, smoothing his sheets and easing him down. "You have all the time in the world to talk—"

"How?" he demands, but he's not looking at me. "How are you... How?"

"I think you three have a lot to discuss," Fabio says, clearing his throat. "I'll leave you to it."

I barely notice him slipping from the room. The slender figure who comes to take his place consumes my focus.

In this moment, there are a million fucking ways she could spin her own narrative. Cry. Gape. Give any indication of how cruel I was to her. How vicious.

She keeps her face blank, revealing nothing and a paranoid part of me scoffs at that. She's just biding her time.

"Saf…" Vin gapes at her like she's a ghost, though hell, to him she is. I can't even recall what exactly I told him. Just that our beloved Safy died in an accident. No funeral. No grave.

For seven years, I let him live with that lie.

"You're dead," Vin says softly. "Uncle Don?"

It's not fair. Even weak, he still possesses the same hope Fabio does. Like the answer to their question has the ability to fix everything. Only if you tell the truth. Lie, and you'll break something in them beyond repair.

"Vin…" I grab for his fingers, but smaller, paler ones beat me to it. She moves to stand closer, stroking the back of his hand with her thumb. I don't argue.

I don't have the right to. It isn't long before I feel like an outsider, intruding on a private moment.

"Get some rest, Vinny." I step back, even though it kills me. "You need your beauty rest."

I walk past her on my way out, but she doesn't even look my way.

"That went…better than expected," Fabio murmurs, appearing by my side the second I step over the threshold.

"Is this your way of gloating?" I can't even put the right amount of anger into my voice. I'm too busy watching her, standing near Vin's bed.

"No," Fabio replies softly. "I'm just glad that everything is going according to plan. A nice, heartwarming visit with your nephew should lift your spirits so that my next news will have a shot of going over a tad bit easier."

I raise an eyebrow, instantly on guard. "Get to the point. What's the bad news?"

"Nothing about Vincenzo," he clarifies. "He's recovering far better than even the most optimistic of estimates."

"So, then what?"

"You know those mysterious purchases in the west end? Well, what I *didn't* mention was that it was a two-pronged purchase. I had assumed that it was all from the same buyer, but I was wrong."

"This sounds like a bitter chaser to a happy reunion," I snap. "What aren't you saying?"

"The larger purchase of the two can't be traced, as predicted. The culprit is most likely our original attacker of the Stepanov family."

"And the other? Spit it out."

He sighs. "It seems as though Gregori Saleri has taken a sudden interest in waterfront development. He bought several of the properties with cash, as well as the rights to several tenant buildings. It was all done rather expertly. I don't think anyone else would have uncovered his name, at least not this quickly."

"Son of a bitch!"

"I don't believe in coincidence," Fabio says in agreement. "And I don't believe that now of all times would be the ripe moment for investment. The Saleris have stayed relatively contained to their corner of the world until now. Why decide to branch out at the same moment a threat against you has risen? Especially one concerning another section of the harbor. It doesn't pass the smell test to me."

"It sounds like you've been keeping tabs," I admit, unsure if I'm impressed or alarmed. "Aren't you the one always telling me not to dwell on the past?"

He shrugs. "How does that saying go? Friends close and enemies closer? That's not all I'm concerned about, though. Think about it from this angle—if Gregori and Mateo made a move to buy up the harbor, even if it's to expand their local business interests, they didn't do it on a whim. A fish market. A meatpacking storage facility. Those enterprises don't exactly scream targets of a sex club owner, do they?"

I frown. "No, they don't. Unless that sex club owner suddenly needs to store a lot of shit."

"Exactly," Fabio says. "Or he's merely serving as a proxy to secure the property for someone else. Someone with a more vested interest, like our mystery man, for instance. Or even… Mischa Stepanov."

I whirl to face him. "And here I thought you wanted to be his best fucking friend. I thought you put your suspicions to rest already?"

"I don't have any evidence he's involved," he says quickly. "But it's a potential theory, and in my line of work, potential theories tend to have a lot more merit where millions of dollars are involved. Mischa's built his empire on importing and exporting weapons that one may not be able to attain via legal means. If he is behind the sale, he could be working to counteract the other mysterious buyer. Or…"

"*Or* he's been working with the bastard all along. In fact, it makes fucking sense if he was." I laugh at the logic. "He and his partners conspire to frame me for an attack on the Stepanovs, giving Mischa the opening to come after me directly. But why hit Vin and not me? Targeting him over me wouldn't make sense, unless…"

"Unless Mischa knows you better than we both suspect, and he counted on you cleaning up the loose ends, such as Antonio Salvatore."

"And with this stupid fucking truce, we're playing right into his hands." I spin on my heel, marching toward Vin's room. If Fabio is right, I brought the daughter of his potential murderer here. Hell, knowing her hatred of me, her aim might be to finish the job.

"Wait," Fabio warns. "That could be the case, I won't deny it—"

"You sound very fucking calm considering this was all your fucking idea!"

"Or," he says over me. "The other possibility is that Mischa Stepanov is an impulsive, though calculating, man prone to reckless violence when those he cares for are threatened. Which means that whoever is behind this, knew *both* of you well enough to manipulate your worst character flaws. The main question is why. Why go through the trouble?"

"Or why the fuck are we still standing here when Mischa could be setting us up to take the fall?"

"Donatello…" He sighs in exasperation. "This is why I've kept these concerns to myself for the time being. I still would if another idea didn't occur to me."

"What? That Mischa's wife was faking her injuries this whole damn time, and we bought it all hook, line, and sinker?"

But if she wasn't… That alone would prove Mischa's innocence. No way in hell would any man knowingly put the lives of his wife and children at risk. Never.

"I won't deny there is a chance," Fabio admits. "But I also thought of another solution. One that only you are capable of enacting, and one that could turn the tables, so to speak on any plans Mischa might have, nefarious in nature or otherwise."

"What?" I scoff. "Have me kiss his ass literally? Hand the harbor over to him? The keys to the Kingdom? Go in there and rip out Vincenzo's oxygen to finish the job he fucking started?"

"Not quite," Fabio says softly. "If Mischa really intends to play us for the fools and was willing to sacrifice his own family to do so, then I have no qualms in suggesting that you forge another path around our apparent negotiations."

I feel my eyes narrow at his tone of voice. It's the sly, cold, calculating one I've only heard him utilize a handful of times, proposing I go along with Mischa in the first place among them.

"So, what is it?"

He inclines his head, and I follow his gaze into Vin's room. A woman stands at the bedside, watching us. She's so damn beautiful my brain blanks before I remember who she is. What she is. God, those eyes…

They're warped mirrors in a carnival sideshow. I look in them and see a grotesque monster staring back.

"Her?" I say absently. "Have you forgotten about the sham of a fucking wedding already?"

"That's not what I mean," Fabio says. "You've been content to parade her around as your toy, but have you stopped to even consider the tool you have in your possession? If you actually chose to utilize it, that is?"

"I'm not following," I snap. "Hell, I'm not sure if I even want to—"

"Don't make me spell it out for you, Donatello. If I were a ruthless sort of man cut from the same cloth as you and Mischa, I'd suggest using the girl to your advantage. Not as a prop, but as a *partner*."

Partner. My brain shies from the term, unwilling to even consider it. "I think you should leave the ruthless calculating to Mischa, Fab—"

"She loved you once," he points out, too softly for her to overhear. "The childish love that only a sick man would take advantage of now. Or a desperate one. You've pushed her away, needled her. In your mind, you've told yourself that you're a heartless cunt, so no harm done, but deep down, I think you know the real reason. You're afraid of your past. You're afraid of the hold she still has over you. I think you should be. But if you truly want to beat Mischa at his own game—if he is truly behind this—then what better way than through his own daughter?"

I stare at him, surprised by the coldness in his gaze. Fuck, he looks like me. "You know, Fab, I never thought I'd live to see the day that you, of all people, advocate for rape and torture."

"Of course not!" Genuine disgust rips through his voice. "Think with your brain and not your cock. Treat her with respect. Gain her confidence, even. Get her to trust you. Open up to you. You'd have a real weapon against Mischa, one he couldn't contest lightly."

"Do you even hear yourself, Fabio?"

He sighs, gritting his teeth. "Do you?"

"Go on and say it. What do you mean?"

"I mean, have you ever stopped to ask yourself why you react to her so strongly? Is it hate, or is it guilt?"

Something in the way he stresses that word stops me cold. "I feel like you're talking in circles, Fab. I was never a fucking intellectual like you, so say it plainly."

"I'm saying that you're afraid of her, and you should try to harness that emotion instead of running from it, for once. It's okay to feel guilty for something you've done. What's even better than that? Acknowledging it and asking for forgiveness from the person you hurt."

"You need sleep, Fab. Your emotions are getting the best of you—"

"If they were, you can bet that my fist would be planted in your mouth right now." He sounds more tired than angry, exhaustion reflected in his bloodshot gaze. "You are not the heartless monster you pretend to be, and I think that's why it's so hard for you to face her and—"

"And what?"

"And risk knowing that she may never forgive you. But you leave that choice to her. You seek out her forgiveness, and you fight for it, not run like a coward. You are not a coward."

I keep walking. "We're done with this conversation—"

"Are you afraid, is that it? Of what she represents? You've never let yourself go back there, not really. Even if you traipse through that fucking haunted house, you never really let yourself relive it. If you could, you would have had the place burned to the ground."

"Relive?" I laugh incredulously. "If you mean 'burn in hell,' then yes, I do that. Every fucking day."

"You don't remember, do you?" His eyes narrow as if he finally solved some complex puzzle. "All this time... This is how you've protected yourself. Turning it all on her. Maybe I was wrong—you *are* a coward."

I turn back to find him in the same spot near Vin's door. "What the fuck are you talking about?"

He gapes at me like he's waiting for something. Then he shakes his head. "Nothing, Donatello. No, you know what, it is something. I have never asked you for anything, but I think I have the right to, at least in this case. You've spent years wallowing in your own pain without once stepping outside of your own head to understand anyone else. You aren't the only one hurting from the past."

His tone resonates with an uncharacteristic note of anger. He's serious.

Rather than counter him outright, I bite my tongue. My feelings toward the woman aside, if anyone deserves to be heard, it's him. "What are you saying, Fabio?"

"I'm saying that I want you to try, if not for yourself, then for me. Try to see beyond your hate and look at her as not a tool but a partner. Though, if you want to use her as your proxy and dwell on the past, then by all means. You're right. This conversation is over."

"Wait—"

"I'm leaving."

He reenters Vin's room, but I follow him. She's still by the bed, her hand on Vin's.

Fabio has always been an optimist, but this time he's verged into fantasy territory. He's a sad old man clinging to hope after a lifetime of suffering. Not only for assuming she would ever forgive me, but that she would stand against Mischa of her own free will, *without* the threat of her family's safety hanging over her head.

No fucking way.

But, I can't ignore how he said those words. *This is how you've protected yourself…*

Turning it all on her.

As if I haven't spent the past seven years hating myself.

When I look at him again, he's fluffing Vin's pillows, his charming grin firmly in place. It's uncanny how easily he can switch out his emotions, suppressing one in favor of another.

Could I do the same when it comes to the blond standing beside him?

Her face is a blank mask, revealing nothing either way. At least not until I catch a glimpse of her eyes darting toward me, probing and elusive.

You aren't the only one hurting from the past, Fabio snarled. He's right, of course. Though he confronted the wrong party to sprout his idea of peace to—it's not a question of whether or not I could use her as a partner.

Would she ever agree to see me as the same?

The answer feels as thready and halting as Vin's breathing, though I'm determined to hazard a definitive guess.

Hell no, she wouldn't—and I couldn't blame her.

15

EVGENI

I wait for her to laugh, proving her morbid statement to be yet another joke.

She doesn't.

So, I bite. "He wants to blow up the city. Why?"

A knowing smile replaces her wide-eyed expression. In the blink of an eye, she's coy again. Gripping the towel around her waist, she skips past me, entering the main suite, dripping water as she goes.

"I wish I had the foresight to pack," she says, frowning at her crumpled dress. "Oh well."

She readjusts her towel to cover her torso and sits on the edge of the bed.

"Enough games," I snarl. "You like it rough, do you? Maybe you'll be more willing to talk if I put my hands around your throat a second time—"

"He wants power," she blurts as I take a step toward her. "He wants to make a splash. Be seen. Be heard. He wants to cause a diversion large enough to move against several big players at once, Mischa Stepanov among them. He won't blow up the entire city, mind you. It's strategic—"

"Do you know where?" I don't know if I believe her in the first place. It sounds insane. Fantastical.

It sounds exactly like the move of someone desperate to shake up Hell's Gambit and make a name for himself. I've worked for Mischa long enough to know the type. Few men can rise to the top of this city's power structure without a bit of shock and awe.

"I don't," she admits. "I know he plans on watching the show, though. From a boat, I think. One of the Saleris'—"

"I know the one," I say. A forty-footer Gregori loves to parade along the coast. "I could head him off myself. Demand answers."

If he resorts to utilizing a lone woman to do his dirty work, how formidable can he be?

As if reading my mind, Briar laughs. "You wouldn't even make it onto the water. Unless it's as a corpse."

Her tone lacks the mocking lilt I'm used to. "You really are afraid of him."

"You would be too if you've seen a fraction of what I have."

"I've seen enough in my day to fear no man."

She scoffs, kicking her legs into the air. "Well, we can't all be as stone-cold as you. What with the things *you've* done..."

It's a statement designed to get a rise out of me. To distract.

It works.

"You know what isn't on that list?" I counter harshly. "Letting my child be taken by someone I deem a madman."

"Oh, touché." She giggles. "I guess you never loved that Willow girl, then. Despite you being faithfully by her side all those years?"

My eyes narrow. "If you won't let me contact Mischa, then tell me. What is *your* plan?"

She scrambles to the other side of the bed to put her back to me. "My plan was to be on a beach in Tahiti by now."

"But you're not. So why stay? Why leave him? Why try to ask a man you hate for help?"

Her response is so soft I have to strain to hear her. "My perfect sister has a wee little accident, and the most powerful man in the city loses his goddamn mind." She makes it sound hilarious, like some marvelous joke. If I weren't used to the cadence of her voice, I'd miss the harsh note lurking beneath. "He should have been smarter," she adds. "He should have seen through it all then. He should have gone after the threat head-on and not be so damn predictable."

"Your Johnathan planned this," I surmise. "But not to get the harbor."

"Who knows?" She scoffs again. "We're all just little pawns to him. Pieces on a game board he believes he can move around at will. And like little puppets, they all fall into his trap. Except for your Willow," she adds, meeting my gaze directly. A hint of what could be admiration sparkles in her gaze. "She's spoiled his perfect plans."

Willow. That name is the least I expect to hear dragged into this mess. "How?"

"She's brought the two men he wanted to kill each other to the same table. I doubt she's smart enough to keep it up, but boy was he pissed when he found out."

"Found out what?"

"About their 'engagement.'" She makes air quotes but doesn't seem to notice my reaction.

Engagement. To Donatello Vanici?

Damn, I don't know why I'm so shocked. Mischa alluded to the bastard's plan for vengeance. I just never thought the son of a bitch truly meant to go through with it…

"But after tomorrow, he'll still come out on top," the woman says. "I don't think anyone can stop him."

"Why tomorrow?"

"He aims to strike several places at once. But like I said, I never knew his plan in full. Just what I've told you."

An explosion in the city.

A ploy to cause a rift between the Stepanovs and Vanici.

Working with both Salvatore and the Saleris.

"There has to be a way to get to him," I say, picturing the marina. I'm not familiar with the area, but no time like the present to learn. "I have contacts I can use."

I withdraw my phone and message Mario again, unsurprised when he doesn't reply right away. Will anyone pick up my call after learning of the rift between Mischa and myself? A question for another day.

Still, I don't let her see my doubt.

"Slow down, hero," she scolds. "There is another way… I go skipping back to him with the information he wants and get close enough to learn what he's planning."

I laugh. Then I turn on my heel and head for the door. "You are smart, I'll give you that. You almost had me duped."

"I wouldn't do it for free, you goddamn fool," she snaps. When I look back, she's lounging on the bed, her arms crossed defensively. "I want something from him as well. Without Mischa, you are my only shot at getting it."

If it weren't for her obvious disgust, I wouldn't believe her. "Why the hell would I present you back to the man you claim to fear?"

"Because it's the only way to save your Willow," she replies. "And Eli, the boy. I'm sure he'll be targeted, as well. He needs him dead, you see? Or do you want both of their deaths on your conscience?"

She smiles when I say nothing.

"Well, then. I can't go to him dressed in a towel. Unfortunately, he doesn't seem to prefer my body naked."

A tacit, or perhaps intentional hint that she isn't sleeping with this man.

"How is that my problem?"

She fixes me with a lethal smile. "It seems you have shopping to do, soldier. Don't skimp on the budget, either. I'm a size two, and I prefer the color red. It looks lovely on the water."

"You want me to buy you a dress?"

She shrugs. "Correction. I need you to buy me a cover. One he won't suspect when I come crawling back. He can't know I left him on my own."

"Wouldn't it be better to look the part?" I rake her over, inclined to provide my own assessment. Beneath the coy veneer, she looks exhausted. Battered. Afraid. If I were a man questioning her loyalty, I'd believe her escape if she showed up on my door like this.

Minus the nudity.

"Why the costume?" I ask.

"Darling, a Winthorp is never underdressed, no matter the occasion. If I went back to him looking like a drowned rat, he'd see through me instantly. He's the calculating type, remember? I need to look like a queen, so confident of my role that I'd take the time to buy myself a new dress before groveling for his mercy. So is the way of *my* world. How did you put it? A spoiled heiress."

Do I believe her? It's a sick, cruel way of viewing the world.

Which means she's right, of course.

After all, she was once a Winthorp—a family of vipers who plotted amongst themselves with the same zeal they ruled the city with.

They'd skin themselves alive rather than reveal their weakness before an enemy. In that line of thinking, a new dress would, of course trump the fear of death itself.

So is the way of her world.

DON

Fabio got one thing right.

She's mine in a way Mischa will never have her —we're too alike. It's a similarity reminiscent of that instinctive rift between cats and dogs—but a bond, nonetheless. We *know* each other.

She thinks she's seen the darker side of me, and I've already glimpsed the forbidden pieces of her. Beyond just her body —I've seen the impulses she's learned to suppress. The fangs she won't dare bare at the fancy dinner parties that populate her future.

She thinks by writing a note, she can get under my skin. It's stupid to play her game by writing in return, but for whatever reason, nothing else feels right.

So, I sit in my study and fish out a new page, unable to squash the impression of being back in fucking high school. How to start?

I know you, little wife, I write. *I know what keeps you up at night. The fears you dwell on inside that pretty little head, hoping your father can't see them. I know you. You're afraid you'll fuck it all up, just like I did. You never felt like you were one of them.*

You never belonged there.

I pause, gripping the pen so tight it rips through the page. *Damn it.* A sudden thought prevents me from trashing it. She'll see that tear, and she'll know. Hell yes, she'll know. What exactly?

The trademark trait we share—rage. Endless, consuming hatred for what we can't control. I can't control her. Spilled ink and torn paper prove that everything I'm writing is the fucking truth.

I want the truth from you. I want you to spell it out for me. Every little thing. Tell me what's in your head. Or not.

Forget Fabio and this sham deal. I'll let you go tomorrow, back to your precious, cozy Stepanov manor. I'll let you go. Just don't respond. Ignore this letter and keep your words bottled up tight. I swear it on my life.

Though what worth is that?

Scratching out that line, I add another—*I swear it on Liv's grave.*

I slip the letter under the closed door of that pink room and enter my own without a second thought. In the morning, her bags will be packed, and we won't have to pretend anymore.

I'm so confident, that for the first time in days, I don't fight to find oblivion. Sleep comes like a one-two punch, pitch-dark and dreamless…

Until I'm jarred awake by the creak of the door opening. Soft, feminine steps resonate next, drawing a groan from my mouth. So much for a peaceful sleep. I'm dreaming of Liv…

But Liv never smelled like this. My nostrils twitch, the scent unmistakable—Roses. Reluctantly, I peel my eyes open to see the culprit standing at the foot of the bed.

Fuck Fabio for giving her these clothes. This dress, in particular, is gossamer-thin, with a conservative neckline; it shrouds her in innocence, the perfect garb of a *mafiya* princess. White wouldn't be the color I'd choose for her myself. Not with those dark, watchful eyes.

She looks better in black.

"What do you want?" I demand.

The answer is obvious—my new little wife took me up on my offer.

Sure enough, she extends her hand, revealing the slip of paper perched between her fingers. Damn her. I weigh ripping it to pieces.

Coward, a part of me snarls, sounding suspiciously like Fabio. *Can you face her or not?*

Shrugging off the haze of sleep, I sit up. The way her lips twitch makes me look down.

Damn. I stripped my shirt, wearing just my slacks, lying on top of the sheets. Her sudden modesty is a puzzle I'll mull over later.

Shifting to sit on the end of the mattress, I snatch the note from her and open it, straining my eyes to make out the scrawled letters in the dark. A sliver of moonlight plays to her advantage, illuminating the tail end of her statement.

You owe me the truth. If you're not afraid of it, then give me the rest of the letters.

"I don't owe anyone a damn thing," I point out, but hell, even I can hear the lie in those words. I owe her more than an answer. If only the truth wasn't far simpler than what I think she's after. She wants a detailed confession, a broad outline of all my sins.

All I can give her are three words—*I don't remember.*

She should crave the lie. It's the only closure she needs. I make a far better villain that way. Still, I promised her.

Inclining my head, I ask, "What do you want to know?"

She inches forward, letting the moonlight bathe her face in its silvery glow. Those eyes convey her thoughts so clearly I grit my teeth. Fuck, it's like…

I'm in her head, able to hear her beg—*Tell me. Just tell me!*

"You want to know why I left you? Really?" The answer on my tongue is a variation of the same one I've grown accustomed to telling. *Because I didn't give a damn. You meant nothing.*

Then I swallow and change tact.

"You want the truth? I… I don't even remember why. I remember what happened," I clarify as she steps forward, unable to disguise her interest. "Gino… Your father was working for the Hortega cartel. There was a trio of them, embedded in the *famiglia*, each taking their orders from a different location at different times so they couldn't be traced. It was smart," I admit. "Smart as hell, but Gino slipped up. I learned he was one of the moles, and I confronted him."

It's funny how some parts of the past are so murky while others? They're crystal fucking clear. Gino had swaggered around, convinced I'd never suspect him. Without direct evidence, I never would have. I trusted him. My right hand, a man I considered a brother, a *fratello*.

For a second, he's in front of me…

Then I blink and realize I'm looking at his daughter. She never resembled him outright, but they have a similar ability when it comes to me—I always underestimate them.

"He wasn't the only one," I say. "Antonio Salvatore was working for the cartel as well, I think—the bastard was just better at hiding it. They wanted to take over. Wanted me dead. But do you know what I did when I found out about the son of a bitch?"

She doesn't react. Does it hurt her to hear this? God, I hope so. At least then, she has something more to hate me for.

"I showed him mercy," I croak. "For you. I didn't want… I was going to let him go. I beat the fucker within an inch of his life, but I didn't kill him. And then… Well, you know what happened next."

She was there. I see her face, tethered to a fragment of memory. I wrack my brain to follow it, trying to remember. *Sea salt. Hot sand.* "We were at the beach, weren't we?"

Her eyes flash with recognition, and it's enough to recall the rest.

"You, me, and Vin. I was teaching you both to swim."

The sun had been shining, the day beautiful. She and Vin frolicked in the sand, and it was damn near perfect.

"Then Liv called. I don't remember what she said, but I went back."

And I found her dead.

"I lost my shit that day," I tell her hoarsely, not that it matters. It's a pathetic excuse, but it's all I can give her. "I must have blacked out. Gone insane. If there was a reason… I don't know. I can't—it doesn't matter. I did it, and I know it's too late for sorry…but I am. I'm sorry for hurting you."

The way her breathing hitches echoes like a train crash. Time hinges on the slow pause before she swallows, stunned by the admission.

It takes effort to decipher the rest of her reaction. I turn and see her standing there, just watching. I will never understand how I can meet that stare and know that I have nothing else to offer her.

I lost the right to make amends seven years ago.

But what did Fabio say? *Try.*

"If you were a man… If you were in the *famiglia,* we'd settle this one way," I say, though I know what she wants—me dead. Soon enough, she'll get her wish. In the meantime, there's no harm in trying Fabio's plan. Get inside her head. Get her on my side.

Find out what the fuck Mischa might be hiding—*and* who the hell tried to set me up.

"I'd let you have an offering," I tell her absently. "I know a man once who demanded the cock of a bastard who violated his daughter. Is that what you want? Castration? Money? Blood? Just say the word, and it's yours."

I mean it. Like hell, do I mean it…but her flashing eyes convey her answer. *I don't want anything from you!*

"Sleep on it," I suggest. "Save it for a rainy day. Maybe Mischa's life would be a good starting point—"

Tears. They don't belong, glistening on her cheeks. I'm on my feet, advancing on her within a heartbeat. Confused, I swipe at one bead of moisture, cradling it on the tip of my finger. I don't believe it's real until it breaks open, wetting my thumb.

I'm telling her what little of the truth I can, but I've only wound up hurting her more.

"You loved me *that* damn much, huh?" I croak. "When I turned out to be nothing more than a piece of shit. I couldn't protect Olivia. I couldn't even protect you. You should have been glad to get rid of me."

I see it now. Why she's really so angry. She's dwelled on this image of who she thought I was, but it was a lie. I'm not the Don she remembers.

Though was that man really so good to her? That much of a role model?

A man who couldn't even please his own wife?

No.

"Was it because of what I did to Gino?" That has to be it. I grab her, pressing my thumb against her bottom lip as if forcing the answer there. It makes more sense for her to mourn her own father than me. "Is that where your grudge stems from? I don't regret killing him. Is that what you wanted to hear?"

She slaps my hand away. *Finally*, I think I have the right answer. Until her eyes meet mine, blazing with more pain. More hate.

The guilt ripping through my chest is only a fraction of what I deserve to feel—a lifetime of pain for hurting her. "Damn it. If Gino isn't the cause, then why…"

Her lashes flutter, and in her eyes, all I see is my own reflection. *Me.*

"Just tell me what you want," I say. Like I'm fucking begging.

But she refuses me, turning for the door.

"No!" I grab her wrist before she's taken a step, easily yanking her back. "Wait. I want to hear it," I rasp against her ear, gripping tighter as she tries to pull away. "I want to know. Fuck. Just tell me what it is. Why?"

Why she held on all these years, letting that rage fester and smolder…

Why the fuck couldn't she move on? Forget me.

"Tell me!"

Her harsh exhale packs the intensity of a scream.

I see her fist forming, but I don't move. The blow strikes the middle of my chest, drawing a startled grunt. I don't even have to look to know it's the spot where her name is etched into my skin.

She extends her fingers, letting the nail of one bite into the flesh. Without her having to say a word, I understand her point. I'm a liar. I tell her she meant nothing, but the evidence to the contrary is here, right beneath her fucking hands.

In the moonlight, the whole thing gleams, starkly grotesque. Her name, scrawled in red, done with a knife and the aid of a mirror. I remember that…

Trembling, I stroke the outline of the first letter with the pad of my finger. I see myself, cutting it initially, letting the blood run rivulets down my skin as I ground the ink into each fresh wound. I remember the pain—searing, burning agony—and knowing that it wasn't enough. Nowhere near punishment enough.

How could I do that to her?

"You want me to cut myself again?" I ask her, gripping her hand so that the palm is flat against my skin. Her muscles tense, threatening to break away, but I grab her harder. "I'll do it, if that's what you want. Tell me!"

Though it's not like I need her permission.

Reaching into my pocket, I withdraw her dagger. I don't even remember carrying it all this time. It still has the Salvatore girl's blood dried over the blade. Regardless, I press the sharpened edge to my chest.

"If that's what you want. I'd slice myself open again—but we both know it wouldn't be enough, would it?"

Anger blazes across her irises—*Hell no, it wouldn't.*

"You should have never put your trust in me." A tall order to ask of a child. Still, it's an argument I feel compelled to make. "You should have moved on. Lived your perfect life. You *deserve* that life."

Symphonies and fancy schools. Money and safety. A father who'd kill for her. A life most would kill *for.*

Only she doesn't agree, for reasons I doubt even she understands. Again, she fights, resisting my grip—but I don't let her, clenching her forearm until she relents.

"I won't insult you by thinking the past can be erased. It can't. What I'm offering you is…"

How would Fabio put it?

"Peace."

I finally release her, but she doesn't run, so close I can smell that inexplicable scent wafting off her skin. *Roses.* I breathe it in and, for a moment, I forget everything between us. The past. The hate. I just smell her as a woman…

Perfect. Beautiful. It's so damn apparent that she doesn't belong here, amid cloying clouds of dust and cobwebs.

She's always been destined for more than me. More than anything I could ever offer her.

"You were never meant for me, you realize that?"

My fingers are in her hair. It's so damn soft, anchored in a skull so delicate it wouldn't take much effort to crush it. "You belong to some pretty, pampered prince."

Someone like Vin. A man who will cherish her. Worship her.

Who won't get drunk off her scent, greedy for more. Unhooking my fingers from her scalp, I find that pulse in her throat instead. It flutters madly as I stroke my thumb against it. Then lower.

Her daring stare is an antidote to common fucking sense. Impulse overwhelms restraint, and I flatten my palm against that slight collarbone, feeling her breath catch. Her eyes darken, revealing nothing, but her body betrays her. She gulps as my calloused flesh grazes her silken skin. Shudders when my fingers slip beneath that gauzy neckline. The globe of her breast is in my grasp before I know it, firm enough to fill my palm and soft enough to squeeze.

She lurches onto her toes when I do, her eyelids fluttering, lips so damn wet.

She's a bitter little vice, sharper than heroin, more virulent than alcohol, deceptively sweet. I'm drunk on the scent of roses. My nostrils flare to steal every drop, dragging her deep into my lungs.

I wonder if she tastes like the flower. Fragrant. Ripe. My mouth waters. With single-minded focus, I remove my hand from beneath the bodice of her dress and go to her thigh instead, creeping under the gauzy hemline. She doesn't move, not even as I brush over the flat of her belly and the delicate curls directly beneath.

"Damn…"

I should stop, but her heat is a searing temptation, guiding my way, growing hotter the closer I come.

Until finally, I touch fire. Wet and burning… So goddamn *wet.*

Her ragged intake of air resonates with the cadence of a scream. All at once, reality comes crashing back.

I rip away from her, running my hand against my side to scrape her off. As if it would be that easy. My cock is threatening to tear through my fly, my lungs swollen with her scent.

To counter the lust, I have to recall Fabio's advice. *Use her.*

"Safiya is allowed to hate me," I tell her thickly, stumbling over my words.

I'm surprised she's still here, panting loudly, swaying on her feet.

"If that's what you want, then hate me. But Willow? She can use me… As a partner," I clarify, stepping back. The less of her smell I inhale, the clearer my head feels. "Do you want to find out who tried to have your mother killed? Then work *with* me."

Her eyes widen as she smooths the front of her dress, tugging the hemline down. My eyes follow, chasing the paleness of her thigh before I get ahold of myself. *Enough.*

"No threats," I clarify, attempting to draw upon Fabio's sense of calm. "No strong-arming. Nothing but your own free will. We work together."

My words aren't calculated, rehearsed bullshit like Fab's. I'm sloppy in comparison, but she understands me anyway.

"Fabio's too analytical to find the asshole in time," I add. "Mischa? He's too reckless. But you and I?"

I swallow hard, picturing how she watched me murder that bitch Paulie Vanetti.

"We know how a sick, calculated motherfucker might think. You aren't the kind of person to sit around, waiting for your future to be decided by anyone else. Either work with me or leave. I won't stop you."

I beat her to the door, heading for the stairs. Down the hall into the kitchen. Out.

The fresh air is a punch to the system, but I relish in it. Every chilling, shocking burst of the cutting wind, is a welcome call back to reality.

A world in which the past can't be overcome by a one-sided conversation. Where a woman who smells like fucking roses can be linked to a monster through no fault of her own.

A world where forgiveness isn't even on the goddamn table.

17

EVGENI

Hours after my last attempt to contact a Stepanov agent, a message from an unknown number flashes across my cell phone screen. *This is Mario. What the hell did you do? You must have been blacklisted, Ev. I don't know why. I can't even reach you through my designated cell. This is a burner. Can't reply. Will contact when I can.*

Despite his warning, I try replying anyway, only to receive silence in return.

Damn. Mischa isn't this petty. Something is wrong, and the suspicion gnaws at my psyche. What the hell am I even doing?

I should be on my way to Stepanov manor. Even if Briar's story is partly a lie, the mentioning of Saleris and Antonio Salvatore triggers several alarm bells. It stinks to hell and back.

A smart man would be hitting the ground running, gathering whatever intel it takes to get to the bottom of this mess.

Instead, I'm entering an overpriced hotel room after dark, my nostrils wrinkling with a distinctive scent. Damn her. I think she showered again.

"You're back," she declares, lying unabashedly naked on the bed. The city itself is her backdrop, the neon lights reflecting off her pale skin in garish shades of red and green. She makes no move to cover her breasts, or the sliver of golden curls between her legs. If I didn't know better, I'd assume she was posing on purpose.

The reality is she's exhausted, in too much pain to move.

"You certainly took long enough," she gripes with a sigh. "Let's see it, then."

I snatch my sole purchase from the shopping bag and raise it in a fist. "Here."

It's a dress, one bought with my own damn money.

She eyes it, wrinkling her nose. "It will have to do. Though I'm assuming your fashion sense isn't what attracts the swarms of women, you must keep."

Ignoring the taunt, I approach the window as if the view alone might snap some sense back into me. The harbor in the distance glows silver in the moonlight, the waves glimmering. Its proximity to the bay is the defining jewel of

Hell's Gambit, the one marker that makes it relevant on the world's stage.

To hear Briar Winthorp tell it, a new outfit is all she needs to take on a man powerful enough to claim ownership of everything in sight.

"What the hell is your plan?"

I hear the swish of fabric and assume she's changing into the new dress.

"My plan? To render you unconscious, escape with your I.D. and van and grovel my way into Johnathan's good graces."

I turn to find her standing beside a floor-length mirror near the entryway, smoothing her hands along her hips. The dress fits her for what it's worth, clinging to her curves, enhancing the shape of her breasts. She's so caught up in inspecting her appearance that I think the impact of her threat is lost on us both.

"You are transparent; I will give you that," I snarl once her words finally register. Am I surprised if this has been a ruse from the start? No. "And predictable. How do you plan to attack me?"

She cocks her head, frowning. Then she laughs. "I don't mean for real. Honestly, you are so paranoid. It's the story I plan to tell to explain my miraculous reappearance, of course. You are gullible, soldier, but with your strength, even I can admit that it would be hard to overpower you without a fight. I need evidence to make my escape believable."

She places her hands on her hips, arching her back to display her cleavage.

"My injuries will help tremendously, though—" she fingers the cut on her forehead, hidden beneath her damp curls. "I can say that you attacked me."

A part of me bristles at her tone. She's so damn nonchalant, as if this is all nothing more than a game. "And then Eli will wind up dead, and I'll be the fool who trusted the word of a penniless whore rather than his gut instinct."

"I am no whore, soldier." Her eyes cut to slits. I insulted her this time. "As paranoid as you are, if you should know anything about me, it's this—I only care about myself. Sabotaging Johnathan's plans are to my benefit, no more, no less."

"What about your son?"

She raises an eyebrow. "And what about your Willow? She's in the hands of a madman while you go gallivanting around the city with me. It seems we both have skewed priorities."

Damn. I can't argue that point.

"What is your *real* plan?"

"What I've said." She steps from the mirror and extends her hand. "You give me your keys and your I.D. I get onto the boat; find the information we need. I'll tell you where the explosion will be. And voila. You rescue me on your shining white horse, and all is well."

"And you just leave potentially hundreds of people to die?"

She blinks. "If you want to waste time being a hero, by all means. I won't stop you."

I can't tell if her indifference is for show. Should I be surprised if it isn't?

Though, her apparent lack of empathy is the least of our problems.

"Let me see if I have this straight—your plan is to go prancing back, ask him nicely what his strategy is, and then escape unharmed? That's childish."

She chuckles. "No. It's *reckless*, dear soldier. And I have found that recklessness can succeed where the best-laid plans fail. Now cough it up, please. Your keys and the I.D."

"And I'm supposed to put my faith in you?" For whatever reason, I'm already fishing one of her requested items from my pocket—the keys. Curiosity could be the sole reason. Is she bold enough to try taking them?

"Yes," she says simply. "Trust me, you don't have a better option."

But I can think of several—all of them requiring resources that would take time and energy to amass. If she's lying, it's no risk to better prepare.

But if she's not…

"Keep your phone on you," she snaps, very much like an heiress commanding a servant. "I won't have long. An hour at most. Then I'll need to run."

"From a boat?"

"That's your responsibility," she says. "Because there's more I haven't told you yet. You want to know? I suggest you keep me alive."

She saunters into the bathroom.

"I should have had you get me some makeup," she scolds. "A natural look will have to do."

Minutes later, she reemerges, her hair dried, flowing in waves down her shoulders, her heels in place.

She saunters past me and pauses, glancing back. "Oh damn. I think I left my panties in there. Be a doll and fetch them for me?"

I'm too lost in thought to argue. I've barely crossed the threshold when I hear the door to the suite open and slam shut.

"Fuck!"

I must get there not even a second later, but when I open the door, the hall is empty.

She's already gone.

I don't have the energy to care. I've probably played into her trap, but I deserve to be burned. Forget the bitch. *Willow* should be my main focus. She's engaged to Donatello

Vanici...

But not for long if I have any say.

I grab my phone and cycle through my contacts. No one associated with the *mafiya* answers. The last number I try is Mischa.

It rings, but he doesn't answer.

For the first time, I'm more alarmed than irritated. What the hell is going on?

You must have been blacklisted, Ev, Mario claimed. Though, how can I be sure he sent that message in the first place? The technological side of the manor's security was never my purview. Is it really so advanced as to block a single caller?

It smells fishy to me. A good way to test that theory would be to get ahold of my own burner and try calling from it—but that would take time. Considering most of the stores are closed by now, anyway, it's time I don't have.

Left with no choice, I'll need to expand my horizons if I want any outside information. Briar Winthorp herself hinted at the perfect method for doing so. How did she put it? *Friends in low places...*

There aren't many whose numbers I still know by heart. Figuratively, I'll have to scrape the bottom of the barrel as far as contacts go. I almost hope the first man I settle on doesn't answer. Unfortunately, the son of a bitch picks up on the first ring.

"If it isn't little Evgeni! It's been a while since I've heard from you."

"Hello Louie," I reply.

The fact that he's shouting—and the clinking glass and murmuring voices audible in the background—suggests he's drinking, most likely at a bar. I'm not surprised.

"Are you too drunk for information?"

"That depends." His tone shifts, suddenly level. "How much are you offering, and what do you want to know?"

I'm not inclined to get into the full story, opting for a quick summary instead. "Stepanov. Vanici. Saleri. Harmon. You keep your ear to the streets. Tell me if any of those names have been heard floating around the usual gossip."

He laughs. "Is this a trick question? What the hell is a Harmon, anyway?"

"This was a mistake." I start to hang up.

"Wait! Wait! That last name I can't help you with, but as for Stepanov… Let's just say that people have been talking."

"What kind of talk?"

"Before we get into specifics, let me ask *you* a question. Why are you calling me, anyway? Aren't you up Mischa's ass these days? Besides, you know my price for information. Lately, you've seemed too high and mighty to—"

"I'll pay it," I say absently. Later I'll worry about the deal I'm making—one with the literal devil. If Mischa and his family really are in danger, I don't have many options left. "Now talk."

"New guy on the block," he says, jumping to the point. "Not much is known about him, but he's been waving money around like crazy, using various proxies to try and get dirt."

"On who?"

"Anyone. Mischa. The Saleris. Vanici."

"Were you contacted?"

"Not directly," he says evasively. "But I know that anyone who has that kind of dough to throw around wouldn't be above bribery. The first thing I'd do is buy off someone high in every circle I'm looking to infiltrate—especially the *mafiya*."

"Mischa vets his men carefully," I point out. "I've worked with them. They're loyal."

And yet, I keep seeing the face of one man in particular— the rookie who, overnight, was promoted to replace me. Jealousy could be why I think of him now. If I were that damn childish, at least. No. There has to be another reason.

"Enough money can buy anyone, Ev," Louie remarks. "Except, probably you. Though, hey, if you and Mischa are on the outs, it would be an easy way to make some money…"

"Not interested. But I will take a name."

"Don't have one. He just utilizes his contacts, but I doubt any of them could give you one either. Not a real name, anyway," Louie says. Judging from how he's slurring his words, I doubt he's sober enough to lie. "I can tell you one other thing, though. Whoever the bastard is, he's been hiring men. Maybe ten guys. Twenty. All to do labor down on the docks, on the west side. I couldn't tell you what, though. Not for free, anyway."

My interest is piqued enough to bite. "Fine. If it's worth my while, I'll owe you a favor."

"A favor, Ev? You must be desperate." He laughs loudly, followed by a clink of glass as if he set his drink down. "I have your word on that?"

I mull it over. Working with Mischa, I haven't had to make deals with scum like him. While his information may be good, the price is always steep.

Again, I can't escape the suspicion that a better option would be to swallow my pride now and return to Stepanov manor before it's too late.

"I don't got all night, Ev—"

"Fine. Tell me."

"I'll do you one better. I'll give you an address. Sixth street. That's where the men have been working mainly. I wasn't lying when I said I don't know the details, but I can tell you that it's manual. Anyone who works there comes back dead on their feet. Like they're trying to mine to China or something."

"Digging? Near a harbor?"

"I didn't say it made any sense, now did I? Anyway, don't forget, boy. You owe me one."

I hang up, not that it will matter in the long run. Louie is a drunk, but he's no pushover. Sooner or later, I'll have to pay him.

For now, I put that out of my head as I leave the hotel. Unsurprisingly, my van is missing from the garage. Despite the late hour, I'm able to rent a car from the hotel's selection, and I head straight for the west end.

Sixth street is a lonely road bordering a row of decrepit warehouses that have seen better days. It should be damn near deserted—especially this late at night.

But low and behold, it's a hive of activity.

At least ten men mill about a yard close to the water's edge. They're only visible due to the bright orange safety vests they wear. Each one reflects what little light there is, blinking in the darkness as they march from a darkened warehouse to the water's edge.

I strain my eyes to make out what they carry. Boxes?

Large, metal crates.

"Hey!" A man I didn't notice steps to the curb, holding a flashlight that he shines directly through the windshield. "This is private fucking property," he says. "No trespassing."

Rolling down the window, I greet him with a nod. "I'm looking for work. Nightshift, too. What kind of labor are you guys into? Shipping?"

His nostrils flare, his expression unwelcoming, to say the least. "We ain't hiring. Now don't make me tell you twice to move the fuck on."

He deliberately reaches for the pocket of his dust-coated slacks. Louie wasn't exaggerating. The man is covered in dirt and grime. Digging to China would probably be a cleaner endeavor.

I'm tempted to dig for more answers, but I nod instead.

"Have a goodnight."

I don't go far, following the water's edge, across the bridge separating the west end of the city from the eastern center. By the time I near the hotel, it's almost dawn.

But still no word from her.

Obviously, because she was lying from the start, using me for her own ends. Fuck Briar Winthorp.

If there is a plot involving the city, there's no reason why I can't get to the bottom of it my damn self. Starting with the Saleris' yacht.

*I*t's already on the water by the time I reach the marina. At least part of her story wasn't a lie.

Luckily for the Saleris, it's a decent day to sail, bolstered by a steady breeze.

Typically, I suspect the marina would be packed with boaters looking to take advantage of the beautiful weather. Instead, it's empty—of the average citizen, anyway.

I don't fail to notice the men scattered at least a ten-block radius, up and down the water's edge. Dressed in black, they blend in well with their surroundings. Too well.

The longer I watch them, the more hairs on the back of my neck stand on end. I know a trained man when I see one. The caliber of this sort looks high enough to match the Stepanovs' private retinue.

And, as if on some unknown cue, my cell phone goes off.

"Volkov."

"6th street to 12th," a woman says in my ear, her voice hoarse. "You have an hour to clear it."

Son of a bitch. I eye the number she's calling from but don't recognize it. A trick?

Then I spy the white vessel gleaming on the water. The only boat on the water, to be exact. "You're on the boat."

"Meet me at the Marina," she croaks. "Be there near the last dock. Row E. Don't try to be a hero, either. Just wait for me. I expect you to bring a very fast horse, soldier. We won't be able to leave the city after. If we don't die, that is."

It's a grittier outlook than any she's revealed so far. She's worried.

Which means I have to reconcile that she might have been telling the truth from the start.

"So, there will be an explosion?" I demand. Sixth street. That's the location where those men were working, carrying God knows what into those warehouses. "What is he planning? Why?"

"Oh, there will be more than an explosion," the woman rasps. "But it's different than I thought. I'm not sure if I can—"

Without warning, the line goes dead.

I'm already climbing from the car, my gaze on the water.

Then I remember her words. *Don't try to be a hero. Wait for me.*

Fine. She can gamble her life if she wants to, but no one else's.

Without taking my gaze from the yacht, I make a call, bringing the phone to my ear.

"Evgeni?" Louie's voice is a shadow of his boisterous tone from last night. "What the hell, boy? First, you run off on me to be Mischa Stepanov's whipping boy, and now you're up my ass—"

"I need another favor," I say. "Same price. Whatever you want."

"Seriously?" He grumbles, cursing under his breath. I imagine him climbing out of bed, trying to sober up. "You must be desperate. Hit me."

"I need you to clear the West end docks of everyone. Now. Call in some favors to the police if you have to—"

"Whoa! Slow down. I told you that some serious motherfucker was in charge of that shit. I stick my nose in there and—"

"And you'll have my balls in a vice," I counter. "You want me on the hook for whatever you want? Then tell me you can do it."

He sighs. "I can try. That's it. What the hell has gotten into you, anyway?"

"There's another thing. I want you to find out whatever you can about a woman. Two, actually. The first is a Safiya Mangenello. That ring a bell?"

"Never heard of her," he replies. Grudgingly, I sense he isn't lying.

"What about the other? Her name is Briar Winthorp—"

"Ice-cold cunt," Louie snarls with a venom that catches me off guard. "A bitch you better avoid if you like your cock intact."

An accurate description. "I'm assuming you've met her, then."

He barks out a vicious laugh. "You bet your ass I have. The little bitch. She—" Abruptly, he breaks off, clearing his throat. "Just stay away from her, sonny boy. The bitch is bad news."

"Bad news," I echo. A sudden thought comes to mind. I should have seen it before. "She mentioned Amina. That's a name she couldn't learn from just anyone."

"Ev…"

"I'm assuming that *you* supplied her with the 'research' she might need to know about my past."

"Ah, fuck. Listen, Ev. I didn't have a choice. The little bitch leveraged a debt from years ago and offered to pay it off. It's a cold world out there, alright? After you left me in the dust for old Mischa, can you blame me for wanting to make a little coin off all our good times? You were a hell of a bounty hunter. The iciest motherfucker I've ever seen—"

"When we meet again, I'll remind you of the importance of privacy," I say, hanging up.

At least now, one mystery is solved. Someone had to pay good money to steer her to Louie. All to get to me.

Do I truly believe she'd go through all of that trouble merely to meet with Mischa?

Hell, no, I don't.

Not one damn bit.

In fact, it's time to get answers from the *mafiya* leader himself. I keep my cell phone in my hand and dial his direct number.

The line barely rings before it goes dead—too quickly for Mischa to have ended it manually. Did he block me?

It's an act too petty for someone like him.

Something's wrong.

You've been blacklisted, Mario claimed.

What the fuck does that mean?

I turn toward my rental, aiming to head straight to the manor my damn self. This mystery has gone on long enough.

But leaving now would mean leaving her. If she is truly in danger…

Fuck. I glare at the yacht, imagining her cackling on the upper deck, amused at making me jump like her little puppet. Her betrayal would be an easy fantasy to believe…

If it weren't for one little slip-up, that's been haunting me from the start. Hell, maybe it's why I've humored her this damn long.

Ali. She referred to her so-called son as Ali more than once —a nickname, conveying a softness that a *completely* heartless bitch wouldn't bother to utilize. I know that from firsthand experience.

My father never called me by any name other than the one he gave me—Evgeni Victorovitch Volkov. Day or night, he referred to me as that. Only that. Pride wasn't his reasoning. Just discipline, the way a trainer would ensure its guard dog never learned anything but the strictest commands. To gain complete control over a living being, you must first strip them of emotion. Humanity. An identity.

A woman who didn't give a damn about her son wouldn't slip and call him Ali while proclaiming her lack of concern.

Though hell, why does it even matter? She's a shitty mother overall, and that should be enough to counter any guilt I might feel for leaving her behind.

The choice isn't that hard to make.

In the grand scheme, I should let the bitch drown.

18

WILLOW

*E*llen once described love as madness. I remember the moment so clearly. We were in my room, and she stood gazing from the window as she spoke, her blue eyes distant.

It's hard to put into words, she admitted. *It's more or less something that you have to experience for yourself to truly know it. All I can say is that one minute you think you understand normal affection, concern, love even. And the next you don't. The whole world becomes lopsided around your perception of one person. Their life becomes yours, their fears and emotions as well. Everything you are takes on a new definition. Wife. Mother. There are so many variations of love, and yet they all boil down to the same, driving promise. You'd die for them.*

I knew she meant every word.

And I felt horrified that I couldn't relate in the slightest. Something had to be wrong with me. I was broken, incapable of feeling anything close to her version of love.

Now, I know the truth. I was just overused. A fried electrical socket, forever defective.

Why? Because Donatello Vanici overwhelmed my young system with more emotion than it could handle. He taught me care and affection.

He taught me hate.

Being around him arouses all of those past sentiments and more in a warped, twisted context. Emotions, in general, feel hotter and more vibrant around him, like I could explode from the sensation alone. Combust. As long as he's alive, I will never feel normal again, whatever that means. His death would be one way to reconcile the damage; I know that.

Or...

Steal back whatever he took all those years ago. Considering that I don't even know how to put that into words...

It's a daunting task. Love isn't a strong enough term—or perhaps too strong. Trust, maybe?

Trust in him when I'd already learned to withhold it from everyone else. Trust that he would never let me down like they had. Never betray me.

It hurt like hell to hear that he never cared, but at least I had something to hold on to. Now he claims to not even remember why he sold me. A pathetic, stupid lie. It *has* to be. Selling a child isn't something you'd forget—unless he truly is a depraved monster.

Or a man with a psyche so damaged he can't truly recall anything. I wrack my brain, trying to square the man in my memories with any one of those scenario Donatellos. Neither fits.

He wasn't crazy, at least not back then. He wasn't cold or distant. Though, I am aware that my recollections don't completely match reality, distorted from childhood and a rose-colored view. Olivia saw a very different man from my Don. Someone she pleaded with, displaying desperation I will never understand.

I miss you. I miss you. I miss you…

Maybe that's what Fabio wanted to hide? His sister had grown out of love with her husband…

A flash of the way he used to look at her appears in my mind in painful clarity—but I refuse to pity him. Instead, I'll take him up on his offer—use him. Take everything he has to give and salvage something from it.

Olivia wilted in the shadow of his indifference, but I won't.

I refuse to.

For the first time in days, my thoughts feel focused. With this newfound clarity, I dress in a simple gray sweater and jeans from the selection Fabio procured for me, and I leave the room with the determination of a soldier facing an opponent on the battlefield. Intuitively, I sense he's already awake, plotting somewhere deep within the house. I follow the impulse downstairs and wind up before the mouth of his study.

Unsurprisingly, he's hunched over the desk, one hand propped against his forehead. The angle alone betrays the lines etched into his face by age and exhaustion. A thrill runs through me, though I write it off as grim recognition. His mouth is in that hard line I remember; his bottom lip skewered between his teeth. He's working on something. Before him is a wealth of assorted documents, spread out haphazardly.

"You're still here." His tone is cold, but neutral. As he lifts his head, I don't find the hostility I've come to expect.

Neither change comforts me.

This iteration of Donatello Vanici is a chameleon. One adept at portraying whatever guise is required to achieve his chosen aim. Last night was all an act meant to lower my guard. The real question is, why?

He sits back without revealing the answer, swiping his hand over the papers before him. A tilt of his head beckons me closer, but his eyes contain a dare I don't have the energy to decipher. With every step I advance, I tell myself that it's on my own terms. Of my own free will.

He hasn't fooled me. I'll turn the tables soon enough...

"Sit." He gestures to the leather chair before him, but I don't move. It's childish defiance. I expect him to snarl his command again, but a slow grin contorts his mouth instead. "Suit yourself."

He shoves a stack of papers at me and picks up a pen. "You are a smart, sneaky son of a bitch out to undermine me from the ground up. How do you do it?"

I blink. His expression remains blank, and his voice lacked the anger I'm used to—he didn't mean that statement literally. It was a question. One having something to do with the documents he nods to.

I scan the nearest one, feeling my brows furrow. The series of numbers and random statements printed on the sheet read as a jumble of nonsense at first. The more I read, however, the more sense of it I can make.

Locations? All for sale, seemingly within walking distance of each other, but their stated designations make no sense when taken all together. A butcher shop. A fish market. A random bookstore a few miles down.

You are a smart, sneaky son of a bitch out to undermine me from the ground up. How do you do it?

I let myself embody that sarcastic hypothetical. How would I destroy him if I had endless resources at my disposal? The first image that comes to mind steals my breath—stripping before him in darkness, forcing him to view me in the one way he shouldn't…

No. To truly destroy him, my plan would be far simpler. I'd buy an army, not buildings. Then I'd drive him out of the city brick by brick and erase any trace of the name Vanici.

"Here—" he shoves a folder before me, containing more documents. These, however, all pertain to one location. A port with his name listed as the owner.

I look up and catch him watching me in return. A shiver runs down my spine, my throat dampening. He's openly transparent, eyeing me like he's waiting for something. Hunting for it. Then, his upper lip quirks, and I almost drop the page in my hand. I haven't seen this expression in seven years.

The smirk he'd sport during the games we used to play, when he was all but sure of his win—until I proved him wrong, winning instead. *I taught you well,* he'd remark after…

"Maybe I was wrong." While I was lost in thought, his smirk disappeared, replaced by a frown. "Give it back—" He grabs for the folder, but I pull it out of his reach.

Eyeing the pages again, I scramble to connect the dots on my own.

Several locations, all within close distance, and one pivotal business owned by him. Without thinking, I rummage through the remaining pages until I find a map tucked amid the chaos.

Donatello loudly clears his throat. He's watching, still waiting. And yet…

I'm too fixated on the puzzle he's presented to care. Despite my better judgment, his dare piqued my interest. *How do you do it?* An answer lurks in the murky bits of information; I can feel it. *You are a smart, sneaky son of a bitch…*

I only know one man who fits that descriptor perfectly. So, I ask myself—If I were Donatello Vanici, what would I see?

Danger. Paranoia would color my outlook of the world in hostile shades of gray. In his eyes, even a harmless butcher shop has ulterior motives.

But would Mischa see things any differently? Yes. Mischa is a crocodile prone to lie in wait for his chosen prey, while the man before me is a lion, apt to go for the jugular as soon as it's presented to him.

My own throat contorts around a hard swallow. This isn't right. No matter which mindset I put myself in, the information refuses to make sense.

But what if I tried a different, untapped outlook?

My own. How would Willow Stepanova see it? Or Safiya Mangenello…

Cocking my head, I observe the documents again. The various bits and pieces blend and meld, but I still don't see a way of making sense of them.

Until I make the mistake of glancing up. Donatello glowers at the center of it all like a blazing bullseye, and my focus shifts. Not as a hunting predator, but something far more calculating. A watchful, careful animal that knows when to lie in wait and when to strike, so still and small it can seem invisible. Yet, dangerous in its own right.

I reach for another document, and then another, arranging them according to the pattern unfurling in my mind. *There.* It's so clear to me now. I'm the one smirking, drawing a single grunt from the man across from me. In answer, all I can do is grapple for a pen and write on the corner of the nearest page.

It's a web.

"A web?" Raising an eyebrow, he stands, moving behind me. His shadow is poison against my newfound confidence. I hate the way I watch him, searching for a hint of approval. *He* is poison. My body prickles with this newest dose, my breaths quickening as he runs his fingers across a document I'd placed in the center.

The port.

Suddenly he slaps his hand down over the map. "Son of a bitch."

I release the breath I wasn't aware of holding. Hidden within the gruff tone was an emotion he couldn't suppress —grudging respect? It vanishes as he grunts again, snatching up another document. "So, their aim isn't to drive me out; it's to box me in. But why? For what?"

I shrug. Why else does a spider spin a web at all?

To catch a fly.

But even I can admit that it would take a rather large web to snare a lion.

I expect him to elaborate more, explain his reasoning at least. Instead, he lifts his hand abruptly, sending a trove of documents to the floor.

"Get dressed," he says. "And not like that—" He nods to the simple sweater I'm wearing now. "Not that innocent shit Fab got you. Find something else. Something…" He seems to fish for the right words as he storms from the room. "Something that makes you *look* like you deserve a seat at the table."

It's a double-edged request, conveying so much of what he thinks of me. Unimpressive. Unworthy. Easily ignored. I bristle, irritated by his assessment, though do I even *want* to appeal to a man like him?

My mind flashes back to that moment in the darkness, and I lose track of everything but the tightness in my chest.

"Show me what I'm missing," he demanded. *"This is how you can hurt me. Show me what I'll never have…"*

"Meet me in the car," the present Donatello calls from the hallway. "I need to have a little word with the Saleris… And I'm taking you with me."

✦

The Saleris. That name sounds familiar, but I don't realize why until I spy the building we approach through the windshield of Donatello's sports car. In the overcast daylight, it looks like just any other midrise structure near the city center.

Not a club. Without seeing the name emblazoned across the front, I wouldn't even recognize it as the lounge where we met those two men. The Saleris. There seemed to be no love lost between them and Donatello—to the point where I felt compelled to kiss him to play the role of his willing fiancée...

This time, Donatello parks directly before it, heedless of the posted sign forbidding the action, or the bouncer who lunges from his post. "Hey! You need to move your car—"

"I need to see Gregori Saleri," Donatello growls as he climbs out and fearlessly mounts the curb.

As I watch him, his prior words echo in my skull. *Look like you deserve a seat at the table.* Only in his world, the "table" is figurative. What he really meant was look like I deserve to stand beside *him*. An unmistakable aura sets him apart from everyone else in this sliver of the city.

Every woman within a twenty-foot radius stops to stare, as the men whip around, sensing the predator in their midst. He's too dangerous to belong. His suit is too black in the vibrant sunshine, his hair wildly tousled and yet coifed at the same time.

He'll always be able to hold one caveat over my head. I don't belong in his world.

I never did.

"Who the fuck do you think you are?" the bouncer demands, and I startle to find that Donatello is frozen before the entrance. It isn't until his eyes cut in my direction that I realize why he's stopped.

Are you coming?

I scramble to join him, smoothing my hand down the front of my idea of an "acceptable" ensemble. A black sundress procured by Fabio, my hair loose. I knew the second I stepped into the car that I had failed Donatello's expectations, though he acknowledged me with silence rather than an insult. Beside him, I'm a rabbit next to a wolf.

"Mr. Saleri isn't in this time of day," the bouncer sputters as Donatello surges inside, revealing the glass doors are unlocked.

"Then where is he?" My breath catches at that fierce tone. I'm a child again, selfishly relieved that his intensity isn't honed on me. "You don't want to lie to me," he warns when the bouncer remains silent.

"On his yacht," the man blurts. "A, uh… A private meeting. I'll inform him that you came by—"

"Do that." Donatello turns, heading outside. When we're back in the car, he says nothing, wrenching the vehicle into reverse.

His speed is reckless. Nearby buildings pass in an alarming blur. Soon, they become sparser, revealing glimpses of the bay expanding over the horizon in between.

"So, what if you're right," Donatello says out loud, though I get the sense he isn't talking to me in particular. "Saleri is acting as a proxy for someone looking to build a net around the harbor. But for what? Why box me in rather than buy me out, or just open up another section of the port? It doesn't make sense, and it's a lot of fucking money to throw around. Maybe that's the point…"

His disgusted tone matches my instinctive reaction. To scoff. This mysterious figure is just doing what anyone with money in this city seems apt to—spend it frivolously.

"But why here?" Donatello continues. "Why now? Why use Salvatore and the Saleris as a proxy at all…"

To cover their tracks. Whoever the culprit is, they aimed for stealth. Their ultimate end goal is something they don't want to be traced to them. At least, not yet. It harkens to my spider comparison all over again—but several creatures, working in unison to create a larger web.

All to catch a very, very big prey.

"You're thinking about something." He risks taking his eyes from the road long enough to scrutinize mine. "Tell me."

I tense, waiting for the impact of what I'm sure was an insult. And yet, the telltale inflection never comes.

"What are you thinking?" This time? He sounds almost…genuine.

I swallow hard, overwhelmed by a reaction that comes from nowhere. Nostalgia? Something uglier, perhaps. A terrifying sense that we've been in this position before, him asking what I'm thinking. In fact, he used to be one of the few people to ever care.

Tell me.

I hesitate, feeling much like a child again, forced to pantomime. I'm acutely aware of him watching as I raise my hands, linking the fingers of both together.

"Your web," he says gruffly. "We established that. So, what's the point of it?"

The point? I extend one finger and turn it on him.

"Me?" He shakes his head. "No. It has to be more than that. I'm nobody as far as the city is concerned. At least by the time these purchases took place. And why rope the Saleris into it? And use me against Mischa? Sure, it makes sense on the surface, but beyond that? It's fucking stupid and reckless."

Unless…

I don't know how to convey the thoughts in my head. I just lean forward, flattening my palms over the dashboard in front of me. Each individual finger could resemble a piece on a chessboard—him on one end, Mischa on the other.

But what if that's the wrong way of viewing it entirely?

I withdraw my hands, triggering a grunt from Donatello.

"Maybe it's not a web after all?"

I shake my head, still sure of that detail. Only he might not be who the trap is designed to snare.

"Mischa?" he guesses, somehow following my train of logic. "Makes sense. He's the biggest player in the game as far as the city is concerned. But he doesn't have a stake in the harbor, so why the fuck would he care? You'd need to strike hard and fast if you wanted to drive him from the city. Not leisurely buy useless property."

He's right, but I try to see past the obvious reasoning. Mischa is powerful; who wouldn't want him out of the way? But how does the spider's web truly operate? It ensnares, trapping its victim until it finally gives up the fight.

Then it drains the husk dry. Speed is an unnecessary factor with such a method. All you need is time.

"You think you know why?" Before I can reply, he pulls into a nearby parking lot and faces me. "Let's hear it."

Communicating with him is a strange exercise, almost like looking at a mirror but in reverse. I move, and he copies the motions, extending his hands, his head cocked expectantly. As I spread each of my fingers, he does the same. Then I form a fist with both.

"You want it all," he says, catching onto the strange pantomime. "It's not the purchases on their own but taken as a whole. It's the long game. Force the target into a corner. Goddamn! It's smart."

Something in my chest constricts, even though I know that admission was for this figurative enemy, not me.

Oblivious to my reaction, Donatello sits back, stroking his chin. "It's very smart, but Fab wouldn't think of it off the bat. It's gritty. Whoever this fucker is… They aren't entirely thoroughbred. You have to be a gutter rat to think of shit like this. Like everything is a game."

His eyes meet mine, and a tendril of understanding darts between us. *Gutter rats.* Those not born into privilege.

Someone like us.

"Fab's parents were bankers, did you know that?" He leans back further, eyeing the roof of the car while I dwell over the fact that he's striking up this line of conversation at all. Even stranger? I don't even think he realizes it himself.

"Yep. Not superrich, but definitely upper crust. He had no business hanging out with a little shit like me. It's funny how we met. My sister, Donella… I loved her to death, but she was a grifter, one of the best. Thought she could rope a fresh, young accountant into funding her latest business venture—but what she didn't know is that Fabio Botelli is no one's pushover."

He laughs with genuine appreciation, smirking at the memory.

"I loved my sister, but she wouldn't know a decent man if he bit her on the ass. When I learned the size of the loan she'd taken out, I went and confronted the idiot who signed off on it. Only to find that Fabio had coded the terms entirely to his benefit. He would own her financially for life should she cut and run. It was sly, but I was so fucking impressed I didn't kick his ass automatically. When I told Donella the game she'd fallen for, the idiot did the smart thing for once and tried to make it right. She invested the money into a small café and ran it for a while, under Fabio's guidance."

I purse my lips, recalling the café where he hosted our "meeting."

"That's right," Donatello says. "Donna's. She did a good job running it too. Hell, I thought she might settle down..."

He trails off, shaking his head to clear it. It's like he forgot he was speaking to me. Forgot everything at all but the sensation of reliving the past. Then he inclines his head, shooting me a look I can't decipher.

"You remind me of her," he admits in a tone that raises goosebumps over my skin. "Wild. Impulsive. Able to read anyone you look at like an open book. I don't know what Fab saw in her, but she couldn't stay on the straight and narrow for long. She skipped town without even saying goodbye. I learned afterward that she 'sold' the café to Fab, which was really his way of giving her the money to run with. Even when she turned up two years later with a baby and no clue of who or where the dad was... He always treated Vin like he was his. A bleeding heart to a fault."

He trails off, and I have a suspicion as to what he might be thinking. Fabio is a bleeding heart, but so was he, taking on the responsibility of a child that wasn't his.

"Long story short, Fabio is smart, but he's not a cold motherfucker," Donatello explains. "He doesn't think like we do. I think you're onto something. Someone wants Mischa out, and they're going out of their way to disguise it. Why? Fab will figure out an answer, but he'll do it the right way. That will take fucking weeks. Would Mischa handle it any differently?"

Yes. He would hunt down any lead ruthlessly.

"There's another way," Donatello says, dragging his thumb across his chin. "We know the Saleris have to be in on it. Gregori couldn't come up with the money or the smarts to make all of those purchases on a whim. Mateo? He's smarter, but has far less tact. There isn't a patient bone in his body. They're taking their marching orders from someone, and they're as good a lead to start with as any. The only question is to confront them now before they can conspire with their puppet master? Or do the smart thing and wait for Fab to finish tracking down his leads..."

I almost make the mistake of thinking I'm the one he's talking to. But that would require him trusting my judgment. Trusting *me*. I wait for his eyes to lose their piercing intensity. For him to look away.

He *will* look away...

"What would you do?" He shifts his weight toward me, and it's as though he simultaneously made the car's interior ten times smaller. I smell him with every breath, feeling his heat prickle my skin. The cadence of his voice resonates through my bones, into my belly.

What would I do? Another taunt, perhaps? Or something far more dangerous.

"Do I even need to ask?" His knowing chuckle sends blood rushing to my face. "You wouldn't think. You'd sneak into the Saleris' hotel room armed with a knife, ready to kill. Wouldn't you?"

His hand bridges the gap between us without warning, his thumb brushing my wrist. Electricity zaps through me, and I flinch.

"Sorry." He didn't mean to touch me. Sighing, he palms his thigh instead. "Honestly, I don't know which option would be better in this case. Patience got Vin shot in the head, and me engaged to a mobster's daughter. But anyone who would go through those lengths must have way more up their sleeve, and I don't think Fabio's smooth-talking can help."

He asked what I would do? Logically I would feel that I learned my lesson when it comes to reacting on impulse. I would wait. Trust things to Fabio and Mischa and lick the wounds inflicted from my last screw up. After what I've done, I don't deserve to take the reins on any opportunity.

But what do I feel? Around him, logic gives way to instinct. It's the difference between watching a lion in a cage and being hunted by one on its own turf. There isn't time to think. Biology rules all, and the human body is such a fickle, delicate piece of machinery. Neutral one minute, and a fluttering mass of adrenaline the next.

His nearness disrupts every normal function I've come to trust, turning bone and skin against each other. Tensing muscle and faltering breaths.

The worst part?

He doesn't even seem to notice.

"Patience it is," he says, putting the car back into drive.

I must do something. Breathe too loudly. Make some kind of movement that has him stopping short. His expression shifts, his eyes narrowing in confusion—only to slowly widen...

"No," he says huskily. "You think we should go there?"

It's wrong. How his inflection dips... *No.* I make my face blank, schooling every muscle into submission.

His eyes dull instantly, losing their conspiratorial gleam as he returns his attention to the road. "Never mind—"

He shouldn't be able to see me nod; I do it so quickly, blaming it on a spasm of muscle. Regardless, his eyes shift back to me, and his smile returns so swiftly it's a devastating lesson in whiplash.

"We'll just *see* if Saleri is at the marina," he suggests. "Just drive by, nothing more. Maybe the bastard decided to spray-paint his fucking plan all over the side of his yacht?" His cold laugh punctuates the statement perfectly, but I can see the irritation he struggles to hide.

This "plan" puts his livelihood at risk—and already put his family in danger. Despite the forced calm he exudes, I know internally he's chomping at the bit, itching to fight. Punch. Draw blood in retaliation. He is a lion freed from his cage, ready to wreak havoc.

In contrast, I don't know how to feel. Between him and Mischa, it seems as though there isn't any room for me to feel anything. In a sense, I'm little more than a pawn.

A pawn he asked for guidance…

"Look at it, the son of a bitch," Donatello exclaims, nodding toward the windshield. "Gregori didn't mourn the loss of his son-in-law long, did he?"

He's referring to a beautiful white boat out on the water, visible from the right side of the vehicle where the bay slices into the city at a rectangular angle. I don't think I've ever seen this part of Hell's Gambit any closer than the view from a plane. To highlight the moment, sunlight pierces the cloud cover, glinting off the waves and reflecting off Donatello's bared teeth. His expression is far too fearsome for a smile.

A snarl, perhaps.

"What are the chances he's out for a lazy waterfront tour after purchasing six blocks of property on a whim?"

His tone sends my mind whirling. He loves this. The threat of violence. The thrill of the fight. Of a battle.

If I didn't know any better, I'd assume I must enjoy this as well. My heart is racing, my interest heightened. It's the same way I felt when…

When I first saw a man from across my family's ballroom, unknowingly intruding into my life again after seven years.

"The fucker's dock has to be close," he says, scanning the area. Not long later, we pull onto a road leading to the Marina's entrance. I can't discern anything from the row of docks and boats, but something makes Donatello hiss through his teeth.

"Son of a bitch. They've cleared it out."

I don't realize what he means until I notice that the yacht is one of the few boats on the water, with most boats still docked. The nearby parking lot is all but deserted, with the marina walkways appearing just as empty.

"There are Saleri agents everywhere," Donatello adds. "Casual tour, my ass."

He grabs a cell phone from his pocket, and whoever he calls answers on the first ring. "Luciano. I need to get onto Antonio's boats. Where exactly are they docked? There's no time—" He hisses, slamming his fist on the wheel. "Don't give me the bullshit runaround; just tell me which dock. I'll make it worth your while. No—" He eyes the water with a steely focus. "You stay put at the house, but if I don't call in an hour, get in touch with Fabio Botelli and tell him that I decided to join Gregori Saleri for a swim."

He hangs up and throws open the door on his end. "Come on," he says to me. "We'll get a closer look."

I follow him warily. I was wrong. The marina itself isn't entirely devoid of people—men in black mill about, their attention on the water. The level of security reminds me of Stepanov Manor. If these men are even half as diligent as Mischa's, they've already identified Donatello by now and alerted their leader.

And yet…they don't raise the alarm or even seem to pay us any attention the closer we come. The web analogy occurs to me again—we aren't the predator they're waiting for.

"Something doesn't smell right," Donatello says against my ear. He's closer than I realized, his heat a warning prickle before I feel a subtle pressure against my lower back. I don't even have to look to identify it—his hand. "Follow my lead," he warns, steering me forward. "I know the Saleris. All this firepower means they either have the fucking president on board that boat, or…"

Or the ringleader responsible for spinning this entire web.

"They're on a fucking victory lap," Donatello growls. His fingers flex, urging me forward to keep pace with his bold series of strides. In this moment, it's apparent just how big he is in comparison to me. So tall I have to crane my neck to fully view his fierce expression.

He's troubled, as if the weight of the world is pressing down, and he's taken it upon himself to bear the burden. Recognition bites at me; I've seen that look before, years ago, though, in a very different context. We'd been out swimming at the beach. Despite his smile, I'd picked up on his worry that grew into full-blown dread when he received a single phone call.

And that day, the entire world changed.

"Stay calm," he warns, snapping me back to the present. "Follow my lead."

We're nearing the entrance of the docks, where a man stands guard. His casual slacks and loose white shirt set him apart from the crisply dressed Saleri men. He must be a manager.

"I'm sorry," he says as we approach. "The docks are closed for uh… Maintenance—"

"We're here on behalf of Antonio Salvatore," Donatello declares. "Taking stock of his assets."

The man sputters. "I'm sorry, but we're closed."

Donatello reaches into his pocket. "Give us ten minutes," he says, extracting a few crisp bills from a gold money clip. "Do you really think we can get up to much trouble? All we need is to check out the boat and square everything away."

"I can't," the man insists, though his gaze flickers toward the money with open interest. "Trust me, man—"

"Tony's dead, and the boat is in his daughter's trust," Donatello says coldly. "You really want to drag this out another day before her father's affairs can be put in order?

You want that on your conscience, or can you spare us ten fucking minutes?"

I don't know what shocks me more. Him, using Kisa's name to his benefit in the first place? Or that it seems to work.

With a harsh sigh, the man snatches the money. "You have ten minutes. Just, please make it quick. I don't think these guys are playing around—" he jerks his chin in the direction of a man standing near the water's edge, his posture rigid, eyes fixed on the yacht.

"We'll just take ten minutes." Donatello urges me forward. Once we're out of earshot, he meets my gaze.

"Don't look at me like that," he warns. "We'll leave little Kisa's inheritance intact. Think of it this way, no one will inherit shit if whoever this motherfucker is takes out your family for good. Or mine."

He has a point. One I feel acutely aware of as I spy the white vessel drifting in the distance.

"We need to get closer," Donatello says. I can almost see the war taking place within him. The need for restraint. The urgency for action. Normally, he'd surrender to the impulse.

This time? He looks at me.

"What? You think we should play the game the right way. Call for backup. Wait for Fabio. But I feel it. Something's off."

His voice touches on that deep, raspy baritone again, rousing a shudder in me. To distract myself, I turn away, observing the boats docked nearby. Does Mischa own one? It startles me to realize that I don't know.

"Antonio kept two boats here," Donatello says, following my line of sight. He hones in on a particular vessel, white with black lettering spelling out "Lady Killer" on the side. "I bet my ass that's one of them."

"Here." The lone worker returns with a manilla folder stamped with the name Salvatore. "These are the keys to Mr. Antonio's two boats. I'm sure the maintenance and upkeep fees will continue to be paid, or we can arrange to have the boats removed—"

"Maintenance," Donatello says softly. "Does that include making sure it's fueled?"

The man shuffles through the documents and nods. "Yeah. It looks like everything was based on Mr. Salvatore's schedule. Since we are in season, I believe the fuel tank was last topped up on the Lady Killer… About two weeks ago."

"So, it should still be good to go, then," Donatello says. He barges down the narrow dock, craning his neck to inspect the larger of the two boats. "When is the last time he's been out?"

"Um, right after the last refuel. He took out the Lady Killer with some acquaintances."

"Anything about it stand out?" Donatello's voice radiates a deceptive calm. Even I fall prey to it, losing track of the aim behind his probing questions.

The man, however, stiffens, his neck reddening. "I…"

"So it *wasn't* a normal visit, then?" Donatello prods.

I marvel at his skill. For someone who can seem so intimidating—like ice—one minute, he still has a unique way of lulling someone into a false sense of security. As though they could tell him anything. Do anything.

"There was a lot more fanfare than Mr. Salvatore usually employs," the man confesses.

Donatello raises an eyebrow. "As in more security?"

The man shakes his head. "No, in fact. Just a woman, but she wasn't the sort like this young lady here—" He nods respectfully toward me. "That one was a spitfire."

"What made that visit, in particular, stand out?"

"Well…" The man chuckles. "They were shouting, for one. Mr. Salvatore mentioned something about 'your little master thinks he can yank my dick, but you can't. Unless you do it manually,' or something of the sort."

"And the woman?"

The man's smile falls flat. "When she left, Mr. Salvatore looked like the fear of God had been put into him."

"They went on this boat?" Donatello gestures toward the larger of the two.

"The Juggernaut, yes. Though I don't think anything has been left on it—"

"Here—" Reaching into his breast pocket, Donatello fishes out another crisp set of bills. "Give us ten more minutes."

"But… I…" the manager sputters, but Donatello is already halfway up the ramp leading to the larger of the two boats.

I follow him, warily stepping foot on the modest deck. It's a surprisingly stable structure overall, swaying gently in time to the waves below.

"In here," Donatello calls from a narrow staircase descending into the boat itself.

This must be the main cabin. It's spacious, stuffed to the brim with gaudy furniture and accents. Dark wood paneling offsets the leather seating and the impractical black fur throw rug in the center of the floor. Square, strategically placed windows allow for a breathtaking view of the water.

While I'm distracted by the sight, Donatello prowls the confined space, inspecting every surface. I copy him, moving in the opposite direction. Upon first inspection, the place is impeccably clean, with nothing seemingly out of the ordinary.

Still, I try to see things through the lens of Donatello Vanici. In his world, death is transactional and strange women wield power over men who own yachts. The manager said that after his discussion with his visitor, Antonio's entire demeanor had changed.

What could she have said?

Or shown him…

"Over here."

I turn to find Donatello standing before a small nook that must have served as a makeshift office. A wooden desk juts from the wall. As I come closer, Donatello wrenches open a drawer, revealing a few pens and a folded slip of paper.

He unfurls it and reads in silence, his brows drawn together.

"Son of bitch." He sits on the edge of the nearest bench, hissing in disgust. "They were blackmailing him," he says in response to my stare. He offers the page to me, but all I find on it is a succinct list of dates and names. The letterhead it's printed on, however, sports a familiar name: *Felicità*.

"It seems Antonio likes them young, supplied by none other than the Saleris. But it doesn't make sense." He stands, raking a hand ruthlessly through his hair. "Why leave evidence like this out in the open? Especially if he was working with the Saleris. Blackmail or not, they wouldn't want incriminating information like this floating around. Though, hell, with Gregori's connections, no one would dare go public against him. Still, they must feel cocky to be so brazen about it. Cocky. Or desperate."

He turns to the window, glowering at the water beyond. "Who the fuck is on that boat?"

Given the security, it's likely we'll never know.

"Well, Fabio will have fun running these numbers at least," Donatello says, crushing the document in his fist. "But they won't do any fucking good if whatever they're planning comes to fruition."

He begins to pace, stroking his chin with his free hand. I hate myself for watching him, enthralled despite my better judgment. No one in the world thinks like him.

In a sense, it's like watching a one-man orchestra perform the most complex of concertos.

"We could stake out the marina," he murmurs. "Wait until they disembark…" Even as the suggestion leaves his mouth, he scowls at the idea of it.

I think I know why. It's too easy. Someone powerful enough —and paranoid enough—to rent out the entire marina for a "waterfront tour" probably wouldn't choose to stroll in and out of the docks in plain view.

"The fucker will probably dock somewhere private," Donatello growls, thinking along the same line. "Meaning they're here now for a reason…" He trails off as his eyes seek mine out. I sense that chilling sensation flash between us. Like we're speaking beyond words in a way only the two of us can understand.

Desperation and rage form their own nuanced language. I swear I know what he'll say even before he opens his mouth.

"I need to see for myself what the hell they're up to. What would you do for the rest of those letters?" he asks, partly taunting, partly serious. "If you want them, then go back to the car and wait for me there—"

I shake my head, my heart racing as I grab a pen from the drawer and write down my own proposal.

I should come with you.

"What do you think the benefit would be of having you there?" I can read beneath his skepticism to what he has enough tact not to state bluntly. *Why would I need you?*

I would slow him down, get in the way. This is a dangerous situation, and the smart thing to do would be to call Mischa and take my chance to return home.

It's selfish to want to stay. To want to watch him in action. What spurs Donatello Vanici to risk his life?

I want to know.

But he has no interest in letting me stay; I can see that. I could always put up a logical argument to state my case. Or curse him. Rage against his dismissiveness. Instead, I put myself in his point of view and think things through just as he would—cut and dry in the most transactional of terms.

I'm Mischa's daughter, I finally write. *They might attack you. They won't attack me.*

He eyes the page warily. Then he scoffs. "And if they kill me and sell you off? You really want to end your night under Mateo Saleri?"

I picture the younger man from that night at the club with cat-like green eyes. My first impulse is to shudder—which is exactly what he wants. I look up to find his gaze smug, his mouth tilted. I simply widen my eyes, conveying a question he can easily decipher.

Will you let him?

His frown unfurls slowly, and he turns away. At first, I assume he's making a show of observing something other than me, but then he leans forward, hissing through his teeth.

"Fuck, they're moving." In a blur of motion, he starts for the upper deck, pausing near the staircase. "You think if I let you come with me, everything between us will be magically fixed? Your father and I, I mean. That ship has fucking sailed, wife. It won't change a damn thing."

But he's wrong. Unraveling the mystery of who attacked my family and why is only part of the equation. The other half consists of learning more of the very subject I am now—Donatello Vanici. What better way to destroy him than to know him inside and out? The reasoning behind his impulsiveness. His recklessness. Perhaps, I might finally understand what led him to treat me like collateral all those years ago.

And he still can, a part of me warns. I could very well end this night underneath Mateo Saleri.

With none other than Donatello Vanici standing watch, unwilling to lift a muscle in my defense.

"Are you coming?" His voice reaches down from outside of the salon. I climb the steps after him and watch as he circles around to the helm. He sits down, his back to the drifting yacht. At first, I assume he's changed his mind, preferring to call Fabio instead of giving chase.

Until I feel the subtle vibration of the engine roaring to life beneath my feet.

"Hey!" Donatello stands, beckoning me closer. "You see those lines?" He points to two distinct ropes tethering the boat to the dock. "Go loosen them."

I stiffen, cutting my gaze up to his.

"Trust me," he snaps, but I think he realizes how hollow those words sound in this context. "The manager has his eyes on *me*. He won't be watching you."

I doubt the validity of that. In reality, he wants to leave me behind, but in this case, should I even care if he does? My entire being is screaming at me to stay. Find Mischa. Run far away from Donatello Vanici and everything he has to offer.

Instead, I turn on my heel, grabbing the railing to steady me as I climb back onto the dock. The manager isn't anywhere in sight, and I grasp the rope, loosening it. Then I turn to the other.

Almost immediately, the boat starts to drift, and I have to lunge to bridge the gap. A sturdy hand on my shoulder steadies me as I do, helping me back to the upper deck.

"Sit tight," Donatello says, returning to the helm. I'm still dazed by the fact that he kept his word. He let me come. Let me stay…

I almost miss what he shouts to me next, "I haven't driven a boat in years."

It's an anti-climactic escape when all is said and done. Despite his supposed inexperience, Donatello easily steers us from the dock, aided by the wind. The manager doesn't seem to realize until we're too far out to stop, and he's just a frantic speck in the distance.

Up ahead, the white yacht resembles an unattainable fortress, larger than expected. A pang of doubt creeps in. He's insane for even trying to track it down.

We're insane…

Those logical viewpoints make sense in my head. None of them manage to penetrate the excitement pulsing down my spine, electrifying my limbs. I blame adrenaline.

Liar, a part of me snarls. Adrenaline isn't a man with piercing eyes that find mine from his seated position paces away. It could be the fresh air, or perhaps the thrill of the hunt, but he's different here. Alive might be too dramatic a word, but it fits. His hair glistens in the sun, his posture relaxed in a way I haven't seen since…

Well, seven years ago. But the past doesn't belong here. The man I knew, and this current creature, are not one and the same. As if to prove it, he averts his gaze to the water, his expression unfathomable.

"You played along. Back on the docks. Then you leverage your status as the daughter of a mob boss. Touché. I'm guessing Mischa didn't teach you that," he scolds. I bristle at the accusation, turning my attention to the water as well.

Mischa didn't teach me a lot of things. He didn't teach me betrayal, for one. How to turn my back on those closest to me, or that no one else matters in the quest to fulfill my own selfish impulses.

In fact, Mischa, as much as I love him, didn't influence me much at all.

I was already infected by the teachings of another.

"Look at me," my original corruptor demands. When I do, he's pensive, wrenching on a dial that must put the boat into the equivalent of cruise control. We're rapidly advancing on the yacht, but at the moment, it's a distant obstacle.

I feel a burst of unease at a sudden realization—we're utterly alone.

"What the fuck are we doing? Jesus, Christ, what the fuck am I doing?" He chuckles, swiping his hand across his mouth. "If the Saleris even harm a hair on your head, Mischa will have every right to fucking castrate me. But you don't care, do you? So, let's turn our attention to something you *do* care about. Why would someone want Mischa to come after me? Is it personal, or business?"

I try to look at him objectively. Donatello isn't the sort of man someone takes on directly.

"They wanted me out of the way," he says. "I thought Antonio was just being a prick, wanting the harbor for himself, but there was more to it. He needed it. Whoever was pulling his strings was doing so to ensure that he was the one to gain control of it from me. Salvatore specifically. Why?"

He trails off, mulling over the question. Suddenly, he cuts his eyes up to mine. "You're thinking of something." His voice is barely audible above the roar of the waves, though no less accusatory. "What?"

I'm thinking that anyone who would go through the trouble had a lot more in mind than buying a few buildings. No. They were laying the pieces of a trap.

Or, I could be overthinking it all, so desperate for his approval.

I start to turn away, only to feel his hand land on my shoulder. "Don't play coy. You don't need words to talk to me—" He grabs my wrist to prove his point. "Tell me."

I slip my hand from his grasp and point at his chest.

"Me. No…" His face betrays his entire thought process. Confusion at first, then gradual dawning until finally, he says softly, "Revenge. Someone wants to prove a point."

But to Mischa or someone else?

"Whoever they are, I think we're about to find out," Donatello says suddenly. He rises to his feet, and I follow his stare to a smaller boat approaching from the direction of the yacht.

"We have company."

Their approach seems to occur in exaggeratedly slow motion. I swear it's hours before they finally draw close enough to make out the two men occupying the vessel, but it must be mere minutes.

"Greetings, Mr. Vanici," one of them calls. They're both dressed in black with sunglasses obscuring their eyes. "Mr. Saleri would like to invite you and your guest to join him this afternoon aboard the Santiago."

Donatello inclines his head sharply, but I'm impressed by his restraint. "An invitation, huh? Can I ask what the occasion is?"

"To celebrate new business ventures," the first speaker replies. "If you two would proceed to enter the vessel, we can return in time for drinks."

I sense Donatello stiffen, though outwardly, he's as cool as ever. It's a strange game, watching him weigh his options one by one. His eyes narrow and widen until he finally settles upon a decision.

"Fine. Lead the way."

His fingers snag my wrist before I can recover, tugging me after him. He heads to the helm first, presumably performing whatever maneuvers are necessary to drop the anchor. Then we step into the other boat.

The Santiago is nearly three times the size of the Lady Killer. As we approach, I have to crane my neck to take in the impressive three deck-structure. One thing that stands out, is that—apart from several men, dressed in black—there are no party guests lounging on the decks. No music playing. It's an eerie, almost somber atmosphere that only intensifies as we climb the metal ladder leading to the main deck.

"Mr. Saleri is inside," the man says, gesturing toward a door I assume leads into the main cabin.

"Stay close to me," Donatello warns, returning his hand to my lower back. "Confronting Gregori and Mateo on their turf in the city is one thing, but this feels off."

I can hear the unease in his voice, but as we pass through the doorway of the cabin his features harden. On the other hand, I wind up blinking while my eyes struggle to adjust to the shift in lighting. Where Antonio Salvatore's salon was drenched in black, the Saleris have chosen white as their accent color. Everything from the walls, to the polished floors, is in the same pristine shade.

Everything but the three people occupying the space. One of them is a tall man leaning against a glass-top bar near the back of the room. His dark green eyes contrast the monochrome background, bringing the image of a snake to mind. His name comes to me instantly—Mateo Saleri, the man Donatello assumed I'd be "under" by the night's end. As he had in the club, he doesn't give off an overly sinister aura. Just a calculating sense that he's watching everything, missing nothing.

The man seated on a leather couch in the corner, however? He radiates nothing but cold, dangerous energy. His eyes narrow as he spots Donatello, and I get the sense that he would like nothing more than to watch him drown in the waters below this very boat.

He must be Gregori.

The third man lurks just beyond the others, seemingly fascinated by the view of the water.

"Vanici," Gregori snarls. Bracing his hands on his knees, he sits forward, his jowls flapping. "You have some damn nerve—"

"Let's be polite to our guests," Mateo says over him. He runs a finger along his lapel, displaying a thick gold ring around his thumb. "After all, we're friends, aren't we?"

"Friends," Donatello echoes in a tone of ice. "Friends, who buy up obscene amounts of property on the sly? Friends, who work with Antonio Salvatore to set me up?"

It's such a bold accusation that I don't understand why he would make it now—until I see the two men's reactions. Their body language alone gives them away better than a signed confession. Mateo maintains his sly, faux-welcoming grin, but the expression takes on a hardened edge. At the same time, Gregori cuts his eyes to the only man in the room I don't recognize.

Donatello seems to notice the stranger the same time I do, his eyes narrowing. "And who is this?" he wonders out loud.

The man in question doesn't respond. He's thin, blond with sleek black glasses perched atop a delicate nose. A tailored navy suit sets him apart from the more casually dressed Saleris. Unassuming, he stands near a row of windows looking out over the upper deck, a leather binder under one arm. At a glance, there's nothing remarkable about his face. He isn't unattractive, but not striking. Until my gaze falls over his neck. A mottled pink mass of flesh forms a vicious semi-circle from his left ear down to his collar, stretching beneath the neckline of his crisp white shirt. Burn marks?

"Him? He's a harmless guest," Mateo says smoothly, turning to the bar. "*Invited* here, unlike some."

"A guest," Donatello snarls, his gaze still on the blond man. "He wouldn't happen to go by J.W. would he?"

The malice in his tone sends a shiver down my spine—but if any of the three men recognize the initials, they expertly conceal any guilt.

"Don't tell me you crashed this little party, Donatello, merely to point fingers," Mateo scolds. Smiling, he fishes a glass from a nearby shelf and pours liquid from a crystal decanter into it. Rather than drink, he shakes his wrist, sending the liquid swirling. "That's not very friendly, is it?"

"Cut the shit." Donatello slides his hand from my back and steps forward. "You played your little word games before, pretending you were in cahoots with Mischa—but don't deny that you've been working with the son of a bitch who tried to set me up all this goddamn time."

"How dare you!" Gregori huffs. "I've had enough. Get him out of—"

"Wait." Mateo raises a hand, silencing him. Setting his glass aside, he turns from the bar, his grin firmly in place. "Before your accusations raise my father's blood pressure, do you have *proof*?" he demands of Donatello. "Or are you determined to do to us what you did to Antonio Salvatore?"

"I should put a bullet in your brain for that alone," Gregori snaps, his face reddening. "After what you've done to my granddaughter, I should—"

"What I've done?" Donatello interjects. "What about what *Antonio* was doing to Kisa?"

I don't know what he means, but the words have the effect of flipping an invisible switch. Gregori's eyes widen with an unmistakable emotion—*alarm.*

Mateo recovers faster, choking out a laugh. "I'll let that insult slide if you return the girl by the day's end. We've indulged you enough."

"Indulged," Donatello says. "You don't let your granddaughter stay with a man who murdered her father to placate him. You do it when you're too busy to give a shit. What have you two been up to?"

"Nothing too nefarious," Mateo says smoothly, but his devious grin undercuts his words. "Otherwise, you wouldn't be so stupid as to come here alone, with no backup. No one to witness if you happened to fall overboard. No one besides your little toy. I'm sorry, your *fiancée*."

"So why extend your invitation?" Donatello asks.

"All in the name of goodwill," Mateo says.

"Goodwill," Gregori harrumphs, but his eyes again dart toward the blond man.

He stands unobtrusively in the corner, watching this entire exchange with little to no interest. But just as I start to look away, I catch his eyes flicker in my direction. They're an unusually bright shade in between blue and gray, enhanced by the lenses shielding them.

"Cut the bullshit," Donatello snaps, drawing my attention. "What are you up to? Don't tell me you make a habit of renting out the entire marina just for three men to take a waterfront tour?"

Mateo's eyes narrow further. "And don't tell me that *you* make a habit of showing up unannounced just for the hell of it."

He returns to the bar and pours two additional glasses of liquor, one of which he offers to Donatello. "Word on the street is you're attempting sobriety now." His grin is anything but supportive.

If the statement catches Donatello off guard, he doesn't show it. "I prefer a brand of liquor I don't think you stock."

"You still drink that shoe varnish?" Mateo chuckles and sips from the glass himself. "It's good to see you on your feet again, old friend. I've heard stories about you. The once high and mighty Vanici hopping from motel to motel, lying in his own piss while his nephew was off to school. There was a particularly nasty rumor that, before you went on the straight and narrow, you needed at least a bottle of vodka just to get out of bed—"

"We all have our vices," Donatello interjects coldly. I watch him, unsure of the emotion rising in my chest. Was anything Mateo said true? His eyes give nothing away. "I think I prefer mine to yours."

Mateo chuckles, swishing the liquid in his glass with a flick of his wrist. "Beautiful women, you mean. A damn fine vice if I say so myself. Though, considering what the rumors say about your union with the lovely Ms. Stepanova here, perhaps our tastes are closer aligned than you think." He drains his glass and sets it aside, grabbing the untouched serving. Holding it aloft, he slinks forward. "If you won't have a drink, what about your friend?"

He's close before I can react. Uninvited, his fingers capture my chin, lifting it. My first impulse is to recoil, but a burst of heat at my back roots me to the spot.

"Don't touch her." That voice…

It rings out like a beast's growl. Mateo's closed lips warn that it didn't come from him.

"Relax, Donny," the man taunts. He runs his thumb along my lip before brutally jabbing the pad between them. I bat him away instinctively—at the same time, my hair rustles, the only warning before another hand latches onto my shoulder.

"Touch her again, and I'll—"

"No need for the dramatics," Mateo says, laughing. He withdraws from me, lifting his glass in salute. Slowly, he takes a sip, his eyes glittering without a hint of remorse. "I merely wanted to see the beauty for myself. A Vanici landing a Stepanov. I wonder what she sees in you. I guess she likes living on the edge, what with your history of losing your wives to mysterious circumstances. If danger is what you're after, my dear, I can more than oblige."

Donatello says nothing.

Denied the fireworks he seems to be after, Mateo frowns. "I hope this union will be far different than the last, at least. You deserve some happiness. Though hell, from the rumors I've heard, I can't lie. I would have done far worse to *my* wife—"

"Enough." The hand on my shoulder withdraws, and I find myself shoved aside as Donatello takes a menacing step forward. "What the fuck is that supposed to mean?"

Mateo holds my gaze with a chilling smirk. "It means that your new little fiancée should know exactly what happened to the last—"

"Sir!" A man wearing a black suit races into the salon, approaching Mateo directly. He murmurs something into the man's ear, and Mateo stiffens, all desire to provoke Donatello seemingly forgotten. "You can't lose someone on a fucking boat," he snarls. I don't miss the way he glances toward the blond man before gritting his teeth.

"Find her. Now." His tone is low enough that I barely hear him.

"Yes, Sir." The guard retreats just as quickly. The second he's beyond view, another figure speaks, commanding the focus of the entire room.

"I think it's time for us to retire to the fresh air, don't you?" The voice is so startlingly different from Mateo's rasp or Donatello's baritone that it takes me a full second to pinpoint where it came from. The blond man. He steps forward, completely unperturbed by the tension in the room. Instead, his focus is on his wristwatch. Looking up, he clears his throat and heads for the exit. "Shall we, gentlemen?"

Mateo and Gregori share another glance. This time I pinpoint what passes between them. Wariness.

"After you," Mateo says, following the men out.

Donatello's hand returns to my back, drawing me to his side. I don't need to see his face to know he's worried. His jaw is clenched as we trail the other men to the bow of the boat. Even after a few minutes, we've drifted further from The Lady Killer, and the ever-present guards remain a visible reminder of the danger.

"A beautiful day," the blond man remarks, running his hand along the railing. Apparently, he senses none of the unease. In fact, though it's far removed from the typical expression, I'd define the slight tilt to his mouth as a smile. "A crisp, clear sky. A welcoming breeze. A wonderful greeting to this fair city."

Mateo clears his throat nervously. "It's good you've found everything to your liking—"

"Not everything," the man corrects, but a subtle shift in his inflection resonates like an off-key note. Or a slap. "The day is far too nice for an argument, don't you think?"

Both Saleris stiffen.

"Yes," the man continues. "Far too nice. I hope any minor inconveniences can be set aside. All in the name of progress."

"Of course," Mateo says in a rush. "Whatever it takes to—"

"Good." After another glance at his watch, the man leans forward, bracing his hands against the railing, his eyes on the horizon. "Progress is a wonderful thing. Advancement. Change."

"You sound like an investor," Donatello interjects. I bet he's remembering the property listings. Could this man be responsible for directing the purchases?

"Investor?" the man replies—one of the first times he's addressed Donatello directly. "Perhaps. An investor in *progress*. In fact, I'm confident that and more is in our near future, ready to commence. Any minute now…"

A low thud rumbles in the distance like a carefully choreographed moment meant to add emphasis to his words. Thunder? A larger boom reverberates next, so loud I'm sure it can be heard through the entire city.

An eerie silence falls in its wake. Even the water itself seems to still, every nearby creature from the men I'm with, to the birds above stunned into a muted anticipation.

And finally, a flash of light battles with the sun itself, emanating from the westward direction. It's so bright my entire vision goes white. Then orange. A brilliant, gleaming orange that licks at the sky in a slow-rising swell.

"What the fuck?" Donatello shoves me behind him as the boat lurches beneath us, caught by a sudden wave. I have to grapple for the nearby railing just to stay upright, nearly knocked off my feet. "What the hell was that?"

As if in answer to his question, an even louder boom rocks through the city. It's so loud. My ears ring as the sensation of the blow resonates in my very bones.

There's no mistaking such a violent crack of noise. A single term comes to mind—*explosion*. Plumes of rich black sweep up to edge the orange licking at the horizon, and I finally recognize the vibrant shapes for what they are—flames. Even from here, a chorus of sirens and alarms begin to swell, audible on the breeze.

"Jesus Christ," Mateo exclaims.

Gregori gapes at the sight, but I get the sense that he's more resigned than alarmed.

The only person seemingly unfazed at all is the blond man. "Beautiful," he says with genuine admiration, his smile more apparent than ever. "Right on time."

"Fuck…" Donatello hisses through his teeth. "Where is that fucking coming from?"

"The West District," the man says coldly. "Far from any residential area, though fatalities are to be expected. Well, what a blaze. I think we're done here, gentlemen."

Mateo snaps his fingers, summoning a guard. "See these two off the ship. This was a pleasant discussion." Sarcasm drips from his tone, clashing harshly with the quiet voice that rings out next.

"Pleasant indeed." The blond man inclines his head as if he just remembered that other people were in the vicinity. Against the backdrop of the blood-red flames, he looks ghoulish, remarkably pale. "I believe the two of us should become more acquainted, Donatello Vanici." He extends his hand, revealing fingers so slim they look liable to be crushed in the firm grasp Donatello captures them with.

"I don't become acquainted with people I don't know," Donatello says in a tone that straddles the line of threatening. "Especially not people involved with the Saleris. What the hell are you up to?"

The man's lifeless grin widens. "Of course. I look forward to us getting better acquainted, then. Gentlemen? I think we should be going if we want to stay on schedule. I will be sure to send you an invitation, Mr. Vanici. We must meet at a later date."

Donatello lurches forward. "Wait—"

"Time's up," Mateo warns, stepping into his path. "I think you better do as the man says and wait for your fucking invitation."

"I'll be looking forward to it," Donatello snaps, his eyes on the blond man. "But I'll need a name to add you to my calendar."

The other man smiles faintly before nodding, smoothing a hand along his suit. "Shall we, gentlemen?" He strolls back inside the main cabin as the sounds of chaos from the city swell, punctuated with distant shouts.

"Branching out your clientele?" Donatello asks Mateo. "He doesn't look like the type to enjoy fucking some kidnapped girl who thought she would be coming to the city as a 'waitress.'"

Mateo's eyes gleam orange, reflecting the distant blaze. "You have no fucking idea." Turning to his guard, he snaps, "Get them the fuck off. Now. Before I decide to not 'stay on schedule.'"

"This way," the guard ushers us back to the ladder leading to the smaller boat. As we pull away, I spy Mateo Saleri storming across the upper deck, a cell phone glued to his ear. His furious shouting is audible, even from here. "Where the fuck could she have gone? Look again!"

A lone figure watches from the bow of the boat, his eyes on the water. A shade of steel, they eye the waves as if they're a sight more offensive than the damage and destruction unfolding in the opposite direction.

I swear I feel him staring as we finally return to the Lady Killer.

"Jesus Christ," Donatello hisses. "What the fuck was that?" He fishes his cell phone from his pocket. "Service is out. Fuck. Look at that…"

I can't look away. The horizon is now black with smoke, the flames flickering higher. The breeze nips at my hair, and I can only imagine how far the fire might spread, aided by it.

"Sit tight." Donatello returns to the helm. "We need to get the fuck out of here... What the hell?"

I look over, startled by splotches of red smeared near the entrance of the cabin. They gleam in the sunlight, still wet, almost like droplets of fresh paint. Did he spill something before we left?

"Get behind me," Donatello commands. His hard tone betrays that he knows exactly what the substance is. I think I do as well, though a part of me shies from what it implies.

Blood.

"Stay close." He moves slowly, descending the stairs into the lower level, his hand on his pocket.

I follow him, feeling dread build with every step I take. Once we reach the salon, it's painfully obvious that my hunch isn't wrong. The salty stench of blood is overwhelming, mingling with the scent of saltwater. Even more puddles of scarlet and water mar the floor, growing larger the further we venture. Some look flattened, oddly formed. Footprints? If so, they blaze a trail across the salon toward a closed door.

"Who the fuck is in here?" Donatello demands. No answer comes, so he wrenches the door open, revealing a narrow bathroom and a woman hunched over the sink, casually dabbing at her thigh with a wadded cloth.

"Could you not point that thing at me?" Her airy voice reminds me of the well-bred girls from the musical conservatory.

From her tone, one might think Donatello's pointing something as trivial as a dirty hand in her direction. Not a gun. I stiffen at the sight of it, unsure of where he retrieved it from. Did he have it on him the entire time we were on the Saleris' boat? Without lowering it, he gapes at the woman. "Who the hell are you?"

Someone slender, with golden hair streaming down her shoulders. She holds herself with so much poise; the scarlet on her skin might as well be makeup. Then she winces, and her act slips.

"There isn't time for introductions, I'm afraid," she says, her voice strained. A glance down reveals why—a gash slices through the meat of her thigh, the source of the blood. "They'll already know I'm gone. Process of elimination states, there aren't many places I could have gotten to—" She angles her head to face Donatello directly. "It's only a matter of time before they're on their way."

Her voice is the lone attribute warning me that my eyes are faulty. This woman standing before me isn't Ellen. Even if their facial structure is eerily similar, their eyes the same shade of blue.

Ellen could never look so cold—not to mention the lack of a scar on her cheek. This woman is someone else, and a name comes to mind, one I heard scarcely spoken at Stepanov Manor. Briar, Ellen's older sister. As far as I knew, she left years ago, before Ivan was even born. Could this woman really be her?

"I know this is a rather dramatic statement, but time is of the essence," the woman snaps. Hissing, she drops her rag onto the ground and limps over it, pushing her way past Donatello. Both water and blood drip in her wake. She's soaked, her dress clinging to her body like a second skin. "If they aren't already aiming to swarm this little dinghy of yours, they will be soon," she says. Bracing herself against a window, she peers out in the direction of the Santiago. "As expected, he's already sent his little henchmen," she remarks dryly. "If we aim to outrun them, I suggest you get a move on."

"Who the fuck are you?"

"That's not important right now," the woman says, waving him off. "What is important is this—do you intend to die in a watery grave with some uninspired explanation such as 'engine failure' to be listed as the cause? Because I can assure you that's what will happen if he knows I'm here."

"Saleri?"

"Son of a bitch!" She moans, grabbing at her thigh. "This stings. Well, I suggest you hurry."

"Shit." Donatello glances from the window and races for the upper deck. Spotting me, he says, "Keep an eye on her."

"I'm sure you both are very formidable," the woman says tiredly.

I don't think her weakness is faked. She stumbles to the nearest row of couches and collapses on one. Fresh blood is already forming a trail down her leg, dripping onto the floor. "I know this bastard had a bottle of whiskey around here somewhere," she says through clenched teeth, scanning the room. Her eyes fall over mine, and she flashes a smile that would seem charming in the absence of blood. "Care to find it for me, darling?"

As the engine stutters to life, rattling the body of the boat, I realize there isn't anything else I can do. I head for the bar, reading the labels of the bottles there. Sure enough, I spy a bottle of whiskey, and when I bring it to the woman, she rips off the lid and pours a majority of the drink onto her thigh.

"We're moving at least," she croaks, glancing from the window. "But can your friend sail this boat quickly enough?" Apparently, she doesn't think so, because she lurches upright, grappling for any nearby surface to stagger her way to the stairs. "I hope you aren't heading for the docks right away," she calls, shouting above the noise of the engine.

Donatello bellows back, "The fuck else am I supposed to go?"

"Shit." She grimaces in pain, biting her lip. "They'll try to kill you if they think I'm here," she says.

"Who the fuck are you?" Donatello snaps back.

Her eyes darken, turning inward. "Someone they want dead very, very badly."

"What's stopping me from tossing you overboard right now?"

"They might kill you anyway," she counters. "Besides, you don't know what I do. Perhaps we could help each other. I'll make it worth your while."

"How?"

"I guess you don't have a choice, but when we get to the docks, stall them until I can leave unseen."

"So much for you making it worth my while, huh?"

"It's not like being dead is a much better bargain, is it?"

Donatello says nothing.

"I'll find a hiding place, then," the woman shouts. Groaning, she inches back into the salon, scrambling to a corner of the room. She braces both hands against it and shifts her weight. With a metallic hiss, part of the wall gives way. A sliding door? "Help me with this," she commands.

Together, we reveal a hidden compartment containing assorted cleaning supplies and a metal safe.

The woman slips inside, dragging her leg behind her. It's a tight fit. She barely has any room to crouch.

"Close it," she warns, nodding to the door. "And trust me, if you want you and your friend to live, you'll do what I say— I was never here."

A statement easier said than believed, considering the blood and seawater all over the stateroom. I return to the bathroom and grab a clean rag, swiping all the puddles I can spot. As I finally exit to the upper deck, the marina dock is already coming into view. Donatello beckons me over, his expression grim.

"She could be full of shit," he says, but his gaze is on the smaller boat still speeding in our direction, this time containing three men dressed in black. "I'd rather play it safe than sorry, though. Follow my lead."

I nod, and as we pull closer to the dock, he grabs one of the lines and jumps from the boat, tying it to the post. As he ties the first one, I hand him the second, trying my hardest not to look back.

"I hope you enjoyed your time aboard the Santiago, Mr. Vanici," a man calls. The other boat has already drawn up beside us. "Mr. Saleri would like to extend another invitation, should you accept. He also wanted to make sure that you weren't too shocked by the events on land. If your boat sustained any damage, he will happily pay for the repairs."

"We're just peachy," Donatello snarls. "Though, you can tell your boss I definitely intend to pay him another visit. Soon."

Two of the men share a look, but the figure speaking seems unperturbed. "Would you mind then, if we took a look around? Just to be absolutely sure. Again, any damage, of course, would be personally covered by Mr. Saleri."

For a second, I think Donatello will refuse. Then he steps back and inclines his head. "Come aboard."

The three men don't waste any time, and I hold my breath as they prowl around the boat, eventually entering the salon with Donatello on their heels. From their body language, to the detail they pay to every corner, it's obvious that they're looking for something other than damage. A person. I can't help stiffening as they near the wall, but they don't try to activate the hidden panel.

"You're welcome to take your sweet fucking time, gentlemen," Donatello remarks after minutes have passed. "But can I ask you to speed it up? Unless your boss can clear a way through traffic after whatever the fuck just happened on the west end?"

"Mr. Saleri thanks you," the original speaker says, finally. In single file, all three return to their boat. "Have a wonderful day, but if you do happen to notice anything out of the ordinary, please remember that Mr. Saleri respects his friends and treats them well."

"What about the other 'friend' there with him?" Donatello asks. "The blond man with the glasses. He didn't seem too chummy with Gregori."

"Mr. Saleri also values his privacy and that of his associates," the man says with a thin smile. "Have a wonderful day, Mr. Vanici. Oh, and I'll take the liberty of informing you that any traffic to the city's west half will be most likely unavailable. I hope you make other arrangements."

"Sons of bitches," Donatello hisses once they're beyond earshot. "They're still watching us. Help me tie up, and we'll go check on our guest when they're out of sight."

We move slowly, taking our time with the lines. Once we finish, advancing footsteps approach, rattling the wood of the dock.

"You have some damn nerve," the manager declares, his hands on his hips. "I would have called the police, but they seem to be a bit busy—" he nods in the direction of the blaze. "I heard that traffic through the entire west end is completely cut off and won't be fixed for hours. Must have been a gas leak or something."

"A gas leak," Donatello rasps, gazing in the same direction. "My ass."

"Well, hopefully, you squared away everything with the boat and are ready to settle Mr. Salvatore's accounts."

"Yeah," Donatello says, turning toward the cabin. "Just let me take out the trash first."

We descend the steps to discover that the woman has already left her hiding place. She managed to find a length of fabric that she tied around her thigh.

"What do the Saleris want with you?" Donatello asks.

"The Saleris?" She forces a harsh laugh, wincing with the effort. "Do puppets truly have their own wants?"

"A puppet," his harsh tone implies he agrees with her assessment. "But whose? The British man's?"

She flinches, visibly paler. "I should probably be leaving—"

"No." Donatello takes a menacing step. "Not until you give me something. Who the hell was that?"

"The real question isn't who he is, but what does he want?" She points to the window where the glow of the fire ignites the horizon, painting it amber. "I'll leave you with a piece of advice—you want to learn the truth? Find the nicest hotel in this area and stay there. I suggest the Norfolk, the highest room you can afford. Enjoy the nightlife and ask yourself why someone might want the city severed in two, even for a few hours."

"What the hell is that supposed to mean?"

"It's supposed to mean that the world is a cruel, cold place, Donatello Vanici. Think of who your allies are, as well as your enemies, and plan accordingly."

"And if I decide to call those men back?"

The woman's smile doesn't reach her eyes. "Then all three of us die. You think they won't drag your little friend on their ship never to be seen again?" She looks at me with a ruthless sweep of her gaze. "It doesn't matter who she is. Stepanova or not, he'll make her disappear, and the most anyone will ever know is some nondescript explanation. But if it makes you feel better, then I'll keep my word. Follow my advice, and by the end of the night, I'm sure you'll get the answers you seek. The Norfolk hotel has a rather lovely view, the perfect place to witness any more 'fireworks.' Take care now."

She limps toward the exit, leaning heavily against the wall.

As she mounts the steps, Donatello asks, "Do you think you can even make it off the boat before they spot you?"

She offers him a weak grin, and yet it stands out as the most authentic I've seen all day. "I'm sure my knight in shining armor is already here." Real pain leeches into her voice. Gritting her teeth, she mounts the stairs to the upper deck as Donatello, and I follow.

Before anyone can question exactly where her knight in shining armor is, she hurries to the side of the boat and climbs over the railing, landing in the water with a splash.

Her golden hair flashes for just a second before she disappears beneath the murky waves entirely.

"Shit!" Donatello tugs open his jacket as if preparing to jump in after her, but she surfaces a few yards away, facing our direction. I swear she winks before diving once again.

Frozen mid-lunge, he readjusts his jacket. "Who the fuck was that?"

I don't respond. If that woman was Briar, why would she be on a Saleri ship?

"Let's get the fuck out of here before we get any more 'invitations,'" Donatello suggests.

I follow him back to the car, where the chaos that rocked the city is even more apparent. The flames swell, seemingly higher than they'd been just minutes ago. Blaring alarms form a deafening clamor that persists even when we're in the car.

"Give me a minute," Donatello says, once again withdrawing his cell phone. This time, he manages to get through.

"Fabio, what the fuck happened?" Whatever the man says makes him growl. "Improperly stored chemicals at a warehouse? That's what they're assuming so far, anyway. Fuck."

I can hear Fabio's voice resonating with authority. "Stay put," he warns. "I can't believe you even went to the Saleris without me. If you won't drive around the blockade, find somewhere to park, and you wait for me there. I mean it, Donatello. Promise me."

After a long moment, Donatello sighs. "Fine."

He hangs up, raking a hand through his hair. "All traffic heading west through the city has been halted. Rumor on the street is that chemicals improperly stored at a warehouse caused the explosion, but I don't buy that shit."

And the blond woman alluded to as much. *Ask yourself why someone might want the city severed in two, even for a few hours...*

"I could go around the blocks and get back to the house, but it will take hours... Something isn't right." He glowers at the horizon. "What do you think we should do?"

I stiffen. He's doing it again, purposefully trying to unnerve me. But then I make the mistake of looking up and find him staring back.

In context, everything we've done so far could be deemed grossly irresponsible. Reckless. Stupid, even. Fabio is right; we should return to the house and relay the information garnered from the boat.

I don't think I move or indicate my thought process, but Donatello sighs, gripping the steering wheel. His lips twitch, but it's in the opposite direction of a frown. He's grinning, his tone conspiratorial. "To the Norfolk hotel, it is, then."

19

WILLOW

To his credit, Gino—my biological father—never shied from the darker reality of his employment with the *famiglia*. In his mind, being a mobster trumped working as a mechanic any day. He gloated about it.

"I won't ever have to do that shit again," I heard him tell my mother once.

Unconvinced, she responded with a line similar to, *"So what? Killing is easier for you than changing a damn tire?"*

To which he replied, *"You bet your ass it is. Forget your fucking morals. A little blood and a hell of a lot of money look better than calluses and blisters any day."*

That line always stuck with me—an example of who I never wanted to become. Someone so bitter and jaded that any mode of success appealed to them, no matter the cost.

I came close to changing my mind, though. In those early days after being sold to Nicolai, I dreamt of killing

Donatello Vanici with my bare hands. Over and over, day in and day out. Imagining his death knell was my nightly lullaby. Who could blame me?

The vibrant red of his blood would have been a welcome sight compared to the horror my life had become.

In retrospect, I might be compelled to thank him in a sick, twisted sense of the concept. That time taught me a lesson I will never forget—the world is cruel. The fleeting kindness a man might bestow on you one minute can be cruelly ripped away the next. Life is no beautiful fairy tale, but a grim horror in which women file in and out of rooms like cattle.

Where men stroll about with weapons drawn and trade money with frivolity children play card games with.

Life in that enclave was a brutal existence, unlike anything I'd ever witnessed of the *famiglia* under Donatello. I have to wonder, was he truly any different?

Or was he just better at hiding the horrific side of his business?

Seven years later, I feel no closer to the truth. The man remains as much of an enigma to me now as he was then—barring one major difference.

I've never seen his mind in action quite like this. The manic cadence of his thought process reminds me of a symphony in disarray, every instrument playing out of tune. Chaotic. Beautiful. Madness.

He is a creature of impulse and action. From a marina, to a club, to a yacht, to an exclusive hotel, the world from the viewpoint of Donatello Vanici is an endless rabbit hole.

I can only go along for the ride and hope that we reach the end with my soul intact.

Luckily, the Norfolk Hotel is just ten minutes from the marina, near the city's center. A gleaming structure of black metal and glass, it overlooks a northern view of the bay. Though, while composed of beautiful architecture, there's nothing overly remarkable about it.

Donatello seems to agree. He says nothing as we enter the spacious lobby, and he proceeds to purchase a suite on the upper floor, as the woman suggested. It's extravagant with a view of the city and the surrounding bay—though I suspect the elegance is lost on the man stalking through the layout with a single-minded focus. He heads straight for the adjacent balcony, bracing his hands over the railing, his hair rustling in the wind.

Juxtaposed against the blackening horizon, he could be a fallen angel surveying the damned world he's been cursed to.

Or a devil, gloating over the destruction sowed in his wake.

"The hospital is near here," he remarks, nodding toward the complex just a few blocks over in the distance. "So is Felicità. A coincidence?" His eyes narrow as he mulls over the connection silently.

I hate myself for inching forward, curious as to what he's thinking. Hours without experiencing his hostility have lulled me into a false sense of security. It strikes me now that today has been the longest we've been together uninterrupted. The longest stretch of time during which he's spoken to me without a tinge of malice.

"Why the fuck would someone intentionally blow up a quarter of the city?" he asks, his irritation evident. "It doesn't make any fucking sense."

I copy his surveying glance and disagree. The reckless destruction is unfathomable if you view the assembled buildings as a city alone.

As a chessboard, however, everything becomes clearer. Amused, I realize it's the way he taught me to see the world. From the perspective of a game player, the various locations around Hell's Gambit could serve as squares and territory.

Pieces up for grabs.

He frowns, stroking his chin as the fading sunlight plays off the panes of his face. Despite the city churning below, I realize that we're secluded. Alone.

But I don't feel the need to run.

I watch him instead, taking the chance to observe him in devastating detail. His eyes serve as a window into his mind like no one else's. I hate that. I can see the gears in his brain turning, the various parts coiling and connecting like the world's most complex musical instrument. Madness is his art form, one he plays expertly, unconcerned by how the result might be interpreted by the outside world.

Watching him, I almost forget… The hate I should feel, the pain he put me through. None of that matters from the mindset of a predator. Such a creature is too ruthless. Selfish. Chillingly analytical.

But there's always a method to his madness, like a wild animal working off its own internal instinct. What could be seen as malicious by an outsider, is merely an act of survival.

"It's clever," he says finally, his voice melding with the roar of the wind. "Create a diversion that will redirect most of the city's resources. The police and fire departments will be stretched thin. So, who benefits?"

He re-enters the suite rather than reveal an answer. A glass bar cart is his first destination, and he fingers a bottle of liquor from the small selection. Frowning, he eyes his hand as if he didn't even realize what he'd been reaching for.

"Come here." Turning to me, he inclines his head and the mask I'm used to returns.

I falter, and his eyes turn to glass. Coldly reflective, they glow orange as he starts toward me. Every step is slow and deliberate, resonating against the dark flooring, somehow louder than the city's noise. Louder than my own heartbeat.

Once close enough, he captures my chin against his palm. His thumb sweeps along my jawline, up to my hair and back, lingering at the corner of my mouth. I know exactly what he's doing.

Retracing the same motions of Mateo Saleri.

"I could have killed him." His tone is so casual that it takes my brain a second to register the violence in those words. The answering shiver in my belly warns me he wasn't boasting.

Kill a man just for touching me?

Not out of a misplaced sense of justice or protection, either. Just pure selfish greed.

Only he can have me.

Only he can touch me.

I don't know if it's the location, far from any other structures that might trigger past memories, but here nothing is tethering him to the old Donatello. He's a stranger, eyeing me through fathomlessly dark eyes. A man who strips me down to a creature I'm not used to embodying.

Not Safiya.

Not Willow.

Just a woman in his possession.

"No one," he says thickly. "No one looks at me the way you do. Like I'm a monster, a villain, and the sheep." He draws away, turning back to the bar cart. "Like I'm worthy of your pity but nothing else."

He rips the lid off the bottle and fills a shot glass. Raising the container to his eye level, he inspects the liquid within.

Then slowly and deliberately, he sets it back down, bracing his hand beside it.

"We need to talk." His voice taints that simple statement, turning it into something else. A darker form of a taunt. A dangerous request. A dare. "Not about the past," he clarifies, approaching a leather couch positioned before the window.

He collapses onto it, leaning his head back against the cushions. I copy him, claiming a nearby chair. As his stare meets mine, it lands with physical intensity, more violating than his hand could ever be. I feel it like a grasping touch, reaching through my skin for whatever lurks beneath. Blood. Bone.

My soul.

"I want to talk about *you*. The new you. Willow Stepanova." He toys with the syllables of my name, tasting them one by one on the tip of his tongue. "What made you choose music?"

It's a seemingly harmless question with a dangerous answer. The short retort would be that I loved to play on my family's piano—the one Mischa bought as a playful joke, promising Ellen that their children would have a future beyond the blood and violence he traded in.

They would have the freedom to be musicians, as he put it, the furthest profession from that of a *mafiya* leader that he could imagine.

The long answer, on the other hand, is far more complex, seeded in reasoning that has little to do with convenience and everything to do with *him*. Not Mischa. Not Gino. Him, the man who taught me that I didn't need a voice to speak.

Who always seemed to hear me...

Until he simply chose not to, that is.

Music is more powerful than any form of speech, too beautiful to be ignored. Too grating. Too boisterous. Donatello Vanici made me feel silenced, so I found my own voice. A way to make myself heard, no matter the number of people in the room. No matter if anyone listened or not.

I defied his last act of brutality against me.

Through the keys of a piano, I learned how to scream—but now, I can't even fathom how to put it into words. How do you convey something so abstract, so childish? You can't. In a way, I feel muzzled all over again.

"I know why."

I'm not looking at him, eyeing the view from the window instead.

"Those pretty little notes can't be overlooked," he says gruffly, and my eyes begin to sting bitterly. I blink and blink, but the sensation only grows. "No one can ignore the girl at the piano, even if she herself is silent. That's why you play. Isn't it?"

I'm on my feet, returning to the balcony. The cool wind hits me at full blast, whipping my hair around and distorting the wails of the sirens still blaring from the west side of the city. It's welcome noise, and I almost think I'm safe.

But even the outside world can't drown him out.

"Was it Mischa…your father's idea for you to go abroad? To Vienna, right?"

Despite every cell in my body warning me not to, I look back and find him still seated, watching me from the shadows bathing the room. His expression is neutral, but I don't trust the question. It has to be a trap in some shape or form.

"I doubt you enjoyed it," he suspects, and I blink again, my lashes fluttering to obscure my view of him. "You had to mingle with sheltered little socialites and people who couldn't dream of belonging to the world you left behind. Why not stay in Hell's Gambit?"

Why? I turn back to the view, exhaling slowly.

"Because the entire fucking world could never feel as large as this city feels small," he says, speaking for me. "A claustrophobic little hell where everything you do and feel is magnified. A cage. But the people around you? They might as well be on another planet. They can't see what you do."

From the corner of my eye, I see him extend his hand before him, grasping at the air.

"Fucking bars."

Mischa would deem his assessment bullshit—the words of a man so wrapped up within himself that everything revolves around his own point of view.

"You know I'm right," he scolds when I turn away. "It's not the city you were running away from, was it? A safe perfect family has safe, perfect expectations—even if your father runs the goddamn *mafiya*. Your life is far different than someone without two fucking cents to rub together. They're like weeds, able to grow out in the open while you get smothered. Am I wrong?"

He is. He… He isn't? Confusion muddles my thoughts. I can't think.

"Look at me, *principessa*."

When I do, his grin is an expression torn between smugness and pain. "I tried to do the same damn thing to Vincenzo." He stands, crossing back to the bar cart.

I don't know why I follow him, re-entering the suite as he lifts the still-full glass again. He inhales near the rim, and I get the sense that he's purposefully torturing himself, playing some kind of internal game. How long can he withstand the urge to smother his emotions?

He sets the glass down unsteadily, causing some of the liquid to spill over the rim. This time, his fingers linger around it.

"You know what I wanted to be when I was a boy? Rich," he says with a harsh laugh. "I didn't care about the why or how, just the end result. I wanted to be powerful. Too big to fuck with."

He smirks at the thought, leaning against the wall, his gaze fixated on the past. Gradually, his smile fades.

"I never sought more, because I never *had* more. I wasn't smart like Vincenzo. Without this life, I would have been nothing. Though who knows, it might have been a better life..."

The pain in his voice startles me, so raw I can almost feel it, chafing against the part of me conditioned to hate him. I've never heard him talk like this. Openly. Drunkenly, without ever having to imbibe a sip of alcohol.

"Most men claim that they did what they had to. For a sick mother or their papa's surgery, or to save a puppy. They *had* to sell their soul and pay the devil for a cause well beyond themselves. But me?" He sighs as if the weight of the world rests on his shoulders, a crushing burden. He's ground down to almost nothing, enduring only through sheer pride. "Me? I wanted this life. The devil never had to twist my arm, you see? He always had a better offer than anything else this world could give someone like me."

He lets that statement hang in the air. His voice echoes off the walls until it's as if a hundred various Donatellos are speaking all at once.

Me?

The devil...

"People like Fabio and Vincenzo have to rationalize it away. The greed. The violence. The hate. They can't accept the fucking truth—at the end of the day, me and Mateo Saleri are one and the same." He extends his hand, crooking a single finger to beckon me closer.

My heart skips, my palms moistening with an unmistakable response—fight or flight. He has a way about him unlike anyone else. An ability to switch from patient to predatory within the blink of an eye.

From vulnerable to vicious.

"Do you want to know what Mateo Saleri sees when he looks at you?" he asks as I stop just beyond his reach.

Sighing, he pulls away from the wall, easily bridging the distance between us. His hand returns to my chin, cupping my jaw entirely. Tension makes his fingers shake, betraying the restraint he's using to keep from gripping a fraction harder. From hurting me.

But he can't. Without warning, his nail bites a hair's width deeper.

"Do you?" he murmurs, staring deep into me. Through me. "He sees a commodity. A body he can buy and sell. A rabbit ripe for the slaughter. But do you want to know what I see?" He draws his hand away, his brow furrowed, and swipes at his own chin, disrupting the stubble there. "I see a little wolf, snarling, snarling... Too angry to decide whether or not to bite. Attack. So, I give you permission—bite me."

His tone is so earnest I think he meant that. Hit him. Hurt him. Give him anything he can use to fight against. He wants more from me than he ever gave.

He craves violence—when I don't even have a scar to show for what he's done.

"I wasn't lying," he says offhandedly, returning to the bar cart. "When I made you that offer. Atonement. Have you made up your mind yet?" He picks up the drink, bringing it to his lips. "How to best make me suffer—"

I reach out before I even realize it just as he tilts the rim, intending to drink from it. My hand is on his, the tension like lightning. Each ripple and coil of muscle plays through my skin, and I'm painfully aware of just how tightly he's gripping this glass.

He badly wants to drink the alcohol within. Not out of habit, or to relax. No. He just wants to hide from me. This is his newest version of drowning me out—altering his mental state if he has to.

Surprisingly, he doesn't resist as I pull away, taking the glass in my hand. I can see in his gaze what he thinks I'll do. Set it down so he can take it again. Play keep-away like Fabio does. Try to save Donatello from himself.

Because this vice? It's his chosen weapon. Punishment via self-destruction.

Him. Him. Him.

It's always about him.

Until I *make* it about me. I picture his reaction to Mateo Saleri, and it's the only thing I see as I throw my head back and swallow everything in the glass.

It's fire. I sputter as my throat contorts to expel every drop while my lips clamp together, selfishly trying to keep it down. As my heartbeat thunders against my eardrums, I realize why they're ringing so painfully—someone is shouting directly into them.

"What the fuck is wrong with you?"

Everything. Being near him destroys everything I thought I knew about the person I'd become. My entire being narrows down to a shadow he seems determined to ignore. Denying him is the only way I have to make him see me.

I would laugh if I could as I wrench away from him, stumbling toward the balcony, my eyes burning, teeth bared with malice. My thoughts are a jumble, dangerously impulsive.

If I jumped, would he see me then?

Or would he still find a way to make himself the victim?

"Stop." His voice is in my ear, his arms around me, and my body goes limp.

For a rare, painful second, it's as if I'm the center of the universe—just as long as his focus is on me. Every little thing I do is under a microscope, nothing missed by him. Every breath. Every shudder. Every dangerous thought I'm only partially aware of thinking.

He smells so good, a stench that merges with the distant hints of smoke…

Abruptly, he pulls away, and I'm cold again. The wind mercilessly batters my flesh as if to punish me for relishing his warmth at all. For wanting his notice even if I have to claw and scrape to get it.

I can't scream.

So, I just snarl soundlessly like the little wolf he accused me of being.

"Get inside." He grabs for my hand, but I pull away and make him chase me to the corner of the balcony. Suddenly drained, I lean over the railing and watch the world sway below.

Tears prickle my eyes, but I can't even begin to decipher why. My emotions are alien, wild things crawling through me with whims of their own.

I feel heavy. Weightless. Like nothing matters but seeking my own stability—the only thing capable of grounding me.

And it's him.

I hate that it's him. Piercing, hollow eyes that make me feel alive even when I'm dangling over a devastating drop. His alarmed shout spurs my heart into beating faster, his attention a drug more consuming than any amount of alcohol. I've been denied it for so long…

And I'm owed it. Every piece of him I can take.

I meet his gaze and hold it, advancing step by step until I'm the one chasing him inside. All he can do is grit his teeth, unsure of my motives. I don't even know my own aim. Relentless, I just keep coming until he's backed against the wall with nowhere to move.

But I don't stop.

I crash into the wall of his body as though I intend to go right through him. I think it's his heat I'm after. His nearness should be repulsive, overwhelming...

But it isn't.

It's intoxicating.

There is no way he can't see me now. Feel me. I don't have to say a single damn word to gain his notice. I only have to touch him, running my hands along his chest, to know everything there is to learn about Donatello Vanici. And for once, he can't block me out. I can't be overlooked.

"Stop it!" He snatches at my wrist as my fingers creep higher. Up his throat, along his chin, following the same path he traveled on me. His eyes blaze, his nostrils flaring, and a part of me screams in triumph.

Finally, I have the one thing I think I've wanted from him all along.

Acknowledgment.

Awareness.

Fear...

Everything.

Greedy for more, I wrench my hand away and grapple for whatever part of him I can reach. His arms. His chest. The proof is in his thundering heartbeat—I'm the one making him stammer. Feel. React.

In a way, I couldn't as a little girl; I have his full attention. He can't turn away from me.

Not now.

"I said stop!" He shoves me back, but my limbs aren't fully connected to my brain. I go sprawling, fighting for balance like a broken marionette.

"Shit." He's near me again, his hand hooking around my waist to keep me upright. Reluctantly, he does so, making me sit on the couch, but I grip him tighter, my nails digging into the flesh of his arm.

He hisses through his teeth but not because of the pain. Because I'm pulling him closer, rattling his unshakable balance. He has to grip the back of the couch to keep from crushing me, but maybe that's what I want to feel? His full weight pinning me down. His full focus.

All of Donatello Vanici.

"Fucking, stop!" He scrambles away, rising to his feet, but something in my expression keeps his gaze riveted to my face. I can see into his mind again, gleaning one new insight after the other. Horror. Disgust. More horror.

Because I've figured out exactly what it is I want from him.

His touch. His taste. I want him to mark me, and I don't even care how. It isn't fair that he's the one with the scars to show for his pain.

I want a token of my suffering, too—a reminder to truly hate him for. To know deep in my soul that I mattered enough to scratch. Even to make him leave something behind that time can't erase.

I want him to hurt me.

I need him to.

And I can see it written all over his face, finally out in the open—it's the one thing he can't give me. How else can he play the victim if I'm the one left bleeding?

"Stop." He wrenches away, turning his back to me, and I go limp. Boneless. His rejection shouldn't affect me the way it does. Like the world has been sucked away. In the absence of his warmth, I'm alone, but it's a loneliness that extends beyond the physical.

It goes deeper into my soul, unearthing something that perhaps is a figment conjured by the alcohol in my system. Or maybe I always knew but never wanted to face it.

I never hated him because he left, or because of his betrayal. My entire life has been a series of betrayals—that isn't what hurt. What's festered all these years until I can feel it consuming me from the inside out.

He took away my ability to hate. To love. To fear—and feel anything at all while knowing that someone understood me unequivocally. Sign language, or music, or the desire to speak at all was irrelevant around him. Until he left. The monster took my voice away.

He made me feel silenced for the first time in my life, and I've been suffocating in that silence for seven long years. I never loved him—I understood him in the deepest, most primal sense of the word, a language that transcends all others. Through him, I could finally accept the twisted, hateful parts of myself I'd grown to fear…

And he stole that from me. He took away the girl I was, his precious Safiya, and he smothered her. Denied me of her. He consumed her.

And it's a crime I can never forgive.

I know now that only one form of retribution can even begin to cover the cost of what he took from me—him. All of him. Those parts of him he's sworn never to let me have. Those broken slivers of his soul he's squirreled away all these years. Through those scattered pieces, I can finally take back the only thing I've ever wanted from him. Needed.

Myself.

"Don't do this to me," he says in a voice I've never heard before. It's an animal's howl, so pained and broken in its utterance that it might not be words at all. A moan. A plea.

A mercy, but one he never afforded to me.

"Don't…"

Don't make him look at me and see the tears streaming down my face uncontrollably. Don't make him stay when every fiber of his being is urging him to run. Don't make him face the creature he's made of me.

A broken woman who can barely stand up. Who staggers to him like a starving creature and grapples for whatever part of him she can reach.

This time, he surrenders, falling back against the couch, and I'm the predator for once.

His heat is my nourishment. I can't get enough. Skin on skin. His breath hot on my neck. His body motionless as I claw open his shirt and run my fingers across the bare flesh beneath.

It's terrifying how you can hate someone so much. Revile them.

And crave the feel of them at the same damn time. My fingers trace him like living beings in their own right, seeking to devour every inch of him. To memorize the scars, too numerous to count, some noticeable only by feel. A surface-level scratch made by something sharp. A deeper, rougher wound that probably took weeks to heal. And finally…

The jagged marks he made himself, spelling out my name as proof of what he tried to ignore. I live in him, this person I've never let myself truly be in seven years. Petty Safiya. Hateful. Vengeful.

But all those good things, too, that I've strived to recall. The joy of sitting quietly in the peace I only ever found around him. The confidence that I no longer had to hide or pretend. I was an open book, and it had felt so good to finally just *be*—without worrying how I came across. No one to pantomime for in the hopes that I was understood.

"Shit." He stiffens as my nails burrow into the ropey scars, but I can see in his eyes the process of him physically holding himself back. He knows what I do.

I'm *owed* this. The ability to explore him to my heart's content. To closely inspect every ridge and drop of ink forming his tattoo. It's mine. Every inch of him is mine.

And all he can do is submit to me.

Exploring him in this way feels like relearning a language I never realized I'd forgotten—only with time it's grown more complex, with far more nuances than I remember.

He is a map of various scars and flaws and old injuries, but he only flinches when I graze what little unmarred flesh remains. Right below his collar bone. Along his throat and up…

It's strange how a face I've seen or imagined hundreds of times can seem so different up close. His eyes are more than just brown, dark enough to touch on black, judging me with a precision that cuts deep.

His stare used to make me feel so small. Like I was just one of a handful of creatures worthy of deserving the attention of Donatello Vanici.

Now, I see myself reflected in those irises, older, sporting an expression I've never seen in a mirror.

I run my hand along his cheek, sensing the strong panes and chiseled muscle beneath. His skin feels worn, speckled with dark stubble. I take my time tracing every inch, every hair, every pore, memorizing them all.

His frown is so much more complex up close, his lips in a stern line, his mouth contorting with the effort it takes to maintain it. A frown that becomes more prominent by the second.

"You're drunk," he rasps, though from his tone, I can tell that he doesn't believe that. One sip of alcohol can't alter a person so drastically.

But years of pain can. If I'm drunk, it's on his indifference. His apathy. His lies. Even now, he can't fully give me what he promised—he still has to maintain control, tensing beneath me.

Lately, I've only found one way to unnerve him.

His lips part as if sensing my intention before I even press mine against them.

I want him to cringe. Recoil. Resist.

But I always underestimate the way my body reacts to him. It's a slow-rolling fire, much like the blaze consuming the west end of the city. Scorching and suffocating all at once. Consuming heat and wicked flames.

Nothing in the world compares to it—the feel of his mouth, the warmth of his breath. He grunts in alarm as I slip my tongue inside, stealing a taste for myself. Then another. More.

It's revenge more effective than anything that could be achieved with a knife or some other form of assault. It goes deeper than any wound, bridging the gap that even words can't breach. I'm in his head, in his soul, privy to all of the subtle things that make him tick, and the fact that he hates this…

At the same time, his body betrays him, relaxing into mine. His hands grip my hips, settling against me with a familiarity that takes my breath away. Desperate for more, I rock into the firmness of those fingers.

Then I grab one, manipulating the thick ridges and firm knuckles.

"What are you…" He grunts in shock when I guide his hand lower. "Stop."

I feel more of him, pressing against me from every possible angle. His chest against mine. His thighs, so thick and rigid with muscle.

"Stop!" He shoves me off, lurching to his feet.

I watch him pace, raking a hand through his hair as if the act alone can help reassemble his control—and it does. His stern frown returns, his eyes darker than ever. "Just stop. Enough."

But it will never be enough. Greedily, my tongue traces my lower lip, hunting for his taste, and I feel the enormity of his loss all over again. He's managed to turn the tables, regaining all the control.

And there is nothing I can do about it.

"Here." He crosses the room, snatching an empty glass from the bar cart. Then he retreats further into the suite and returns with the glass full of water. "Drink this," he demands, shoving the cup into my hand. "Sober up."

He leaves again, and I hear a door slam.

But he's still in the suite somewhere, regrouping.

Regaining his composure.

Regaining control.

20

EVGENI

*J*can smell the city burning from here. The acrid stench is chillingly familiar, unlocking a swath of memories I've spent years suppressing.

Fire is a tricky, beautiful element. So slow to build. Quick as hell to rise. Before you know it, the blaze is beyond control, devastating in its destruction…

There's nothing on earth like it. I've seen how quickly it can consume sticks of wood—and yet how sluggishly it can creep over a human body, licking away skin and bone at a leisurely pace. The smell haunts you forever.

Hands down, it's the most gruesome death I can name.

Drowning would be a close second.

I shake my head to clear it and refocus on the sole reason I'm *here*, and not closer to the blaze. I *should* be there, helping any way I can. Let Briar Winthorp find her own way out of the trap she's set with her secrets and lies.

No matter how deeply I believe that, I don't move. Instead, I scan the water, hunting for the equivalent of a needle in a haystack. Or, to be more specific, a woman in an ocean.

The bitch set me up, I'm sure. Most likely, a sniper is perched somewhere nearby, waiting to take a shot, while she lounges on the boat floating in the distance, cackling over how well her "reckless" plan worked.

I can't even blame her for gloating. She got to me. Got inside my head…

And, speak of the devil.

What I mistook at first for a trick of the light, turns out to be a mass of golden hair, floating just beneath the water's surface. Her body? *No.* A glimpse of pale limbs reveals she's very much alive, propelling herself through the current.

She rises slowly like some fucked up mermaid, her skin so pale she glows against the water. Her hand grips the edge of the dock first, fingers grappling for purchase. A heartbeat after, she surfaces with a gasp.

I lunge, grabbing her wrist, but I sense that my strength is the primary force lifting her from the water. She lands on her side, coughing up greenish liquid in between her pants. I marvel at the sight of her, measuring the distance from the yacht.

Did she really swim all that way?

"Run," she croaks, her chest heaving, dress glued to her body. "Now!"

She doesn't need to tell me twice. A glance along the marina reveals that the guards are suddenly alert, patrolling the docks.

Crouching, I lift her in my arms and head for the rental, shoving her into the back seat. It quickly becomes apparent that I won't be receiving my deposit upon return.

"Damn." I thought she found another dress at first, longer than the one I bought. The extra scarlet is just blood, coating her legs. Too much. I inspect her for the wound, zeroing in on her left thigh. It's deep.

"What the hell happened?"

"No time to play hero now," she scolds, her voice so tight I barely hear her. "We need to move."

I don't have to look over my shoulder to know she's right.

"Fuck." I lunge into the driver's seat and take off, merging into the thick of traffic. It's already slowed to a crawl, jammed in every direction. We're sitting fucking ducks.

But so is anyone who happens to follow us.

That good news, however, is quickly tempered by the glaring reminder darkening the horizon on my left. Though her initial phrasing was rather ineloquent, it sums it up.

The bastard blew up the city.

"What happened?" I look back in the rearview mirror, and I can take a guess. "He hurt you?"

She laughs weakly, gesturing to her leg. She managed to tie a length of fabric around the wound, but it's already soaked, dripping fresh blood. "This scratch? It was inflicted during my daring escape. I'll be fine."

She won't be. There's too much blood, leeching the color from her skin at an alarming rate. She'll die without treatment, and soon.

Rather than say as much, I focus on weaving through the traffic and manage to advance at least a block. Now the only question is where to go.

"I'm assuming you learned something?" I ask her, glancing back to make sure she's still conscious. "What is he planning?"

"The hospital," she croaks, her head lolling every time I hit the brake. "But we won't have much time. I managed to find out that little tidbit, at least. Though I don't know his aim. The boy, I'm guessing."

"The hospital? Eli." In the chaos of the explosion, the police will be stretched thin, and Mischa's men will be cut off from the rest. Judging from how long it's taking me to go a block, it will be hours before they can reach the hospital in time.

"He'll want him alive," she adds. "For now. His plan, however… It's complicated. He could attack tonight. Or tomorrow. It could be a coincidence. Or strategic. I know he has a mole in the Stepanov ranks—"

Exactly what I feared. But who?

"Did you get a name?" I prod, hissing as a car cuts me off before the next intersection. "Fuck! Did you get *anything*?"

"He's… He's difficult to predict." She's breathing heavily, every word a struggle. "This all could be a diversion. I don't think he bought my act for too long, either." She croaks a watery laugh.

A diversion. Only a madman would go through these lengths for no good damn reason. There *has* to be a reason.

"What else is he planning? Another explosion?"

She shrugs. "I don't know. He had me watched like a hawk and gave me little direction. I had to get creative with my methods. When things got too hot… Let's just say I 'jumped' out of the frying pan."

Meaning that she jumped off a forty-foot yacht into the bay with no life vest? I choose not to question her now.

"Damn it."

There's no way I can get to the hospital in time. Still, I grab my cell phone and try calling one of the men. The connection won't go through at all.

"Service must be out," I assume, hissing. Though my device claims to have full bars of connection. Could there be some kind of jam through the Stepanov network? "I wonder if he planned *that*."

I slam on the brake as traffic stalls again, and an ominous thud comes from the back seat.

"Briar?" I look over my shoulder to find her lying on the floor, her breathing heavier. A low groan betrays she's still alive.

"Your…driving skills…leave much to be desired, soldier."

"We're not going to get there in time with this mess," I hiss, scanning the road for a spot to pull over. "I have to move on foot—"

"If I can make a suggestion," the woman says tiredly. "I know someone who might be able to get there in time. Two someones, in fact. How much use they'll be, remains to be seen…"

My eyes cut to slits as I weigh the dangers of trusting her again. The short answer? I don't have a fucking choice. "Who? If the phone lines are jammed, I probably can't reach another cell phone—"

She smiles, her eyes glazed. "Call the Norfolk hotel. I'm sure their landlines are still working."

The same hotel she requested I book.

"What can they do?"

"Connect you," she rasps. "Ask for Donatello Vanici."

21

DON

The water I'm splashing on my face is ice-fucking cold, but nowhere near cold enough. I'd need actual ice to counter her. Still, I cup handfuls of the liquid until I'm dripping wet, my shirt almost soaked through.

Fuck. Like a coward, I contemplate waiting in here until the roads clear. I should let Fabio deal with her. Better yet, send her back to Mischa.

As if she'd be that easy to get rid of. No…

Facing her is inevitable.

But today isn't that fucking day.

I step back from the sink and reenter the main suite, heading straight for the balcony overlooking the city. As if from miles away, I hear a musical chime that doesn't belong amid the backdrop of sirens coming from outside. A telephone? One designated for the room, perched on a glass table that I pass on my way out.

I let it ring, turning my focus to the city, ignoring everything else.

Already the evening sky mimics the unnatural orange glow from the fire. It feels more pressing than ever to decipher the riddle of its meaning. From the Saleris, to their "guest" to the woman who snuck onto the boat, it all feels too calculated. Too complex, like some elaborate fucking scheme that I'm only seeing a sliver of.

By the time I unravel the web itself, I'll already be caught in its snare.

Lost in thought, I miss the exact moment someone approaches, watching from beyond the doorway. The wind plays devil's advocate, bringing their scent to my nostrils. *Roses.*

Indecision leaves me grappling with the need to go, versus staying regardless of the tension. Will we have to reconcile whatever the fuck just happened? Yes, but later. For now, I throw myself into solving the problem presented to me.

The only time we seem capable of tolerating each other is by working together.

"This is the Saleris' territory," I say, thinking out loud. In fact, most of the city center they control is viewable from this very height and location—I doubt it's entirely by coincidence, either. That woman, whoever she is, suggested this place for a reason.

"The hospital is there," I reiterate, spying the building in the distance. "Felicità is over there... Why the fuck would someone want the city severed in half, even for a few hours?"

I lean against the railing, pondering that very riddle.

"The Saleris make most of their money from the club. They traffic their women from all over, arranging escorts for high-class clients. Thanks to Gregori cultivating 'friends in high places,' the police don't dare to look in their direction."

It's only as I hear my own voice echoing back that I realize I'm spouting this shit, not for my own benefit, but for the figure inching closer, her smell so potent I can taste it. I'm choking on it.

She's so eager for information, able to overlook anything else between us. Curiosity is her true vice, not liquor. All things considered, I'm inclined to give her another dose.

"No one knows where they keep their 'inventory,'" I say. "If I had to hazard a guess, I'd assume something mobile. A truck convoy, perhaps. I've heard rumors of the tactics they use, setting up 'work placement' agencies under the guise of scoring their girls legitimate employment. Once they arrive in the city, they find themselves wearing a thong in Felicità instead. If the Saleris were in on the explosion, cutting traffic off for an unforeseen amount of time wouldn't be very beneficial to their business model. Unless…"

I find my attention being drawn to the corner of the bay wrapped around this part of the city like a noose. The water sparkles like a blaring beacon, under my fucking nose all this time.

Of course.

"Unless they have another method of entry. The docks. They smuggle the girls in through there. And, with the land they snatched up, they'd have the ability to store whatever they bring in. That would set up Gregori to expand his establishment well beyond Hell's Gambit."

But that wouldn't explain the explosion.

"Mischa's territory forms a noose around the Saleris'," I add, turning my focus to the swaths of land extending beyond the city center. "If he were gone, they could claim the entire city."

Nearly every fucking thing this side of the fire, to be exact. A damn good bargain for playing the role of someone else's patsy. But what is the ultimate goal?

Why would someone go so far as to use the Saleris, let alone empower them with so much territory?

"They stand to gain a lot in the end," I muse out loud, answering my own question. "But whoever is pulling the strings must stand to benefit much more."

I keep seeing the other man who had been on the Saleris' yacht. Someone unimpressive enough, but I've learned from my days with Giovanni Rossi that looks can be deceiving.

"Who would benefit from the appearance of a fire drawing resources and attention away from the city center?"

I see her move from the corner of my eye. She grips the banister, drawing up beside me, her gaze fixed in one direction. The hospital.

"Mischa's wife and son are still at Mercy," I say, putting the pieces together for myself. "If I wanted to stage another hit on the Stepanovs, now would be a perfect time. Mischa has some men stationed there already, but a small number, I'm assuming. On a typical day, it wouldn't take long for backup to arrive."

But now?

"Given the chaos, reinforcements could be delayed hours at least," I suspect. "Any other day, Gregori or Mateo would have to make the call to slow any traffic through the city center. With enough firepower and the right timing, someone could stage an attack in the heart of Saleris' territory without implicating them on the surface. The hospital is a sitting target."

I look to the woman beside me, curious if she's come to the same conclusion—but her gaze is turned toward the interior of the suite. My ears pick up what has her attention—that noise again. The phone.

It could be a hotel employee calling about some matter related to the suite. I'm tempted to let it ring, but something makes me answer it this time.

"Vanici."

"If you truly want peace with Mischa Stepanov, now is your chance to prove it," a man says. His voice is too gruff to belong to a concierge. It's not Mischa or Fabio, either.

"Who the hell is this?"

"That doesn't matter," the man replies, his tone short. "Get to Mercy hospital before it's too late. The Stepanovs might be a target, and I'm sure your nephew is too."

"What the fuck am I supposed to do?"

"Traffic is at a standstill," the man says. "You'll have to run there. Stall long enough for me to arrive."

"Who the fuck are you?"

Rather than answer, the bastard hangs up.

Son of a bitch. I eye the receiver, weighing my options. I'm not inclined to take orders like some whipping boy—at the same time, I don't like the idea of the hospital being a target. Not one fucking bit.

Getting in touch with Fabio is the smartest course of action —or even Mischa himself. I grab my cell, trying to call those particular people in order.

Neither one goes through, and time is ticking.

As it stands, my only backup is the woman behind me.

"Here—" I reach into my pocket, knowing full well that I'm giving her more than a weapon—her own knife, to be exact. I'm giving her *control,* a chance to turn the tables if she wants to.

Attack me. Run.

Her eyes gleam as though she's weighing those very options. Which appeals to her more?

"We need to get to the hospital," I say, offering her the blade. "Your family could be in danger."

So could she. Rethinking my plan, I start to withdraw the knife. "Or you could stay here. Wait for me—"

She shakes her head, her eyes blazing. When she offers the flat of her palm, I know that whether I allow her to or not, she's leaving.

"Fine." I press the blade against her hand. She has nowhere to put it, though. "Here—" I shrug off my jacket and shove the knife into the pocket. "We'll have to run there. You stay with me, you got that?"

She nods, chin jutting in the air, gaze fixed with determination. Looking at her, I have to admit—as stupid as a thought it might be—when it comes to her, I know better than Fabio.

Black is the only color that suits her.

WILLOW

I have no idea who he spoke to, or what about. I only trust the truthful way he conveyed those words—*Your family is in danger.*

When he lunges for the door, commanding me to follow, I do without question.

We can't have been in the hotel for more than an hour, but as we exit the building, it's apparent just how sheltered we've been within those walls. One step from the main doors and the chaos stemming from the city's west end is deafeningly intense.

Smoke tinges the air as sirens continue to blare. People congregate on corners muttering, their faces turned in the direction of the blaze.

But beneath it all, I can't escape a feeling of wrongness. Donatello senses it as well, his eyes narrowing. Without warning, he grabs my arm, pulling me closer to his side.

Selfish thoughts intrude in a moment where my sole concern should be on my family. I hate him for touching me. At the same time, I *need* him to. His nearness is an anchor against the pandemonium, bolstering me when otherwise I'd be too anxious to think straight.

With his scent in my lungs, my thoughts are crystal clear. He's worried; I can see it in his eyes. For Vin? For my family, even? …For me?

Fearlessly, his steps propel him from block to block. I'm panting in my haste to keep up, but the further we go, the more obvious it becomes that driving would be out of the question. Traffic is bumper-to-bumper, and I know a grim possibility he doesn't mention out loud.

If Ellen and Eli are in danger, the small retinue of Stepanov men stationed at Mercy is all they'll have for protection. Beyond the city, in Stepanov Manor, Mischa won't be able to reach them.

"We're almost there," Donatello warns. His composure alone dispels the fear threatening to choke me. He turns calamity into clarity, his voice persistent, somehow easily audible despite the noise.

"I don't know what to expect," he cautions as the Mercy Hospital complex comes into view. When we near the main entrance, he grips me even tighter, lowering his mouth to my ear. "We'll get to your family, first. Move them toward Vin's wing."

A fact easier said than done once we reach the lobby.

The spacious area is packed with concerned visitors all clustered around the front desk, shouting various questions. Only a few of the lights remain on to illuminate the usually bright space.

"Yes, there was a power outage," I hear the receptionist say, her strained tone desperate to convey calm. "The hospital is running on a generator for now, but there is no risk to patient care. However, patients on the fourth floor are being evacuated to another wing for their safety…"

My heart lurches. Vincenzo's floor.

Donatello must realize as well. His jaw clenches as we pass the receptionist completely, but he doesn't slow, heading straight for the elevators.

"Shit," he snarls when we reach their location.

A yellow caution sign has already been affixed to one, warning they're out of service hospital-wide.

Already pivoting, Donatello heads for a nearby stairwell instead. "This way. Wait—" His eyes flash with indecision as we mount the first flight of steps. Overall, the stairwell itself is eerily deserted, every breath and sound amplified times a thousand. "Vin… I need to make sure he's okay."

But if there's a threat against my family, there isn't time to waste.

He must see that in my eyes because he hisses through his teeth. "It will be stupid to split up. But if you want, you can get there first," he says. "Keep the knife on you. Stay out of sight. Wait for me—"

I nod, already starting up the staircase.

"You wait for me," he warns. "We don't know what the hell to expect."

Meeting his gaze, I marvel at what I find. Concern? So brief and fleeting I could have imagined it. Still, it shocks me to my core. In that moment, he…

He looked like himself again.

"Did you hear me?" he snaps, his tone as gruff as ever.

I nod a second time.

"Good." He continues up the steps, keeping pace with me until we reach the second floor. "Your family's wing is here," he says. "Vin is two floors up. Get to them if you can, but you stay out of sight otherwise. Understood?"

He doesn't move until I start past, entering the floor proper. The door closes behind me with a deafening thud. When I look back, gazing through a pane of glass providing a view of the stairwell, he's already gone. All that's left to do now is try to remember the way to Mischa's wing on my own.

Was it through this corridor?

Or the next?

Mischa's paranoia proves a detriment in this instance. Due to the privacy of Ellen's ward, there's no one else in view to ask for directions.

When I finally find a wing that looks vaguely familiar, I can't ignore the ominous feeling building in my gut. Something isn't right. It's *too* quiet here, with the partial lighting casting shadows that make the hallway feel as spacious as a crypt.

Every step I take echoes, magnifying the undeniable feeling of being alone.

He left you again, a part of me hisses. *Not because he believes you'll be any help. He knows your useless. Perhaps he'll hope this building explodes as well. You'll finally be out of his hair for good…*

No! I bite back the thoughts and focus. Finding my family is my sole concern, though I can't escape the feeling that the quiet interior doesn't resemble a target under siege. There are no men with guns like the figures who guarded the marina. No screams or gunshots.

Maybe Donatello had it wrong?

Either way, I have no choice but to find my way alone. Up ahead, the corridor forks into two, but I don't know which way to go. Left? Right?

Unsure, I bounce on the balls of my feet. Then I hear it—a masculine voice coming from the left-hand direction.

"…everything secured," he says, though I don't hear anyone respond. He could be speaking into a phone. Or a headset, I realize as I round the corner and spy a familiar figure dressed in black.

Mischa's guard. He's alone, still at his post near the door, but his voice is strained. Gruff. I doubt he would speak to Mischa like this. "The fuck are the others? They can't expect me to move them by myself—" He breaks off, his eyes widening as he sees me. In the blink of an eye, his demeanor changes, his posture straightening, voice deepening. "Ms. Willow? What are you doing here?"

Unease wars with relief. Again, I can't ignore the suspicion that he wasn't speaking to another guard so informally. At the same time, I can admit that extended time in the orbit of Donatello Vanici has heightened my paranoia.

Either way, I approach him.

"Are you alone?" He eyes the hallway behind me, and I note the way his hand goes to his hip. Where his weapon is holstered? Again, new alarm bells go off. Another side effect of Donatello's influence?

When I draw near enough, the man plunges that same hand into his pocket. I stiffen, but instead of a weapon, he withdraws a set of keys, fumbling for the door. "Ah… Allow me. Your father isn't here. The rest of the men are… They're on break." His words are disjointed, as if he's speaking purely out of habit.

Jostling near the lock, his hand shakes, and it takes him two tries to successfully open the door. As he does, he shoots another glance over his shoulder.

"Is…ah, Mr. Vanici with you? Or your father?" Something in his tone raises the hair on the back of my neck.

I ignore it, racing down the hall into Ellen's room. She's still there, lying in bed, Eli beside her.

"Will!" He flashes a grin, lurching to his feet. A book falls from his lap to the floor, not that he seems to notice. "Did you hear that boom? It was so loud! We tried to call Papa, but—"

"We didn't know you were coming, darling," Ellen says, but her expression is constrained. She's worried. Does she suspect something's wrong as well?

"Why is your face like that?" Eli demands.

My face…

A nearby mirror provides more insight. My hair is disheveled, my eyes bloodshot. Donatello's jacket dwarfs my body, a glaring reminder of the urgency at hand.

Turning to Eli, I raise my hands. *Where are the other guards? Evgeni?* I sign.

He shrugs. "There were three guards overnight. But only one came to replace them."

"We were supposed to leave today," Ellen says, her eyes alert as they cut to the doorway. "No one has explained to me why we haven't. I've asked for my phone—"

"But the guard said the lines are down," Eli says over her. "This one won't work—" he points to the landline beside Ellen's bed. "Papa hasn't been here yet, either."

A rare note of unease colors his tone.

We need to move, I sign to him. *Can't explain.*

"Move?" His eyebrows wrinkle.

"What's wrong?" Ellen demands. She's regained enough of her strength to haul herself upright, bracing her hands against the mattress for support. "Willow?"

"She says we need to move," Eli explains, racing to her side. "Something's wrong."

Ellen meets my gaze and nods, rising to her feet. "Unhook the IV from the wall, darling," she tells Eli. Gripping the pole, she uses it for support to enter the hall.

I lead the way to the door, but when I push it open, it doesn't budge. Locked. I pound on the glass, but the guard doesn't move. I see his eyes flicker in my direction before cutting away. He's ignoring me.

And the building dread becomes an avalanche of terror.

"Excuse me," Ellen calls, her voice conveying the full authority she commands as a Stepanova. "Open the door."

The man doesn't move. Not even when she raps on the glass with what little strength she has. Slumped against the IV pole, she's no match for his insubordination.

"What's wrong with him?" Eli demands.

I think I know, though I don't try to convey it. He must be working for the men who caused this diversion.

And Donatello knew, of course, a part of me snarls. *Once again, he's led you like a lamb to the slaughter.*

No. I shake my head, quashing the guilt. There isn't time to dwell. I need to think.

They can't expect me to move them by myself, he said. Does that mean he's working alone?

Why?

And who is "they"?

"Hey! Where are you going?" Eli demands as the man moves without warning, venturing from the door.

Through the pane of glass, I catch a glimpse of him with his hand at his ear. He's on his headset.

But Donatello said the cell towers were down, interfering with his ability to use a cell phone.

This guard must be speaking via a local connection. Which means whoever he's communicating with must be somewhere on the hospital grounds. Waiting to attack?

Or is their plan more nefarious? What I overheard him say before keeps echoing in my head. *Move them.* Eli and Ellen? But where…

"He's coming back," Ellen says.

Sure, enough the guard is returning, approaching the door directly. As he wrenches it open, something in his expression makes me step back.

"There's been a breach at the manor. I need you to come with me," he says, reaching for Eli. "The other men are on their way for Mrs. Stepanova and you, Ms. Willow."

No. I step in front of Eli. Objectively, I'm not even sure why. It's a pulse, surging through my blood as strong as my heartbeat. Or maybe it's a voice whispering through my skull in a baritone suspiciously resembling Donatello's. *Don't let him go.*

"Please…" The man sighs, glancing over his shoulder. He looks impatient, like he's waiting for something. Expecting something.

"We should all move together," Ellen declares, her eyes narrowing. "What kind of breach happened? Let me speak to my husband—"

"There isn't time." The man grabs for Eli only to grunt in shock, clutching his hand to his chest. Blood drips from it, stemming from a jagged cut sliced into his forearm.

The strange thing is that I don't even remember grabbing the knife. Sure enough, it's in my hand, trembling with how tightly I'm gripping it.

I'm flashed back to the last time I brandished this very dagger against another person. With Donatello beside me, his voice rasping against my ear. *"He deserves to be punished,"* he told me then. *"You know that as well as I do. So where should we start?"*

"Willow!" Horror wracks Ellen's voice, but the guard has my attention.

"Fuck." He slides his hand into his pocket again. This time, he withdraws a gun, aiming it at her.

"Please get back into the room Mrs. Stepanova," he commands. "The boy will come with me, and more men will come to escort you to safety. There isn't time for argument."

He's lying.

I know that in my gut, though I can't explain why.

Eli's eyes meet mine, and in them, I see bravery. A hint of fear. Overall? Trust. The same trust I once felt, confident that the man before me could never let me down.

Never leave…

"Come on," the guard commands. Digging his fingers into Eli's injured shoulder, he yanks him back.

I don't think. I just react. The blade flashes through the air, raised high. Then, with a sickening thud, it strikes something firm. It resists at first, then relents with a heart-wrenching sensation.

The guard shoves Eli aside, grasping a chunk of my hair in a fist. He staggers, dragging me with him, so brutally tears prickle my eyes. "Little… Bitch…"

Suddenly, a force slams into me from the side, knocking me to the floor. Crushing me. The stench of blood is overwhelming, an oppressive weight pinning me down.

The guard? He's too heavy. Unmoving.

As if from miles away, I hear Eli and Ellen talking, but their words overlap, impossible to decipher.

But then a louder voice cuts through the din, impeccably clear. Probably because it's spoken against my ear, persistent as the pressure weighing me down is suddenly withdrawn.

"I've got you," that voice continues as I lurch onto my hands and knees, twisting my head to get my bearings. "It's okay." An arm goes around my waist as I spy the guard nearby, lying on his side. He isn't moving.

Which means, he isn't the figure whose strength spreads through me as a stabilizing force, his voice so soft... Softer than I've ever heard it. "Don't look at him. I've got you."

Tears spring to my eyes, impossible to keep at bay. I just let them fall as the unseen figure continues to hold me, repeating those same three words over and over. "I've got you."

It's a lie; I know it is. He'll have me until he no longer has any use for me...

But for the time being, his presence drowns out the guilt.

And I don't have the energy to resist him.

EVGENI

We're too late. I sense it the second we pull into the parking lot. Roughly an hour after the blast, and I'm sure the bastard has already made his move.

Though what it might be? Who the hell knows.

Without any contact with any of the men inside, I'm blind to what we might be walking in to. My gun is my only backup.

And her. She's been so quiet, I've almost forgotten she's here.

"You learned nothing else?" I call to her.

When she doesn't answer, I turn and find her slumped on her side, her eyes closed.

"Shit."

I climb into the back seat, focusing on her thigh. Up close, the severity is worse than I could have imagined. It's deep, almost down to the muscle. Whatever cut her, must have hit an artery. Or two. Beneath her, the floor of the vehicle is soaked with blood, but the fee for a damaged rental is the least of my concerns. I think she's dead. Her skin is so pale I can see the map of veins snaking beneath.

I feel along her neck, shocked to feel a faint, but steady pulse.

"Not dead yet, soldier," she rasps. Her eyelids flutter, but she only seems capable of opening them halfway. "It seems you face…a dilemma… Am I worth more to you dead or alive?"

Dead, warns the part of me that knows better. But damn her. In that mocking hue of blue, I see a flashing hint of relief. And greed.

She wants to die. Because she did her job, leading me into whatever trap she and her boss have set?

Like hell, will I give her the satisfaction.

"You owe me answers," I warn. After a glance around, the bloodstained seats reveal nothing else to use as a bandage; I strip my shirt and cover her wound, applying enough pressure to make her wince. "No dying until I say so."

"Funny," she rasps, chuckling in between panting breaths. "I think you have more pressing matters…"

She trails off without finishing that statement, but I can guess well enough.

And she's right.

This is the parking lot Mischa's men use. If it's empty, that means only a fraction of the men must be inside. Ten? Five? Fewer?

"Come on." I hook an arm beneath her waist, dragging her from the van. When she slumps, unable to stand on her own, I sling her over my shoulder and approach the hospital, heading for the back entrance near the Stepanov's private wing.

I don't even have to set a foot inside the building to sense that something's off. There are no patrols on the outer perimeter. The door to the stairwell is unlocked.

"What the hell?"

I enter it, instantly on guard.

"He moves fast," Briar murmurs into my ear. "I suggest you keep that gun of yours handy, soldier."

"Like minds." I'm already drawing the weapon from its holster.

As I mount the staircase, the stench of blood tinges the air, irritating my nostrils. Hers? Or someone else's?

I've barely gone another flight, when I see the body slumped against the outer door. I recognize his face—one of

Mischa's. I don't even have to feel for a pulse to know he's dead, his throat slit.

The method sticks out to me. No gunshot, meaning the attacker prioritized stealth over speed. It's sloppy. The work of one man?

A mole.

"Damn." I readjust the woman, pressing my ear against the door to the ward. It's quiet. No…

I hear shouting. A woman and child. And I hear a man's voice answer them.

"Shit." There isn't time to regroup. I shrug the woman off and leave her on the bottom step. "Wait here."

She's too weak to argue, her blue eyes glued to the dead man slumped just paces from her.

Ignoring any emotion, I hold my gun aloft and kick the door open, steeling myself for whatever I might see beyond it.

Nothing.

Mrs. Stepanova isn't in her room as I race down the wing. They're just beyond it. I move entirely on reflex, rounding the hallway to find blood on the floor and a man, his arms around a woman I recognize instantly.

"Willow!" Without hesitation, I aim at her attacker. "Let her go."

But he doesn't, and when his eyes meet mine, I'm sure he never will.

The last time I saw this face was on a grainy video as he tortured a man to death—and yet I have no trouble identifying him. Donatello Vanici.

"Get the hell away from her!"

It's like the bastard doesn't even see me.

The man lying nearby is a Stepanov agent. I recognize him —the newest recruit. He's still breathing, his face contorted in agony. The knife embedded in his chest, gives a clue as to why.

But when I see the handle of the blade, I stop short.

What the hell?

"Look at me," Vanici demands, his hand on Willow's cheek.

I lunge for them, my gun at the ready, but I never pull the trigger.

Willow's expression has me paralyzed. I've never seen her look at anyone the way she is now. Like she's drowning, and only his touch is keeping her afloat. Keeping her breathing.

My gaze cuts to the injured guard. Then I turn my attention to the rest of the ward. There's no one else around. Where the hell is everyone?

"It's over," I hear Vanici tell Willow. "It happened. There's no use dwelling on it."

"What happened?"

"Evgeni?"

I swivel in the direction of the voice and sigh in relief. Further down the hallway, two figures lurk in shadow. Mrs. Stepanova and Eli. Both seem unharmed but wary.

"Something was wrong with him," Eli says, pointing to the guard. "He tried to take me."

"We need to get in contact with Mischa," Mrs. Stepanova demands, her tone authoritative despite how frail she appears overall. Which reminds me.

"The baby?" I ask. Yet another potential member of the Stepanov family who could be targeted.

Mrs. Stepanova's strained look of relief eases that worry. "She's been discharged already. Mischa and Anna have been getting her settled."

"Good. But we can't stay here long," I say, thinking fast. Until I know what the fuck is going on, even the traffic jam would be a safer place than the hospital. "We should leave. Come with me—"

"I'll cover you," Vanici says, lurching to his feet. Willow copies him, but her gaze is distant. I doubt she even realizes I'm here.

I take a step toward her. "What happened?"

"Go!" Vanici says, inclining his head toward the stairwell. "There isn't time. We need to get them out of here." He nods to Mrs. Stepanova. "Worry about them. I'll get Willow clear."

"Wait…" I grit my teeth, my fingers clenching the handle of my gun.

It's hard to think clearly without a clearer view of just what the hell is going on. "We need to—"

A sudden noise from down the hall draws my notice. Reinforcements?

But Mischa's or an enemy's?

There isn't time to question.

I look back at the Stepanovs. Ellen seems far too weak to move on her own. Picturing Briar, I'll need all the help I can fucking get.

"Help me carry them," I tell Vanici, weighing strategy over common sense. "I have a car. I know somewhere we can regroup."

And yet I have a suspicion that, no matter where we go from here, we'll still be ensnared by this twisted web.

DON

An injured woman, a child, and a surly guard enter a hotel suite.

It sounds like the start of a bad fucking joke. Yet, here we are, and no one's laughing.

"It doesn't make sense," the man says from across the sitting room situated near the front of the three-bedroom suite. Evgeni, the Stepanova woman, called him, though we haven't been properly introduced. Judging from his voice, he's the mysterious caller who sent me to the hospital in the first place. "One man kills his partner and tries to take a Stepanov child out of the hospital alone? It's insane. It's reckless. It's…" He lowers his tone, shooting a glance down the hall where said child is resting with his mother. "Mischa will be here soon. Maybe he'll have more insight."

It's already after midnight. Apart from one stabbed guard and one dead one, there was no other attack on the hospital from what information we've gathered when the cell phone service returned roughly an hour ago. To put it bluntly, no "fireworks."

"Care to enlighten us?" I ask a figure lounging on a leather chaise near a row of windows that provide a breathtaking view of the waterfront.

I almost didn't recognize her at first, the blond who smuggled herself onto Tony's boat. Somehow, I'm not surprised that her "knight in shining armor," turned out to be a Stepanov guard. Now that I can pair her features with those of Mischa's wife, the resemblance is uncanny. A sister?

It doesn't seem the mystery will be solved any time soon. Considering Mrs. Stepanova collapsed from exhaustion the second we entered the hotel, I can't question her directly, and Evgeni doesn't seem inclined to strike up an in-depth conversation.

My knight, she called him. He stands in between us more like a bulldog. His stance is angled toward her, his hands at the ready to repel any potential assault. Does he aim to protect her? Or is his intention more possessive? Like a predator disinclined to share his kill…

"Enlighten?" the blond echoes with a shrug. Despite her swim, she looks none too worse for wear, though her leg is wrapped tightly with towels taken from the bathroom. How she's still conscious is a miracle.

"I'm as in the dark as you are," she says, her voice a rasp. "Maybe I was wrong after all? I could have made a mistake—"

"Bullshit." I take a step toward her, but the guard moves to block my path.

"We'll let *Mischa* question her," he suggests. At least my unasked question has an answer—he's her guard dog.

Apparently, he was able to get in touch with the *mafiya* leader after we left the hospital. Though why the hell were his wife and child left with just two guards for protection in the first place?

Yet another mystery.

"I need to make a phone call of my own," I say, heading for the hall.

I see a flicker of movement near my side, and smell roses. Since we left the hospital, she's been damn near unresponsive. Considering her knife was stuck in the living guard, I assume she stabbed him.

Without reinforcements, we had to leave him behind to be treated. Knowing Mischa, he won't get far.

But it still doesn't make any damn sense. Why send a lone man to kidnap a child? Though, hell. Without being tipped off ahead of time, would I even have had the foresight to think the hospital could be a target?

No.

That question and more weigh on my mind as I open the door to the suite. Time alone to think is as much my reason for leaving as the need to call Fabio. If anyone can make sense of this, it's him.

"You should stay here, Willow," Evgeni says as she starts to follow me into the hall. "I'm sure your mother would feel better with you here—"

"No." I snatch her hand before she can move, making the decision for her. "She stays with me."

We go far enough from the room to prevent being overheard.

I call Fabio, and he picks up on the first ring.

"What the hell is going on? I've been trying to reach you for hours—"

"You're not going to like it," I preface before explaining everything that happened since we reached the docks.

"I've heard from Mischa as well," Fabio admits. "It seems the network his men were using to communicate has been hacked. Calls were blocked, signals scrambled. Sometime directly before the blast, most of his men were called back to the manor via an emergency message. They thought it had come from him."

Well, that's one question explained. Whoever set this plan into motion must have ensured only two guards would remain, exempt from the fake message.

"Can someone do that kind of shit?" I ask. "Hack an entire network?"

"I haven't heard of such technology," Fabio admits. "But who knows? I don't like this. You should come home. Vincenzo is safe—"

"I know. I made sure of that."

"But I don't want you staying in that godforsaken city any longer. I've already ensured that Vin will be covered around the clock—"

"I'm not leaving the city while he's here," I say. "That's final."

"At least promise me you'll try to get some sleep. It won't do Vincenzo any good to spend the night lurking around the hospital. I own a property not too far from—"

"There's a hotel," I say absently. "I already booked a room. It's close by."

I hate the idea of leaving Vin alone, even for a few hours, but I can't shake the sense that being in a central location is better overall. If the hospital was just a diversion, who knows where the real "fireworks show" might be. And when…

"Good," Fabio says, drawing my attention back to him. "A part of me wants to question how you could be so reckless. At the same time, you turned this situation around better than expected. Mischa owes you his son's life. That can't be denied. I'm sure any previous 'disagreements' can be forgotten. You might not need this sham engagement after all."

I have to chuckle at that. "Same old Fab. Won't let a little thing like a foiled abduction, a bombing, and a plot to take over the city get in the way of business—" I don't miss how the woman flinches, still watching me. The look in her eye resembles the Salvatore girl's. Miles away.

I can't resist running my thumb across that delicate chin. She jumps, her eyes flitting to mine. Still glazed, but the longer I touch her, the more life returns to them.

"Donatello?" I hear Fabio say.

"I was calling you shrewd," I reply.

He laughs. "You're damn right I am. But I'm pleased to say that we'll live to see another day thanks to you. Though I do have to wonder the effect this all might be having on your…guest."

I'm looking right at her, wondering the same damn thing. Her eyes seem darker than ever. For once, I can't tell what she's thinking.

"She'll need support, Donatello," Fabio says. "In fact, a good show of faith would be letting her return to her family—"

"I'll keep that in mind," I say.

"Stay put and get some rest."

I hang up, heading back down the hall.

The guard, Evgeni, is still waiting in the doorway, his arms crossed. "I still think she should stay here. Her father is on his way."

"Tell Mischa that one little instance of cooperation isn't enough to fix everything." I step closer to the girl, grabbing her hand. "The engagement isn't off yet."

She's still mine.

To prove it, I keep walking, feeling her fall into step behind me. Until a figure exits from an elevator up ahead, flanked by two guards. Sympathy is the last emotion I expect to feel for a man who put me through hell. In this one instance, perhaps I'll make an exception when it comes to Mischa Stepanov.

He looks haggard, more of a zombie than a man. When he spies his daughter, he lunges for her, crushing her to his chest.

A heartbeat later, he seems to notice the blood smeared across her wrist. Blazing, his eyes cut to mine.

"It seems like the guard stationed near your wife and son attacked them," I say. "She... Willow defended them on her own. The bastard is at the hospital—"

"I already have him secured," Mischa growls. "He'll talk soon enough."

"And he has plenty to answer for," someone declares from behind me.

A look over my shoulder reveals Evgeni, still in the doorway, his expression even more guarded than it'd been a minute ago.

Reluctantly, Mischa releases his daughter, advancing toward the suite.

"Your wife and son are safe," Evgeni adds, stepping aside. "Though there is a…guest, we will need to discuss."

I can't help but notice that the blond has vanished from her perch. Could she be hiding again?

Evgeni's eyes meet mine before I can be sure. "Willow should stay here, with her family," he suggests for the third time.

Maybe he's right.

Knowing that doesn't prevent me from grabbing her hand, though, pulling her with me. I'm sure he'll follow, but I don't fucking care. I drag her into the elevator, striking the button for the penthouse floor.

Only when we're back inside my suite, do I finally face her.

I expect that blank stare, but when I cup her jaw against the flat of my palm, she comes alive, her lips fluttering, confusion widening those dark eyes.

"I should let you go with them. You got what you wanted," I tell her. "Your family is safe. Mischa is in the clear. Everyone is fucking happy. We're even."

I don't have to look in her eyes to know that we're not.

Stepping closer, I force her to crane her neck just to hold my gaze. "What the hell do you want from me?"

Her flashing eyes convey the answer. She already named her price. She wants my fucking soul.

Well, she can have it.

I turn my gaze to her hands, slim and pale, bruised from her struggle. "You can stab me if you want."

It's the wrong choice of words. She flinches, and I grit my teeth, surprised by the guilt I feel. "Or you could beat me," I suggest, changing tact. "Sell me on a platter to the Saleris. Take your pick."

But again, her choice is obvious. She wants me to bend to her will and give her the one thing I can't.

And I won't. Pride aside, not because I swore not to—but the morality of it, if I even believe in that kind of shit. It's wrong to take her throat in my hands, sensing the pulse surging beneath. Wrong to toy with that palpitating little artery until a hint of fear appears in her eyes.

But it's worse to want her. To feel her heat on my skin, sense her taste on my tongue. It's wrong to crave her.

"Do you really want to play with fire, *principessa?*"

No. She wants oblivion. To forget the hell she's been through. Because of the attacker. Because of me.

As greedy as ever, she inches closer, pressing her face to my chest first. Then her searching hands crawl up to my shoulders, finding my jaw. Her fingers shake, as if she's fighting against the contact with all her might—but she can't resist whatever impulse drives her to stay near me. To touch me. With gentle pressure, she makes me face her.

In her eyes, I see another glimpse of the same emotion I felt the night she climbed into bed and crawled beneath me. Is it pity?

Or something far more dangerous.

"Take what you want," I tell her. "I don't care anymore. Just tell me what you want from me. You can have it. Just take it!"

She runs her tongue along her bottom lip, and I hiss through my teeth. Of course, she'd want the one thing I've denied her all along.

Corruption.

I can see it in her eyes, mingled there amongst her hate— the very emotion that's haunted me all this damn time. Because it *shouldn't* be there, not in her. Not after what I've done.

Even Liv lost that gleam after a while. I remember it now like a punch to the gut. One day, I looked into her eyes, and they were guarded against me. I'd lost her, long before she drew her last breath.

Because I was never worthy of her, worthy of anyone.

So love can't be what I see in the woman standing before me now. I'll prove it, no matter the cost. Even if I have to hurt her to do so.

The next time I look in these eyes, I'll make sure that hate is all I find.

My hand latches onto the back of her skull, dragging her closer. Our lips meet, but this kiss is no chaste peck. It's painful. Gnashing teeth—hers, seizing my lower lip as if in punishment for calling out her habit for doing the same. I groan at the bitter sting, hoping she pulls away. Relieved when she doesn't. Her taste is hell, her touch like sin.

And my motives for indulging her blur. The scent of roses is a drug more potent than alcohol. I lose track of my thoughts. I lose my goddamn mind.

I only crave more.

Pulling her against me, I slide my jacket from her arms, grasping for the slender body beneath. Her dress has thin little straps that are easy to flick aside. It's even easier to grip the front of the material, below the neckline, and rip it open. The fabric parts to reveal swaths of pale skin, and I'm choking out words I can no longer hold back. "Damn… You're too beautiful. Beautiful."

And she is. A body formed from sin, designed to entice. To entrap. To torment.

I'm tired of living a life of repentance. Tired of exercising restraint when it comes to her.

Those dark eyes dare me to do it. To cross the line we've both been toying with all this time.

So, I slide my hand over her hip, down the porcelain length of her thigh, then up between her legs, and I earn my ticket to hell.

Her flesh greedily envelops my thumb, hot enough to burn. It's nothing like the first time I touched her. Her body relents, those tight muscles dragging me deeper, her hips arching so violently I have to wrap my arm around her waist, tethering her to me.

Mine. It's an impulse so strong I feel it with every pulse of my fucking heartbeat. A need. A promise. A curse.

We're linked. Two damn twisted souls who only feel sane around each other. I don't even have to look into her eyes to know what I'll find there, glistening behind that sheen of tears. *Relief,* building as I shove my finger inside her, and she takes every inch I have to give.

Sweet fucking relief.

I reclaim her mouth with such force our teeth click together. Her taste fills my tongue, and I choke her down in desperate, deep pulls.

For the first time in so damn long, the buzzing chaos in my head feels silenced. My thoughts are clear, my head lighter, the world smothered for once.

But it's not enough.

Feeling her cunt quiver in the palm of my hand isn't enough. I shove her back onto the couch she dominated earlier, pinning her down, those hips beneath mine.

A part of me craves to savor her. The louder part demands I claim. My brain is a rush of need. No rhyme. No reason.

Returning my attention to her cunt, I slide another finger alongside the first. She shudders, her nails sinking into the leather of the couch, her eyelids fluttering, lip clenched between her teeth.

"I… I should take my time," I tell her, hating how I sound. Broken. Guttural. Mindless. Like a goddamn animal.

But, fuck, her body reacts, her cunt growing slicker with every pass. She's molten, weeping for me.

And I can't take it anymore. Hissing through my teeth, I ease my hand from her, wrenching open the front of my pants. I grip my cock, groaning at the feel of her. Two strokes, and I fear I could come from this alone. Watching her. Smelling her.

But then I see her eyes, widening at the sight of me.

Slow the fuck down. I shake my head to clear it and grip her thigh, dragging her closer. Carefully, I guide both of her legs apart, fixing my gaze on the pink flesh awaiting beneath a swath of golden curls.

It's mine.

She was *always* mine.

And I deserve to savor her.

WILLOW

Nothing on earth compares to the sensation of feeling him pin me down, crushing me to the couch. His body is a heavy, rugged burden to bear—and yet a part of me feels crafted for this very purpose. To endure him.

Be devoured by him.

If only this moment were more terrifying. Then I'd have the sense to fear it. The cruel truth is, that his weight isn't stifling the way I think it should be. My body conforms to him, providing softness where he is all hard muscle. Fragility against his brute strength. Even, my curves fit perfectly within the contours of his chest, almost *too* perfectly.

Like I was made for him alone, no one else…

The thought is too dangerous to consider in full. I try to suppress it, fighting to clear my head, and keep my focus on him. I've barely gotten my bearings when he crouches, spreading my legs, his gaze between them. His expression sends a thrill through my belly as I realize where he's looking. The door to the balcony is still open, allowing the cool air to replace his touch, heightening every exposed inch of flesh only he has ever explored. Defiled.

Like a starving man's, his eyes rake over me. Ravenous.

I grapple for the nearest armrest, using it as leverage to watch him as my thoughts blur, head spinning. Then…

He lowers his mouth, and I feel the contact hit like a bolt of lightning. Instantaneously, I explode. Combust. Whatever word can describe every nerve frying at once—a sensation so overwhelming you go numb at first. Perception is a slow, torturous battery of one new feeling after the other.

The moist heat of his mouth, followed by the pulsing pressure of his tongue…

My brain is slow to catch up, piecing together exactly what he's doing. Just when I think he can't possibly do more, his fingers fearlessly navigate flesh and nerves to find a bundle of skin that makes me arch into his grasp.

It's cruel what he does to me, playing my body like an instrument only he has ever learned to tune. I feel things I've never experienced—stomach-churning pressure aching between my legs. His tongue lashing like a whip. The sinful heat of his breath.

All at once.

I'm falling. Flying, all while being held by thick, trembling hands that grip me tight as if they never mean to let go.

Through all the chaos, some internal impulse warns me to breathe. Gulping for air, I look down and shudder.

His teeth glisten, tongue tracing his lips before he delves between my legs for another mind-bending swipe.

He feels so good. *Too* good.

Like the sting of alcohol times a million. I go limp, surrendering to the onslaught. My nerves overheat, my muscles spasming in anticipation of something... Something terrifying, the threat of which turns my belly into knots.

All I can do is grit my teeth and wait for the impact.

And it's devastating when it comes.

My spine curls back on itself. I think I'd levitate if his weight wasn't here to crush me down. I'm on fire, each stroke of his tongue a drop of gasoline, chased by a sharp grating pressure that makes me jump. His teeth, I think, raking and teasing.

Grinding and taunting.

My thoughts are a formless mass, my body rocking amid the pleasure. For a moment, it feels like it will never end.

And then it does, so suddenly it's like being raised to the height of the moon and left to fall.

Dazed and heavy lidded, I glance down and realize why.

He's rising onto his knees, cock in hand, an expression on his face like a man being slowly tortured. Without mercy or the hope of salvation, his torment must be. He groans, the sound so dangerous my head spins.

"I need to be inside you…"

I close my eyes, overwhelmed by the sound of his voice.

I never knew…

Now I do. This is what I've wanted. Him on his knees, begging me for relief. Needing me. Craving me.

If I tell him no, it will shatter him. Hurt him beyond physical means. He's in the palm of my hand.

For now, a tiny voice whispers. *But for how long?*

I don't think it matters.

I blink, and his mouth is on mine, his breaths heavy, his hands snatching my waist, dragging me beneath him. He feels too solid. Too heavy to ever make this work without crushing me. As if he's reading my mind, his mouth finds my ear.

"It will hurt," he warns, his tone unapologetic.

Pain between us is nothing new.

But when he presses against me, demanding entry, it burns. The sting takes my breath away—and then, in the next instance, a burst of pleasure comes like a wave to demolish everything in its path.

I was made for him. It's the only way to explain how he fits. How good it feels when he moves, rocking his hips into mine. Then away.

Then harder.

I can't make a sound to tell him what I feel. My mouth finds his ear anyway, my teeth snagging the lobe and biting down, converting my pleasure into his pain.

"Fuck," he grunts. "You feel so damn good…"

His pace increases, each thrust deeper than the last. Deep. Deeper. Endless.

Suddenly, he throws his head back, throat cording around a groan as fire floods my belly in dangerous spurts.

And this is true destruction—what he did to me in the past was nothing.

At least then, he left my body whole.

This time, he destroys me from the inside out.

And I will never be the same again.

Corruption, in reality, turns out to be far different from how I envisioned it. I always imagined shame and chains. An existential dread and an overwhelming sense of defeat.

In actuality, all I feel is…

Tired.

So damn tired. His body is a support I never knew I'd needed. Almost like finding a raft after years spent swimming against an unforgiving current.

Salvation is surprisingly quiet. There is no fanfare. No heralding trumpets or soaring arias.

Just steady, slow breathing. Endless quiet. Warm lips that brush my earlobe with devastating softness, and a voice that grates, "You've gotten what you wanted."

Have I?

No. The realization stings, threatening to shatter this fragile cocoon of peace. I ignore it, squeezing my eyes shut and turning further into the comforting heat beneath me.

His body is a symphony of muscle and bone, his heartbeat the steadying metronome at the center of it all. It hammers in a consistent, constant rhythm, revealing what he will never admit out loud.

I let myself be lulled into a daze by the beat, hoping to steal away a few more minutes at least. A little longer…

"We need to go."

And just like that, the moment ends, his heavy sigh serving as the finale. Gently, he nudges me aside and stands, crossing the suite to enter the bathroom. I hear the distant spray of running water, and he returns a few minutes later with a wet rag in tow.

My pulse stammers. This isn't fair. Not the way he crouches, grabbing my knee to ease my legs apart.

I don't think he even understands what he's doing. To him, he's merely dragging the rag in between my thighs, washing away the blood and sweat and traces of him.

The truth is more destructive—he's making it more real. I'll never be able to smother the memories of his touch. His smell. The disarming gentleness with which he swipes the rag across my skin.

Once finished, he retreats to the entryway, salvaging the remains of our clothing.

My dress is beyond repair; the neckline torn.

"Here." He drapes his suit jacket over me, wearing just the shirt, and slacks himself.

When we return to the car and leave the city, an eerie dichotomy becomes apparent. Part of Hell's Gambit lives on, thriving as if never disrupted while the other half smolders. In a sick way, it reminds me of him.

All this time, his body has lived on despite the ravages of his psyche and broken mind.

Fabio's warning echoes now, louder than ever. *Some memories are better left buried.*

Though for whose benefit?

The past doesn't belong here. I resist its pull for as long as I can, but it's no use—I keep thinking of those letters. What secrets was Olivia hiding?

And what horrors have Donatello Vanici's brain thought to suppress?

And why…

DON

We return to the house and find Fabio already waiting on the porch. He looks worried as hell, his hair unkempt as if he spent the entire night tearing his hands through it.

I'm clenching my jaw, eyeing the woman beside me.

"You should go change," I warn.

The last thing we need is for Fabio to suspect what happened between us. Without looking my way, she holds the front of my jacket together with both hands, obscuring her body beneath. The second we exit the car, she heads inside, rushing past a startled Fabio.

"What the hell happened?" he asks, descending the steps to approach me. "Is she alright?"

"No," I admit. Though it could be because she almost killed a man.

Or because I'm a sick, twisted fuck who took advantage of the aftermath.

I watch her go, compelled to follow her. Delve inside that brain and see the truth for myself. She's an enigma, unfathomable almost to the point of insanity. Sometimes we're on different fucking planets.

And then the next second, we're a goddamn hive mind, thinking in sync, breathing in harmony. Fucking like the world might end if we didn't.

Damn…

"Don?" Fabio's staring at me, his eyes narrowed with suspicion. "Is everything okay? Don't tell me you took advantage of your little vacation and threatened her—"

"You should get in contact with Mischa," I suggest, turning my attention back to him. "So we can reassess the terms of this fucking insanity."

Though there's no need for any further discussions.

It's over. I broke my own fucking rules—and perhaps that was her goal all along? Yes. That's all she wanted. I let myself play into the paranoia for a heartbeat before reality sets in.

I keep seeing the way she looked at me, covered in blood, staring into the distance like some lost puppy.

No one could fake that.

"Don? Don, are you listening?"

I shake my head to clear it. "What?"

"I said I already spoke to him," Fabio says. "Mischa. Now that his own family was in danger, I think he's finally convinced that we've all been played for fools."

"But the game isn't over yet." I turn my attention inward, trying to sift through the scattered bits of information for the umpteenth time. None of it makes sense.

"We should talk inside," Fabio warns, leading the way. "I have something to show you."

I hate that I catch myself approaching the stairs the second we enter the house. She's on my mind, a part of me craving for her input. She sees the world like no one else.

Or at least in a way no one else would admit. Someone like Fabio would rather live in oblivion of the darker side of human nature.

The universe is beautiful to him.

To her? It's paradise and hellfire—with both beauty and damage being different sides of the same coin.

"Where are you going?" Fabio asks.

I've already mounted the first few steps and have to physically force myself to turn around. "To think," I say, entering my study instead.

The drawer draws my attention like a fucking beacon. Ignoring it, I riffle through the stack of documents Fab left, trying once again to see order amid the chaos.

"I've been reading through them all night," he says, nodding toward the overflowing piles of papers.

I must lose track of time, poring over each page for some key bit of information I could have missed. When I look up again, Fabio is gone.

Sighing, I take in the mess of scattered pages again. Tucked beneath a random folder on the corner of the desk, I find a familiar set of documents.

My insurance policy.

Sex isn't a magic cure. One night shouldn't be enough to shatter my entire perception, and have me reevaluating everything that felt like perfect sense before.

What the hell was I thinking? Leaving Vin, whether or not it would benefit him in the long run.

I must have lost my fucking mind.

Though maybe, I'm still just as crazy—just in a different way. This life may not be as fucked-up and worthless as I thought. Sure, I broke my own damn vow—I fucked her.

But the little witch has more secrets in her head to discover. No one could blame me for wanting to try, prolonging this engagement a little longer...

"Did you?" The voice is Fabio's, but too soft to be directed at me. Maybe he left me to interrogate my fiancée in peace?

Warily. I enter the hall, noting that his voice is coming from the top of the stairs.

"...I think it would be better for everyone to leave the past in the past," he says.

I frown, recognizing his tone. Fabio is inclined to recite his little speeches ad nauseum, but this is overkill, even for him.

I mount the stairs, intending to tell him as much.

"I need you to retrieve those letters," he says. "Please."

The letters.

It's several seconds before those words sink in. Those fucking letters. Olivia's letters, that Fabio somehow knows about. I'm sure he put Willow up to reading them— probably gave her the damn things in the first place.

They must not notice me yet, their heads together, scheming and trading their fucking secrets.

Well, no more.

Turning on my heel, I start down the stairs. "You want those fucking letters?" I call loudly on my way into the study. Circling around my desk, I wrench open the drawer, grasping every folded page.

They must have heard me this time. They're waiting at the base of the stairs, wearing twin expressions of shock.

"You wanted these so badly?" I lift my fist, brandishing the pages in my grasp. "And here I was thinking you wanted the past left in the past, Fabio."

"Donatello," he rasps, but his gaze is on my hand. "I just...
I don't think it's a good idea to dredge up these old
memories."

Old memories, though he looks anything but nostalgic. No.
He looks like he's seen a ghost, instead. Or that he fears
one...

Liv.

I feel invisible around you, baby, she wrote. *Sometimes it's like
I'm a ghost...*

Fabio isn't the type to fight over old trinkets. No. There
must be something in them he's wary of. Or something *she*
told him. Perhaps she left one of those messages for him as
well?

If so, she doesn't even have the decency to convey a shred of
guilt. Standing beside him, she keeps her eyes on me, but I
can't get a read on her at all.

Even when I offer the letters to her directly. "You want
them? Here—" She reaches out, her fingers grasping, and
for a heartbeat her mask slips.

Bingo. Those wide, dark eyes are the window into her soul
—through them, all I see is desperation. She can't disguise
how badly she truly wants these fucking snippets of paper.
Badly enough to extend her fingers with greedy intent.
Badly enough to fuck me? To follow me onto a Saleri yacht
and toy with my head, pretending she understood me?
Agreed with me...

Just as she fingers the edge of a page, I change tact and throw them. Every last one. Let her gorge on the past to her heart's content.

She's always been a scheming snake—thank fucking God. At least now I know the meaning behind that searching, desperate look she always wears. It's greed. She only ever wanted something from me.

She never wanted *me*.

It's like a weight has been lifted off my fucking shoulders.

Her using me, I can understand.

Nothing more.

Not redemption.

Not love.

"Donatello!" Fabio starts after me, but I barely hear him.

I'm too busy laughing. Loud, boisterous fucking laughter.

"I'm going to see Vin," I say, starting down the porch steps. "I don't need your fucking permission for that."

If he argues, I don't stick around to hear him. I'm done playing by his rules like a spanked child.

It's time to live my way. For Vincenzo.

Only for Vincenzo.

"You staring at me like a mother hen isn't going to make me eat any faster," Vin grumbles while stabbing at a mass of scrambled eggs perched on the edge of his breakfast tray.

"Fine. I won't stare." It's a lie. My focus remains glued to him, analyzing every inch of his pale expression. Apart from the bandages, he almost resembles his old self. My Vinny with the mischievous brown eyes and a smart-ass mouth.

The doctors claim his progress is "unprecedented."

I'm selfish enough to deem it too damn slow. Despite how well he's healing, the damage done to his body is undeniable. He's still too exhausted to stand on his own, capable of holding a conversation only for a few minutes at a time. True to form, he suppresses the discomfort the only way he knows how. With snark and humor.

"You should be more like Saf… *Willow*," he says, nodding toward the other side of his bed where she's seated. "She knows how to make me not feel like a fish in a bowl."

Her lips twitch into the shadow of a smile, but it's thinner than Vin's watery eggs.

He doesn't seem to notice, smiling wider in return.

Fabio must have been the one to tell him her new identity. I suspect he's the same force behind why—despite my visiting him every day—he hasn't mentioned the past once.

A good man, worthy of him, wouldn't need the prompting to come clean.

But me? I'm savoring every fucking second I can withhold the truth.

I didn't just lie to him.

I ripped his childhood apart, and I couldn't even begin to tell him the reason why. I'll be lucky if he ever speaks to me again.

Hunting down the real puppet master behind the attack on him is the only damn thing I can do to make amends—and I can't even do that. Two weeks later, and we're no fucking closer to the truth.

This J.W. son of a bitch might not be much of a mastermind at all.

Or you've missed something, my gut tells me.

Fabio must think the same. Since the explosion, he's been poring over documents related to the docks, consumed with examining the damage done to the west end. As well as pretending that our little standoff regarding the letters never happened.

I don't know what he's done with them. Or why he even cared. Olivia's belongings never interested him before.

As for the woman, she's been elusive for once, lurking in the corners of the fucking house like a specter. For all I know, she could be a ghost, with the real Willow Stepanova having snuck back to her family two weeks ago when we left the hotel. It feels strange to admit the lack of contact after that night. It's been two weeks since I've felt her skin up close. Weeks since I've smelled the nuance of her scent in full detail. Two fucking weeks of silence, both literally and figuratively.

Good riddance. I want to give into that reflexive anger again —make her the enemy. No matter how hard I try to feel it, the remnants of that hostility ring hollow.

None of this was ever her fault. Just mine. If I were like Fabio, I could find a way to talk to her. Bridge the gap I created. So, what if she only aimed to get close to me to gain the letters?

A few notes from the past are the *least* I can give her. I owe her so much fucking more. Shame alone could explain my avoidance of her. The void between us has always been too vast to fill. We can't play this game forever.

It would be better to let her run.

Sooner or later, she'll return to Mischa anyway and claim the future promised to her—as an heiress to a fortune, sheltered by a powerful name.

The only thing I should do is hasten that inevitability. Show her mercy, for once…

But mercy has always been a foreign concept in my world.

When we finally leave Vincenzo and return to the house, I turn my focus to the one subject I know better than anyone. Plotting self-destruction.

The little princess deserves to return to her castle, and Vin should have the means with which to build his own.

The insurance policy has already been updated…

"It doesn't make sense," Fabio remarks from the corner of my study he commandeered.

I blink, startled from my thoughts. I don't know how long he's been sitting there, poring over the morning paper.

"Even the explanation of the fire is being whitewashed," he snaps. "Public officials are still claiming it was most likely an 'industrial accident,' though the investigation seemed to last barely twenty-four hours. So far, the death toll stands at ten workers caught in the blast. They won't even name who they were employed by."

"It feels too neat," I say in response. Too clean.

If the purpose of the display was to attack the Stepanovs, or even make a dent into the *mafiya's* territory, they failed. Mischa's family is safe, and everything else seems at an eerie standstill.

Even the Saleris have gone quiet. Though at least one thing seems clear after the dust has settled.

An engagement is no longer necessary. Mischa owes the lives of his wife and child to me. In retrospect, little Willow should have gone running back to him the second I broke my vow.

But she hasn't…

Every time I recall that night in the hotel, the more aggravated I feel. She won. She got her wish.

But these past weeks, she's lurked within this house like a ghost. The only time she dares to appear is when Fabio and I go to see Vin. Every day, like clockwork, she waits by the door when we're ready to leave, dressed in one of the outfits Fabio supplied her.

And every goddamn time I try to look at her, she shies away —whether it's in the hallway of Havienna or in the car on the way to the hospital.

Even when we arrive at Vin's, she nearly lunges around the bed to put space between us, but she isn't the only one on edge around me.

As I enter the room after her, Fabio hesitates, avoiding my gaze. "I'll be right back," he says before slipping away, and I'm instantly suspicious. He's up to something.

I start after him, but from the corner of my eye, I see a flash of golden hair and lose track of everything else.

Vincenzo isn't shown the same avoidance she reserves toward me. She's already by his side, taking up her usual seat. He's awake, pulling himself up higher in bed to face her.

His lips part into their usual smile, but the sight of it hits me differently than before. Despite his sallow skin, and the bandages still draped over his head, he looks...

Happy. That's not all. Day by day, I've noticed the subtle changes when it comes to her. His eyes sparkle a little more, what little color he has flooding his cheeks.

Watching them, I don't know what the hell to name the emotion shooting through my chest. Guilt? Jealousy? Both?

Weeks ago, I entered Stepanov manor, Vin in tow, convinced that a marriage to Willow Stepanova was his only ticket to a good life—but I was wrong. Not because of the shitstorm that followed, but because he never needed me to decide his match in the first place. In a perfect world, they would find each other naturally.

The same way Olivia should have found a nice politician, or doctor, or banker, Vin deserves a woman like her.

Not me.

I don't know how long I watch them. Long enough that when I finally turn away, Fabio has already returned.

He isn't alone.

Rage is my impulsive reaction. Then I remember the shit we've both been through, strung along by the same bastard. Knowing that, I bite my tongue at least, letting them approach.

To his credit, Mischa seems to be heeding the same unspoken boundary. Our eyes meet, though I can't get a clear read on his motives. Walking alongside him, Fabio implores me through his wide-eyed gaze. Instantly, I know that he's up to something.

The awareness of someone beside me distracts me from the two men long enough for a new arrival to rattle my mindset entirely. She probably noticed her father before I did. When I look at her, that stoic mask cracks, revealing the pain lurking beneath. Longing.

It's the first time in weeks that I've sensed anything from her at all. The sensation rippling through my gut could be jealousy. Or maybe selfish acknowledgment of a truth that shouldn't catch me so off guard.

Mischa will always have her loyalty. Her trust. I forfeited the right to anything of the sort seven years ago.

"Donatello?" Fabio's tone is fittingly cautious. When I look at him, he skirts any eye contact, staring at the wall behind me instead.

"What a lovely day for a family reunion," I bite out. So much for the attempt at restraint.

Fabio sighs. "I think it's past time that we finally arranged a meeting—"

"I don't need permission to see my daughter," Mischa growls, his eyes cutting to slits. Apparently, I'm not the only one struggling to let bygones be bygones.

Though, if our past meetings serve as anything to go by, we're off to a damn near calm start.

"What do you want?" I ask, skeptical if I've read him wrong. Though, this is perhaps the wrong damn place to test the patience of a man like him. From the corner of my eye, I remember where we are, and my mind goes straight to Vincenzo. Maybe Mischa's changed his mind on peace?

"I've learned information of my own," the man says, his tone less harsh than I've become used to. "From the traitor. He's been talkative these past few days. Fabio will relay what we've learned once I verify it."

"Of course." Fabio nods, clearing his throat. "Mischa has also offered to pay for all of Vincenzo's medical expenses, as well as contribute resources toward—"

"What's the catch?" I can't help the cynicism.

"No catch," Fabio says in a rush.

I laugh. "You mean there's no caveat to drop the engagement? Or the blood test?"

Peace or not, no one could blame me for the anger that seeps into my voice. That stunt was a low fucking blow from the outset.

Unapologetic, Mischa's expression doesn't waver. His olive branch, must only extend so far.

We can work together to find the source of the chaos that has affected both of our lives—but where his daughter is concerned, we're both enemies.

Though, what did Fabio suggest the day he first mentioned the blood test? *Do you want to know why Mischa really asked for this asinine request? It's because he thinks it will tip you over and that he has the upper hand. He wants you to drop the charade first, giving him the opening to go for your throat...*

The ironic part is that—as far as vengeance goes—I've already beaten him at his own game. He aimed to use my dead wife and child as a tool to hurt me?

I've already countered with an underhanded move of my own.

I sullied his own damn daughter. A true bastard would gloat over that.

A coward, on the other hand? He'd try in his own twisted way to make amends.

Mischa wants my blood? He can have it.

"You know what?" I say to Fabio's visible horror. He starts forward as if afraid I'll voice a threat. Instead, I shrug. "I'll do it. That blood test you wanted. In fact, we can arrange it now. Mine and hers. Just to square everything away." Baring my arm, I head for the closest nurses' station.

Fabio stammers. "B-But…"

"Can you direct us to the department responsible for blood tests?" I ask of the startled receptionist. "I want mine, and my fiancée's tested. For DNA. Hell, run it for everything, just to be fully transparent. We'll make it a family affair." I try my damn hardest to inject the vitriol in my voice that I don't feel.

This is just a pathetic way to assuage my own guilt and toss Mischa a bone. My humiliation? He can have it, one last show of goodwill before I let his daughter go for good.

If not for her, then for Vincenzo.

The Stepanov name has enough pull to command a blood test with ease. Perhaps, Mischa is playing along merely to save face. Or perhaps he truly believes that something nefarious will come from it—something he can use to turn his daughter against me.

It's already too damn late for that.

I might as well be dead to her. Those eyes stare past me, her silence like a hammer driving in the vast gulf between us.

This is more than that shit over the letters. More than morning-after regrets. I almost reach out to her as we're shown to a room where a nurse prepares to perform the procedure. My fingers are outstretched, her arm within reach…

"Donatello?" Fabio calls from the doorway, as wary as ever. "Are you sure this is really necessary?"

It isn't, not to me, anyway. If anything, going through the motions of this charade just drives home how insane this plan was to begin with.

Marry a woman too young to even decide her own future. Her entire life has been guided by the strength and power of the Stepanov name. Who the hell am I to fuck with that, even out of spite?

The answer seems to lurk in the scarlet liquid the nurse takes from my arm.

I'm not blood to her. In the grand scheme, I was only ever a stranger who did the unthinkable and left her to die.

Once it's over, now feels as good a time as any to approach Mischa directly without Fabio's intervention.

He's in the hall, waiting in silence. If he even still wants the damn blood draw, he hasn't said a word either way. As I approach, he eyes me warily, one of his guards close by.

All I do is meet his gaze, hiding nothing. "You want this sham to end?" I ask, knowing that I'm far enough from the exam room that neither she nor Fabio can hear me. "Make me a deal. You can take her tomorrow, but you keep your word."

His upper lip twitches, his eyes narrowing. I can see him cycle through the pros and cons of believing me or not. Finally, he crosses his arms, shooting a glance across the room where his daughter sits beside a nurse.

His voice is so gruff I nearly miss his reply. "Name your price."

WILLOW

There is beauty in madness. In insanity, even. The human mind has an almost whimsical way of spinning reality into whatever narrative it desires.

Hate becomes interest if you want it to be hard enough. Interest can be lust. Lust can…

Seem so real. Feel so real.

Until you realize that, in a sense, it was all a daydream, conjured by a naïve mind. In the end, I was no better than Olivia in her letters, pining for a man who never existed.

The real Donatello never gave a damn about me. I was only ever a tool he could use to his own benefit. Any connection I thought I felt on the yacht, or that night in the hotel meets the hard wall of his disinterest—and then it shatters into a million pieces.

Weeks later and he can barely even look at me.

The letters are a festering wedge between us. I haven't been able to bring myself to read them. Though I should. I *should* fearlessly stalk any hint of the truth—Donatello's feelings be damned.

I should look for any further justification to hate him more than I already do. He had no right to feel betrayed over some silly old letters. No right to look at me like I was the monster for wanting to read them.

No right to ignore me all over again.

His hate is poison—I physically feel the effects, weighing me down, turning every waking moment into an exhaustive effort. Sleeping is the only thing that holds interest.

At least then, I don't have to fight so hard. Try so hard.

I can imagine him in any way I want and trust that, at least until I wake up, that man will follow a predictable pattern. Only in dreams can I ever understand him.

The days devolve into a monotonous loop split between Havienna and the hospital. Ironically, despite the uneventful hours trickling by, I sense something building in the background, swelling to the forefront of everyone's consciousness.

Fabio seems to feel it. Mischa. Vin. Even Donatello.

Something is happening—though no one seems to know exactly what.

I can taste the tension prickling in the air, like lightning crackling before a storm.

And yet, the world seems at a standstill.

Until the second everything comes crashing like a dam breaking. It happens one morning, too quickly to even track. As soon as I wake up and spy the figure standing over me, I know in the pit of my soul that everything is about to change.

If he looked angry, I could understand that. Hateful, even. Vengeful—the way he appeared after he nearly let me fall off a cliff to my death.

Instead, his expression is eerily blank. I can't read him.

"Willow…" Even his voice lacks its characteristic cadence, so…cold. "The engagement is off," he says next. "You can go."

I hear each word resonate in slow, excruciating detail, but my brain can't match the meaning with his expression. There's no smile. No gloating taunt. Just a blank, lifeless mask that sends a punch of déjà vu through me—I've seen it before.

"Your father already sent a car to take you home."

Home. I blink, knowing that he's not referring to these decrepit, dusty-coated walls, but Stepanov manor. Away from here. From him.

You can go…

I have to hear those words replay in my mind a million times before they finally settle. All the while, he looks at me as if waiting for something. A reaction. For me to scream.

Jump. Attack.

Deep down, I think I always knew it was coming.

I saw the way he watched me with Vincenzo. Always watching, every time we traded smiles or interacted.

Lurking just beyond the bed, Donatello would stare, agonized. I'd ignored the expression at first, trying to rationalize it as concern for his nephew, nothing more.

But I think I've always known the truth.

The same way I never belonged in Mischa's world, I never belonged in his, either.

I was always a thorn in his side. A burden he never wanted.

Whatever happened at the hotel was a brief lapse in judgment—but just that. Brief.

He never wanted me. Not then. Not now.

Seeing me with Vincenzo must make that sink in for him, clearer than ever. I think that's why he might have sold me in the first place, in the aftermath of Olivia's death and my father's betrayal.

I was of no use to him anymore. Just a reminder of his pain.

A burden.

By the time I fully process what he's said, he's already gone. Alone, I crawl from the bed and dress blindly without even examining exactly what I'm putting on. There's nothing of mine to take anyway—everything in this room has been borrowed or stolen.

Still, I can't resist grabbing a silver box and the contents I'd painstakingly returned to it. With it hidden in my fist, I move on autopilot, descending the steps to find a car already waiting for me.

My heart swells as I see the driver. Evgeni, but the only greeting I can muster is the shadow of a smile.

He wasn't bluffing this time—he truly wants me gone.

Racing from Havienna in the direction of Stepanov manor, everything that happened since I left could have been some vivid, horrifying nightmare. An endless dream.

When the house is just a speck in the distance, it feels as good a time as any to finally read the letters, fishing them from the silver box.

By reading them, I can finally put my curiosity to rest and leave the mystery of Donatello Vanici behind for good.

With every page I consume, more of the world falls away. The past words of Olivia and Donatello entrance and consume. Soon, I'm stuck in the past, my heart racing, throat so dry it's painful to swallow.

I don't love you, Olivia wrote on one of the final notes. *I don't. I don't know what this is. But when I'm with you, at least I'm not invisible for once. You see me. Maybe that means something.*

Maybe it means nothing.

It's wrong, either way. I know this is wrong.

But Donatello's name isn't written across the top of the crumbled note. It's shorter, and I read it a million times before my brain finally makes sense of it.

Gino.

DON

I'm ready for Fabio when he arrives, waiting on the porch as he drives up. The knowledge that at least one person will revel in my supposed change of heart is a surprisingly pathetic crutch, but I lean on it anyway.

Fabio will reaffirm what I know in my gut. Letting her go was the right thing.

"Where is Willow?" Fabio calls out the second he parks in the driveway.

There's no point in drawing it out. "She's gone," I say as he exits his car. "I sent her back to Mischa this morning. In exchange, he'll provide Vincenzo with security and a trust from the Stepanov estate."

I should sound happier. That outcome is all I wanted from the very start.

"You can help tidy up the details, but it's done," I add.

"Donatello." Fabio's voice is stern enough that I lose track of the relief I should feel. Fuck, he should look happy, at least. Not…

Terrified.

"What?"

He observes me for so damn long. I'm almost convinced he's frozen in place by the time he finally inclines his head toward the house. "We should discuss this inside."

"Discuss what? Don't tell me you plan to advocate for this fucking marriage after all?" I laugh at the thought. "I did what you wanted. I chose peace—"

"The bloodwork came back," he says, but he sounds too stiff. Cold. He fishes a folded document from his pocket, clenching it carelessly in a fist. "I have to even wonder if you planned this. Maybe you did. Maybe you're really sick enough."

"What are you talking about?"

He extends the page to me. Printed on it is a brief list of medical terms. The blood test results.

As expected, there's no familial relation. Though I doubt that revelation is responsible for Fabio's disgusted glance.

"Mischa hasn't seen it yet, I'll have you know," he says tiredly. "This time, you can face him alone. I'm done trying to clean up your messes. Frankly, I… I can't even look at you."

"What am I supposed to be reading?" I demand.

Then I realize that one line is highlighted. **HCG: abnormal**. That term…

"I peed on a stick," Liv told me, her eyes sparkling. *"It was positive, but the doctor still did a blood test to check my HCG levels. They're elevated, Don…'*

"Don't be stupid, Donatello," Fabio snaps, pulling me back to the present. "It's early, but a blood test would detect something. I'm sure even you knew that."

He waits.

Then he sighs.

"Willow is pregnant. Congratulations."

MENDED CROWN

1

WILLOW

I understand just how fragile the world is. So delicate, in fact, that even a simple drop of blood can tip the scales.

It's happened before. Seven years ago, blood ties were the catalyst to what turned my life on its head. I lost everything, and in the aftermath, became someone else. These recent events are merely history repeating itself—though, laughably, this time based solely on a mistake.

I'm sure of that, despite what everyone else thinks.

Why waste any energy getting upset over a lie?

Mischa did. Anger was his initial reaction, and he shouted in a voice so booming it reached the furthest wings of the manor. I had no idea what he might do. Ironically, a silence fell afterward, so thick that not even the children seemed willing to break it. For days, that suffocating quiet lingered.

I was sure it would last forever.

Finally, a giddy sense of denial broke through. It's like some internal switch was flipped within everyone, and they all woke up determined to ignore and forget. The past few weeks could have been written off as a crazed, shared nightmare—if it weren't for the injuries Ellen and Eli still sport.

And the subtle tension looming over everything like a sharpened knife, waiting to descend at a moment's notice.

Even so, I should be the most eager to play along with the shared denial. Ignore and smile and clamor for breakfast like nothing has happened.

Live on as though Donatello Vanici isn't lurking somewhere beyond these walls.

But he is.

So, I don't leave my room. Not to eat. Not to mingle with the others. I just sit in a corner by the window and read the same series of crumbled pages over and over. They've become worn beneath my fingertips, creased so badly in places the slightest pressure could tear them apart.

I've come to know each passage by heart, anyway. They're my only tie to reality, reinforcing the darkness lurking beyond these walls. Greedily, I scan the gnarled handwriting and sniff the cologne faintly clinging to the paper.

I tell myself that the pain I feel stabbing through my chest with every breath is just a necessary evil in a quest to know more. The truth? Some sick part of me has grown addicted to the agony aroused by anything connected to him.

Masochism alone explains why I keep re-reading these letters more than anything else. The fact is, despite days of study, I still haven't deciphered their meaning in full. At the same time, they remain my only clue to the past, and what really served as the catalyst to the downfall of Donatello Vanici.

I used to think my memories held the answers, but I was wrong. This stack of crumpled letters does, because Olivia, Donatello's wife, wrote them to another man—my biological father, Gino Mangenello. They lack the emotional passion of her letters to her husband. They're blunter, more honest, conveying stark desperation that strikes me to my core.

I parse through the potential explanations, ignoring the obvious answer. Maybe she was lonely and desperate enough to seek out the companionship of her husband's closest ally? Perhaps Donatello disapproved of their friendship?

Or she betrayed him by sleeping with his righthand man behind his back.

I keep picturing her, that beautiful face and hazel eyes. I can't ever recall seeing deception in them. Just sadness. A sadness so heavy a child could never comprehend it.

Years later, I'm only getting a mere taste of that despair. It's emptiness. A hollow agony you can only feel after loving someone so much it desolates you by the end. Then, to top it off, you watch them throw that love away. Throw *you* away as if you never mattered. In the grand scheme, you were worth nothing.

And you'd do anything in the world to fill the gaping wound left behind. Anything. Even tell yourself that you hated him from the very start. If you have to turn that man into a monster, you will. No matter how you distort the past to believe it, you do until it becomes the only truth.

Until the pain can diminish to the point that you can breathe again and even dream of saying his name without screaming.

He's already taken so much from me, and yet it feels like this is his final, cruelest game played at my expense. Take from Mischa something he can never, ever erase and rub his nose in their twisted feud.

I want to believe that. Over the past few days, I've convinced myself that it might be true. Revenge is all that drives him. That and hate. He hates me…

Then I remember that Donatello wasn't who pushed our relationship past that invisible boundary.

I did.

In this instance, he isn't the monster.

I am. Only my victims are far more numerous, and unlike Donatello, I didn't have the decency of leaving them behind. Every day, I serve as a living reminder of the damage I've caused, and nothing assuages the guilt.

"Willow?" A tiny knock on the door heralds the presence of the only person more persistent than Ellen in striving to visit me every day. He sounds winded as if he ran here, forsaking playtime with the others. Still, I hear the thud of him resolutely claiming his place in the hall, most likely sitting cross-legged with a puzzle or book to pass the time.

For a moment, he's as silent as always. Then he sighs.

"Willow... Are you sick? Is that why you're going to a hospital?"

A hospital. I haven't heard of such a trip directly, and I can't ignore a sense of dread prickling down my spine.

"I hope you feel better soon," he adds. "But I don't want you to go away. Okay?"

I don't move to reassure him. Deep down, I can't ignore the small voice in my head warning that my going away might be the best option for everyone involved.

The only option.

"Willow?" A stern series of knocks rattles my door.

I must have drifted off, because at some point, Eli was replaced by a taller figure who isn't content to hold their vigil in silence.

"Willow?" The doorknob is tested once more before the door itself opens from the outside, revealing Ellen, framed in the doorway.

I barely manage to shove the letters under my bed before standing to take her in. This isn't a regular visit. She looks tired. Her hair is loosely piled atop her head, her plain blue dress overbearing amid the gray daylight filtering in from outside. With a sigh, she wipes her hands on her skirt and enters the room, closing the door behind her.

I stiffen. She isn't one to barge into a situation unannounced. For days, she's let me hold my silent vigil, respecting the unspoken boundary of a closed door.

One look at her face, and I know that whatever drove her to break that truce is serious. Serious enough that her forced, thin smile doesn't even reach her eyes.

"You haven't been eating," she says tiredly, glancing at the plate left on my bedside table. The untouched oatmeal looks ice-cold now, flanked by a bowl of sad-looking fruit and deflated toast.

"Willow..." With a sigh, Ellen turns the full brunt of her gaze to me. Her lips part, only to purse before parting again. Finally, she swallows as if gathering up the nerve to speak. "Tomorrow, we've arranged an appointment with a doctor," she says softly.

I don't know how to process that—though at least Eli's statements make sense. It seems he's been eavesdropping again, though at least he felt fit to tell me. Apart from knocking on my door throughout each day, neither Mischa nor Ellen has spoken more than a handful of words to me directly.

Not that I can blame them. I've buried myself in old love letters and silence—but they can't escape reality so easily. My heart pangs as I meet Ellen's gaze and examine her delicate features in full.

It kills me to see the hurt in her eyes. At the same time... I can't feel anything. It's like I'm numb, an observer unconnected to unfolding events. I merely watch.

"I know that this isn't a comfortable conversation, but it's one we need to have," Ellen continues. "Whatever decision... We should get confirmation."

There is no mention of whether Donatello will be there.

Because, even if invited, he wouldn't come.

DON

"You look like hell," a voice declares, startling me awake. "Don't tell me you've slept here all night, Don."

If the speaker is referring to the hard as hell leather chair I'm slumped in currently, they're right. Groaning, I open my eyes to a dimly lit room where a scowling figure watches me from beyond an open door. "Fabio? You decided the first fucking thing you wanted to do at the ass crack of dawn was visit me?"

Apparently so, not that this is shaping up to be a pleasant visit. He's standing with his arms crossed, that judgmental look on his face. The same one he's been sporting for the past two weeks, in fact—not that I can blame him.

The truth is, I'm lucky he hasn't cut me off completely.

Still, I bristle at his arrival, feeling like a child on the verge of a scolding.

"Why are you here? Let me guess. Mischa's decided to launch another attack on my life? Let's hope he doesn't go after Vin at least."

I'm only half joking.

Thankfully, Fabio doesn't seem like someone desperate to prevent an assassination attempt. If anything, he looks more like a man dragged here against his will.

"There have been some developments," he says, utilizing the stern tone he prefers to deliver bad news in. "Gregori Saleri is dead. Best to get the good news out of the way before giving the bad."

"Good news," I say, swiping at my eyes as I sit upright. My brain sluggishly processes the bombshell. Unlike Fab, I don't consider it good news at all.

"What happened? It seems too much of a coincidence if the old man dropped dead of a heart attack."

"It happened last night, apparently," Fabio says grimly. "There aren't too many details out now. The only bit of information we can be sure of is that Mateo is now solely in charge."

"That is bad fucking news." I brace my hands over the desk before me, scrambling to get my bearings. As Fabio insinuated, I fell asleep here—again. If sleep is even the right word for maybe an hour of unconsciousness. "You're only this morbid when you're stressed. Even if he was working with our enemy, I don't see how his death is a good thing. Especially for the girl—" I jerk my chin in the vague direction of the room where Kisa Salvatore is sleeping. First her father, now Gregori.

"Good news is relative," Fabio says with a shrug. "In comparison to the bad, at least. Keep in mind, Don, that I'm not telling you this because you deserve to know," he adds to preface this unannounced worse news than the death of my enemy. "Call me naïve, but I still think you should have a heads-up…"

To heighten the drama, he sighs before pursing his lips in disapproval.

"Any minute, Fabio," I snap.

"Word is the Stepanovs have booked a private appointment at the hospital for some time this week—"

"When?" I'm on my feet as my brain jumps to the obvious conclusion as to what that private appointment could mean. Son of a bitch, I was hoping even Mischa wouldn't go that route. "What time? Tell me!"

Fabio sighs again. "I'm not telling you when. Not even which day."

"But you know?"

He raises an eyebrow. "Could be tomorrow. Could be ten days from now. It doesn't really matter. Don't get the wrong idea, Donatello. This isn't a heads-up so you can intervene. If anything, I want you to show restraint. This is just so that you can prepare yourself in case…"

His low tone alludes to an outcome even he has the tact not to voice.

"In case they terminate the pregnancy." Saying it out loud guts me. Could Mischa really be that cynical? Though, hell, if I had a daughter, would I encourage her to do any different?

"Don…" Fab frowns, wringing his hands together. He's wearing a suit as usual, but the tie is crooked. He probably rushed here to make sure I heard it from him first. "I honestly don't know the details. We're lucky that one of my contacts at the hospital thought to notify me. But if it is to… At least this way, it won't come as a shock."

"A shock?" I hiss and slam a fist against the desk, so hard pain shoots through my knuckles. So much for restraint. "Do you even hear yourself?"

"Do you?" Fabio counters, crossing his arms. "I'm trusting you to handle this maturely. Barging into the hospital will only result in you having some startled nurse alert the authorities. This is for the best, Don."

The best.

God and Fabio must share the same sick fucking sense of humor—because that's all this is. A twisted joke at my expense, and Mischa gets the last laugh.

Ha ha.

But it's not one damn bit funny. No…

The potential consequences of this mess are too twisted to explore in full. It *must* be a joke. If only I could get ahold of Mischa or his lying daughter, confirm the ruse, and put this all to rest.

Fuck.

"If I could just be there," I muse out loud—but I'm not thinking of the hospital. Instead, I picture Stepanov Manor and its intricate layout. "Mischa's security is good, but no structure on earth is impenetrable…"

"Not this again. You need to slow down," Fabio warns, surging forward. "Listen to me, Donatello. Plotting and scheming won't help anyone—"

"Don't tell me what the hell I should or shouldn't do."

Fabio winces at the fury in my tone, but so do I. Anger toward him is unwarranted, but I can't fucking help it. "Not after your 'advice' got me into this fucking mess in the first place. I think I'm done listening to you—"

"Are you saying that this is my fault?" He inclines his head, his eyes narrowed to slits. Somewhere at the back of my mind, an alarm bell goes off. I've pushed him to an emotional state the man rarely reaches. Enraged. But, like always, his true emotions are hidden behind such a carefully crafted veneer that it's hard to tell what he's thinking at all.

My own expressions aren't so fucking polished. In the reflection cast over the blade of a small knife resting in front of me. It's hers—who knows why I've kept it all this time. I grab the hilt to see myself more clearly, and goddamn what a poor son of a bitch I make. My eyes are bloodshot. I haven't really slept in… I can't remember. My hair is a mess, but it's the look in my eyes that I find the most unfamiliar. The most unsettling.

I don't recognize this pathetic son of a bitch. Deep down, this man knows exactly what Fabio's been hinting at.

This is my fault. And hell, I deserve it after all the shit I've done. My punishment.

Absently, I stow the blade in my pocket, running my thumb over the sharpened edge.

"You need to think clearly," Fabio insists, coming to stand before me. He braces his hands over the desk, his expression contorted into a forced imitation of his usual calm. But he isn't calm now. A blind man could see that. "Plotting a way into Stepanov Manor isn't going to fix anything," he insists. "What we need to be focused on is Vincenzo. Getting him out of the hospital, for one. According to his doctors, he's ready to be discharged as long as we arrange for daily visits from a nurse. Have you even been to see him lately? He asked about you…"

Fabio's gotten his wish. Instead of Willow Stepanova, someone else just as important takes center focus. Guilt is a gnawing parasite feeding off what little sanity I have left. Since that bombshell about the blood test broke, I haven't set foot in the hospital, not even to visit Vin.

I'm too much of a coward to face him.

"Don?" Fabio waves his hand in front of me. "Did you hear me?"

I stopped listening. Not even my old friend has the answer to the problems facing me now. Still, I'm driven to ask, "How can I even look at him?"

"Don…" Fabio blinks, baffled by the question. In truth, there's no good answer.

After seven years of believing the worst—thanks to my lies—he finally has his Safy back. Only now I've gone and…

"I'll tell you how." Fabio slams his hand over the desk, sending a nearby pen rolling off the edge. "You focus only on what you can change. Getting Vincenzo somewhere safe? That's fully in your control. As for the rest? You put it out of your mind. You have to, Donatello. You'll drive yourself mad if you don't. One thing at a time, and only what's within your control."

But he's forgetting that Safy… Willow—she is fully in my control. If I can reach her, I can demand an answer either way.

What will she do if she really is pregnant? End it?

"You want me to focus? Then I need to know the truth. I'll ask you one more time to get me an audience with Mischa. Nicely," I add, meeting his gaze. "If you want me to do this your way, then you owe me that. If not, I'll do it on my own, and I don't think you'll find my methods very diplomatic."

He raises an eyebrow. "You think that this is the time to be giving out ultimatums?" His polished mask cracks further. "Seriously? I know that deflection is one of your primary tactics, but I don't understand how you can even turn this on me."

"How?" I incline my head sharply, eyeing him up and down. "You insisted I work with Mischa one on one. *You* agreed I should marry her—"

"And you promised me that you wouldn't touch her," Fabio counters. "Don't turn away one of the few allies you have left, Don. I know that self-sabotage is another one of your defining traits. Frankly, I'm not in the mood to have you go on a downward spiral. You want to play with ultimatums? How about I set one of my own? You owe it to me to do what I say. Stay out of this. You let Mischa and anyone associated with him come to you, but you don't go looking for a fight. Not in this instance, because I can tell you, Don, that you don't have a leg to stand on anymore. If this was what you wanted all along, then congratulations, you've truly made Mischa pay for what he did to Vincenzo. At least you didn't kill anyone."

His face is red, the veins in his neck distended. I've never seen him this riled, not even during my lowest trips to rock bottom. It figures. Even high on heroin and drunk out of my mind, I still showed better judgment than sleeping with Willow Stepanova.

"I'm sorry, Fab," I say. "But if it's true? If she really is…" I force myself to grate the word through gritted teeth. "If she really is pregnant?"

Fabio looks away rather than answer. He knows what will happen. If it's true, I couldn't just ignore it. I can't stay away and wait for Mischa to stew and plot his next round of revenge.

I couldn't ignore her, either. If Fabio thinks I've won this war, then she's gone and crowned herself the grand champion of it. She got exactly what she wanted all along —revenge.

She may not have my life in her hands, but it's damn close. Would she be cruel enough to lord that control over me?

Could I even blame her if she did?

Fabio's right, though even he has enough tact not to state it outright. This is my fault. I fucked up, and in this scenario, there is no easy way out. Not for me and not for her. No one wins at the end of this game, and neither Mischa nor I have a damn say in it.

Just her. Willow Stepanova.

Her choice controls everything hanging in the balance, and for the life of me, I have no idea what that means.

But I know exactly what it is that I want.

Badly enough that even Fabio and his logic can't derail me.

I need to face her. I need to see her.

And for what it's worth, I need to state my case.

If not for myself, then for *them*—an unborn child brought into existence through no fault of its own.

To do that, I'll flaunt whatever norms I have to.

I'll fight Mischa Stepanov himself.

EVGENI

"It's like this motherfucker doesn't exist," Mischa snarls, slamming his hands over the surface before him—a desk overburdened with tax documents and property listings, all stemming from the attack on the harbor.

In the span of time since, we've come no closer to unearthing the figure at the heart of it all. In a sense, Mischa is right. Whoever this mystery figure is, he's damn near invisible, on paper at least. The only clue we have to go on is a name. Jonathan.

That, and the secrets held by a woman who seems determined not to reveal them.

"There hasn't been any sign for weeks," I point out, frowning at the prospect of what that could mean. "There's always the possibility he's gone underground."

"Or, he's planning something," Mischa says. "I've kept eyes on the Saleris, and they've been far too quiet lately. Word is

Gregori has gone silent to his allies. We need to know why. I want you on it. You haven't gotten anything from *her*?" His disgusted tone alludes to exactly who he's referring to.

"No," I say stiffly. I can't resist casting a glance toward the corner of the manor Briar Winthorp has claimed as her own. "It could be that she doesn't know. Or…"

"She's been playing us from the start." Head cocked, Mischa eyes the materials scattered before him as if they might contain the answer. Abruptly, he looks up, fixing me with a probing stare. "You still want to handle this your way?"

My way being sans torture or more brutal methods. Turning my gaze to the ceiling, I mull over the answer. "I think using violence would only give her more of a reason to lie. She seems like the type who won't break easily."

"Fine. Then you find a way to make her cooperate," he growls. "I don't trust anyone else around that witch."

His voice booms to the furthest corners of the study, but the Winthorp woman is the source of just a fraction of the rage simmering within him.

The main culprit is a topic I know better than to broach without tact. To stave off the inevitable, I bite my lip hard enough to sting—but even the taste of blood doesn't serve as a big enough deterrent. Finally, I ask, "And what about Willow and Vanici?"

He doesn't answer, but what can he say?

With a swipe of his hand, he clears the desk instead, sending an array of documents and pens to the floor. The resulting thuds serve as a symbolic representation of the bellowed insults he doesn't voice. Amid the chaos, he strolls to the window overlooking this half of the property.

"We can't afford to be caught off guard again," he says with his back to me. His voice is eerily level, but I feel myself tense, unnerved by the display of calm. "I trust you to handle the Winthorp whore—but I need you to find out what she's hiding. By any means necessary, short of killing her. You have my permission to do whatever it takes. In the meantime, I will handle Vanici."

That statement rings far more ominous than it should. Mainly because I doubt he'll be under the same restrictions I am.

I can't kill Briar Winthorp.

But when it comes to the mess Donatello Vanici may have caused, who knows what Mischa will determine to be adequate punishment.

Something tells me that even death won't be good enough.

The potential consequences of another cold war weigh on my mind as I leave the study and turn aimlessly down another hall.

I nearly run into a figure racing from the opposite direction.

"Sir." A man in black fatigues skids to a stop paces away—but his sheepish expression warns me that he isn't here on official business. "Your guest wanted me to tell you—"

"My guest?" Damn it. Mischa apparently wasn't kidding about the level of control I'd have over a certain unwelcome visitor. As far as the rest of the manor is concerned, she is *my* responsibility. "What does she want?"

"Uh… Tea," the man says. His lips twitch, contorting his mouth into a pained grimace. Though, I suspect his discomfort stems from holding back laughter more than anything else.

"I'll get it," I say, heading for the kitchens.

With Mischa's vague permission of "any means necessary," to go off of, I contemplate if poison would be a sanctioned method.

***

I always hated the saying "when shit hits the fan." It seemed like a lazy summation when a simpler expression would suffice.

Until now. The only terms that come remotely close to describing the mess that has become the relationship between the Stepanovs and Donatello Vanici is a comparison to literal shit flying in every which direction. Never in my worst estimations of how bad things could get did I ever calculate something like this.

At least now I can finally grasp a fraction of the irrational anger Mischa must have felt all this time. To have a danger so close to the very family you'd do anything to protect. Any man with a soul would give in to that rage.

And only God knows what Mischa might be driven to do now. I should be by his side to minimize the risk—not here, on the opposite end of the manor, playing babysitter to a woman who serves as just as big a threat as Vanici.

If not bigger.

My steps slow as I round the deserted wing Mischa ensconced her in. I smell her before I even reach the room. Her presence is like a fucking viper's or some other insidious creature meant to ensnare and poison.

She is poison. Even her voice, seeping through the door as I approach, has corrosive properties.

"Did you bring my tea?" The door opens before I can knock, revealing her leaning against the doorframe, her eyes narrowed, blond hair piled loosely on her head.

The disheveled appearance takes a back seat to another glaring detail—she must have been in the bath, the most likely explanation for the towel slung across her hips— leaving the rest of her bare. Water drips from her body onto the polished floor beneath her feet. She must be freezing, and a quick glance at her breasts reveals hardened nipples alluding to that very fact.

With an exaggerated sigh, she extends her hand toward me without attempting to cover herself. "I hope this time you didn't forget the honey or the sugar."

"You still owe me answers," I point out, keeping my gaze focused on her face. For the past two weeks, that void has loomed between us, not that she seems inclined to fill it.

With Mischa preoccupied, she's been able to go unnoticed, keeping her secrets close to the vest. But who knows when he'll come to his senses and recall the thorn nestled in the heart of his family?

Or decide to destroy her completely.

"You're grumpy today." She reaches for the mug, but I step past her, forcing my way inside.

For all her bravado, she's barely made herself comfortable here despite the passing weeks. Apart from the water dripping over the floor, the rest of the room looks untouched, the bed neatly made. Remove the woman from view, and this room could be as abandoned as the rest of the wing.

But judging from her ripe, slow grin, she's right at home in the Stepanov mansion. It's her mystery that confuses more than anything else. She hides her secrets well behind those glinting blue eyes, but I'm tired of waiting.

I slam the door behind me and cross over to a wooden table positioned near a row of windows overlooking a part of the east lawn. There, I set the mug of tea down.

"Forget the honey," I say to her, claiming a nearby chair. "I would much prefer honesty. You've had days to lurk in the shadows, avoiding any direct questions, but time's up. I want to know everything about your little friend. And I won't accept the excuse that you're still healing. In fact." I grab her tea before she can reach for it, taking a sip of it myself. "If you don't start talking, I'll inflict an injury of my own."

She laughs, slinking into my line of sight. At a glance, no one would be able to discern the wound on her thigh from this angle. But lurking behind those glittering eyes is a shadow that grows more prevalent the closer she comes. With a sigh, her smile falls, revealing a glimpse of the real woman beneath the poise and smirks. Instead of mocking and secretive, this woman?

She's terrified.

But not of me. Her eyes dart to the windows, and I imagine her picturing whatever she believes lies beyond these walls. Perhaps another sniper waiting to silence her forever.

"You're safe here," I say grudgingly, though, in reality, I should want her scared and skittish. It might prompt her to open her mouth a little faster than she seems inclined to. "But if you want to test your luck on the outside, then I suggest you continue not to give Mischa a reason to keep you around."

Her upper lip quirks, reviving that cat-like grin. "He seems to have plenty of reasons not to remember little old me at the moment," she murmurs, toying with the edge of her towel.

Damn. I risk taking my gaze from her face to watch her twisting fingers, envisioning just how many messes she's had her hands in. The more I've mulled over her connection to the violence plaguing Hell's Gambit, the more convinced I am that she's played a much larger role than she's alluded to.

The only question is how.

"Have a seat."

"Give me my tea." She stalks forward, swaying her hips to jostle the positioning of the towel. Deliberately, I suspect. Whenever she's threatened, resorting to her sexuality seems to be her one tried and true trick. Running is the other tactic she loves to employ.

I focus on her eyes again, unsure of which method she'll fall back on now. Heavy-lidded. Her gaze sweeps over me, lingering on any potential spots I may be concealing a weapon. Even while feigning poise, she's still on guard. As expected, her sexuality is her chosen crutch. She runs her fingers across the length of her towel, drawing attention to the pale legs exposed from the knees down.

Gritting my teeth, I don't take my eyes off of her face, ignoring anything lower. Like the pale throat jerking around a hard swallow...

With bold, sure steps, she approaches me and wraps her fingers around the handle of the mug, easing it from my grasp.

I let her take it, noting everything from the way she takes a furtive sip down to the fact that her eyes keep drifting to the door.

"Run if you want," I tell her, leaning back into my chair. "I'm sure Mischa will remember your presence if you come traipsing past his children's nursery half naked and dripping wet."

She laughs, spinning to face me as she continues to sip from her tea. "If I'm dripping wet, I can assure you that it wouldn't be for his *children's* benefit. Just yours."

My eyes narrow before I remember to school my expression. Damn her. I've known women like her before, at least in their beauty and confidence. I've just never met anyone so damn bold in flaunting it. If she thought that by stripping herself naked, she could manipulate me into doing her bidding, I have no doubt that she would.

Honestly, I should probably be alarmed that she hasn't. She must think I'm above such a display, which means she has a different ploy up her sleeve. Luckily for her, I have my own in mind.

Bluntness is the only option worth trying.

"Tell me the truth now or so help me God, I'll drag you from the manor myself and see who comes to claim you."

"Ah, but you don't believe in God," she remarks innocently before taking another sip. Her blue eyes sparkle with mischief. "After all, how could an omnipotent being be so cruel as to put you through the life you've endured? Tsk,

tsk, Evgeni. What a life it's been. No wonder you're so mistrustful and, dare I call it jaded?"

I bristle at the reminder that she knows more of my past than I'd like. In fact, I don't even know how much she's aware of. Which brings up another important factor weighing against her continued presence here.

"You seem to have a close association with the sorts of men who know about my past. Men, I might add, who I wouldn't consider allies of Mischa. Another mark against you in the friend or foe column, and I'll give you a hint— I'm not leaning toward friend."

"So, what are you leaning toward?" She sets her mug down, arching her waist to strain the state of her towel a little further. "Should I inform you that two weeks is more than enough time to wreak havoc if I wanted to? And yet all is well." She gestures around us with a wave of her hand. "No more explosions. No attacks. No kidnapped daughters or injured little boys. While I've been around, everything has been safe and sound."

Which is exactly what I'm afraid of. The fact that she's taken care to point it out, only alludes to how strange this momentary peace has been. It feels less idyllic and more unsettling—like the calm before the storm.

And something tells me that the woman before me is the equivalent of a dark cloud, heralding the first drops of rain.

"I want you to tell me what you're after. What you want. Why you're here. Considering you've barely left this room, I don't think you're inclined to spark much of a family reunion, either. So, if you aren't planning to 'wreak havoc' and you've changed your mind about supposedly wanting an audience with Mischa, then why are you here?"

Her eyes flit away from me, and an answer springs to the forefront of my mind.

"You're hiding."

She laughs, but her smile isn't quite so wide anymore. "You certainly do love to play detective—"

"I do," I say over her. "In fact, I've done my fair share of research on you these past few days." Utilizing Louie, one of the men she pumped for intel on me, in fact. "I've learned that you haven't left much of a paper trail since your initial disappearance over seven years ago. There is no record of a marriage. In fact, there seems to be no record that you've had a son at all. Can you tell me what kind of woman would lie about something like that?"

Though if I did have any doubts about that last part, the way her lip quirks into a frown gives me reason not to. She's a good actress, but not that good. The boy wasn't a lie, which means she's been off the grid since before he was even born. Why go to such lengths? I don't think the fear of Mischa alone explains it.

"If you think I'm such a liar, then why am I still here?" She extends her hands and shrugs. "It seems like you must need me for something, Mr. Evgeni. I think I should be the one asking you to explain your motives."

"My interest is in *information*," I snap. "Tell me everything you know. Unless... That's been your plan from the start. To stall and obscure."

She smiles wider. "Now, why would I want to do a thing like that?" Her tone alone would be enough to confirm my hunch—that's been her game from the start. But no... There's something in her eyes...

And the real answer comes to mind as if planted there.

"You're afraid. You don't know what he's planning, and you can't anticipate his next move. Staying here isn't your ideal course of action, but you don't have a better idea, and you're too afraid to confront him directly or try to weasel your way back into his inner circle. That's the real truth, isn't it?"

She's still smirking, but a glimpse of emotion flashes in those blue eyes, and I feel confident enough to name it this time. *Fear.*

"You're as much in the dark as we are, and, even worse, you aren't sure which tidbits of intel you know could prove your case as an ally, or damage you further. I don't think you're half as innocent in this as you pretend to be. My guess is that you never planned on sticking around this long, and now you're in a bind. A smart man would call your bluff and attempt to glean from you whatever he could; however, he could."

"Is that an allusion to torture, Evgeni?" She crosses her arms, her head inclined. "I wouldn't be surprised if it were.

It's only natural for a man such as yourself to revert to his old ways when challenged."

My spine goes rigid. She got the rise out of me that she wanted, and it's too late to disguise it. Damn her.

"However, I will spare you the dramatic descent into your old naughty habits," she scolds mockingly. "Perhaps you're right, and I've depleted my bag of tricks, forcing me to rely on the kindness of Mischa Stepanov—" She laughs, her serious expression cracking. "Does that even sound likely to you?"

"No, but then again, nothing you've done seems to square with anything most women would be 'likely' to do. Most women would never presumably leave their young son in the hands of a monster, for example."

"I suggest you leave your opinions on women and your expectations for them to yourself," she replies dryly. "I don't think you're in any position to judge anyone—"

"So then tell me the truth, and there will be nothing to judge. What are you after? Why stay here and not try to leave? Not even to find your son, if you're so afraid of this man. This Jonathan."

If I'm not mistaken, she cringes at the name. "I think the question you should be asking is, what kind of man would inspire so much fear in a woman that she wouldn't seek out her own child? That she would rather hide behind Mischa Stepanov, the man who is responsible for the deaths of her own father and brother."

"If I had a child of my own, no one would keep me from them. No one."

She frowns at that, turning her back to me. I've spoiled her game. Deep down, I think she's been dancing around the truth—there's no grand master plan to explain her presence. She's merely a coward.

"I'm going to approach Mischa directly and see what he wants to do with you." I brace my hands against the table and stand. It irritates me to realize that if her aim has been to hide and stall, I've done more than a little to assist her in that effort. I convinced Mischa to take her in and give her a room that isn't a jail cell. I've submitted to be her errand boy.

No more. There are far more important things to deal with, other than Briar Winthorp. Willow, for one. With a sigh, I head for the door—and nearly run into the woman who darts to block my path.

"Wait!" She places her hand on my chest, and I swear I can sense her pulse through the trembling fingers. For once, she doesn't attempt to disguise her nervous energy—it seeps from her, and her expression openly displays one overriding emotion—terror. "You want to hear me beg, is that it? Fine. You send me away, and he'll kill me. Want me to tell you the real reason why I've allowed myself to hide out here like some goddamn criminal? It's because I don't know what he's planning next. I don't!" Her voice breaks, rising in pitch.

No one is this good of an actress.

"Then what are you so damn afraid of?" I demand, pushing against her until she lets her hand fall away.

Her bottom lip trembles, but she fights to keep her expression blank. "I… I'm afraid that I'm next on his list of things to blow up. He has no reason to hurt Ali, but frankly, I've been waiting for him to storm this place since the day you brought me here. The fact that he hasn't isn't a comfort, and especially not after this long. The truth is that I don't have a damn clue what he might be up to. And I can assure you, Evgeni, that's not a good thing. Whatever happened at the hospital must have forced him to change course—"

"Stop speaking in riddles!" I grab her arm, dragging her closer.

Unlike our past encounters, she doesn't pull a knife out of her ass. She gasps instead, her eyes widening.

"You are going to tell me everything you do know," I warn her. "Starting from the beginning."

"Oh, I am?" That smirk returns, igniting a fire in those blue eyes. For a second, she appears as bold and confident as the first day I met her in Mrs. Stepanova's hospital ward.

And that smugness lasts the entirety of five seconds until I palm the back of her skull. A shudder runs through her, and I briefly consider how easy it would be to press too hard. To squeeze this delicate structure between both hands.

I've never killed someone in this way, but some detached part of me isn't unwilling to try. She would make for a tempting target.

"Tell me, or I'll—"

"He contacted me a year ago." The confession spills from her lips as that smug grin falls.

I step back, letting her go, and she scrambles to compose herself, wrenching her towel up to cover her torso.

"My life didn't end up like my darling younger sister's. I wasn't lucky enough to find myself a husband capable of funding the lavish lifestyle I'd grown up accustomed to. After what that monster did to my family, I was lucky to escape with pennies to my name."

"But you were married at some point," I say, hazarding a guess.

Her eyes gleam as she turns to the window, gazing at the impassive fields below.

"Married," she says dryly. "I found someone I thought I loved. I stayed with him. Lived with him. But, as it turns out, I don't know much about love after all."

"You left him," I say, another guess, but she shakes her head.

"No. He died… But the world kept spinning." Her brows furrow as if the concept is one she can't comprehend. "I thought everything was supposed to come to a crashing halt or something. That grief would consume me, and I wouldn't be able to go on. That I'd turn myself into a martyr and end my life in a nice, hot bath." She sighs and shrugs. "But I didn't. I felt nothing, and there were bills to pay and a life to lead. No time for tears or worry. No chance for heartbreak."

"But you had a son."

She nods. "I didn't expect him, mind you. In all honesty, my first impulse wasn't perhaps the most maternal. I never saw myself as the motherly type."

There's a blunt note of honesty in her voice I wouldn't expect. It's blatant and raw, with none of her usual bravado slathered over every word. It's brutal.

"What changed your mind?"

She shrugs again, her head tilted thoughtfully. "I had nothing left to lose, did I? No one else, and I'll admit to you, soldier—I may not understand love, but I'm not meant to be alone."

I raise an eyebrow. Is loneliness what drove her to a man who supposedly stole her child and sent her on the run for her life? Her expression is unreadable from here, and as if aware of me watching, she tilts her face further away.

"I can practically smell you judging me, such a noble man like yourself. But I have to wonder if my little niece, Willow, might be wondering the same things I was at that point in my life. A child brings so much change with them. And yet, sometimes the alternative seems just as daunting."

"Don't bring her into this," I warn, hating the anger leeching into my voice. She knows she hit a sore point, and like any worthy opponent, she's bound to dig in to inflict the deepest wound.

"Why should I? In fact, I think I know far better what she might be going through than you. Though, to be fair, I never had a child with a madman crime lord, merely an ex-Stepanov guard, if you were curious."

"We aren't talking about Willow," I warn. "We're talking about you."

"Yes." She nods. "And you want to hear all the nitty, gritty details, don't you? Well, I had Alexander, and I didn't turn into Mother Teresa overnight. Children are harder than they look. I knew early on that I wasn't cut out for it. I lacked my sister's nurturing instinct, you see. Perhaps I carried resentment toward my own neglectful mother? Who knows, but I found it hard."

"And so, you gave him away to the first man who came asking for him?"

She turns to face me slowly, and I realize that the brief glimpses of anger I've seen from her until now were part of her carefully crafted façade. Real rage on Briar Winthorp is volatile and ugly. Her eyes narrow, her upper lip pulls back from her teeth. Just as quickly, she banishes all emotion beneath a thin smile.

"Why, of course, I did. You've cracked the code, dear Evgeni, and figured me out, motives and all. What use is there for me to explain any further?" She throws her hands into the air and saunters past me for the door. "Our conversation is over, apparently—" She wrenches on the doorknob, revealing the empty hallway beyond. "Now get out—"

"I want to hear," I admit, hissing the admission through clenched teeth. "Or are you just afraid that the full truth will make you sound even worse than you already do?"

"Because you know everything." She laughs, inspecting me with a cold, raking glance. "You've birthed a child alone in a foreign hospital where only the janitor spoke broken English and helped you translate the stacks of paperwork the doctors dumped on you without explanation? You went through labor alone, with only the ashes of someone who gave a damn about you to keep you company? Then yes. You know exactly what that feels like."

The pain in her voice is evident, displacing the charm and leaving it harsh in the aftermath. This is the real Briar Winthorp. A woman left bitter and scarred by life, too cold to see past her own pain.

"Have you?" she prods.

"No. But I'd like to think that I wouldn't abandon any child of mine, no matter the circumstances."

"Oh?" She juts her chin defiantly. "Even if you had no love for the mother? My own dearest mother certainly felt that way when it came to me. She was forced to marry my father for survival, you see. I was just a casualty of that. But my sister? Did you ever hear the tragic story of sweet Ellen's conception?"

She laughs again, but it's a harsher sound. As the seconds tick by, it's as if she's shedding more of her carefree persona, exposing the simmering fury beneath.

"I'll skip the dramatics and give you the short version. My mother had an affair with one of my father's sworn enemies and birthed his child in secret. The catch? She actually loved him, and begged to keep her precious illegitimate child, no matter the cost. I think she convinced herself that I never knew."

She returns to the window, bracing her hands on the sill. As if in a choreographed motion, her hair uncoils from the mass atop her head, falling down her shoulders. Instantly, she resembles more of the disheveled woman lurking beneath the haughty act.

"She thought I never realized that I was always an afterthought to her. That her real daughter lurked in the basement, and while she treated me with care and affection, I never really had her love."

"Is that your justification for everything you've done?"

"Perhaps," she snaps. "Maybe I just like hearing how it sounds out loud? My poor little rich girl story."

"How does this tie into your relationship with this man you're so afraid of?"

"Because I learned that parents show their affection via money," she says coldly. "I have none. Had none. Perhaps the only way I knew to be a good mother was to give my son the only semblance of security and affection I understood."

"So, this man promised you money. Security. The Winthorp fortune?"

"I thought my mother was the only one to stray from her marriage," Briar continues as if I never spoke. "As it turns out, my father might have done the same long before she did. A man approached me when I was at my lowest, with a child I could barely care for on my own. He offered me a way to get Ali everything he was rightfully owed and more. I had no idea the price I would eventually have to pay."

"And what price is that?" I advance on her slowly, expecting her to dart out of reach—but she stays, her back rigid, eyes on the field.

"My soul," she says simply. "As it turns out, I had one left after all."

"So, this man, he claims to be a missing Winthorp heir?"

She exhales slowly and shrugs. "I have no definitive proof. He only showed me a birth certificate, but it seemed real enough. My father never legally recognized him, so he couldn't claim anything on his own."

Suddenly, one piece of this twisted puzzle makes sense. "He'd need a proxy if he hoped to get near the inheritance. Like your son, or Eli."

She nods. "Children from two known and registered Winthorp heirs. He could make a claim to the fortune and wrestle it away from Mischa Stepanov's grimy hands."

A decent plan—yet it sounds too damn simple, all things considered.

"What is it you aren't telling me?"

She spins to face me, but we're too close. Her breath grazes my lips as her eyes find mine, steely and impenetrable.

"I thought I knew what I was in for. That anything was worth securing Ali his future."

"And let me guess." I lower my mouth near her ear. "You had a miraculous change of heart and realized that you'd made a grave mistake."

"No," she says without an ounce of emotion. "I went along with whatever he wanted. I all but shoved my son into his hands, and I waited for the peace I think I was meant to feel. But do you know what happened instead? I looked upon my son one day, and love wasn't what I saw in his eyes. I saw myself staring back at me, and then I had a miraculous change of heart."

She is a damn good liar when she needs to be. I can't decide now if she's telling the truth. Maybe it's a little of both. She's still concealing something, dancing around a larger issue, and I'm tempted to wrap my hands around her throat and wring from her what I can. Anything.

But then she steps into me, pressing her body against the contours of mine.

"If you were a simpler man, this would be the part where I offer my body to you in the hopes that you'd take pity on me and bend yourself to my will. I could distract you…" She trails her fingers along my shoulder, down my chest. "Lure you into bed to dislodge everything I've said from your memory."

I shrug her off, and she chuckles, stumbling back a step. "But I forgot. You are Evgeni Volkov, the stone-cold soldier, loyal only to Mischa Stepanov and his family. So, I would need to devise a Plan B when it comes to dealing with someone such as yourself."

"And what is that?" Too late do I realize I've stepped right into the trap she's set.

Sure enough, a slow, ripe grin unfurls over that pink mouth. "Jonathan's plans extend beyond Mischa, and even me. He has his sights set on the Saleris for now, but I suspect within these past few weeks, both sides have worn out their welcome."

I frown. "I've had my men watching Mateo, but they've spotted nothing unusual."

"Because they aren't stupid enough to operate out in the open," she quips, her head cocked knowingly. "You'd need to look a little deeper to unearth anything they might be hiding. Underground perhaps."

"That hunch you had with the docks proved false. They've been abandoned, and there's been no sign of any activity whatsoever."

"On the surface," she murmurs. "But I suspect they're more active than you think."

And suddenly, I have a suspicion as to why she's hidden out here for so long. "You're waiting for a signal, aren't you? But it hasn't come. That's the real reason why you're cowering beneath the roof of a sister you resent. You're afraid he's written you off completely, and you have no other backup plan. You've been cut off."

"Oh, you make it sound so devious. But it's a good thing you initiated your interrogation when you did." She crosses to the bed and crouches, reaching beneath it. "I was just about to seek out my own answers, but I'd much prefer your company."

I try to hide my shock when I see just what she has—a rolled object that looks like a sleeping bag, dark enough to blend in with the shadows and initially go unnoticed. She unravels it from one end, exposing an array of equipment that seems eerily similar to the various items Mischa's detail are issued.

A flashlight, batteries, a dark jacket most likely stolen from one of the men, sturdy boots, and one object that draws my notice in particular—a knife.

"It seems like a strange tactic for a thief to divulge their stolen goods before one of the people they stole from," I point out.

Her smile resembles that of a cat toying with a baby bird. "If I believed you were willing to do anything about it, I wouldn't have shown you in the first place. But perhaps you aren't as rigid and chained to your rules as I thought. You came here, without your master, for a reason, and if you want answers, you'll come with me."

This woman… It's disarming how hard it is to predict her, and yet she somehow manages to act in a way that isn't the least bit surprising. Selfishness seems to be her one true motive, but—at least on the surface—her current proposal doesn't make any damn sense.

"Why wouldn't I have you tied down and beat the answers from you myself?"

"Oh," she purrs, rising to her feet. "I might have thought you were that sort of man once, but now I've changed my mind. It seems that you might be more…unorthodox than I gave you credit for. You were willing to torture me, after all. That is the kind of initiative needed to outsmart a man like Jonathan."

"You keep speaking in riddles."

She scoffs in exasperation, and once again, a hint of the real woman beneath the bravado peeks through. "Because you aren't listening. If you want answers, then come with me and find them. Otherwise, you can pretend to lock me up and throw away the key, but you know I'll find a way out. Somehow. Someway. Think of this offer as a truce, and believe me when I say that I won't extend this chance twice. Come with me."

"And what was your plan?" I demand, eyeing the items she stole. Among them is a packet of crackers. "Hide out in the woods and hope he forgets your existence?"

"No." She looks up at me, teeth bared, expression fierce. "My plan was to look past the maudlin Stepanov family drama and try to make up lost ground. He's planning something. I know Mischa has his own little plans in motion, but he doesn't know Jonathan the way I do. If you want to find out as well, then come with me."

"Why?" I'm genuinely curious—and on guard. "So you can lead me into a trap?"

Her smile widens. "No. Because, as you pointed out, I'm desperate, and the more silence comes from his end, the more uneasy I become. Something isn't right."

"If I come with you, it will be on my terms," I warn. "Not yours."

She grimaces, and I wonder if she truly thought I'd follow her lead with no questions. Then her resigned sigh gives me an answer—she was hoping I wouldn't.

"Fine. Tell Mischa so he can send out the hounds and make it painfully obvious that we're suspicious. That will surely lead to answers and totally won't drive Jonathan further underground."

"I said I'd go with you on my terms," I say. "But I never said I'd call in reinforcements. You've gotten your wish. I'll babysit you myself, though I think a smarter move would be to act on my previous suggestion to strap you down."

Her throat twitches, and I know that I hit the mark. Still, she expertly conceals any fear beneath another brazen grin.

"That would only slow us down," she says slyly. "I have a much better idea. We go see firsthand what Mateo Saleri and his papa are up to and garner answers. I have enough sense not to take silence as a good omen. So, are you with me or not?"

If I value my sanity, I should lock her in this room and mount my own search. But I can't deny that her intel hasn't proven false so far. I'm sure she has another motive up her sleeve. I'd be a fool not to take her hunch seriously.

Besides, Mischa's orders were crystal clear—any means necessary.

"Get dressed," I say, though she's already shimmying from her towel. "We'll leave within the hour."

"I knew you'd see reason," she simpers, now stark naked.

Internally I'm questioning everything she told me about her so-called past. As much as I want to ignore her completely, I can't escape the feeling that some sliver of truth was lumped within a few carefully crafted lies.

The hard part is to decipher which were which…

Without getting myself killed in the process.

4

———

DON

I love Vincenzo with all my fucking heart—literally. There shouldn't be room for anyone else in that shriveled, beaten shell. For a long damn time, I believed there wasn't.

Lo and behold, the chaos with the Stepanovs opened up a new space after all. Within that neglected crevice grows something I never in a million years would have expected to feel again. It's so fragile and alien I don't even know what to name it.

Hope? That's too strong a term. Maybe just a chance. A chance for something different, something new.

And now that "chance" lies at the foot of Mischa Stepanov himself. Son of a bitch, no one could have planned this better—but I have no choice but to face this mess head-on. Only, considering my usual methods of conflict resolution, I can't brandish a fist at this problem or kidnap its daughter. Once again, Fabio and his unrelenting logic has a point.

497

There is no easy way around this other than confronting it directly…

Willow Stepanova is pregnant, and it's mine.

It's a dangerous statement to admit, even inside my own skull, but there it is.

Fabio, to his credit, hasn't been nearly as disgusted with me as he should be. If he punched me in the face, it wouldn't be punishment enough. A good man would cut the cord and leave me out to dry for this.

And there is no telling what Vin will think.

I can't worry about that now. The only thing that matters is getting answers. I spent all morning convincing myself that I would handle this as Fabio suggested and avoid the hospital. Maybe even make a diplomatic appeal to Mischa directly? By sunset, I finally settle on a course of action…

And I wind up in the car.

The hospital is my only lead, but I know before I even put the key in the ignition that it's a waste of time without a definitive date to go off of. I'm heading there for nothing, which means there is no reason at all to alert Fabio. The man isn't my babysitter, and—in this instance, at least—he has no say.

This is my battle to fight. My mistake to salvage.

My future on the line.

I've had seven long years to bury any hope of a legacy beyond Vincenzo. That prospect died with Olivia, and I never regretted that. I never once tried to seek out a different outcome with another woman.

I didn't deserve a second chance at a family, so, on its face, this present reality is too cruel to be true—it has to be a lie.

No one could blame me for wanting confirmation, not even Fabio.

With one last glance at the house, I start driving. Predictably, I've barely left the driveway when my cell phone starts ringing. My first impulse is to ignore it. Keep going. The less he knows of this, the better.

Still, maybe guilt is what finally makes me wrestle the device from my pocket and answer.

"Another scolding for today, Fab?"

"Where are you going, Donatello?" His voice is carefully restrained, falling into that calm cadence. I'm not fooled.

"You're spying on me now, Fab?"

He doesn't even try to deny it as he usually would.

"I know that you wouldn't be heading for the hospital," he says tightly. "Because causing more trouble is the last thing you need right now."

"Of course not," I say, matching his tone. "But this is one issue that doesn't concern you. We tried it your way, and now I suggest you stay out of it."

"Doesn't concern me?" Anger breaks through the pleasant façade. Usually, I'd take it as a warning not to push him further.

But right now, he can just get in line.

"Donatello, I hope you do realize how hard I've busted my ass to keep you out of the frying pan thus far—and that you are dangerously close to worming your way into a situation that pretty words and fast-talking can't get you out of. I think you should turn around right now, get back to the house and wait for me there—"

"Have a good night, Fab." I toss the phone aside and consider throwing it from the car altogether.

Though I can't deny that he's right. There is no turning back from this, but that's been the lesson learned from the very minute Safiya Mangenello came back into my life.

We're tethered together whether we like it or not.

I can blame Fab all I want, but I'm the one who touched her, who kissed her. Who took from her something that I didn't have the fucking right to.

I started this mess.

And I know that nothing I could ever say or do would make this right again. The options are limited in this situation, and some would claim I don't deserve a say in anything.

I don't.

At the same time...

I can't slink into the shadows and watch from a distance. Not this time. I can't wait seven damn years for the consequences to catch up. I can't pretend like this isn't fucking happening.

It's happening.

Even if I don't have the balls to admit it outside of my own head.

Alone in this moment, I try to, only to wind up laughing at the insanity of it all. The cruelty of it all…

My life ended seven years ago. I'm not entitled to more.

And now…

God, it's like the universe is mocking me.

I swerve to the side of the road and slam my foot on the brake, parsing the jumble of thoughts and emotions tumbling through my skull. Impulse is the overriding force, urging me to storm Mischa's manor and confront him directly. Mow down the front gate if I have to. Make my case. Shout. Threaten. Demand.

It's harder to push all of that aside and listen to the small sliver of Fabio I've internalized. Maybe it's my actual conscience? That faint voice warning me to slow down, that this situation is far too tenuous to risk relying on rage now.

Rage started this mess, blinding me to everything but the need to salvage my own pain. But looking back, I can say that I was never alone in this. I was never the sole victim fucked up by the hands of fate.

I hurt her first. I opened the initial wound that she had to suffer and let fester for seven damn years.

And this time, I can't use Mischa as a scapegoat.

Barging onto the Stepanov property would indulge a part of me desperate to react, but in the long run, it would only cause more damage. More fucking chaos.

I can't avoid reality either. No longer can I shun my responsibility.

So what's left? The sad part is I don't know how to even begin to answer that question. For so damn long, I've relied solely on fighting for Vin—either out of vengeance or trying to protect his future.

But when my own future needs protection, I don't feel that same fire. I've drowned myself in alcohol and drugs to ignore the pathetic creature I see whenever I look in the mirror. I've clung to my past as a monster and reflected only on that aspect of who I was.

But *Il Monstro* was a fraction of who Donatello Vanici is at his core. Another version of me existed once. A man who was willing to trust those he cared enough about. A man who dreamt of a family, and cherished his wife more than his own life.

I thought that man was dead and buried—and I preferred it that way.

Resurrecting him is an agonizing process. Hell, it's almost impossible to think back to that mindset, and picture what someone might do if his entire reality wasn't consumed by violence and anger.

When I met Liv, my tenure with the *famiglia* was still in its infancy. I was just a few years in, the youngest recruit to climb the ranks as quickly as I did. She was so damn beautiful. In the midst of running a job, I stopped dead in my tracks, spying her leaving some building downtown. She wore a tiny yellow dress, her hair spilling down her shoulders. Damn, no one else could draw me in the way she could with just a fucking smile.

Our first date was more like an extended car ride where we drove around for hours just talking.

I sink into the memories as I put the car into drive, heading for the city. In those days, it was just as looming, a concrete jungle of skyscrapers. The restaurant we used to eat at. The park we walked through. The hospital…

I can see it towering in the distance, but it isn't the building I find myself parked in front of.

The sprawling cathedral seems untouched by time as imposing as ever. Being here could be a sign from my subconscious, driving me to repent. Or it could be a nudge toward the only damn solution left to me regarding Willow Stepanova.

Ironically, I think back to that night when I first entered the Stepanov Manor feeling some small shred of hope, willing to put my own pride aside for the chance of forging a lasting connection. What had I done then?

I brought myself, unarmed and unguarded.

I brought a gift, wrapped with a white fucking bow, and I told myself that was enough to impress the mysterious Willow Stepanova.

No gift can even begin to heal this rift now…

But it's the only method I have left to try.

And it's the only way she might hear me.

5

EVGENI

Discover the woman's secrets, Mischa commanded—a task easier said than done.

These days, the world outside of Stepanov Manor is a parallel universe where tension and mystery meld into a gnawing sense of paranoia I can't shake no matter how hard I try. The presence of a viper in the passenger's seat doesn't help any.

I've never seen anyone handle their nervous energy the way she does. Her careful mask conceals her anxiety expertly—from the outside looking in, she's the picture of stoic calm. It's the nuance that gives her away. Her silence. The stiff way she holds herself, straining that debutant posture. Mainly, it's evident in the way her eyes keep darting from the windows to me, as though she isn't sure which factor terrifies her more.

Me? Or whatever might lurk beyond this van?

I'm willing to suggest it's the former.

"So, you want to stake out the Saleris," I say, breaking the silence that's lasted since we left the manor. It's dark enough to obscure most of her expression, and I'm rendered blind as to how she processes those words. For all I know, she could be leading me into a trap. I wouldn't be surprised—I think I'm counting on it. "Why them? And how do I know you won't turn around and present me to Gregori or Mateo on a silver platter?"

"You don't." She's damn good at feigning confidence. Her eyes glitter in the darkness as she cuts her gaze toward me. "For all you know, I could be planning to kill you. Ah! Maybe right at this moment."

I'm watching her, already primed the second she extends her hand my way. The fact that she isn't holding a weapon is the only reason I allow the contact.

Her fingers shake, twitching as if waiting for the second I'll recoil. Or attack.

I find her reaction more amusing than her audacity. This woman seems to be nothing more than illusions and contrast. Bold one minute. Fearful the next. Poised with confidence, and then snarling with anger a heartbeat later. I don't think I've ever met anyone quite so volatile.

"Word of advice. You want to kill me, then you do it now. No fanfare. No hesitation. It's the only shot you'll ever have."

"You sound like you're speaking from experience."

I recognize the probing lilt to her voice. She's not making a low jab at my expense. She's curious.

"And if I am? You were the one who claimed to have done your research on me," I say. "I'm sure you've heard all of the gory details."

"I did," she admits. "But considering how skewed your image of me is based on hearsay and gossip alone, I'm curious as to your side of things. Perhaps you see yourself as the tormented hero of your story and not as how you appear to the rest of us."

I can't resist taking her obvious bait. "And how do I appear, exactly?"

She inclines an eyebrow. "Like the monster. I don't think you can blame anyone, either. Most would hear 'man kills innocent young girl in cold blood' and come to the same conclusion—"

"And most would hear 'woman abandons her son to a supposed long-lost brother she barely knows,' and come to a different conclusion."

"You do that a lot," she points out softly, leaning back against her seat. The shadows obscure her enough to disguise her expression, but her voice is cold. "Deflect when you think I'm getting too close to the topics you deem too personal to talk about. This time, I won't let you deter me so easily. I want to know."

"Know what?" I scoff, hazarding a guess as to her true intentions. "If I'm capable of murder?"

"I want to know if, deep down beneath that self-righteous, pompous exterior is a man who might truly know a thing or two about regret and desperation. What could drive someone to commit an act they can never outrun. That is what I want to know, but I think I'm leaning more toward you being just a pompous ass."

Her laughter adds a musical flair to the sting of her insults. A part of me is impressed.

"Rarely does someone make such a scathing assessment of me outright. Bravo."

"Well, if you aren't capable of killing a woman, you certainly do seem to enjoy mocking one. Fine. I'll let you keep your secrets, Evgeni Volkov. You'll have to prove yourself to me in another way."

"Prove myself?"

Fuck. I slam on the brake, skidding to a stop in the middle of the road. Luckily, this section of the highway is deserted enough that the nearest cars are just blips of color on the horizon.

"I'm getting the sense that we aren't on some secret jaunt to merely spy on the Saleris."

Her reply is soft. "And if we aren't?"

I swerve onto the shoulder and park, aware of the city blinking up ahead, a mismatched array of glimmering lights.

"If you aren't..." Any threat dies in my throat, and I'm startled by the laugh that erupts instead. "It serves me right for believing a goddamn thing you would say—"

"I want you to help me kill him."

The casualness of her speech catches me off guard, and my brain belatedly processes those words seconds after she's gone silent. Kill him. Mischa is my first guess—the man she's proclaimed more than once to have no love for.

Because the more obvious answer is far too reckless, even for her.

"You want me to help you kill the man you've spent days hyping up the intelligence and cunning of? The man who blew up part of the city for seemingly no reason. The figure you claim to be terrified of to the point that you sought refuge with your estranged sister, and her family, whom you hate. I don't know what's more insane? That you think I'd go along with it so easily, or that you'd think I would consent to doing a damn thing with you."

The anger in my voice is partly for show, considering I've already agreed to her plan—we're here, after all. And as dangerous as this man is, death may be the only feasible way of ending the threat he presents for good.

"Well, when you put it that way, the self-righteousness really shines through," she says dryly. Then she lunges for the door on her end, shoving it open.

I don't move to stop her. "What are you doing?"

"I'll take my chances getting struck by the next passing semi and put myself out of my misery," she says. "I thought dealing with a madman was hard enough, but a condescending murderer? That takes the cake."

For all her bravado, she doesn't move, just allowing the night air and sounds of bustling traffic to flood the space between us.

Sensing yet another trap, I decide to tread carefully. "What do you really want?"

"Do you think you can stomach hearing it, in your perfect, heroic brain?"

"You're afraid of him," I reiterate, ignoring her jabs. "But not because of what he might do. You don't like being out of his loop. You're afraid he's already written you off as a lost cause."

"Which means I'm not of any use to you anymore, lucky me—"

"No," I reply. "It means that you're worried that even Mischa's protection won't be enough. I'm sure you'd run if you could, so the fact that you haven't yet means that you feel your options are dwindling. Your last, desperate action is to go on the offensive; consequences be damned. It seems, Briar Winthorp, that you believe you have nothing left to lose."

The door on her end slams shut, but with her still inside, breathing out harshly. It seems I've hit a nerve.

"So then, if you know everything, tell me that you also know that it's better to nip a threat before it can strike rather than let it bloom."

"But if you thought you could strike on your own, you would have done so already. You wouldn't need a babysitter, and you certainly wouldn't need me."

"Ah, but therein lies the catch. I've never killed anyone before."

It's not the truth. Her face is what gives her away, in the dark.

"I almost believed that," I admit.

"Not intentionally, at least." She smiles wickedly, brandishing her teeth. "So, it wasn't completely a lie."

"Luckily for you, I'm not curious as to the real answer." I grip the steering wheel and turn back onto the road—only to cut across two lanes and swerve into a U-turn.

"What are you doing?"

"I'm taking you back to the manor. I'm done with your games—"

"Mischa is merely a stepping-stone," she blurts in a rush. "His real end-goal is much bigger, involving way more pieces. The fact that he hasn't acted yet means that he's cutting out the middleman and going straight for the jugular. All of that to say, if we follow the Saleris, they'll lead us straight to him."

"And what else?" I demand, sensing more.

Her grudging hiss reveals that suspicion to be spot on. "Fine. I think the bastard's changed course, and I need to know how. I know you don't trust me. Hell, I don't expect you to. But I do expect you to care about your Mischa and his precious family. If not them, then yourself. You've made yourself quite the target. It's only a matter of time before he comes at you directly."

"Is this your way of convincing me to help you?"

"Yes, but that's not the part that will convince you. This will —I think my son is in the city, and I need your help to find him."

I process the request for only a second. Then I laugh so loud, I drown out the honking of a car that speeds past. I've been idling down the middle lane, giving that distant traffic plenty of time to catch up.

Still laughing, I slam on the gas, picking up speed. Internally, I'm kicking myself for even trusting her this far. Of course, there's another tale to be spun. Another lie to be woven when the first falls flat.

She's nothing if not predictable.

But, fuck, I'm the idiot who fell for it.

"When we get back, I think I'll try my hand at that dungeon and torture scenario. You think I'm a murderer now? You have no fucking idea—"

"My, my, you almost sound like the kind of man who would mean a threat like that." She laughs me off, but her voice shakes. From the corner of my eye, I see her grasp the door handle, but she doesn't force it open. Yet. "If you truly didn't believe me, you wouldn't bother to take me back," she points out. "You would throw me on the side of the road and drive off without a second glance. The fact that you listened at all tells me that, not only do you believe me, you want to help me—"

"Do I?" I toy with the idea of following through on her suggestion. Leaving her behind would be the best option for everyone.

Especially if she were always a spy. She would crawl back to her master, having failed with nothing useful gained.

But if she is telling the truth…

He'd kill her. He's already tried to more than once, and I don't believe that attempt was faked.

So, fuck it.

"Give me a reason. Lie, and I'll throw you out. Tell me what you're really after."

"Alexander was always better off without me," she says bluntly. "So, I'll spare you the maternal waterworks. I left him willingly, and up until recently, I didn't second guess it. Everything I've done has been for him. For his future—"

"Even teaming up with a man you fear?"

She chokes out a scathing laugh of her own. "And how would you explain your relationship with Mischa? Don't tell me that you work for him because you admire his rousing people skills. No. Someone as high and mighty as you must believe that he's somehow working toward a larger goal. You're doing it for a reason beyond the money, don't lie and pretend like you aren't."

"So, you admit that you're a terrible mother, and now I'm to believe that you've suddenly grown a heart and transformed into a caring one?"

"If he's bringing Ali into the country, he'll do so using the Saleri contacts. He'll want it under wraps, secret from everyone. The Saleris probably don't even know what they'll be transporting, but they own enough land to safely land a private jet, I'm sure."

"Why would he even go through the trouble? Why now?"

She hisses in exasperation. "Because Alexander is integral to his end game. If I am right, and he's bringing him into the country now, it means that he's ready to make a final move. Even if you don't believe me fully, you can't deny that it feels suspicious. I bet you'll find your way to the Saleri properties anyway, with or without my assistance.

But I can assure you that I know both men far better than you do."

I raise an eyebrow at that. "You sound confident. So, what is your hunch? What do you plan to do? Storm onto a Saleri tarmac and kidnap a child from under their noses? That sounds far too reckless for a caring mother."

"No," she says softly. "That's not what I intend at all to do. We will skip the guessing game and get answers straight from the source."

I feel my eyes narrow, and driving is the only distraction I have from either shouting, or strangling her with my bare hands.

"You want to kidnap and interrogate one of the Saleris?"

Her silence conveys a rare amount of modesty on her end. I don't trust it one damn bit.

"Are you insane?"

"No. I'm desperate, as you so kindly pointed out," she snarls. "And I'm tired of sitting and waiting around. He's up to something, and I intend to beat him at his own game."

"So where do I factor in? As your muscle?"

"Don't be so hard on yourself, Evgeni." She chuckles. "But if the shoe fits..."

"And if I refuse to be used as your pawn?"

"You won't," she says confidently. "Because no matter how hard you deny it, you can't resist the chance to play the hero. And you know that I'm not lying. I would conjure a much better sob story to pique your bleeding heart if I were. So, turn around."

"Fine—" Another U-turn sets us back on course for the city. "But we do this my way."

Impatient, I ignore the speed limit, heedless of the consequences—but our destination isn't one of the many residential properties the Saleris own. Instead, we arrive at the heart of their operation—the club from which they conduct the more salacious of their business ventures.

This time of day, the place is dead. Only a single bouncer guards the front, scanning anyone who comes within view of the gilded building.

"They won't be here," Briar scoffs against my ear. "I didn't think you were stupid as well as righteous—"

"Gregori and Mateo aren't my focus right now," I hiss back. "We're here only by coincidence."

I claim a spot in a parking lot across from the club, unnoticed by the sentry. Luckily, my real destination is a block down, out of his line of sight.

"What the hell do you mean?" the woman snarls.

I shrug. "You want to go barging into a guarded fortress without intel, but that simply isn't my style."

"So, we skulk around a dead club and hope that someone just tells us what we want to know?"

"No—" I exit the van, keys in hand. "We do this my way."

"Wait!" She scrambles out as well, racing to my side. "What the hell are you planning? To waltz in there where they most likely aren't."

"No." I withdraw my cell phone and watch her eyes narrow. "I get intel. You remember our good friend Louie? Well, you should know his haunt is a bar not too far from here. He'll be able to get us more info on what the hell the Saleris may or may not be up to. *Then* we make a move. Understood?"

She's smart enough to see the benefit of that plan. Still, her expression can be politely described as skeptical. "Why bring me?"

Because I don't dare leave her at Stepanov Manor alone.

"Because he'll be resistant to telling me a damn thing without payment," I lie. "I'm sure you'll be able to use your Winthorp charm to convince him otherwise."

She doesn't seem to buy that explanation. "Oh?"

"You're collateral," I admit. "I'm sure the bastard will try to play both sides. You're the tempting carrot he needs to reach out to our enemies—and we'll be waiting."

"Sneaky, sneaky," she taunts. "I wouldn't think you'd have it in you."

She sounds impressed, even.

Which makes me feel dirty rather than amused.

"Let's go," I say, heading for the main street.

Just beyond my reach, she slinks into step behind me.

The second we enter the bar, the bastard tries to run. I have to corner him in a backroom while the woman blocks the door.

Admittedly, Louie is a sneaky son of a bitch in the best of times—but this is unusual, even for him. He's spooked.

"That isn't a very nice way to greet friends," I hiss, grappling with the collar of his stained gray shirt. The bastard reeks of alcohol, and this struggle feels less like I'm fighting to keep him here, and more like I'm helping him stand at all.

"Word on the street is you've been poking very big hornets' nests, Ev," he chokes out, his bloodshot eyes comically wide. "The people in your crosshairs seem to wind up dead. Even more so than usual."

"What do you mean?"

"Gregori fucking Saleri is what I mean. He's dead."

"What?" I couldn't hide my shock if I tried. Glancing over my shoulder, I note that Briar Winthorp, however, doesn't look surprised in the slightest. Suddenly her "hunch" regarding the Saleris isn't so farfetched.

"Yeah," Louie croaks. "Gutted like a fish in his own fucking club. Word on the street is that Mateo did it himself. The motherfucker's gone crazy—"

"Mateo…" Whatever happened sounds like far more than the average family squabble. "When?"

"Last night? I don't fucking know. The point is, who the hell is next?"

"And that's all you know regarding the Saleris?"

His eyes dart to the woman. "I know they're taking their marching orders from an outsider. And I know that *she* turned back up around the same time he did. This shit reeks, Ev. I'd get rid of her if you can."

"And that's it?" I release him, stepping back.

He sways on his feet, pointing a trembling finger in my direction. "I've been too busy trying to get the fuck out of here!" He pushes me off, tugging at his collar. "Now, can I drink in peace?"

He staggers for the doorway, and the woman standing there comes to my side.

"Au Revoir," she murmurs, blowing him a kiss.

But her eyes are on me, unmistakably smug.

When we return to the manor, I regret ever leaving in the first place.

"You know more than you're saying," I snarl while driving up to the gates. "I should shove you in the darkest, deepest room possible and demand real answers. Enough games. Enough lies."

She laughs, but her eyes blaze. I suspect that she's only revealing a fraction of what truly has her so on edge. Regardless, I shouldn't give a damn. If she wants to play coy with the answers, one of my men can drag them out of her.

Slowly and painfully.

Surprisingly she's silent as we near the front of the manor.

"It looks like the darling family is refusing a visitor," she finally remarks, sitting forward.

I follow her gaze, instantly on edge. Another car bars our path, but I don't recognize it as belonging to the estate. The door to the front seat hangs open, and I assume the driver is the same man standing nearby, his back to me.

"Son of bitch!"

There is no mistaking that posture, nor that characteristic bulk.

I lunge from the van, grasping for my gun.

"I'm not here for a fight," the man says, turning to face me. "I'm just here to give this to her. Only her. Please."

Confusion goes to war with the adrenaline surging through me, demanding I fight. Instead, I settle for pointing out the obvious. "You don't have the right to even show your face here—"

"So don't let me in the house," Donatello Vanici says tiredly. "But let her have the choice to accept these or not."

I crane my neck to view the items in his arms. Both are surprisingly innocent, but I'm not fooled. His true intent is far more sinister than delivering some harmless flowers. He wants to pressure Willow and play more sick mind games at her expense.

After all, I have an expert in manipulation behind me.

Ironically, her presence is why I don't feel compelled to drive my fist through this man's skull.

As much as I care about Willow, this is her fight, not mine—and it would be wrong to play the role as a pawn for either side.

The only right course of action is what I should have done in all matters concerning Briar Winthorp in the first place.

Stay out of it.

"I'll have my men search whatever you've brought for explosives," I suggest, but the man doesn't flinch.

"Do whatever the fuck you have to. Just give her the option of whether to accept them or not."

"Then leave them," I say, jerking my chin toward the pavement between us. "And go before I change my mind. But realize that I can't guarantee they won't burn them. As they should."

"Fine," he concedes. "I'm not asking for anything more than that."

Seconds later, he drives off.

"Strange," Briar murmurs in my ear.

I jump, having almost forgotten her presence. "What is?"

Her cold laughter rings hollow. "That you trust a madman more easily than you trust me."

6

WILLOW

I've never realized how heavy silence can feel when it's stretched over days. Weeks. And when a sound finally breaks that quiet, it rings out louder than a gunshot.

Alarmed, I jolt to awareness, lifting my gaze from the crumpled page in my grasp. My room is bathed in shadow, and I race to the windows to find the sky beyond is a hazy twilight with only hints of the setting sun peeking through. The guards out patrolling don't seem on alert, though, strolling at a leisurely pace. The booming noise could have been thunder.

But then it echoes again, far louder. A few distinctive, piercing notes betray the sound for what it really is. Voices, coming from below.

Shouting.

My first instinct is to ignore it, even as my heart races. It feels safer to lurk within these four walls and disregard the world beyond. I try to, seeking out the same handwritten scrawl I've come to memorize, desperate to find meaning in it.

I don't love you, I don't. I don't know what this is. But when I'm with you, at least I'm not invisible for once...

"She deserves to know." That gentle murmur easily transcends the commotion of voices, despite being the softest. *Ellen.* "If she wants to burn them, she can, but it should be her choice."

"None of this was *her* choice," a man growls in response. Mischa. "You don't even know what the hell that monster might have sent to her. Or what he's written in that fucking note—"

"She's an adult, Mischa. We have to trust her to tell us—"

"Fine. If you want to let that bastard continue to fuck with her head, be my guest. But what happens next will be on you."

"This isn't our fight," Ellen warns, her tone unwaveringly gentle in the face of her husband's rage. "All we can do is be there to support whatever *Willow* decides. Please. You've handled this better than I thought you would so far. It means a lot."

Better than she thought? Perhaps that explains why Mischa's visits to my room haven't been nearly as frequent as hers. He's been restraining himself. From saying what, exactly?

If he replies to his wife, I don't hear it. Just soft footsteps, advancing toward my room, ignoring the invisible boundary I've set. Without a knock this time, the door opens, revealing Ellen, her expression constricted.

"I know you want to be alone," she says softly. "But these came for you, and I thought you might want to know. If you want to refuse them, you can."

From her position, I can't see what she holds. Not until she enters the room fully with an apologetic frown. "Just leave them outside the door, and I'll have them taken away."

Them, being a vase of roses propped against her hip, nearly large enough to dwarf her in comparison. I gape, thrown off by the beauty of them. Red, white, and pink blooms in various sizes spill from a glass container shaped like a teardrop.

It's an extravagant gift, all things considered, but I puzzle over her hesitation.

Then the answer hits me like a slap—they aren't from her or Mischa. Without admitting as much out loud, she approaches a table in the corner of my room and sets them down, along with a small white box wrapped with a matching bow.

Both catch the snippets of lighting filtering in from the hallway, tinging their pristine white. They look so sinister sitting there, deceptively lovely. Considering who sent them, the intention behind the delicate blooms could be more dangerous than a simple gift.

"We didn't open anything," Ellen warns—judging from the shouting, it was her who insisted on that. "I want to believe there's nothing nefarious in it—" She seems to bite off the rest. "If you need anything, I won't be far."

She switches on the overhead light and leaves. As the door closes behind her, I warily approach the table. The floral scent floods my nostrils before I even reach them, betraying a beautiful quality. After everything that's transpired, they almost seem surreal, and I can't place the building dread that has my fingers shaking before I reach for a small white card affixed to one of the stems.

I would be a fool to think that this alone could change the way you feel about me, reads the first line. The stern, sloping script might appear beautiful if I wasn't already well versed in pages of similar writing. I know the author's signature stroke, and how the darker ink betrays how tightly he pressed the nip of his pen to the page.

I know this scent too, mingling faintly beneath the aroma of roses.

He wrote this, every word.

Shock knocks me back, and I trip over my own feet. Suddenly the beautiful colors conjure a more menacing imagery. The red resembles blood, the white unblemished skin ripe for abuse. I wonder if this is his way of mocking me—a parting gift, meant to add salt to the wound.

I can't explain what drives me closer regardless. Perhaps a morbid curiosity to see the rest of his message—especially when his past notes are still fresh in my mind. His old letters have become engrained on my psyche, every word. Every last punctuation mark.

His gritty composition haunts my nightmares, and some masochistic part of me can't resist consuming this newer dose of poison.

I steel myself for more vague rejection and callous disregard. Or maybe he'll refer to the glaring reality that has turned me into a leper in my own home.

But, like always, whenever I hope for clarity from Donatello Vanici, all I'm given is more doubt and confusion. More pain.

We should talk. In person, alone. No threats. No ultimatums. I need to see you. Come to the café we met in before. I'll be there all day tomorrow. I'll wait for you.

Damn him.

I'm on my knees beside the table, the card in my grasp. I don't know how many times I read those words, branding them into my brain much like I've memorized the stack of letters from the past. He's written in this tone before, pleading and demanding in the same breath—when he urged Olivia to open up to him.

Trust him.

And then she died.

Of all the responses, this is the least one I would have expected, but I'm not comforted in the slightest. I'm uneasy.

He's planning something. Plotting something. Men like Donatello Vanici don't beg, not without a reason.

And I can think of several why he would want to meet with me now, alone.

Would I put it past him to make a demand or an ultimatum? Or worse, would he dare to use me against Mischa to further his own selfish aims? Yes.

After all, I've only ever been a tool to him.

That's what this really is about—using me. He can't truly expect me to come to him, even if Mischa would allow it. No, true to his self-deprecating nature, he'll relish the rejection as an excuse to see himself as the victim. It's been his aim from the very start—going back seven years ago. Even now, he has yet to tell me the whole truth of what happened then, but I can guess. A variation of what has become his life story, in a sense.

Donatello got overwhelmed.

He got angry and vengeful.

And then, when the consequences set in, he got regretful. Unable to accept responsibility for his actions, he blamed me, turning the little girl he abandoned into both a martyr and an albatross around his neck. He told Vin I was dead and used my memory as a shield.

But when I came back, what did he do? Act as though I were the enemy—anything other than accept responsibility.

I should take a page out of his book and do the same, hurt him as he hurt me. Lie. Deny. Ignore him. Erase Donatello Vanici from my history.

Our history…

I suck in a breath as everything that's happened recently comes rushing back. It's all too much. So, I shove the most terrifying issues aside and fixate on what little I have control over now.

Donatello wants a meeting, if only to use a refusal against me. But I'm done being his punching bag. He wants to see me? He will, but not on his terms.

Mine.

A shocking sense of calm washes over me. I can think clearly, at least in this limited capacity. Taking a deep breath, I even manage to stand, still facing the table—but then my gaze falls over the box, and I lose what little resolve I had.

It would be one thing if I could write it off as some careless gift he had Fabio purchase and wrap. Something without any of his input. In that case, it would be obvious, with telltale signs of perfection, to give it away.

But the wrapping is…sloppy in places. One side of the box is crooked as if the person who prepared it misjudged how much paper they'd need. In vain, they attempted to hide their mistake with more tape, and they even tied the bow off-center.

Seven years ago, I used to receive birthday presents wrapped in the same haphazard but thoughtful manner. Tears sting my eyes, burning and acrid, too many to blink back. They spill unbidden, landing over the open card and smearing the ink scrawled across it.

I lash at the gift with both hands, nails drawn, ripping through the ivory casing to the object resting beneath. There is nothing he could ever give me that would change my opinion of him.

Nothing but this.

I drop it, watching it hit the floor with an ominous thud. My first thought is that he meant it as a joke. A mocking way to taunt me with the one method of communication we managed to forge over my last few days at Havienna. Yes, it must be. A cruel joke. His way of proving that the only things remaining between us are meaningless words and crisp parchment.

I'm sinking to my knees anyway, reaching for the wooden box with a clear glass lid. Visible beneath it is a swath of stationary and a golden pen.

I would have preferred something worthless. Or priceless. An expensive necklace or trinket that would mean nothing to me.

This gift is too tailored to ignore, and I lift it carefully, bringing it to the bed.

He's gotten his wish. I'll acknowledge him, but in my own way. This time, I'll make it easy for him to hate me.

I'll make him face me.

The following morning unfolds almost too normally for the current circumstances. Even with the added visit to the hospital, the day itself could be described as boring at best. If it weren't for the fact that no less than ten men make up the guard accompanying Ellen and me from the manor.

And the fact that Mischa is nowhere in sight to send us off. Eli and the other children aren't milling about either, and I assume he's entertaining them in another part of the manor.

Ellen smiles despite the circumstances, treating this trip as though it's a usual occurrence.

"We can get tea after," she suggests. "There is a place not far from the hospital. If you don't mind the escorts."

Said escorts remain vigilant even when we reach the hospital, lurking outside the exam room. Their shadows loom beyond the doorway, creating an ominous contrast to the sterile white walls and scurrying nurses.

The doctor is a smiling woman who enters the room chatting aimlessly about the weather before sternly detailing the parameters of the exam. Still smiling, she draws a vial of blood and cheerfully attempts a conversation even on her way out. Only when she returns, the smile has vanished.

"Is something wrong?" Ellen's voice is strained, but the doctor shakes her head.

"The HCG levels are in the right range, but the lower end."

"What does that mean?" Ellen asks. "Is… Is there no pregnancy?"

I flinch at the word.

"Not quite. It's a bit unusual, but potentially nothing serious," the woman explains. "Still, I think it would be best to have another appointment soon."

Her tone doesn't convey the same hope as her forced smile, but I can't focus enough to follow the conversation. Unusual. That word could contain so many things, but that numbness prevails. Nothing breaks it but one persistent thought.

Donatello.

I need to find him.

"Another visit in a week is all that's necessary," the doctor declares. "Then we can make more definitive decisions. In the meantime, here is some documentation."

We leave, documents in tow, returning to the car, flanked by the retinue of soldiers.

"I know I promised tea after, but…" Ellen sighs, her smile gone. Looking at her stirs that unease again. That desperate feeling to avoid anything beyond the numbness. "Maybe we should head back?"

No. I grab her hand, shaking my head.

"It would be good to get some fresh air," she says warily.

The café is small, near the heart of downtown, eerily close to where Donatello wanted to meet. Does she know that?

I can't tell looking at her blank expression. She's worried, though, but it's a full second before I realize that Donatello has nothing to do with it.

"Are you okay?" she asks, catching me staring.

I nod, but she has a faraway look as if the answer only disturbs her more. By the time we leave the car and approach the café, she's frowning. In silence, we enter the luxurious dining room where plush burgundy carpet inspires a calm, cozy aura. Within seconds, a grinning waitress shows us to a table and reappears with steaming cups of tea.

As Ellen samples her drink, I finally gather up the nerve to move, lifting both hands.

"Bathroom?" Ellen asks as I sign.

Nodding, I stand, aware of the soldiers posted around the room.

The bathroom is near an exit door, and I don't think before entering a stall, withdrawing a paper and pen from my coat pocket.

The note I compose is short and pathetic in retrospect, nothing like the detailed missives of Donatello.

Knowing him, this meeting won't last long, and I might be back before she even notices.

534

7

DON

The hospital isn't my destination today. Fabio should be proud of my restraint—but I've never felt like a bigger fool. Or, in this case, a sitting duck.

It doesn't help that I'm sweating like hell. I can't remember the last time I've been this nervous—stretching back to my early days working for the *famiglia*. Serves me fucking right.

I came alone, without backup or even Fabio. It could be a trap, but I'm here despite the risk. If this is the only way to get some ounce of fucking clarity, then so be it.

I'll wait out in the open and take whatever comes my way, be it a bullet or answers. Hopefully, it's the latter.

Though how I can face either is another question. Any other time, I wouldn't dream of confronting this shit without a bottle of vodka and a cigar. Devoid of both, all I can do is try my best to process it all one step at a time.

Doubt is paramount for the most part.

She won't come. Could I even blame her?

Hell no.

The other possibility is that Mischa shows up instead, unwilling to compromise. Were I in his place, I don't know what I would do. Not that letting me see her will make much of a difference. Some goddamn flowers can't fix a damn thing. I know that.

But dwelling on the mess won't solve anything either.

So, I wait, eyeing the street beyond the café, unsurprised as the minutes tick by without the sign of a Stepanov cavalcade.

More doubt feeds on the dread building in the pit of my stomach. How the hell could I have been so damn stupid? Not even with just her. With Vin, and even Olivia. Over and over, I've failed to protect anyone who means anything to me. Over and over, I had to watch them be injured or die.

And yet, I'm the one who remains unscarred.

The right thing to do would be to fall back, like Fabio said. Let her live her life, whatever choice she decides to make, in peace. Sink into the shadows and turn my focus onto Vincenzo. His is the only fate within my control. The merciful thing I could do when it comes to Willow Stepanova is to let her go.

Like hell, I will.

The dark impulses I've fought so hard to smother break through, and I form a fist, slamming it against the narrow table. Already a million other options unfurl in my skull, threatening to push out that fragile desire for peace.

I tried diplomacy already.

The next obvious step is something a little more direct. Like returning to Mischa's manor and driving straight through the gates like I originally planned. Then I'd demand that she talk to me. Even for a fucking second. If only to…

What?

My mind goes blank. It's easier to fantasize about an impulsive course of action and run with it. If she won't see me, then I'd find a way to see her.

I *will* find a way.

Determined, I brace my hands against the table and prepare to stand. Mid-rise, I smell it. Roses. The faint scent hits my nostrils at full force, inexplicably fresh despite the lack of any such bloom in sight. Instead, a flash of gold draws my notice to the front of the café.

Damn.

If Mischa chose her outfit, the bastard has a cruel streak. Though why would he? No… *She* picked this dress, a delicate shade of yellow with lace trim visible beneath a dark coat. Her hair hangs loosely. Overall, she looks the same way she did the day she left Havienna.

Fucking perfect.

Warily, I scan her face, unsure of what I'll find. If I were honest with myself, I'd expect her eyes to be bloodshot, her mouth twisted in an expression of abject horror. Maybe then I'd be able to meet her gaze like the coward I am and face the damage I've wrought?

Instead, her eyes blaze, like burning coals incinerating whatever expectations I had of this meeting to ash.

So, this isn't a friendly reunion, then.

Swallowing hard, I tear my gaze away from her, expecting to find an army of Stepanov guards waiting to descend. All I see is the street behind her and the average pedestrian mingling on the sidewalk.

Only the lone proprietor of the café serves as the buffer between us, quietly bringing a pitcher of water to our table.

There is no Fabio. No Mischa. Not even a smiling Vincenzo to siphon off the tension.

In short? I have no one to hide behind.

"Here." I lurch to my feet and wrench out the empty chair across from me, nearly knocking it over. "You can sit."

She doesn't move. I can see now that while she came into this building alone, she doesn't trust me a fraction. Not even enough to go beyond the safety of a quick exit.

It's odd, but some sick part of me finds that comforting. Her hesitation shortens this meeting. There's no time for small talk or awkwardness. Just getting to the heart of the matter.

If only I knew what the fuck to say.

"You… You look good," I croak, hating myself the second the words leave my throat.

I might as well have voiced an insult. She flinches, her eyes more guarded than ever, concealing any hint of what she might be thinking. I can't stop myself from eyeing her waist, flat beneath the fall of her dress. Though it would be, wouldn't it? It's only been two weeks. It would take longer for anything to become more apparent.

If she didn't choose another option in the meantime.

For all I know, she could have, and my chest constricts at the thought. I've spent days avoiding that outcome, but now it's all I can think about. Would she have done that without even telling me first? Why wouldn't she?

Fabio all but hinted that he thought it would be the better option. For all I know, he conspired with Mischa to make the decision without my input. He'd deem it was for the greater good.

Do I have a better idea?

As the seconds tick by, I can't even bring myself to say a damn thing, let alone offer up a solution. The million different lines and explanations I came up with before now scatter like dust.

I owe her something. I need to say something.

"I… Uh, do you want something to drink?" I gesture helplessly to the water.

Her blank expression doesn't waver.

"Are… Are you okay?" It startles me just how much I crave even a hint of what's going on inside that head. Something. That she hates me? She'll always fucking hate me.

I deserve it.

Another heartbeat passes without a move on her end. So much for handling this on my own. If Fab were here, he would know what to say. He was always good at this shit.

I, on the other hand, just clear my throat and force myself to meet her gaze directly.

Facing her again is like tearing open a festering wound and letting the puss drain out. There is no hiding from it. The disgust. The pain.

She hides it all for as long as she can—but those eyes always give her away. They blaze, glimmering too brightly, and I stiffen at the threat of tears. Damn it…

"I'm sorry." The words slip out, pathetic and hoarse, but there they are. It's all I can say, over and over again. "I'm sorry."

I collapse onto the nearest chair, unable to even look at her. Groaning, I dig my fingers into my temples, questioning whether this really is a setup and Mischa will come storming through the door. I almost wish that were the case.

I know how to handle violence. I know how to defend myself, even against an armed man, and I know the ins and outs of the political scene of Hell's Gambit.

But this…

I can't even compare this moment to the day Liv came to me, tears in her eyes, and told me I would be a father. That was meant to be. Olivia signed up to share her life with me, and her future should have been spent with five more kids —however many she wanted—in a house she loved with only grandkids and peace to look forward to.

Liv made her choice. It wasn't forced on her.

My own sister wasn't so lucky, getting pregnant by some punk who abandoned her in the end. She loved Vin in her own way, but motherhood didn't bring her the same joy Liv craved. It overwhelmed her, driving her deeper down a rabbit hole of vice and decay. She died high on God knows what, slumped in an alleyway while I was the one left to mix up the formula and fill Vin's bottles. Caring for him was the last fucking thing in the world I wanted.

And it turned my whole life on its head.

I couldn't ask someone to take on the same responsibility.

"I didn't want this. Do you realize that?"

I hear her breathing out, every exhale ragged and unsteady. Surprisingly, the distorted soundtrack helps me gather my thoughts. Each negative, twisted realization I should have admitted from the start.

"I didn't want this. I… I didn't. Fuck, I don't even… You went to the hospital. Did Mischa—"

What? I can't even say it. Did he do what most fathers would demand in this instance? Deep down, some part of me insists that would be the best thing for everyone involved.

A larger part of me, on the other hand, can't even consider the thought. It's driving me mad not to know. Fuck…

Or hell, I'm already insane, I must be—crazy enough to imagine the warm touch ghosting the side of my jaw. I glance up, just in time to catch a small, pale hand rear back and land palm first against my cheek. I've barely registered the attacker's identity—the only other person in the room —by the time they rear back for another blow.

I lurch to my feet, grabbing her wrist out of reflex, only to immediately let her go.

"What the hell?" I demand, but one look at her face renders me silent. A slap is the least of my concerns.

She's angry. So goddamn angry, practically levitating on the tips of her toes. Without even trying, I've hurt her again.

"I'm sorry."

An apology seems to rob her of the anger—along with whatever energy she has left. She sways, and I barely manage to throw my arm around her waist before her knees buckle completely.

I shouldn't touch her, let alone hold her. Not like this.

It's harder to think clearly with her scent flooding my nostrils, her hair like silk beneath my fingertips as I cradle the back of her scalp. She's shaking, and I feel like an even bigger fool.

Why wouldn't she be angry?

"I'm sorry." I voice it directly against her ear, feeling her shiver in response. "That was a selfish thing to say. This isn't about me. This is about you."

Her face is angled away, but some of the tension leaves her body, and I'm fully supporting her weight. In her absence, I've convinced myself that it was for the best. That I didn't miss her touch. Her smell. That I didn't crave the sight of those dark fucking eyes. That I could wait until Vin fully recovered and leave Hell's Gambit, never to look back. Never to see her again.

Only now can I realize how fucking egotistical I've been. The only course of action that matters is the one she decides on. For all my scheming and planning, I never once considered asking her what *she* wanted. I didn't have the courage to.

"Tell me what you want from me." I don't make her face me, not yet. I just hold her, raking my fingers through her hair, trying to ignore any preconceived notions I may have. "It doesn't matter what I want, or Fabio, or your father. The only person whose opinion matters is you."

If she heard me, she doesn't react, her gaze presumably on the window across the shop. It overlooks a sliver of green field, and as if enacting some mocking cliché, a small family picnics there in the sun. The woman even has blond hair, the man towering over her with his hand on her lower back, and their children playing on the grass before them. It's like looking into a twisted mirror—that's what this situation should be.

Not this.

But here we are, regardless. No amount of pretending or wishing can change a damn thing.

"What I want doesn't matter," I tell her hoarsely. My jaw throbs with the effort it takes to chew out every damn word. "But I think you deserve to hear it anyway, if only so that you know where I stand."

I find myself enthralled, watching that family, seeing them interact without a care in the world. A few years ago, I was convinced that would have been the future awaiting Liv and me. Happiness. More children than we could possibly stand. Freedom. Serenity. Safety.

I wanted it all so badly I could have killed for it.

But somewhere along the way…

I found myself in my office or hunting down enemy leads instead of in my own house. My nights were spent nailing down deals rather than beside my wife. I could rationalize it if another woman had gotten my attention. Something less cliché and far more fucking enticing than chasing money and prestige. But, God, I wanted it all.

"I missed my shot once," I say, though I don't even know exactly what I'm referring to. A shot at a family? At happiness? At life?

Liv's death took so fucking much from me, that the creature left behind might as well be deemed a ghost. Beneath the drugs and the alcohol lurks a truth that I don't think either Fabio or I wanted to face—those vices merely enhanced a descent into madness I gladly welcomed. Death was my end goal, and recovery wasn't even on my radar, then. Misery was the only state powerful enough to drown the guilt.

I thought nothing could ever dig me from that despair, but for the first time, it's like the storm cloud raining down on my life has let up just enough for me to take notice of the world around me, drenched as it may be. This mindset is a new form of sobriety, and I'm not even sure if I like the feel of it.

I can think clearly again, and one solution feels so fucking obvious, the realest concept I've been able to grasp outside of hate and violence.

"I want…"

Childish laughter seeps through the walls as if taunting me with the sheer magnitude of everything I've lost. Everything I could find again. It almost feels wrong to crave that faint lifeline. I don't deserve it.

That doesn't mean I don't desire it so badly my voice breaks over the admission, "I want a future."

I feel her shiver in my arms, and I loosen my grip, waiting for her to pull away. But she doesn't. Somehow, I find the nerve to ease a finger beneath her chin, guiding her to face me.

That anger is still there, burning bright—but beneath it is a glimpse of something that resonates in me like a kick to the stomach. I don't dare name it.

"I do. You have no reason to trust me. No reason to believe me after everything I've done. Ignoring this won't fix it, and I don't want to. You came here, and I thank you for that. I have no right to ask you for more…" My throat thickens, and I tear my gaze to the window, clinging to that mocking image of family. "So, look at this more as another choice. You come with me, and we can find some way to make this work. You and I, no one else. Not Fabio. Not Mischa. This doesn't have to be a tragedy. But it's your choice, and I will respect whatever you decide, I swear on my life. But if you want another option, you come to me. Or… You could leave."

To reinforce that choice, I pull away, putting my back to her. Regardless, the thought of letting her go now triggers the paranoia constantly at the back of my mind. I could always take her to Havienna now, preempting anything Mischa might do to convince her otherwise.

But therein lies the fucking dilemma. To earn her trust, the first step is to acknowledge that I don't have control.

"I'll let you decide." With that said, I start for the door, but a flicker of movement from the corner of my eye draws my notice. I stop short with my hand inches from the doorknob, only to feel a familiar touch graze my forearm in response.

She doesn't have to say a single word to make her feelings clear—annoyance. Once again, I've aimed to have the last word with no input from her, contradicting everything I've said. Even now, I can't let her state her own case, her own thoughts.

And that was the offer I made to her, wasn't it? Before she even came here. We both know what giving her paper and a pen meant.

It meant she would have her voice.

And I would finally listen.

8

WILLOW

I'm a fool. Coming here was a mistake, and nothing has made that sink in like the sight of his retreating back for the umpteenth time. Him leaving now is a stark reminder that nothing between us could ever change. He's still determined to assert control and set the terms for whatever truce we might be able to build.

Seven years later, and he's still treating me like a little girl.

But no more.

I sense in my soul that if I let him go, I'll never see him again—but the choice won't be my own. No, Donatello Vanici will continue to do what he does best and spiral into a downfall of his own volition.

In fact, I think someone like him would crave a moment like this, only to compound his own despair and truly make himself the victim. He's so damn selfish, but I wasn't able to see it until today.

Tears of rage blur my vision, lashing down my cheeks in an unstoppable torrent. It's cruel how he does this, how easily he can turn the tables while offering the semblance of control. But to him, control is merely a word he can use to assuage his own guilt.

From day one, he's taken everything, giving nothing in return.

Until now. A strange expression breaks through the rigid mask he wears, bringing a rare hint of softness to those dark, imposing eyes.

"I'm sorry," he croaks, the only phrase he seems capable of voicing without guilt or rage. The words ring hollow, and as much as it stings, I can hear the truth in them. "I'm sorry. I... What do you need to say?"

There's too much, but, ironically, I didn't bring any more paper with me. Just his pen and the handful of documents the doctor provided.

And the letters...

Not that he'll read them. Trusting him should be impossible. How could I take anything he says at face value?

I'm too tired. Drained, I cross over to the nearest chair and sit, rocked by the reality I haven't had time to face. Or perhaps, ignored is a better word. I've ignored how my life has changed because of him.

And because of me.

That's the element of this that everyone else refuses to consider, and one that he could easily throw in my face. The prospect of him doing that very thing unnerves me more than anything else. We both know the truth.

If it were up to him, our relationship would have ended on his terms. He would use me as a pawn and nothing more. I made him cross that boundary out of some twisted sense of revenge.

I made him break his own foolish rule, but the consequences affect us both.

It's too much. The walls seem to close in, and I can't breathe. I can't think. The air is too thin in here. Too hot. I'm burning alive, suffocating…

"Look at me."

Again, he so easily asserts himself, but when I do look up, his expression is far from the stoic mask I'm used to.

Wincing, he drags his hand across his chin, drawing notice to the dark stubble there. Blinking, I take in all of the minute details I didn't have the sense of mind to notice before. The dark circles beneath his eyes. The slight unkempt appearance to his hair and the fact that his suit jacket is wrinkled, the collar crooked. I have a mental image of Fabio fussing over him, bringing him clean clothing to wear, and it hits me that he isn't here this time. Donatello is alone, devoid of his posse for once.

"If we are going to make this work, I can't read your mind," he says gruffly. "We can't keep playing with half-truths and misunderstandings. There needs to be some level of trust. Clear communication."

He makes it sound like I'm to blame for said miscommunication. Maybe he truly believes that.

I plunge my hand into my pocket without processing the action clearly. Then I feel my fingers close over the pen he sent me, and something clicks. He wants clear communication, does he?

He frowns as I withdraw the pen and rip off the lid. His eyes latch onto my trembling fingers, tracking their every movement as I reach for one of his hands.

He stiffens, curling the fingers tightly before slowly unfurling each one until his palm is bared. He must know what I intend to do as I press the nib to the calloused surface because he doesn't move, even as streaks of ink mar his flesh.

Voice gravelly, he recites each word as I form them. "You don't listen."

A grimace disrupts his pained expression. Then he sighs, leveling me with a searching glance I'm unprepared for. "You haven't exactly tried to talk to me."

His brows draw together. I've seen this look before, though not recently. It's the spark of the cunning man he used to be, unwilling to let any opportunity pass without a fight.

"We've been too busy listening to Mischa and Fabio," he continues. "Doing things their way when neither of us were ever known to be the thoughtful type. We're reckless. It's how we operate together, like with the Saleris…" His voice trails off as he recalls that day on the water, one of the few we were able to interact in relative peace. When he meets my gaze again, I swallow hard, sensing the intention lurking behind that distant expression. "We work best when we throw caution to the wind and do things in our own way. Should I tell you what I would do, Mischa or anyone else be damned?"

He has a way of sounding so damn enticing even while speaking insanity.

"I'd marry you," he confesses, raising the hand I've written on, tracing each scribbled word. "Secure the future I want. Our feelings don't matter—only the reality. I can protect you better that way."

But I'd be under his control again.

He must read that suspicion in my face because he nods. "And it would make things easier for me, but not if I offer you a lifeline. You stay with me on your own terms, and I will never deny you anything. I will never lie to you. Anything you ask of me, I will grant. I swear it on my life."

He's made this boast before, but under duress with Fabio in his ear. This time sounds different. There's a note of exasperation in his voice that I can't deny. Something raw and strained.

Warily, he approaches the table, keeping his hands in sight, his expression open. Those eyes contain a hint of the man I remember, and it stings. God, it stings like hell to see that piece of him lurking within the stranger he's become real enough to touch. Believe. Trust.

Only so I can be burned again.

There should be nothing in this world that he can offer me. Nothing.

But there is.

I reach for his hand again, brandishing the only weapon at my disposal. Surprisingly, he lets me use it, presenting the back of the hand I've already marked. Slowly, I etch each word, hating how badly my fingers shake. The lines wobble, so distorted that he wrinkles his mouth in concentration as he reads. "You want the truth."

I nod, unable to hide the desperation I can feel seep into my expression.

Answers. Answers to the questions gnawing relentlessly at the back of my psyche, demanding to be resolved. Did he know about Olivia and my father? Was their relationship as fractured as it looked on paper?

Not that it matters. I know that. The past should remain dead and buried. If I truly want to heal and focus on my future, the only logical course of action is to go home—my real home. For the first time, it strikes me how drastic the next few years could be, no matter what choice I make. Donatello's method, however, leaves no room for education, no room for music.

No identity for myself beyond my ties to him alone.

"I wish I could explain what I mean without sounding like a dumb son of a bitch," he admits with a sigh. He claims the chair across from me and sits sprawled, his head tipped back. Dark and unreadable, his eyes scan the ceiling as if hunting for an answer among the white plaster. "I was never good at this shit. I think it's a testament to my true nature that I was only married once. God knows what she saw in me. Frankly, I never wanted to venture down this road again. I didn't want this…"

It's strange to hear him admit as much out loud. If anything, some part of me craves this honesty. It's one way that differentiates him from the past. Safiya was never exposed to the real man, apart from the caring protector.

"I could deny it. Claim that it's a lie, and I never touched you. I could tell Mischa to go to hell. I could walk away. I can't lie and say I haven't considered it. I have no right to come to you and ask for you to give me anything more than I gave to you. I know that."

He frowns, his gaze so constricted. Worry lines wrinkle the planes of his face, displaying his age. We've spent so much time in the past, that it still shocks me to realize that seven years have passed. We're different people, no longer tied to who we once were.

"If I marry you, it shouldn't be like Fabio suggested. It shouldn't be carefully planned and thought out. We're not like that. With us… There is only action. Only moving forward, damn what happens after. I caused this mess. But I can't deny that… For the first fucking time in only God knows how long, I feel like myself again. Whatever that is worth. Whatever that means. If we make this work, then we make this work. No thinking it over."

I can't follow his logic. I don't want to. It's dangerous when he talks to me like this, freely without preconceived notions or hatred tainting his voice. When his tone falls into that raspy, easy murmur as if no one else is meant to understand him but me…

He inclines his head, lowering his guard, so I have another glimpse of the figure behind the hard mask he shows the rest of the world. The man beneath is exhausted and battered. He's desperate.

Whatever thought weighs on his mind is so dangerous he doesn't voice it right away. He toys with the phrasing, mulling it over, lost in thought. Absently, his tongue traces his lower lip twice before he finally croaks, "Marry me tonight."

He doesn't move. Doesn't laugh to reveal the request to be a joke—though it has to be. Stubbornly, his gaze returns to the ceiling above, eyeing the shadows painting the surface in varying shades of gray.

"There's no time to talk ourselves out of it. No going back. No more silence. It will be done, and then we move on. We make it work, and we do this the only way we both seem capable of doing anything. Recklessly. Impulsively. We do it now."

He doesn't look at me, not once, and his real motive becomes clear. He wants to scare me by voicing something so insane it can't be plausible. This must be the easiest method in his mind of turning me away. Propose something rash and watch me recoil.

Though what are the alternative options? Go home. Wait. Continue to hide and know that eventually, Donatello will find some excuse to leave.

"It wouldn't be for nothing," he adds as if reading my mind. "This way, you would be protected. I could die tomorrow, and you'd be left with something—not that you'd need it with Mischa… But I want you to have it, what little I can give to you and Vin. And the house, not that you would want it."

Again, he speaks as though he's the only one in the room. The only person whose life has been thrown into chaos. I feel my anger rising, but the second it starts to flare, he shifts.

He's watching me again, his gaze reflective, head still cocked.

"If I were to die tomorrow, I'd want you to have those things with no effort. But that's not the real reason why I'm asking for you to at least consider this."

He pivots, sitting forward, so we're eye to eye. His breath sears my cheek, and it's a nearness that churns my stomach. I shouldn't have so many different versions of him in my head to compare and contrast. The man is a chimera. Calm one minute. Raging the next. Looking at me as though I'm the only woman in the world.

And a heartbeat later, like I don't even exist.

His impression of me has shaped my life for so damn long. Would it be so bad to erase any trace of Donatello Vanici completely? The sad part is that I think it would be the best revenge against someone like him. To cease to exist for once. To be abandoned without a reason.

"I know that you have every right to hate me." He sounds like he's speaking to himself more so than me. Lost in his own world, consumed by his thoughts.

Inhaling raggedly is the only way to make him hear me and reinforce that I'm actually here. He blinks, fixating those dark eyes on my face, scanning intently for whatever he hopes to find. He's dwelling on something, I suspect, hesitating once again before finally spitting it out.

"I'm a horrible fucking husband, if you couldn't tell."

In the background, the lone proprietor rummages through mugs and glasses, returning to quietly replace our pitcher of water. It must have gotten too warm, or maybe she just feels the same instinctive need to fill the silence that I do. I fidget uneasily in my seat, triggering the wood to creak in protest.

He has that look in his eye again.

"I'm no good at love. I'm not good at any fucking thing that doesn't involve killing or money. You'd be a fool to marry someone like me, like this. But all I know is… I need to do something. You don't owe me a damn thing, but I'm willing to try. Something. Anything. Can you give me that chance?"

I flinch. It's strange to hear this note from him. Not a command or a threat, but a question.

Pleading.

My eyes narrow. I can't help the skepticism.

"You're right." Abruptly, he pushes back from the table and stands. "I should go."

Wait. I'm on my feet again, playing right into his hands. He must love how easily he can jerk me around like a puppet on strings.

But he isn't smiling.

When I reach into my pocket a second time, it's with the full knowledge that this is the last card I have left to play. My only remaining method to unnerve him.

The old note is one of the last ones Olivia ever wrote, and his eyes widen as he makes out the crumpled ridges and dried ink. A tremor seems to run through him, making him sway.

"You want to make me read those?" he demands, his voice a dangerous octave deeper. "Fine. You trust me, I'll do it. Whatever you want."

I feel the pen slip from my grasp as those three words hold the weight of so much. A twisted offer that no woman in her right mind would ever take him up on. And yet, it's the promise of the same answers he's been dangling over my head for so damn long.

And…

I'm scared.

It's the emotion I can't admit to Mischa, or even Ellen. I'm so damn scared. The level of fear that paralyzes and freezes the air in my lungs when I think about it. The kind of fear so thick that I constantly feel on the verge of tears.

I'm so sick of feeling afraid because of Donatello Vanici.

I'm so sick of the loneliness, the sleepless nights, and hating him so much it physically hurts. God, I should want to hate him. Every inch.

But for the first time in days, my brain is working again. I can think clearly. I can finally name this "problem" in my head for what it truly is.

I will potentially be forever tied to this man, whether I like it or not. Whether I acknowledge it or not. Whether I return to Mischa's home and lock myself away until I grow old.

I will never be able to escape him.

So why not finally face him on even ground? Take whatever he's willing to give. Anything and everything. Drain him dry of whatever he has left.

I don't have to love him.

I don't even have to like him.

But could I ever trust him?

The answer rings through my skull, hollow and bitter.

No, I couldn't.

I can't.

I stumble past him for the door, aware of his gaze on the back of my neck. Beyond a pane of glass, I can see the streets idling with light traffic. If I hurry, I might still be able to reach Ellen before she leaves. That family loves me. I believe that.

Though, I couldn't say the same were I in their shoes. Especially Mischa's. I've made his life so much harder. I owe him loyalty, and for that alone, I should run now never to look back.

I take another step. Then another. Another.

But I don' t leave. My jaw aches; I'm gritting my teeth so tightly when I turn to face Donatello.

He stands rigidly, his expression pained—like he understands that I'll walk right out of this door. I should.

And he'll let me, that's the confusing part. For a man so hellbent on his own relentless crusade, he'll let me go if I want to leave.

And I should.

9

DON

Theoretically, knocking up the daughter of a powerful rival should be low on the list of crazy shit I've done. I've faced the Hortega Cartel alone, been betrayed more times than I can count, and witnessed the death of my own wife and child. Somehow, amid all that suffering, I remained standing.

Morals aside, I have no problem admitting that this might be a new low. Apparently, rock bottom has one final layer hiding beneath it, paved with good intentions. Surprisingly, it doesn't lead to hell, but a church.

The road leading to this lone cathedral is remarkably devoid of traffic, as if the universe conspired to have all obstacles to this insanity removed. Mischa doesn't come falling out of the sky to stop this, and neither does Fabio even think to ring my cell phone. It's a brief respite from the din of arguments and outside voices. For the first time in a long damn while, the only voice I have to listen to is hers.

Figuratively, anyway.

Her speech is expressed in delicate lines of ink spider-webbing my fingers like a literal example of her hold over me. The hold she's always had.

She sits stiffly on the passenger's seat, her face tilted toward the window. I bristle at the imagery. The illusion that she's here against her will, the picture of a nineteen-year-old girl in the grasp of a madman.

Of course, that's how this appears from the outside looking in. I'm a fucking madman.

"We don't have to do this," I say thickly, though it's a lie. *We* don't have to do this—but I do. "You don't… You could still refuse if you wanted to. Leave."

In fact, her appearance without a retinue of guards in the first place should have been a warning sign. I flit my gaze to the rearview mirror, scanning the empty road as paranoia urges me to question her. Demand answers.

I bite my lip in a bid to remain silent. God, she's the only person in the world to rattle me in this way. Even around Liv, I didn't feel so fucking scattered.

Adjusting my grip on the steering wheel, I scan the street for the nearest place to park. I'll let her out. Call Mischa. Forget this insane plan and fall back. There are other matters to focus my attention on. As Fabio claimed, there's still the pressing need to find the crazy son of a bitch who plotted against me in the first place. With Gregori Saleri suddenly dead, who knows what the sick son of a bitch is planning.

So, I stop the car, still gripping the wheel. "I should have never made you come here. I shouldn't have—"

Her hand lands on my forearm gently—but with the force of a slap. I go rigid before the impact of her silent request hits me. She doesn't need a pen to make her point, at least.

Shut up.

I've selfishly made this about me. Again.

"Fuck…" I tear my hands through my hair, feeling the fingers tremble. I wish like hell assembling my thoughts could be as easy as parting the thick, unwashed strands. Logical reasoning hasn't been my strong suit for a while, but it takes twice the effort around her.

When some semblance of coherence does peek through the chaos in my skull, it's an irrational, childish fear.

Bringing her here could just confuse her further if I don't make my intentions crystal clear.

"I'm not supposed to want more from this," I rasp, watching her go rigid in my peripheral vision. "This isn't about love, but I do care about you. What will happen to you."

Out loud, the words sound more pathetic than they did inside my head. It's a confession I haven't made even to Fabio, and the real reason why my desk has seen more use than my own bed.

Every fucking night since that night in the hotel…

She's been on my mind. In my head. I can smell her. Taste her. Still feel her. Denying it all feels like trying to ignore a festering bullet wound. Sooner or later, the infection will take over.

And I lack the strength to fight it. I'm too damn tired. Too weak against the first damn thing to make me feel even an ounce of humanity after years in the dark. I don't deserve it.

But I never deserved a damn thing I've ever gotten. I've just taken it all.

"I should tell you that all I want is to do the 'right' thing and take care of you. I do… I'm not supposed to want more than that. I can't. But if you think I don't care for you in my own way. I do. God, I do. It's nowhere near enough to make up for everything you've been through, but… I've failed you so many times in the past. We aren't those people anymore, and from here on out, things can be different."

She doesn't react, but follows my gaze to the cathedral.

Ironically, I haven't set foot in this place in years. The last time was…the day I married Olivia, in fact. The memory robs me of breath.

I remember coming here with her, mounting the steps of the gothic-style building with the giddy excitement of a young boy. I held her hand in mine, sporting an idiotic grin as I envisioned her walking down the long aisle to meet me. The kiss we'd share.

The night we'd have after.

I had so much damn hope for the life we would build. Nearly a decade later, Liv is gone, but the building we forged those dreams in looks unchanged. I can't take my eyes off it, towering above like a mocking fixture of how much I've lost since my last visit.

When I finally open the door and exit the car, I'm shaking like a leaf—much like the way I was on that day. But the woman beside me then cracked a joke to lighten the mood, a naughty one about what we'd do to each other once we were finally husband and wife.

I can hear her voice so clearly. Hell, I almost expect to see her as I incline my head. I blink instead, caught off guard by the figure standing by me now. She's inches shorter than Liv, her hair a sun-kissed gold, her body even slighter. Like me, she isn't the same person she was back then. No. Maturity has transformed her features in ways I haven't noticed until now. Her lips are fuller, her chin more rounded, her jaw a firm line given how hard she has it clenched.

For once, I can't even begin to get a read on her. Perhaps I shouldn't want to. Confessions aside, this moment extends beyond our feud or even attraction. It is primarily survival. Protection. All the nuanced shit I've spent the past few years striving to secure for Vincenzo.

The future awaiting Kisa Salvatore is a fate no child carrying Vanici blood should ever have to face.

Not this unborn child. Not Vin… Though, there's no telling what he'll think of me afterward. Or how Fabio will react, let alone Mischa. For the time being, I do my best to ignore anyone else as I reach for the woman by my side.

To my shock, she curls her fingers around mine, and together we start for the cathedral.

Apart from the overcast sky, it feels so…normal. Children laugh nearby, playing tag on a field as the city around us bustles with life at the heart of the mid-morning rush hour. In an unusual twist, Hell's Gambit makes for a cheerful backdrop after the shitstorm of crime that's wracked it the past few weeks.

We enter a cathedral devoid of the tension I feel lancing up and down my spine. From the second I pass through the door, the back of my neck prickles. Something's off, but I don't know if it's paranoia or instinct.

I push it aside and approach the back of the main cathedral. It's dead silent, every footfall echoing like a gunshot. There's no telling what might happen once we leave these walls.

But for now, there's some sense of direction in my life after a long fucking time of confusion and darkness.

Even if it's wrong, I can't deny how it feels…

Better than hiding in Havienna, desperate for a drink.

WILLOW

The prospect of planning a life with Donatello Vanici is a cruel, sick joke. Ironic even, considering I once believed my brain was defective in my inability to envision my future the way everyone else seemed to. Sure, I could construct an idyllic one out of abstract ideas, such as performing before an audience of thousands, at one of the more prestigious concert halls scattered across the world. Perhaps in Paris, or Milan. I'd play to accompany some famous soprano, and that would be a highlight of my career.

I could visualize it all, but only a distant image, as though it were happening to someone else.

It's funny how everything came to a screeching halt after the viewing of a simple billboard. Knowing that Donatello Vanici was still in my life, and so close in proximity...

That day exposed that mental defect for what it always was —a stubborn acknowledgment that no future could ever suit me without first facing my past. The instant I admitted that to myself, all my pretty hopes and dreams burned to ash. Nothing mattered but erasing this stain on my soul. I truly thought that I had to in order to move on. Live. Return to those dreams and never have him darken my thoughts again.

But now, everywhere I look, my future only seems to have Donatello Vanici in it. Whether directly or indirectly, I will never be able to escape him or his influence.

But I'm tired of running from him.

At least in this way, he can't ignore me either.

If anyone had told me months ago that I would be contemplating elopement with any man, I would have considered them insane. And if they mentioned the name Donatello Vanici…

I would have deemed myself the insane one.

The strange part is that I've never felt more firmly rooted in my thoughts than right now. It's like a light has been turned on in the depths of my mind, exposing all the feelings I've been ignoring. The dirty little emotions I should be too mature to feel. Jealousy. Hatred. Regret. Pain.

So much pain that I've felt blinded by it. Devoid of it, I can finally face the man beside me and see only a figure who looks far too old. Exhausted. Broken. A man who might have never been worthy of my admiration in the first place.

"Two days," he says with a harsh laugh that echoes off the walls of the car's interior. "There goes our reckless plan. Two days until a priest can be secured, along with the necessary documents."

He has a habit of doing this, stating the obvious out loud. I guess it's his way of filling the silence that extends between us.

He makes the delay sound intolerable, but it could be reality's way of exposing this reckless plan for what it truly is. Even the priest seemed taken aback. The man, slightly older than Donatello, barely took his eyes from my face. I could sense the thoughts he had enough tact not to voice.

What hold does this man have over her?

She's too young.

"We won't make it ten hours before your father or Fabio come after us with knives drawn. And maybe they should." Laughing darkly, Donatello swipes a hand through his hair, his expression twisted in contemplation. He's falling back into his self-deprecating mindset. Donatello Vanici hasn't met a problem he couldn't turn onto himself. "What the hell was I even thinking?"

He drags a hand across his lower jaw, disrupting the brown stubble growing there. While doing so, he meets my gaze, and his expression transforms for a second time. "Should I take you home?"

He should. That's what every logical cell in my body is warning me to do. Let him take me home and go back to the shame and guilt, and doubt.

No. I shake my head and watch how he processes the answer. His eyes narrow, taking on that thoughtful gleam. "I thought so."

With a sigh, he sits back, bracing his hands behind his head, his gaze on the church looming above.

"I wouldn't assume that you would be willing to go back to Havienna?"

Havienna, my old home now overrun with strangers. Is the little girl, Kisa, still there? I picture her and shiver. Though, as it turns out, I don't even have to shake my head to make my feelings clear because he takes one look at me and scoffs at the notion.

"I'm in too deep, regardless," he muses. "Why not go all in and leave a paper trail for Fabio to follow. We can't hide from him forever. We'll wait for two days and then…"

He trails off, eyeing the sky for a long while before he finally moves to put the key in the ignition. Without another word, he drives off, and a part of me isn't surprised when, minutes later, we pull up to a familiar skyscraper in the heart of the city.

It's the same hotel where everything began, in a sense. A cold sweat breaks out over my neck, dripping down the back of my dress. I blink, wondering if this is a joke on his part. A mocking quip.

But when I look over, he seems just as apprehensive as I feel.

"Staying here might not flag as easily as a new hotel," he explains, a cunning scheme despite the connotations this establishment holds for us both. "Fabio will still track us down eventually, mind you, but it might buy a few hours, at least. Plenty of time for us to…talk." He frowns at the word choice, eyeing his scribbled-over hand. "I need you to hear me out. At least that way… Just hear me out, please."

Despite the plea, he's silent as we enter the building, and he reserves a room with a cheerful receptionist. Minutes later, we're in the elevators, ascending to the upper floors.

There's a grim sense of déjà vu in retracing these steps, this time without the threat of danger looming overhead. I can still recall how it felt to stand beside him, unsure of his motives—much as I am now.

And how desperate I'd been to make myself feel seen. Heard by him. Understood.

For so long, I've stopped myself from touching the memories of that night. There is no point. He even took pains to make sure I knew that it meant nothing. Nothing…

So why is the only thing on my mind now him? My chest aches in a way I'm not used to, and I nearly sigh in relief as the elevator doors finally break apart.

I scramble out first, sensing him on my heels, his silence oppressive. When we finally enter the room, one small detail I take comfort in is that it's not the same one from that day, at least. The color scheme is different, with accents of cream instead of black, and the view from this suite displays a swath of the city with the bay in the distance.

It's still beautiful—no doubt expensive—and I cringe from the thought of how most women might venture here with a lover on their arm. Not a man they've spent nearly half of their lives hating.

"I… Make yourself comfortable," Donatello says.

He moves awkwardly, crossing straight to the bar cart positioned near the door of a spacious balcony. He reaches for a bottle of liquor, only to pause with his hand inches from it. Slowly, his head roves in my direction, his eyes meeting mine. Abruptly, he withdraws his hand and sighs, raking it through his hair instead.

"I haven't even asked you." His tone is level, but I don't miss the way his eyes dart away from me, examining the view of the city. "Have you decided on a course of action? Before today."

His tone conveys exactly what he means. A course of action. An answer. A solution.

There are a million different ways I could respond to him. Slapping him is by far one of the most tempting. In the end, I merely settle for lifting my arms into the air, though I'm aware of another set of documents burning a hole in my pocket. That's right. There might be no need for any "course of action" beyond letting nature run its course—according to the doctor's vague explanation.

I can recall only snippets of what she said, and something that might be guilt pinches at my chest. Despite Donatello's newfound willingness to accept responsibility, this whole mess might be for nothing, in the end...

All I'd have to do is hand over that proof and let him process it.

But I don't.

In the resulting silence, Donatello sighs. A ball of restless energy, he fidgets with another bottle of liquor, lifting it from the cart completely, only to set it back down. Heavy footsteps carry him toward the center of the room, where he begins to pace. There is such a sharp contrast in how he holds himself compared to what I'm used to. Gone is the swagger. The bold defiance that always made him seem invincible. In this moment, his usual bravado is nothing more than a fractured shell.

Not for the first time, I get a glimpse of the real Donatello Vanici, and he is a stranger I barely recognize.

"I didn't ask," he says, whirling on his heel to face my direction. He has his head cocked, eyes narrowed cautiously. "If you even wanted this. I didn't ask you directly."

His attention sears my skin, fixed on me so intensely. There is nothing I can do that won't draw notice from him. The second I start to exhale, he tenses.

"I'm sorry for that. I..." He advances, moving slowly as if to give me the chance to avoid any contact. When I don't withdraw, he reaches out, bringing his hand within inches of my face. His fingers waver, inching closer...

Then he curls each one into a fist and turns away, storming to the other end of the room. He nears the bar cart for a third time, running his hand along the edge of it. "I don't know what to say," he admits, his back to me. "I'm sorry for that. I should know at least what to fucking say."

Shoulders rigid, he continues to pace.

That chilling sense of déjà vu grows stronger. He's done this before, withdrawing inside himself, dwelling over his own internal struggle, blinded to everything else.

I don't realize I've taken a step toward him until he stiffens, stopping mid-step. He watches me, and I think I'm just as uneasy as he is—equally confused when my hand lands against his jaw too softly to be considered a slap. I feel the rugged contours of his face beneath, vibrating with whatever words he's keeping himself from voicing.

There is something so familiar about him that, at times, it physically hurts to be this close. A part of me is still drawn to his stern features, compelled to seek out the hints of softness I know lurk beneath the stoic exterior.

I start to pull away, but then I change my mind and continue to explore the bristly stubble along his cheek. Then down around his mouth.

He watches me, his expression constricted—as though it hurts to have me touch him like this. Regardless, he doesn't resist. Doesn't slap my hand away. It's one of the few moments of power he's ever allowed me, and I extort every last second.

Internally, I mull over my reaction to him, parsing over every nuanced emotion I feel. Confusion mostly. Then remnants of old anger and primarily just...

Pain. It hurts to look at him. Judging from how his frown deepens the longer I touch him, he feels the same.

"I should have been able to face you like a man," he says, the movement of his lips disrupting the placement of my fingers. "The first time. When I saw you... I should have let you drive that knife through my chest like you planned to. None of this would have happened, and you would have... I don't fucking know. Some semblance of clarity. Closure. You could have moved on with your life for once without me holding you back." He reaches up, capturing the back of my hand against his cheek. He holds it there for so long, basting the side of my face with the heat of his breath.

"You deserve that," he admits, his voice rough. "Maybe it's best if I get it out now. So, we can move forward, and there's no more... Chaos."

He pursues his lips with renewed determination. As he cups my jaw against his palm this time, there is no hesitation. I shiver at the warmth emanating from it. Slowly, he guides my head back, forcing me to meet his gaze directly.

"The first day I saw you. Saw you again... My mind went blank. You were beautiful, yes, but that isn't what stood out to me. It was your eyes. Those fiery, hellcat eyes. Even if you weren't who you are..."

Both a Stepanov and Safiya.

"I would have been drawn to you regardless." His voice deepens, betraying a hint of that elusive truth he's avoided voicing out loud. The validation of the persistent part of me driven to find him. See him. Smell him. Taste him.

We're drawn together by something more than hate. He felt it too.

"Though, even in an alternate universe where we never met previously, your father would have every right to kick my ass for being attracted to you."

Not because of a shared horrific past, just that he's simply far older. That age is apparent more than ever in the wrinkles etched around his eyes. And yet, despite the weathered features, they're still objectively handsome.

I hate my body for reacting to him the way it does. My heartbeat quickens, my pulse hammering like mad.

Whatever this attraction is, it isn't reciprocated. He looks at me like he's physically in pain. Agony. As if the mere sight of me torments him in a way I could never understand. Finally, he withdraws his hand, spinning around to face the door of the balcony. He approaches it slowly, lacing his fingers together behind his back, head inclined.

"There is a future you could have, should you choose it. Either way, you deserve more than this. I should take you back home myself—"

I lunge forward, but it's like I'm not in control of my body. Something else has taken hold, and I can only watch on helplessly as my hand flies out, connecting with his cheek.

The slap startles him into silence, but I can't seem to lower my stinging hand. It hangs in the air between us as he roves his gaze from my twitching fingers back to my face.

"I deserved that," he admits. "I deserve a punch, too. Hell, far more than that."

He grabs my hand, startling me. Rather than bat it away, he guides the fingers into a fist, stroking each bared knuckle.

Alarm shoots through my chest, warning me to pull back. Retreat. Run.

Nothing good comes out of letting my guard down around this man. After everything we've been through, I can't risk losing any more of myself than I already have.

But he won't let me escape so easily.

I feel his breath on my shoulder before I even sense his face beside mine, his lips near my ear.

"The right thing to do would be to let you marry Vincenzo," he says, and only shock keeps me from recoiling as violently as I want to. I'm frozen in place, unsure of how serious he even is. Deadly serious, judging from the heavy exhale he releases next.

"A good man would insist that you do that. He would stand aside and know… Your future isn't one he should have any damn part in."

I'll never get over just how damn unpredictable he is. Open one minute, closed the next. Before I can react, he pushes past me, moving stiffly toward a hallway that branches off this part of the suite. "I requested two bedrooms," he adds. "You can have the larger one."

I hear a door slam, and knowing him, I'm sure he locked it. Not out of any gentlemanly concern, either. Merely out of his own selfish fear that I might defy him. That I might creep into that room after him and deny him the last word. That I won't let him hide from this or escape his guilt.

Why should he be able to?

When I can't.

I don't know if I'm surprised or relieved that hours pass without Mischa breaking down this door, or without Evgeni coming for me. It could be that Ellen took my note seriously enough to intervene on my behalf as I requested.

Or that Mischa's finally done what he should have years ago and written me off as someone else's problem. It was never his responsibility to take me in, and everything that's come after is my fault and mine alone.

The guilt I feel is like a noose, constantly pressing on my throat, but never quite hard enough to suffocate me completely. I can only imagine how both he and Ellen might feel. Leaving again is just constant cruelty to them.

And yet, the selfish impulse driving me all along insists that I have every right to handle this on my own. It's my life, after all. My future in question.

And Donatello Vanici has always been my cross to bear.

I can't seem to leave this main room of the suite, even as darkness falls, and the only illumination comes in the form of moonlight, paired with the neon glow of the city at its brightest peak.

I can't even read the letters I fish from my pocket and scan in the dark. Over and over, I stare at them anyway.

Over and over, my gaze flickers toward the exit.

I keep toying with the thought of running, and with every passing second, it seems more tempting. I even start to stand, wincing as my sore muscles protest after sitting for so long. Warily, I take a step. Then another. Another.

And almost as if on cue, I see his shadow, engulfing the mouth of the hallway nearby. Then I hear him, that perpetual low, heavy sigh.

"If you left now, I wouldn't blame you," he says, inching within a beam of moonlight that cuts across his face. I can make out his eyes, intense and yet unreadable. He takes another step, and I wonder if he truly intends to stop me. "But you must be hungry. We can talk over some food."

Talk. This illusive conversation we have yet to have. This time, however, he doesn't seem too willing to give me the chance to refuse. He crosses over to a phone perched on a table near the door. He must dial for room service, because a minute later, he's reciting a handful of meal items.

Once he hangs up, he switches on the main light and retreats to a small dining area positioned near the windows.

Perhaps it's the tension distorting time, but it feels like I've barely blinked before room service arrives. A smiling man enters, carrying our meal on a tray—various steaming items that I doubt he put any thought into ordering. Pasta. Fish. Fruit. Sandwiches.

As the server retreats, we both take places around the table.

And another battle in our unending war commences.

"Eat." Donatello snatches up something seemingly at random—a sandwich that he hastily takes a bite of.

I reach for a set of silverware and fix a serving of pasta on a plate. But I don't eat it. I observe him instead.

That strange sense of familiarity sinks in again. Like we're the only two in the world, nothing else matters beyond these walls, for better or worse.

"If you could live anywhere else, in or outside of the city, where would it be?" It's a question far different than any I would expect, catching me off guard.

Lost in thought, I turn my gaze to the window, inspecting the city beyond. The truth is I haven't pondered where I might wind up after my schooling in Vienna. Few places in the world seemed to hold the same allure of Stepanov Manor, or even Hell's Gambit. It's a rare gem—a mess of a city that glorifies its flaws as much as its beauty.

"This place is a cesspool," Donatello remarks as if reading my mind. "But it has an appeal you can't deny. Even if you go beyond its borders, you never truly leave." He follows my gaze, propping his fist beneath his chin. "I never thought I'd consider returning for longer than a few days at least, to help Vin settle in…"

He trails off, no doubt recalling one of the events he supposedly returned to attend. My debutante ball.

It feels like another lifetime ago. In another world, with far different worries than the ones plaguing me now. Back then, my only concern had been getting through that party and the few months I'd have home before returning to the conservatory.

"I could sell Havienna," he proposes, still facing the balcony. "Find another place somewhere else. A house in the country… A place fit to live in. Hell." He laughs darkly. "Before now, I'd thought my future living arrangements would consist of hopping from hotel to hotel. This place is hell on earth, but it's in our blood—" He nods to the jumbled array of concrete buildings and neon lights.

I stand, drawn toward the balcony to get a better view. The door opens easily, and the warm night air is a jarring slap in contrast to the cooler air inside the suite. Out here, the noise of the city assaults in a barrage of honking horns and distant voices.

It isn't loud enough to disguise the advancing figure who follows me out, coming to grip the railing beside me. He leans against it, tilting his head back to eye the impassive sky above.

"A change of subjects seems to be in order," he declares. "I never told you what sparked my change of heart, did it? Why I reached out to you in the first place…"

He didn't. I shake my head, sensing an ominous tremor wrack my spine.

"You remember Gregori Saleri? That pompous prick? Well, he's dead."

I picture the older counterpart of the duo we've confronted more than once.

"I never got the details, but the point is his granddaughter —remember her? Kisa? Well, despite being born into that godforsaken family, she might not inherit a damn dime. Poor kid. The point is, what use is money or power or any of that shit if it dies along with you?"

While most people would consider the emotional side of a young girl losing most of her family overnight, this is what truly bothers him. Her lack of resources to show for the tragedy. Not the monetary aspect, I suspect. Just the failure of a family's name for protection. The lack of control wealth or power gives anyone in the end. That reality disturbs him enough that his eyes are downcast, his knuckles protruding as he tightens his grip over the railing.

"You still have those letters," he says haltingly, and I feel my throat thicken at the audible pain he doesn't even try to hide. He has another reason for broaching this topic, it seems. "Did she write about how I was never there? That I told her I loved her at night, but spent more time at my desk than in our bed?"

He captures my wrist without warning, shifting to face me. From this angle, his features are bathed in shadow, robbing me of any hope of reading his intentions. Intuition is my only guide. His posture is relaxed rather than hostile, at least. The low, unsettling tone of his voice doesn't even near the enraged growl I'm used to. Even his touch is oddly gentle, providing more than enough give to pull away if I wanted.

"I was a terrible husband," he admits. "A selfish bastard who didn't deserve love."

My breath catches as sweat slicks the back of my neck. Is this his way of confessing what Mischa's alluded to more than once? That he played a larger role in Olivia's death...

"I don't think I'm capable of loving anyone," he continues, his nearness sending my pulse surging. "But I will make you a promise, here and now. No matter what happens, we can do this together—"

A noise sounds from inside the suite. Banging? I whirl around, recognizing the persistent thud—someone is at the door.

Donatello, however, sighs. "Goddamn it, not now."

His shoulders slump, and I suspect he recognizes who our insistent visitor is before he even reaches the door.

I follow him, but it doesn't take long for a familiar voice to emanate from the hall.

"You open this door, you son of a bitch!" If it weren't for the faint hint of polish to that voice, I wouldn't even guess it could be Fabio. He sounds furious, following up his demand with more fierce pounding. "Donatello? Donatello! I know you're in there. How the hell could you do this—"

Donatello wrenches open the door, revealing the man alone on the other end, his fist raised mid-pound. His voice aside, I barely recognize Fabio from his appearance. His usually crisp suit is rumpled, his hair tousled. His eyes look bloodshot, and the faint hint of alcohol wafts from him, another alarming change.

When he sees Donatello, he raises his still brandished fist, slamming it against the larger man's chest. "Have you lost your mind?" he demands as the other man grunts, rocking back on his heels. "You must have. You've gone fucking insane. That's the only possible explanation that might see you out of this with your life, at least. How the hell could you even think of doing something so reckless? Do you know the amount of ass-kissing I've had to do just to keep the Stepanovs at bay? And if you even dreamed of so much as touching the girl, I swear to God, I'll—" He breaks off abruptly as if realizing that I'm here. Blinking, he steps back from Donatello, smoothing his hand down the front of his jacket. "Willow. My dear, I'm here to take you home, and I apologize for whatever ordeal you've been through. I will—"

"No," Donatello says. The calmness of his tone alarms me more than Fabio's frazzled nerves. He stands tall, the picture of poise, and it's as if the two men have swapped personalities for the moment.

"You don't have a say in this, you son of a bitch!" Fabio curls another fist, but Donatello shakes his head before he can launch an attack.

"I don't," he admits. "But *she* does." He gestures to me, and Fabio blinks as if struck dumb.

"She?"

"You once warned me to let her have her peace," Donatello adds. "Why don't you listen before you gripe at me?"

Whether he intended to or not, his right hand is in view, exposing the missives I wrote across it, the ink now smudged and faded.

"You really think you have the higher moral ground right now?" Fabio scoffs at the idea. Still, he turns to me, and I can see him working to compose himself. "Willow…" He breaks off, glaring at Donatello. "I think it would be best if you let me speak to her in private."

Donatello ushers him inside. Then he strolls to the balcony, stepping out into the night air. His stance gives the appearance of relaxed confidence—but he didn't shut the door, ensuring he can still hear every word said.

Seemingly oblivious to that fact, Fabio sighs, raking a hand through his hair. "I'm sorry. God damn him…" He glowers in Donatello's direction, only to seem to remember where he is. "If he brought you here against your will, I'll kill him. But first, I will return you home. I have my men downstairs and a car ready. Your parents are aware, but I've managed to convince them to let me speak to Donatello first." He reaches for my arm, and I nearly trip in my rush to back away.

My thoughts are a blur, and I can't even make sense of them. Helpless, I grit my teeth, eyeing the wall in front of me.

"You don't want to leave?" Fabio sounds somewhere between shocked and fearful. "I… If you are afraid of Donatello, I can assure you that—"

I shake my head again and turn to find him gaping at me. I don't even know how to convey the rush of emotions racing through my head. Maybe shame is the best way to describe it. A fear that I can't go back to hiding in a room alone. Donatello Vanici is one monster I am no longer afraid of.

But shame? *That* is what haunts me. I can't bear the thought of what I've done to Mischa and his family. No longer can I burden them, either.

"I don't… I guess it's not my place to understand," Fabio admits, tugging at his collar. "You have the right to make your choice, and I can't stop you. Even if I don't agree. Not in the slightest." He clears his throat and raises his voice, presumably for the benefit of the figure on the balcony. "You can come back in, you son of a bitch—"

"Keep cursing, and you might shock yourself into a heart attack, Fab," Donatello remarks as he reenters the suite. I don't miss how he brings himself within the dangerous orbit of the bar cart, only to turn at the last minute and perch himself on a leather couch instead. His eyes flit over me before settling on the figure pacing a few yards away, but he hides whatever he might be thinking behind an impassive stare. "Maybe you should have a seat."

"Maybe you should stop fucking up the lives of everyone stupid enough to love you," Fabio snaps back. His cheeks flush the second the words leave his mouth. "I didn't mean it like that—"

"Yes, you did," Donatello says softly. "And you're right. I won't deny how much you've done for me. So, believe me when I say that this isn't your fault. I don't expect you to bail me out of this mess. Maybe that's been the problem all along. I've been too busy letting you fix my fuck ups. It's time that I take the helm on this one at least, don't you think?"

If anything, Fabio's cheeks become even redder. "Oh, don't be a fool," he snaps, throwing himself onto a nearby leather armchair. Groaning, he tips his head and exhales sharply. "Funny of you to want to be noble now, of all times. As much as it pains me to admit, this is a mess that even you, with your vast talent for fucking up, won't be able to get out of alone. You'll need a smooth talker just to buy enough time to develop a plan, let alone anything beyond that. Unless…" He swallows hard, darting his gaze in my direction before returning to Donatello. "You've settled on—"

"No," Donatello growls before he can even voice the option out loud. Then he frowns. "I don't know. It's not my choice to make."

"Yes, well, knowing, either way, will certainly limit our options," Fabio says grimly. "Not that I would be crass enough to voice an opinion either way—"

"Only one person can make that choice," Donatello interjects. I can feel his gaze on my neck as I turn away. It's far more unnerving to hear them dance around this mysterious final option rather than just say it.

Especially when this entire conversation might be moot after all.

"Yes, well, we don't have to focus on that now," Fabio says sardonically. "There are more pressing issues. Things that you and I definitely have control over. If you plan to go unnoticed, you can't stay here, that's for damn sure. Trust me, I'm not the first person to guess that you would return to this hotel. You aren't as brooding and mysterious as you think, Don. You'll need somewhere more secluded, but just as easy to secure. And not that god forsaken Havienna—"

"I'm open to other suggestions," Donatello says gruffly. "But don't use Mischa as your excuse. I plan on facing him directly and making my intentions clear soon enough."

"Like hell, you will," Fabio says with a harsh sound in between a laugh and a scoff. "No. That is one stupid decision I will override. The last thing you need to do is offend the man. I will handle all direct communication with the Stepanovs. And Willow, of course."

"So much for being done with cleaning up my messes," Donatello says with a grim smile.

Fabio doesn't return the expression. "This is so much more than a mere 'mess,' Don," he warns. "This is beyond anything I could have ever thought you capable of getting yourself into. Jesus Christ, a child—"

He breaks off abruptly, his eyes wide. "I'm sorry. God, I'm a fool."

No, he's honest. This is the first time anyone has put it so bluntly, rather than dance around the topic with wordplay.

A child.

Mine.

And Donatello's.

"Willow!" I hear Fabio cry out, but his hand isn't the one I feel cinch my forearm a second later.

"I've got you," Donatello warns, his voice a murmur. He easily rights my balance, but I pull away from him the instant I can.

His nearness is a taunting reminder of everything I've lost, and for a second, I wonder if Fabio is right. I should go home now.

"Whatever you decide to do, it's your choice," Donatello says as if reading my mind. "But know that you have my support no matter what. Whatever you decide, I will respect it."

I swivel my head to inspect him, skeptical of that. Could someone like him truly stand aside and let someone else take the reins of a decision that might go against his own desires? I can't help but think of Olivia and what was revealed in her letters. Did he respect *her* wishes?

Hell, he just confessed that he knew she was unhappy…

"I'm a fool," Fabio insists. I look back to find him returning to his seat, grimacing apologetically. "We don't have to discuss the particulars for now. What we really need to do is cement a plan of action. Make the necessary arrangements to keep you both safe and go from there. Perhaps it might be best to leave the city for a while—"

"We can't," Donatello says softly.

Fabio inclines his head. "Oh? And why not?"

Sighing, Donatello returns to his position on the balcony, letting his voice drift back. "Because I've already scheduled an appointment with a priest in two days."

The room goes dead silent, and I almost fear that Fabio did have a heart attack after all. He stares blankly, his head cocked in disbelief. Then he stands, smoothing his hands down the front of his suit. "And why on earth would you need to see a priest?" he wonders, his tone still composed.

"To arrange a marriage, of course," Donatello replies.

Of all the responses Fabio might experience, the last one I expect is for him to laugh. Loudly in long, booming cackles. He has to clutch his stomach, his head thrown back. Seconds into the display, he seems to realize that no one else is smiling. Slowly, his playful grin falls flat.

"You aren't serious," he says as Donatello reenters the room. "Tell me that was some sick attempt at a joke. Donatello?"

The man in question doesn't respond, instead returning to the bar cart for the umpteenth time. With determination, he snatches a bottle by its neck. Then he spins and throws it so hard it smashes against the wall in a spray of amber liquid and flying glass.

"Jesus Christ!" Fabio exclaims, covering his head. "Have you lost your fucking mind?"

Donatello eyes his trembling hands before wrestling them into twin fists. For a long moment, he doesn't move. Doesn't seem to react at all.

"I'm sorry," he says finally. "I'll clean it up."

"I know this is a lot," Fabio says gently. He crosses the room and cautiously places a hand on the other man's shoulder. "And while it is primarily your fault, I won't let you go through this alone. Either of you. But honestly, do you think that a hasty elopement will help to solve this mess any quicker? I can assure you that it won't. If anything, it will make life way more complicated."

"So, what do you suggest?" Donatello counters. "Keep hiding in shame and pretend this isn't happening? Wait until it's too late? Ignore this mess for another seven years and then deal with the consequences? I'm not willing to do that, Fabio. Not this time."

"Donatello…" Fabio throws himself onto the nearest couch. When he finally lifts his head, he's dropped his polished persona completely. He looks haggard and exhausted, a man pushed to his breaking point. "If you would stop barging into these situations head-on, you might actually realize that more people are on your side than against. You don't have to push me away. I will support you no matter what. But I also can't quietly stand by every time you act so impulsively. Have you considered what Willow might want? What her family would think? How this might play out a week down the road, or a month, a year?"

"I'm thinking of the here, and now; you're right," Donatello admits. "I'm wondering what would happen if I were to have a bullet slam into my skull this instant. How might Vincenzo and anyone else I care about be protected? Sometimes reckless decisions are the only way to circumvent the possibility that life won't always follow some neat plan devised by an accountant, or on a mob boss' timetable. I think you and I know better than most that life rarely follows a particular order. Don't believe me? Ask Gregori Saleri."

"So that is what this is about?" Fabio sighs for the umpteenth time. "You think a wedding solves anything? Though I can admit, this doesn't feel quite the same when it was a way to screw Mischa over and keep him from killing you."

"Which means it should be easier to plan," Donatello counters.

"And what about you?" Fabio turns his focus on me. "Though I assume that if you weren't at least partially in agreement, you wouldn't be here in the first place."

There's nothing I can do to counter that, not that he truly seems to want the reassurance.

"Running away, however, isn't the way to do this," Fabio insists, stroking his chin. "This should be handled correctly, through all of the proper channels—"

"You really think a sanctioned wedding makes much of a fucking difference now?" Donatello interjects coldly. "I don't think Mischa will be lining up to be my best man, either way, Fab."

"Mischa isn't the only one who matters here," Fabio says softly. "I think it's time you start to realize that. Take Vincenzo, for example. What the hell is he supposed to think if you go gallivanting off without a word? No, this must be handled in the right way. No more games."

"So, then what's your suggestion?" Donatello demands. "Keep groveling for forgiveness? I think it's a little late for that as well."

"No groveling," Fabio replies with more of his usual stoic calm restored. "No running away, either. Instead, I suggest you *inform*."

Donatello inclines his head, those dark eyes narrowed. "Inform?"

"I'll arrange another meeting with Mischa—but not to get his permission or agreement," Fabio hastily clarifies. "But merely to inform him of these latest developments and issue an invitation should he so choose."

"Which means?"

Fabio raises an eyebrow. "It means, you position yourself as an arrogant son of a bitch confident in his actions. Mischa could object, of course, but this way, you eliminate some of the appearance of guilt."

"How so?"

Fabio winces, visibly uncomfortable with whatever he's about to propose. "You set a date, but whether or not Mischa attends is irrelevant—" almost apologetically, he cuts his gaze toward me. "What matters is the appearance of propriety. Frankly, though, I'm disgusted with your behavior Donatello. Morally, I'd recommend that you cease this charade completely and make amends—"

"Or?" Donatello demands. The firm set to his shoulders reveals he has no intention of either outcome.

"Or you own the damage you've caused, and you live it. No more hiding. No more running. You own this choice, no matter how disastrous it may prove to be."

"Does that mean you'll help?"

Fabio's pained expression doesn't clearly broadcast either confirmation or a denial. "It seems I don't have much of a choice, do I? I can make arrangements with Mischa, but other than that, I can't control what happens from there. Only the two of you have that choice—and I do hope that it is a consensual choice between the both of you."

Again, he turns his gaze on me as if hunting for any hint of disagreement. When I don't give him one, he shrugs.

"I'll head to my office now and see what I can do. And Donatello? Be careful."

He leaves the suite, but everything looms larger in his absence. The distance between Donatello and me seems almost insurmountable, despite consisting of only a few short feet.

In the absence of Fabio, whatever confidence he displayed diminishes. Silently, he eyes the floor, his jaw clenched in thought. When he finally meets my gaze, I can't decipher his expression.

"Well, Fabio may be prone to theatrics, but he does have a point. What is it that you want?" He sits on the leather couch across from me, palming his chin. The look on his face is pensive but confused too. He's uneasy. God, it hurts how easily I can decipher him in some moments—and yet others, he's a stranger.

"Even if it's… The choice is yours."

I think he believes he's offering me some great favor. A glorified means through which he can wash his hands of any responsibility. His tortured expression suits that image perfectly.

Until he frowns before I even realize why—I've shaken my head.

"No?" He sits back, his head cocked in the way he used to inspect any of his men who dared to question him. "I'm assuming you don't mean that in the obvious sense. You're angry."

It's unfair. Even now, he can read me like an open book when his own motives are so hard to discern.

But he's right. Anger is exactly what I feel surging through my veins, heating my cheeks.

"It's not my place to demand an answer from you at all. Is that what you mean?"

I swallow hard. Then I copy him, leaning my head back against the leather cushions, observing him from this newer angle.

The action draws a choked laugh from him. "You're right." The hoarse note in his voice makes my chest clench. "I don't get to swoop in like some fucking hero and put you in the place of a child. You are not a child. I think you've made that clear more than once." He rubs his jaw as if recalling my most recent slap.

I don't remember if he's said those exact words so bluntly before. If so, they didn't resonate like they do now. It's as if that fact finally dawned on him. No longer can he regulate me to a position easily overlooked.

"Fine," he grates, still running a hand over the stubble on his chin. "We're on the same playing field. This is a fucking mess."

His voice loses the patient, gentle tone that strained it before. He's cold, but honestly raw. I never thought I'd crave to see this side of him so damn much. The unpolished, unrestrained Donatello Vanici.

The cruel bastard capable of leaving me behind. In this instance, he claims we're on an equal playing field, but I'd be a fool to take him at his word.

I sit forward, and his brows draw together with open curiosity. "You don't believe me."

I shake my head again, and he laughs.

"I shouldn't expect you to."

Damn him. This newfound freeness with me is a double-edged sword. His stoic mask slips further, his eyes openly wounded.

"You don't have a damn reason to trust me, do you? Especially not now. Fuck!" He stands, turning on his heels to pace. With this polished, luxury suite as a backdrop, he looks more imposing than ever—a man unraveling. Gone is the false confidence. That reassuring calm.

Perhaps all along, it was merely an act. The truth is, he's just as terrified as I am.

Because I am terrified. It seeps in when I least expect it, sending my pulse racing, coiling my stomach in knots. Watching him storm across the room unravels what little resolve I had. It's humanizing to see him like this. And disarming. This man is far more dangerous when he seems vulnerable.

For the next few seconds, we coexist in strained silence—with me watching him while he sneaks glimpses of me in return. His thought process is a chilling beast to behold. His eyes narrow, his brows wrinkling as his pace overall slows until he comes to a stop just feet from me.

"You don't want me to treat you like a child," he reiterates ominously. "Then I'll be as honest with you as I can. You're pregnant." He breathes out the word. "And it's mine. You can't even begin to understand how fucked up that is—" He seems to stop himself, grimacing as if he has to choke back the words and start again. "You should know how bad this really is."

The look in his eye catches me off guard. It's so stern, and yet that openness remains. For the first time, I can see beneath the cool exterior to just how unsteady he is underneath. He's shaking, his jaw clenched.

"Not only because of how young you are." He inspects me, once again grappling to accept what he admitted—I am not a child.

"It's who you are. Who I am. Frankly, if Mischa wanted to put a bullet in my skull, I wouldn't blame him—"

I'm not sure what I do to make him stop mid-word. Frown? Flare my nostrils? Whatever it is, draws his focus, and he sighs, his mouth tilting downward.

"You're right. Fuck Mischa. This isn't about him. This is about you and me…" He turns with a grace a man with his bulk shouldn't be capable of, coming to stand before me directly. "You don't want to be coddled? Then I'll spare you the false sympathy and the restraint. I'll tell you what I want —I want my child."

His voice rips through me, stealing my breath away. If I weren't convinced by the dark conviction in his tone, then the look in his eye would be proof enough. He's serious.

"I could lie to you and paint you a false picture of what your future will be when the inevitable comes to pass. That I'd step back. Give you time. That you could scurry off to Vienna and leave my child sequestered in Stepanov Manor, pretending I never existed. I'll tell you now—you're wrong if you believe that. No one will keep my child from me. I won't patiently lurk in the background. I will be there. Do you understand me?"

I do. And at the same time…

I don't.

Where the hell was this same man seven years ago? Though, it's not like I need any further proof of what I now know to be the truth. He never gave a damn about me.

And he still doesn't.

He stiffens as if sensing exactly what I'm thinking. Rather than counter me outright, he shifts his gaze to the window displaying the city's waterfront.

"There's more," he says gruffly. "You don't want to be treated like a child? Then enough with the naïve mind games. You tell me what you're after. The responsibility is mine; I'll accept that. But *enough*." He growls the word, his anger apparent in every grated syllable—and pain, too. It lurks beneath the gruff notes, reinforced by his heavy breathing. "I refuse to be the monster anymore in your little game—" He looks at me and grimaces at whatever he spies in my expression. "You don't know what I mean? Fine. I'll spell it out for you."

He advances, reaching me in seconds. Before I can react, he snatches my hand, drawing me to my feet. I sway, off-balance, as he grips both of my shoulders, leveling me with a stern, searching glance.

"Do you have that pen?"

I do. It's still in the pocket of the coat I have yet to take off. When I withdraw it, he snatches it, tossing the lid aside.

Then he lashes out with the nib drawn. I suck in a breath as I watch the metal tip connect with my palm. Within seconds, his intent becomes clear—not to attack but to use my own weapon against me in another way.

He writes, taking his time to form each word so that I feel the lash of ink with the same intensity as if he shouted. *You fucked me.*

"I'm not sick enough of a bastard to blame you for what happened," he adds, releasing me. We're close enough that his breath rakes over my cheek, searing hot. "I know better than that. But what I refuse to allow anymore?"

He strokes my chin with the pad of his thumb, tilting my face for his inspection.

"There it is. That. *That* innocent little glance as if you don't know damn well that you've been playing with fire all along. You know how babies are made. So don't pretend like you don't understand the pull you have. I'm not blaming you. I'm asking…" He looks down, exhaling harshly. "I'm asking you to show me an ounce of mercy in that respect. You stay here; there are boundaries to follow. Rules we will both abide by. Do you understand that? I've told you what I want."

He pulls away, his hands outstretched in a gesture of surrender. With a metallic clink, my pen hits the floor, rolling out of view.

"Just show me that one, small shred of fucking mercy and make it clear what you want. Do that for me, and I'll do whatever the hell it is. I swear to you."

He turns away, retreating swiftly toward the mouth of the suite.

"There are two rooms," he reminds me. "I'll take this one. You take the other. We keep them separate unless invited in."

No such invitation comes as he barrels down the hallway and out of sight. A second later, a slamming door alludes to which of the two rooms he's taken.

I should be relieved, I think. Flattered by his honesty. And his rules. And his assertions. And his lies.

Any other day before now, I'd retreat into the empty room and wait for the morning like a dutiful captive. But therein lies the flaw of his summation of our "situation."

I'm not a child. I'm not his captive. I'm not allowed to question his rules and ultimatums.

He merely expects me to behave however he wants me to—however is convenient to fit the narrative. He doesn't want a real equal playing field.

But if he accused this of being my game, then I alone can make the rules.

And break them.

I don't think; I just follow him down the hall and grip the knob of the only closed door. It isn't locked, opening easily the second I turn the handle.

His back is to me, his jacket already off. I spy it slung over a leather chair behind him as he wrenches at his collar next. Then, he must hear me because he freezes.

There are no words to adequately describe what I feel watching him. It isn't hate—not anymore. Something more wistful than that. Maybe it's simply frustration?

The man is a walking contradiction when it comes to me. *Do this. Don't do that. You're not a child. You're too young.*

There seems to be no in between among the extremes he's willing to slot me into. Not that I can blame him. I've let him take my voice in more ways than one.

But, as he said, *enough*.

The right thing to do would be to end this now. Show him the medical paperwork and let him revel in the fact that our futures might not be linked after all. Squaring my chin, I cross over to the chair sporting his coat and sit down, facing him with my hand in my pocket. The tumult of emotions crashing through his expression one by one are almost comical to witness. He's angry. Angry enough to grit his teeth, his nostrils flaring as he rebuttons his collar and lets his hands fall to his sides. Then frustration becomes evident as he clenches his fists. Finally...

His eyes take on that faraway hue of brown.

"What do you… I don't know what the fuck you want from me." His inflection shifted so drastically over those few words it's dizzying to decipher each nuanced phrase. It's as if he went from cautious coddling to callous and demanding, grappling with his promise yet again. We're on an even playing field, supposedly, but I'm not willing to let him retreat just yet.

It's not fair.

There are so many damn things I need to say, but the method eludes me. It's sadly ironic in a sense. He was the first person who ever made me feel as though I didn't need a voice to be heard. But now, interacting with him is much like trying to communicate through a wall of solid concrete.

I let myself wallow in the self-pity for a heartbeat before I recall the few times I ever managed to get through to him without the benefit of being his precious, charming Safy. I made him listen, either through violence or…

My cheeks flame as he clears his throat. I'd been so wrapped up in my own thoughts, I didn't notice him cocking his head as his expression finally settles on one overarching emotion. Hostility.

"I'm guessing this is your way of making it known you don't want boundaries. Fine." He stalks to another corner of the room, where a chair sits before a small desk. He grabs it, dragging it to me. Then he perches himself on it, leaning forward with his weight precariously balanced on his toes as if he's aching to leave. Run from me.

Instead, he snatches my hand, running his calloused thumb over my palm. I suck in a breath, though I already know what his real intention is. To unnerve. To rouse the shiver that snakes down my spine and make me second guess my own motives.

It's been his method from the start.

This time, I don't give in, leaving my hand in his grasp. Instead, I look up, holding the inquisitive stare that greets me.

"Alright. You have me," he warns gruffly. "So, what now? We rehash the past again? You threaten to leave. Or…" His eyes widen for a split second betraying that this next guess disturbs him more than he will ever admit out loud. "You've changed your mind."

The scary part is that I haven't. Sitting here now, I don't feel that oppressive need to run. Or the guilt or the pain that suffocated me for days. Alone in this room with Donatello Vanici, I'm just…

Tired.

He is exhausting, with his web of secrets and lies. My own experiences with him aside, there's the looming mystery of what happened to Olivia. And my birth father.

And to me.

So no, running isn't an option anymore. To prove it, I manipulate my fingers to squeeze his in return. He doesn't seem startled by the gesture. He stiffens, a sigh hissing through his lips. Rightfully, he sees it as the challenge it is.

"I promised not to coddle you," he reiterates. "Should I explain what that really means? I won't sugar-coat things, either. You go through with this, you marry me, and you won't receive some happily ever after. I could never love you in the way a woman should be loved."

He reverses course, withdrawing his hand from mine. I stare down at the pale, slim digits that seem so frail in comparison to his larger, darker ones, scarred with the remnants of the life of a crime lord.

"I can't," he adds, turning away. The windows in this room are smaller than in the main space, displaying a clearer view of the waterfront and the moonlight painting its delicate surface. He eyes the water with a desperation that chills a part of me to the bone. "I can't love you. I can't protect you. And… I can't give you the closure you want. I can't." He shrugs, but I've never seen a man look more helpless. "So, if that's why you're here, I suggest you leave."

He wants me to, more than anything. Sometimes, he's so good at hiding his real feelings. But every now and again, he slips, and the volatile reality peeks through. Beneath this stoic mask, he is in turmoil, scrambling to cling to that composed bravado he's sported for so long.

He wasn't lying—there is no more coddling, just cruel honesty. But it doesn't sting the way I thought it would.

He's right. Love isn't the name for whatever festers between us; it's something uglier and stubborn that refuses to diminish even in the face of logic. It's greedy and selfish, and hateful.

It's honest and real.

It's… It's better than nothing at all when it comes to him.

Abruptly, he bolts to his feet as if sensing the direction my thoughts have taken. A restless energy radiates from him as he crosses to the window, bracing his hands against the glass, leaning his full weight forward as if he wants nothing more than to crash through the structure entirely and fall.

My throat constricts as I stand and follow him, copying his motions, watching my palms flatten over the cool, unyielding surface. The words he wrote reflect off the polished glass.

You fucked me.

Even with our combined weight, we don't go crashing through.

We just stand in silence, waiting for destruction that never comes.

EVGENI

This is my fucking fault—there is no escaping that truth. As expected, Vanici's gift had a more nefarious aim, and now Willow is missing. Nothing should be enough to draw me from the search for even a second. Nothing.

Save for an order not from Mischa, but from Ellen Stepanova herself.

The second she returned to the manor, I was there waiting, ready to send out every resource at our disposal.

"No," she said tiredly. "Here."

She then handed me a slip of paper I still can't take my eyes off. It isn't a detailed list of Vanici's crimes, but a note, presumably written by Willow herself.

I need to speak to him alone, please. Give me a day. I'm not running away, but I need to do this for myself. I hope you understand.

But I don't. More importantly, I don't understand how Ellen managed to convince Mischa, either, because while I wait for his signal, it never comes. When I finally approach his office, ready to demand an answer, I just find him seated at his desk, his head bowed, hands braced over the wooden surface.

"A day," he grates without looking up. "In the meantime, you follow whatever leads you have on the Saleris. Gregori's death was unexpected—and I don't like it. Something feels off. That being said…" He lifts his head, and I swallow hard at the visible exhaustion etched into his features. "We stay in the shadows for now. That means no attacks on the Saleris or anyone else without my permission. In the meantime, I will cultivate other resources."

"You really think I'm more useful to you playing wild goose chase with a conniving witch?"

He purses his lips as if mulling it over. "I wouldn't trust anyone else to find the truth."

A more tactful way of stating the obvious—find out what Briar Winthorp is hiding. Now.

But after last night, I'm not in a hurry to interact with the woman again.

To buy more time, I enter the service wing, where most of the guards spend their off-duty hours. I've barely stepped inside the modest suite assigned to me, when a knock rattles the door.

"Please," a woman demands, her voice tense.

Damn. When I finally face my unwelcome visitor, I'm unsurprised by who I find. This time she's fully dressed at least, sporting a black shirt and modest skirt.

"Shouldn't you be somewhere gloating?" I demand.

If Vanici weren't a big enough threat on his own, I'd assume she was somehow behind his stunt with the flowers.

Surprisingly, she lets the jab go by without even a smirk in response. "Not gloating. Begging. Trust me, soldier, it hurts my pride far more to ask for your help than you know. But there is no other choice. So, hear me out."

I raise an eyebrow at her gall. "You mock me. Lie. Spin your mind games and somehow believe that you can still manipulate me to your will."

Some of that elusive coyness returns to her gaze. "If I wanted to manipulate you, I'd be willing to try far more desperate methods than asking you outright," she hisses. "But I know that you are far too prideful to be seduced. Even if I presented myself to you naked on my hands and knees, the great Evgeni Volkov would take greater pleasure in denying me. This way robs you of that ability to gloat, at least. Nonetheless, the effect is still the same. Help me. I think that Saleri bastard holds the answer, and I need your help to capture him."

"Why not ask Mischa?" It's a question gnawing at the back of my psyche, lending credence to the suspicion that her true aim in requesting my "help" is far more nefarious.

Then again, she could be telling the truth. Something big is lurking on the horizon—I can feel it. Like the unending calm before a storm when lightning crackles in the air. The only question is, will I be ready when the rains begin, or caught off guard, unable to withstand the onslaught?

Irritatingly, the key factor to everything seems to be Briar fucking Winthorp.

"Frankly, I'm not in the mood for a suicide mission," I tell her, preparing to slam the door in her face.

"No!" With surprising strength, she forces her way in, slamming the door after her.

"No one else will get me close enough. You will." Panting, she faces me, her chest heaving, cheeks speckled pink with exertion. Those blue eyes blaze, and my suspicion grows. She wants far more than a lapdog to accompany her on a wild goose chase.

"I'm to believe Mateo Saleri matters that much to you?" I snarl.

"No." She doesn't even flinch. "And you are smarter than I want to give you credit for. You know how men like this operate, and I don't trust anyone else. Not with this."

I recognize ego stroking when I hear it, despite how much of a shock it is coming from her.

"Get out." I reach past her, aiming for the brass knob still clenched in her grasp.

"Wait! Fine. I'll tell you the real reason I'm willing to undergo this suicide mission. Ali is Jonathan's last and most important leverage. Without him, the bastard has no claim to the Winthorp fortune—"

"So, we switch gears to your son instead of the Saleris," I point out, increasingly skeptical. "Now you've suddenly decided to shoot for mother of the year?"

"Of course not," she says coldly, meeting my gaze without a hint of guilt or shame. "I haven't been a mother to him since the day he was born. But without him, Jonathan has no tool to secure more money. Without that influx, he can't secure the allegiance of fools like the Saleris. They've joined him for their own gain. If that house of cards looks like it might topple, they'll be the first to scatter from the ruins. You can unravel whatever scheme he has in place simply by intercepting my son when he arrives. After that, it will be too late. He'll have him surrounded by security—"

"And you don't care about the risk you might be putting him in if we succeed in getting him out by your so-called brother's men opening fire?"

"He won't," she declares, but I can see the doubt in her eyes.

"Tell me the real reason. Now. Stop dancing around the issue. I want to hear you say it. Do you plan to ransom your own son back to him for a cut of the profit? Or do you want to lead me into a trap while your little cohort mounts an assault on Stepanov Manor? Don't lie and claim that your motives are anything but selfish."

"Oh, they are very selfish," she hisses. "Pride."

The intensity in her voice alone is what stops me from shoving her into the hall. Her cheeks flame as if she regrets that admission, eager to play it off as a coy bit of manipulation.

But somewhere in the forming of another playful grin, her lips fall into a frown instead.

"Congratulations, Mr. Volkov," she says softly. "You've wounded my pride with all of your petty little jabs. I am a terrible mother with no real love for my son. I'm a horrible, selfish bitch, and I only care about myself. And I care if some smug murderer calls my character into question because he has no idea what it is like to birth a child. To be willing to do anything for that child, even if you don't know how. You think you know me, and maybe I'm bitter enough to lure you into a trap out of spite. Or maybe…"

Her voice softens, and I brace myself for the shift in her demeanor. I'm expecting her eyes to take on a more limpid sheen and the low purr she slips into when she's priming to manipulate. I have this woman nailed down from head to toe.

Until she raises her hand abruptly, sending it colliding with my cheek. *Thwack!* The stinging pain draws a hiss from my throat. She didn't hold back.

"You are a fool, and I'm forced to relent to the fact that of all the brawn Mischa employs, you happen to be the smartest, but not by much. You want me to beg and plead?

I'll do you one better." She saunters past me, her eyes on the window. I can't name the emotion I sense from her—something more elusive than anger, perplexing enough that I don't chase after her and wring that slender neck.

"I believed that Ali and I had no allies. That we were alone in a cruel, cold world. Being here, while I do believe that Mischa is a brute, I don't think my dear sister would let him turn away Alexander even if he tried. That makes this place a better home for him than being used as a pawn by Jonathan. Think of this as a mother's prudent judgment, but the game has changed. I don't care what you think of me, or what assumptions you've come up with. But you should realize that I could still go crawling back to Jonathan if I believed he were a better option."

"Even after he's tried to kill you?"

She scoffs. "I've done worse. You have no idea of the ways I've debased myself. All for…" She bites off the words, her eyes blazing.

I could blame curiosity for what draws me to her side. "For what?"

"Oh, dear." She hums low in her throat, that smile quicker than ever. "Isn't this the part where you comfort me, and I seduce you and convince you to help me in my little crusade? All without telling Mischa, of course. Because a man like you can't resist the chance to play the hero."

"Who is the one being pretentious now?" I counter. "I keep warning you. You don't know a damn thing about me."

"Oh?" She places her hands on her hips. "I know that your father was a rebellion leader in a small European country most people have never heard of. Especially not in a city like this one. That you fought for him, and in the process, you participated in the murder of an unarmed family of farmers, including a young girl, barely seventeen years old. Some would consider you a war criminal, Evgeni Volkov. They might wonder how such a man could ever judge anyone, let alone someone like me. I may be ruthless, and spoiled, and cunning, and so on. But I can tell you for a fact that I have never directly killed anyone."

She steps up to me, boldly prodding the center of my chest with her finger. That mocking smile is brighter than ever, her head cocked in contemplation.

"And I wouldn't presume to think I'm better than you because of a few rumors whispered by men every bit as unscrupulous as you. I wouldn't take their word for something I could see for myself. You are a vicious, dangerous man, Evgeni. But for some silly damn reason, I keep believing that you might not be like the rest of them. Hellbent on killing out of the pursuit of money or fame or prestige. Dare I say it? I think you might be a tiny bit less repulsive in your motives. So, sue me for believing that."

"You aren't that trusting," I counter, aware of how damn close she is. The stench of her floods my nostrils. Faint perfume that she must have hidden somewhere in her room. Fresh air. Lies.

She's such a good damn liar that it's almost too easy to forget her original aim. She's more cunning than I gave her credit for, nowhere near as shallow—which isn't a good thing. A shallow woman wouldn't be quite this shameless.

"I see that you've resorted to your so-called plan B," I point out, matching her grin with one of my own. "Seduce me. Manipulate. Spin a sob story about how you've had a revelation. You've changed. And you need me to put my life on the line as your hired muscle. I'm not that gullible—"

"Will you stop?" Her nostrils flare, her hiss too unbecoming to be faked. "I don't want gullible. I want reliable. You followed through for me at the docks when you could have looked the other way. I need someone like that to even have a hope of breaching their security. Too many men will tip them off, and Mischa's hoard has been breached once. Who's to say that more men haven't been bought to the other side? It's not very heroic to have me beg, but I will if I have to. Come with me. You know I'll go on my own otherwise."

"No." I step back, but I see her coming for me, her hand grasping for a fistful of my shirt. I don't know why my first impulse is to suppress the urge to fight. Why I let her scramble to stand in front of me.

"Fine," she snarls. "I shall have to resort to my plan C."

Her lips are on mine before I can process the motion. My hand goes around her throat reflexively, and her teeth graze my lip in a warning. But she never bites. She tilts her head instead, taunting me to chase her. Step into her. Tighten my grasp on her throat so that she has nowhere to go.

I've denied women like her before. Sexy as hell. Tempting. Lying bitches.

None ever got this close, and maybe I should have entertained those previous trysts. At least then I'd have something to compare her to. This lying mouth…

It's a goddamn sin. She beckons with her tongue, inviting me in. The second I relent, her teeth clamp down without an ounce of restraint. *Shit!* As I recoil, her laugh slips into this mocking excuse for a kiss, and her fingers latch onto my collar.

She tugs so fucking hard she could choke me, sucking in a breath as I flex my fingers in return. Her body conforms to mine, and I'm painfully reminded of how long it's been since I've slept with…

Anyone. I can't even remember the last woman, her face a blur. Some one-night stand met at a bar.

Women are a vice I've learned it's best to ignore. No cunt is worth the heartache. The headache. The hell.

Certainly not her.

She grinds her hips against mine, shameless. Damn good. Her nails scrape my chest as she readjusts her grip on my collar.

"Stop." I shove her back, blinking to get my bearings. "Just… Get out."

Turning to the window, I wait for the sound of her retreating footsteps and another sly jab at my expense. The soft hiss of fabric is unexpected. I crane my neck as alarm tightens my spine. Either she just wrestled a gun from the folds of her skirt, or…

Or she shed the fabric entirely, the next pair of soft footsteps marking the moment she stepped from the pile left on the floor. Even as I drag my gaze over her narrow frame, it doesn't sink in that she's fully naked. Not until she advances, her head tilted, her eyes shrouded in shadow.

I've seen her stripped before, but in those times, it was a more obvious ploy. A blatant game on her part. In this moment, the expression on her face differs. She's not smirking. Her throat quivers around a hard swallow as she draws even with me, but her eyes glow with more determination than I saw in her the day I fished her from the water at the docks.

As though she's pledged herself to tackle a new enemy, no matter the cost.

"Don't deny that you want it," she warns, taking another step while reaching out to cinch my collar in her fist. "There's no honor in playing coy now. You get your fix, and then I'll leave to do what you are too much of a coward to do. But don't pretend as though you don't want me. After tonight, we will never see each other again, unless I deign to come and laugh over the smoldering remains of your precious Stepanov Manor."

"So why sleep with me?" There's only one obvious answer to that question, but she laughs.

"I'm selfish and childish. I want some way of proving that I got one over on you. I got you to break down your precious boundaries—" She tightens her grip, wrenching on my collar so hard a ripping sound issues from the fabric. "You aren't so high and mighty, though you certainly do a good job pretending to be. You still want me. Like any man, you are just as weak."

"You are beautiful; I will give you that."

I risk taking another glance at her, hissing through my teeth as my abdomen tightens in appreciation. That was a lie. She's heads above any other women I can remember. Too beautiful.

That's her problem.

"But I wouldn't dare stick my cock in you, even for a quickie."

She should laugh, unbothered that I refuse to play in her little scheme. Her expression ripples instead, her lips pressing into a firm line, her eyes an even colder blue.

She doesn't recoil and saunter away. She holds my gaze unflinchingly, probing for whatever she expects to find.

"I was wrong," she says softly, disentangling her fingers from my shirt. "You aren't as brave as I thought you were. You are a coward. So afraid of breaking your little rules and straying from the straight and narrow. You think that I'm the selfish, foolish one, but I at least know my limits. I know who I am, and I don't go around pretending to be someone that I'm not. I can admit that I'd want to fuck you if only to see what it felt like. But I can only assume that your flaccid personality extends to other parts of your being. So fine. You get out—" She strolls to my bed and makes a show of stretching with her back to me. From over her shoulder, she nods to the door. "I'm tired. That bed in my room is atrocious, and I'd rather get some sleep before I leave. Oh, and tattle to Mischa if you'd like. Don't think he or any one of his goons can stop me. So long Evgeni Volkov."

I'm tempted to deny her. Drag her out of this room by her hair. Or push her onto that bed and show her how heroic I can be. But that's exactly what she wants—to play her game to whatever ultimate end she has in mind.

Well, I'm done being her patsy.

"Goodnight, Briar Winthorp." I head for the door, wrenching it open without looking back. Until I do.

She's still standing by the bed, her body glistening in the moonlight, her eyes fixed in my direction. Her prideful, confident laughter should be what chases me from the room as I finally leave.

Not a sigh.

12

DON

I've committed hundreds of crimes in my lifetime —and I deserve to suffer for every one. This latest transgression merely adds a few more sins to the massive pile, but in contrast to the rest, they stand out. Corrupting the daughter of Mischa Stepanov. Roping an innocent woman into a mess, she doesn't fully comprehend…

I should burn in hell.

The guilt is all-consuming, threatening to swallow me whole. Until I make the mistake of looking over into a pair of watchful brown eyes. Condemnation isn't what I find there. Just a similar guilt she shouldn't reflect so easily.

I may be a fucking animal, but there isn't a damn thing "innocent" about her. She wouldn't be able to inhabit the same room as me if she were. Not for hours, with only our breathing to pierce the quiet.

I keep waiting for the second she'll demand the answers I've promised her. Answers about Olivia. About her. About her choice.

Instead, she watches the sunrise, her cheek pressed to the window, her legs outstretched in front of her, our bodies side by side with only a sliver of space between us. So much for boundaries. We've broken them already, despite no real physical contact. Yet, I might as well have touched her. I feel just as dirty, just as selfish.

Hearing her soft breaths scrape at the air is a corrupted intimacy I know I shouldn't extend. Every time I inhale her scent in return just reinforces how twisted it is that I get to experience this moment at all. Nearness with another person. A night spent in the presence of someone else who doesn't aim to scold or stab me.

It's a fragile peace I'm too much of a coward to break—so I never tell her to leave as I should. I don't exit the room, either.

I relish one more sin, and my damaged soul buckles under the weight of it.

Finally, a ray of sunlight pierces the cloud cover, intruding upon the shadows like a warning. This reprieve is over.

It's time to face the consequences, whatever they may be.

"We should go." I stand, smoothing my hands over my rumpled shirt.

It's no use. I still look like shit, but luckily fashion isn't my aim today. Aware of her watching, I cross over to the chair and grab my jacket, pulling it on. I turn to find her unmoving by the window, those eyes as unreadable as ever. "We'll leave Fabio to attend to his meetings and politics. If you don't mind, I'd rather not deal with your father just yet, either."

Frankly, I'm surprised no Stepanov agents have come barging in during the night. Beyond the window, the morning looks pale, with dark clouds heralding rain looming over the horizon. It's as good a day as any to make yet another bad decision.

"We should discuss our course of action together before involving anyone else," I suggest. "In the meantime, we get out into the city. Keep our ears to the ground for anything out of place. Gregori Saleri's death could be the start of something bigger. You'll be safer with me."

It's a pathetic fucking lie. If there were any intel worth scouting, she would be the last person I'd bring with me. Still, I can't escape this impatient itch biting at my spine. I need to move. Think. More importantly…

"We need to continue our conversation from last night."

That gets a rise out of her. She stands, smoothing a hand down her rumpled dress. A good man would procure her fresh clothing to wear—and something to eat. She needs to eat.

God, my head hurts. I haven't entertained these concerns in a long damn time, perhaps outside of nagging Vin. Caring for someone apart from myself. Remembering the simple things that a human being needs, like nourishment and liquids other than alcohol. It's strange, like flexing a muscle I haven't used in years. So long, in fact, that it's atrophied from neglect.

"I should take you to lunch," I say. "We can get a few things for you to wear too before getting down to business."

Thanks to Fabio, I still have my money and access to my accounts, at least. Shopping will be a good excuse to leave before the accountant returns to continue his scolding.

"You can wash up," I suggest, entering the foyer. "I'll wait."

I've barely left the room when she appears by my side regardless. The stern tilt to her mouth makes her thoughts painfully clear. She doesn't trust me.

Not yet.

Rather than argue, I exit the suite, sensing her fall into step behind me.

I'm half-suspecting to find an awaiting Stepanov cavalcade as we descend to the lobby. Silence greets us instead. The muted tones of classical music playing throughout the lobby feed on this unstable paranoia. I can't shake the need to scan the empty hall, hunting for anything out of place.

Or it could be that I'm just that damn desperate for a distraction in any form. I crave a fight. A confrontation.

She presents the next best thing, though. I can sense her, watching me with those unspoken questions dancing in her eyes. Two months ago, if anyone asked me who I feared most—though a bit too strong a word—I'd probably say Mischa Stepanov.

Now? It's her. This woman from my past, haunting me with that soulless gaze. Looking at her is like reliving Liv's death over and over again. Not just because she shares that twisted history with me. At the core of it, I feel guilt. Guilty as fuck for betraying the only woman I ever loved.

For replacing her with someone who shouldn't be with me in the first place.

This isn't the time for self-pity. Not anymore. It's time to prove to Fabio, and anyone else who might be skeptical that I can function like a normal man for one fucking day at least. The blond head I catch a glimpse of in my peripheral vision serves as the only person who should command my focus right now.

I owe it to her.

As we enter the hotel's garage and find the car where I'd left it, climbing behind the wheel feels ghoulishly symbolic. It's time to take the reins of my own life again, starting with something deceptively simple.

"Today, we'll set the bullshit aside for a moment," I tell her as she claims the passenger's seat. "We'll just…"

I let the statement hang there, unsure of how to finish it. A sloppy beginning to a shopping trip, but hell.

It's better than kidnapping her.

13

EVGENI

I spent the night in the van, watching the house from the shadows, ready for the moment she'd sneak out in the darkness. By morning, there's been no sign of Briar Winthorp.

Either she's developed the gift of teleportation, or she never left.

By the time I reach my room in the service wing, an answer comes in the form of a slender woman lounging on my bed, eating from a bowl of grapes she presumably stole from the kitchen.

She's dressed herself again, her blond hair tied back into a poised bun. To anyone on the outside looking in, I'm the intruder, determined to disrupt her peace.

"You're still here," I say gruffly. My throat is dry after inhaling the crisp night air. If I slept at all, it was for an hour at most. Cautiously, I keep every inch of her in view, envious of the lack of shadows beneath her eyes and her seemingly well-rested state.

"Change of plans," she says, shifting into a sitting position. "If you won't help me take on Mateo Saleri, perhaps you need a demonstration of just what he's capable of."

"And what would that be?" I cross my arms, leaning against the doorframe.

"If the man killed his father, it means he's becoming impatient." Her tone takes on a scolding note reminiscent of a teacher informing a problem student of a difficult subject. "If I know the man—and I do—it's only a matter of time before he strikes out on his own. And if he does, I think I know where he'll attack."

"And where would that be?"

She leans back, smoothing her hands over the rumpled sheets beneath her. "I couldn't help but overhear that poor little Willow's run away again."

I bristle at her mocking tone. "I'm surprised you haven't run to your master to let him know."

"Ah, but I'm sure he does know." She wags a finger at me. "While you were gone in the night, I took the liberty of pilfering this—" She reaches beneath a nearby pillow, withdrawing a slender, black device.

I curse in recognition. "Son of a bitch." It's a cell phone—not mine, but a similar model, most likely taken from another guard.

"I'll return it," she says with a playful giggle. "But Louie wasn't my only special friend capable of providing information."

"A fact that you purposefully hid," I point out. Not only that, but I'm sure she saw through my plan to track her last night.

"The point is, my contact let me in on a little secret you might want to be privy to."

"Which is?"

"Take me shopping, and you'll find out." She tosses the phone at me and lurches to her feet. "And by that, I mean, let me shop in peace while you watch from the shadows like a good boy. Bring your weapon, and I'll even let you keep the rest of your hoard on standby."

My interest is instantly piqued—as is my alarm. "This sounds less like a shopping trip and more like an assault."

She winks. "You're the fool who left me alone all night. Blame yourself."

Damn her, she has a point. I thought to gain the upper hand by calling her bluff and following her straight to her master.

But—grudgingly, I'll admit—she managed to turn the tables.

But to what end?

Briar Winthorp is many things. She's reckless and impulsive like a child denied a sweet. And she's apparently suicidal.

But what does that make me? The idiotic bastard tracking her movements from afar despite every ounce of common sense warning me away. The only upside will be if I catch her red-handed in a scheme against the Stepanovs.

So far, I'm forced to admit that outcome doesn't seem very likely in this location. Rather than a yacht or a crime lord's mansion, she's dragged me to a boutique just near the city's center. More puzzling, it's not located in Saleri territory or within the boundaries of another power player.

I'd almost assume she decided to partake on a carefree shopping spree in between supposedly running for her life.

But she's too smart, and for her to risk being out in the open…

She must have a good damn reason.

Or, she's led the Stepanovs and me into yet another trap.

To distract myself from the folly of trusting her, I take in my surroundings, hunting for even the smallest detail out of place. The boutique itself has a front formed entirely out of a row of large windows that provide a clear view of the interior. There are several similar establishments up and down this block—and by noon, she's visited most of them.

This could all be a game on her part. Watching her observe a red dress near the back of the store, I'm starting to believe that.

The suspicion makes me turn away and scan the rest of the street in the hopes that Mateo Saleri himself will come strolling into view, if only to prove that this isn't a waste of my time.

And, hell… I must be so desperate that my eyes are playing tricks because, while not Mateo Saleri, the figure exiting a black car just a few blocks down looks strikingly familiar. So familiar, in fact, that I push through a passing couple to get a better look.

A man and a woman step onto the curb—with him bracing a hand protectively over her waist. Together, they enter a nearby boutique. Only then, do I get a good look at the man's face. Wait…

Son of a bitch.

There is no mistaking the bastard. Donatello Vanici—nor is there any denying who the small, blond figure accompanying him must be. Willow.

Does her family even know where she is?

I reach for my pistol while grasping for my cell phone with my other hand. I've barely pressed it to my ear when a flicker of movement draws my notice.

Briar Winthorp has positioned herself at the front of the store, seeming to admire a dress hanging in the window display. But then she looks up. I swear those blue eyes find mine despite the decent foot traffic and the distance I am from the store. I even see her lips move, mouthing a silent command.

"Wait."

Maybe it's shock that stops me in my tracks. Either way, the hesitation gives her enough time to hurry from the boutique empty-handed.

I cross the street, braving moving traffic, and head for her, stealth aside. The second I'm close enough, she strains on tiptoe to murmur against my ear, "Easy now, soldier. Put your anger aside and use that brain of yours."

"You knew they would be here."

Her coy smile confirms the accusation.

"How the hell did you—"

"They aren't important," she says dismissively. "But those men? They are." She inclines her head a few blocks down.

I hesitate only a second before following the line of her gaze, down the street to where a gray van lumbers around the corner. Something about it raises the hairs on the back of my neck, and I feel the woman tug on my arm, pulling me into the mouth of an alley so that she's out of the driver's line of sight.

Whoever they may be. The windows are tinted, obscuring a view of anyone who might be lurking inside, but no one exits the vehicle. Instead, it lingers near the store Willow entered.

Waiting.

"You see how gracious I can be, soldier?" Briar taunts. Her voice is that characteristic mocking purr, but I can sense the tension ripping through it. She's worried. Hell, maybe more than that. She's terrified. "You want proof of the danger you and your precious employer are in? Here it is. Now I suggest we stay out of sight and see what they might be planning."

"You think it's an ambush?" When she doesn't answer, I take my eyes off the van long enough to snatch her wrist. "What the hell are you playing at?"

She smiles, though her eyes widen. "You want to spurn my gift? Or do you want to save lives? There isn't much time."

Common sense tells me to break her wrist and grab Willow now. My gut instinct, however? I can sense the unspoken danger tainting the atmosphere, warning me to stay on guard.

The question is, how did she know?

"I asked you what you're playing at." She doesn't resist as I grab her throat next, applying pressure to her windpipe.

Her eyes meet mine boldly without a hint of fear. Either she has a death wish, or she's convinced I won't hurt her. A foolish mindset either way on her part.

I grip her tight enough to make those beautiful eyes bulge. Hard enough to cut off her air completely and risk drawing notice from anyone passing by. Only when her cheeks turn an alarming shade of pink do I let go.

"You have five seconds to tell me what we're doing here—"

"You want to know?" Wincing, she rubs at her throat before shrugging off the discomfort entirely. Then she advances, rising on tiptoe to bring her mouth to my ear. "Then I suggest you employ some *patience*. So, let's get in that van of yours and stay out of sight."

It's stupid to trust her.

But I don't have much of a choice.

14

DON

Considering my credit cards go through without incident, Fabio hasn't cut me off out of spite just yet. All for the better. It's been so damn long since I've done anything this…

Normal.

Every piece of clothing I've owned the past few years was procured by Fabio in some fashion. In this arena, I'm woefully out of practice, and it's funny in a sense. Willow believes that I think of her as a child, when I've barely had control of my own life as of late.

And in the same amount of time, she's matured into a different person entirely.

Setting off on a mundane errand feels almost as momentous as the day I bought my first suit with money earned from my work with the *famiglia*. This store isn't a shady tailor, but a ritzy boutique in the upscale part of the city specializing in women's clothing.

As it turns out, I'm not that invested in shopping after all. I barely notice whatever the saleswoman sends our way.

I only see her face.

She looks just as out of place as I feel. Hours later, she still does, seated across from me in a restaurant somewhere on the city's outskirts, hopefully far enough from Mischa's domain that he won't risk barging in unannounced. Though if Fabio worked his magic, the *mafiya* leader should be swayed from any murderous plots.

For now. Not that being out in the open feels any less risky. Because of the danger of outside enemies, and the danger of interacting with her. Alone. Sitting in this chair across from her is a struggle. It's too quiet. Too damn close in this private dining room near the back of the restaurant— secluded enough that Fabio can't make a scene should he come strolling in unannounced. I've covered every base but the obvious.

I'm still dancing around the topic at the heart of this matter.

What will her ultimate decision be?

I promised not to influence her choice, and I meant that. That doesn't stop my brain from dwelling on it. I lost one child, and it damn near killed me. Is it selfish not to want to experience that pain again?

Maybe not. Ignoring my feelings on the matter won't help anyone. Oddly enough, I don't even know how to put it into words. I just speak. "I bought him a toy once."

She's staring at me—probably has no fucking clue what I'm talking about. I feel this impulsive need to keep speaking anyway.

"Nico. A ball, I think it was. A baseball with a tiny mitt he wouldn't be able to fit for years at least."

I laugh, startled by the sound. It sounds genuine.

"I think that was the happiest fucking day, buying that stupid ball. I could already see him as a grown man, playing in the major leagues. Though hell, he could have wound up like Fab. Still, I would have loved him. I still do. I'm not telling you this to guilt you," I add, looking up.

Her eyes are like mirrors, reflecting how I must appear to her. Unwashed. Unshaven. A man barely capable of taking care of himself, let alone a baby.

I can't argue that it might be an accurate portrait of who I've portrayed myself to be until recently.

"I've spent nearly the past decade letting my life go to shit. If I wasn't surviving on beer and liquor, then it was something far stronger. It's no secret that Fabio's been the one chasing after me, wiping my ass and cleaning up my messes. He got my life back on track, and I know what he wants me to do now."

I don't feel the need to clarify. Her grimace is confirmation enough that she knows damn well what I mean.

"Let you go. Let you take care of this problem and fly back to that polished little school of yours and forget I ever existed. He'd lock me away himself if he thought that would work. He's afraid. I can see it in his eyes. Afraid that this might tip me over the edge and history will repeat itself."

And he has a point.

"I'm not going to pretend like I know any better than he does, and, either way, you don't owe me a damn thing. Whatever your choice is. I can't stop you. I can't even promise you a better future. The reality is you might have to put your entire life on hold and deal with me for God knows how long. But what I can tell you is this. We're in this together."

I reach for her hand—and instantly regret it. She's on fire, radiating heat that burns as if in punishment for daring to touch her in the first place. I want to rip my hand away.

But I don't. I grit my teeth and let the contact linger, sensing every nuance and curve in the delicate fingers trapped between mine.

"I don't want to be bound to the past. I want a fresh start."

Even if I'm not entitled to one in the slightest.

"Do you want the same? Yes or no?"

She hesitates. Then her chin jerks downward, and I have my answer. *Yes.*

"Fabio will be pissed," I admit, feeling a corner of my mouth twitch upward. "Perhaps your parents as well, but what they want doesn't matter. All that does is—What the hell?"

A scream comes from the front of the restaurant. I start to stand as the sound of breaking glass echoes. More screams. Shouts…

Before I know it, a shadow falls over the doorway, moving swiftly in our direction.

There isn't time to think.

"Get down!" Instinct kicks in as I lunge across the table, grabbing a slender wrist before we both plummet to the floor.

I've barely pulled her beneath me when a deafening roar confirms my suspicion in the worst fucking way—this is an ambush.

The potential attackers are too numerous. The Saleris? The Rossis? Someone else? It doesn't matter who.

They're good. I've barely gotten my bearings when another shot whizzes past my head, taking chunks of wood out of the wall. Instinct saves me as I withdraw my gun, aiming blindly.

"Stay down," I hiss to the woman beneath me. Then I stand, racing to put as much distance between us as possible.

Boom!

Pain rips through my shoulder as I stagger to my knees—but the bastard still in the hallway is already falling to the floor, his body lifeless. His face is bared, but I don't recognize it. Groaning, I haul myself upright, raising my weapon as someone else comes to take his place.

Only, this man I recognize instantly—and only one fact keeps me from pulling the trigger.

He works for Mischa Stepanov.

15

EVGENI

A detour to the hospital is too risky, given the attack. That's the excuse given to Vanici for why he has to settle for a private doctor to inspect his wounds, anyway. The good news is that he was only grazed by a bullet, not hit. He'll live.

The bad news is that his exam takes place in an abandoned wing of Stepanov Manor under the watchful eye of at least a dozen guards—all of whom await Mischa's arrival. I'm not a fool. The fact that the bastard came here of his own accord means he has his own motives for meeting with Mischa on his territory.

Either way, Willow is home where she belongs, and Vanici won't be here for long if I know Mischa.

"Is your job to play nursemaid to me?" Vanici himself snaps as he pulls on his bloodied shirt. A row of bandages encircles his left shoulder, but apart from that, he's unharmed—though apparently not very grateful to the man who saved his ass. He glowers in my direction, his posture tense. "Or to find who the fuck did this?"

"We're searching the bodies now," I snap, but he has a point. It wasn't a coincidence that I happened to be there in time to intervene.

And for such a sloppy hit to take place in broad daylight…

Well, if Mateo Saleri was behind it, that only gives more credence to Louie's claim that the man has lost his fucking mind.

Though one person was able to predict him—and I don't think it was due to her innate gift of feminine intuition.

"Watch him," I tell one of the men posted near the door.

Before I step into the hall, I look back at the only occupant of the room other than Vanici. She leans against the wall unobtrusively. Our eyes meet, and she flashes a weak smile, but she doesn't move to follow me out.

I don't push her to. There will be plenty of time to speak to her later.

My nostrils flare as I turn my attention to another woman, trying to picture where she might be. I move swiftly, intending to hunt her throughout the manor. Instead, I find her staring from one of the windows just a few rooms down.

"You knew," I say coldly. "How?"

She inclines her head as if she didn't notice me until now. "I assume you appreciated my gift," she says coyly. "Believe me or not, but that was just the first attempt. There will be more. There is only one way to stop them. You defeat one cell, and another will spring from the ashes. The game is only beginning."

"Stop speaking in riddles." I grab her wrist, spinning her around to face me. "I want answers."

"And you'll get them," she says, stone-faced. Her eyes don't even blink, and it's a rare show of resolve on her part. "Once you uphold your end of my little request. Help me find Alexander. No extra force. No sloppy tactics involving the *mafiya*. You help me alone."

"It's sounding more and more like you really want to isolate me in particular, Ms. Winthorp." I don't intend for it to sound as suggestive as it does. "I have to wonder why that may be."

"Don't flatter yourself," she says with a simpering smile. "Your skillset is of use to me, nothing more. Considering your current standing with your employer, I doubt you'd be of use for any relevant information. Even under torture. I need you because, frankly, you're the only man capable of performing this task that I have leverage over."

At least she's honest.

"And, Mr. Volkov, time is running out," she adds. "If you refuse, just tell me now, and I will most definitely do it on my own. But you might not catch the next time a strike team is called on one of the many, many Stepanov family members.”

“You want my help?” My common sense bristles at even entertaining the prospect. I'd only be springing the trap she no doubt has in mind. “Then tell me one damn thing. How did you know?”

She smiles, but her eyes take on a hard gleam. She's on edge. “I already told you. You have your 'friends in low places.' So do I. I had a hunch, and it happened to pay off to your benefit. You should be thanking me for being so thorough.”

“So much for your story of being a poor, hunted woman all alone in the world.”

“I never claimed to be lonely. Your imagination is running away with you, Mr. Volkov. All I claimed was to be desperate. Desperate enough to keep tabs on whoever may be of interest to the men 'hunting' me.”

“If I do this, you tell me more than a few hypothetical hunches and riddles. You give me everything. All of the intel you know.”

“I thought you'd never ask,” she counters. “But I'll honor that request, only regarding what is necessary to complete your task. Be a good boy and do your job admirably, and you might earn another reward.”

“And if I were to go to Mischa and tell him of your little scheme—”

"Pardon my use of such trite phrasing, but that would be the equivalent of sending a raging bull into a china shop. You do anything to risk Alexander's life, and a sniper team will be the very least of your concerns."

"Does that mean you aren't planning to bring your son back to the bosom of this manor? You plan on going on the run."

"And if we do, trust me, it will be better for everyone in the long run. You deny your enemy of his leverage, and I miraculously get out of your hair. Everyone wins, as they say."

And yet, I get the sense she's deliberately holding one or two details back. The suspicion gnaws at me, clashing with curiosity. But I can't take the risk of another attack.

"When?"

Her smile falls, and a hint of her genuine fear crosses her features for a split second. "Tonight. Thanks to you, we've lost ground and time. I'll need to meet with my contacts and devise a new plan of attack—"

"That undercuts your desperate narrative."

"Desperate, but not stupid," she snaps. "A trait I'm sure you can appreciate."

"So, I'm supposed to just turn my back, let you meet with your 'contacts' in secret, and blindly do your grunt work like a good boy."

"Now you've got it." She places her hand on my shoulder. "Be ready by midnight."

"You think I could just sneak away after what's happened?" The guards will be on red alert tonight.

"That's your problem," she counters, swaying her hips with every step. "Don't be late."

16

WILLOW

This homecoming unfolds nothing like the first. Ironically the circumstances are no different. Violence. Bloodshed.

With my life precariously in the balance by a cruel twist of fate.

It's as if I'm being punished for my crimes, too numerous to name individually. This chaos is all I deserve.

But I wish I could undergo it alone.

It doesn't feel fair that the Stepanovs keep getting caught in the crossfire. If anything, only one man deserves to be punished alongside me.

Donatello Vanici.

He promised me answers, but they feel more elusive than ever. In the end, I'm not even sure which outcome would provide closure. If he played a hand in Olivia's death, it would cement every vile, horrible thought I had of him and then some. I would be justified in hating him.

But if he were capable of such a heinous crime, then everything I thought I knew would shatter right along with his lies. The memories of my past will collapse. Everything will have been an elaborate lie colored by my own naivety.

Another fear is more selfish. He loved Olivia enough to forgive even a transgression of that magnitude.

And yet, he condemned me for something that wasn't even my fault.

In both scenarios, I wind up hating him.

And yet, here I am, watching him wince through the pain of his injuries, still striving to live up to his unshakable persona. I'm getting better at seeing through the act, though.

He's in real pain. Though the bullet grazed his shoulder, the wound stings whenever he moves. He must crave a painkiller to take the edge off, and yet I saw him deny what the physician offered. His stoicism could be the cause, but I doubt that in this case.

Much like me, he's punishing himself, though he doesn't feel the need to resort to dwelling on the past and his own shortcomings. He prefers to suffer.

"Let me guess," he says gruffly. "I won't be able to stroll off this property, huh?"

A man lurks near the doorway, gazing stoically ahead. I know that look. He's received his orders. Now he's merely enforcing them.

"Thought so." Donatello scoffs, and I can't tell if he's apprehensive at all for the inevitable.

I am. My palms sweat, my throat so tight it hurts to breathe. While Donatello seems content to wait patiently for his punishment, I'm not so calm. I'm dreading seeing Mischa again, knowing I put his family in danger.

And I'm afraid he'll ask me to stay.

I can't ignore a growing part of me determined to resist that request no matter what. Shame is merely part of the reason. The other is greed.

I'm so close. To what? I have no idea, but it's a taunting, elusive prize. Deep down, I sense that I'll never be able to move on without facing it.

The truth?

Mischa could beat an answer out of Donatello for me. He is more than capable of that.

But I don't want him to. It needs to be me, and I can't avoid the confrontation anymore. Donatello owes an explanation to me and me alone.

He stiffens as I stand and approach the old bench that's become his makeshift hospital bed. This room is in the lower level of the manor, easily accessed by the servant's entrance—and out of earshot of the main part of the house where the children might be.

Coming here was strategic, but I can tell by looking at his rigid stance that Donatello doesn't intend to stay here for long. Hissing through his teeth, he shifts to face me.

"You can go if you want," he grates, wincing. "I'm not keeping you here against your will. I can face Mischa alone without using you as a shield."

I blink, thrown off by the statement. Belatedly, I dissect it, homing in on his coarse, grated tone. Go. He thinks that is what I want. To scurry away and let him leave.

No. I shake my head, weighing the option of brandishing those letters again. I still have them. With him bloodied and trapped, I could force him to read each one. Make him react. Make him answer.

"I don't think you'll have a choice," he says, and I flinch at that. Even now, he keeps forgetting the promise he himself made me. To let me stand on my own.

His eyes narrow in alarm before I realize why—I've jerked my chin defiantly. But that's only part of what has him on edge.

Footsteps approach our direction swiftly, echoed by a voice.

"Get back," Donatello warns just as the door flies open.

I don't even recognize the man standing on the other end. Mischa? Or a monster. Only a flash of blond hair registers before he surges, crossing the room in a heartbeat to reach Donatello.

A monstrous crash shakes the very foundation of the house. At the center of the commotion stands Mischa, grappling with a man every bit his equal in terms of bulk and size. The only difference?

Only one of the men is actively attacking the other.

"Mischa!" The shout comes from another figure racing through the doorway. "Stop!"

Ellen—but I doubt he even hears her. Fully enraged, he's singularly focused on driving his fists into every part of Donatello he can reach. Over and over again.

Impulse drives me forward, within his line of view.

And he goes still, his fist raised. "Willow... Leave," he commands in a harsh tone I've never heard him direct at me. "Get her out of here!"

"I suggest you listen to her," someone interjects.

I don't recognize the voice at first, nor the figure speaking. His nose is bleeding, painting his face in swaths of scarlet that obscure any defining features. Except for his eyes. That hue of brown is unmistakable. "I'm not here to fight with you—"

"I know why you're here." In the blink of an eye, Mischa is composed again. Only his disheveled blond hair reveals the violence he enacted just seconds ago. That, and the blood on his hands.

"Willow." He meets my gaze, his jaw stern. "Go—"

"I said you should listen to her," Donatello warns, swiping at his jaw, painting the sleeve of his shirt a brighter crimson. "She isn't a child."

"And you claim to speak for her?" Mischa pivots toward him, his fists clenched. "I think you've done enough—"

"I second that." This voice isn't Ellen's, but the newer figure who appears in the doorway, briefcase in hand. That's right. Fabio was meeting with Mischa originally. Both must have been aware of the ambush soon after it happened.

"In case you gentlemen have forgotten, an attack was just launched on both families in broad daylight. That was an elite team. No identification. No easy way to trace their origins. Hell, they don't even seem to have fingerprints. Paired with our recent troubles, and the death of Gregori Saleri, to say I'm concerned is an understatement. Now isn't the time to fight." He enters the room, broadcasting his trademark confidence, but I note a tremor in his usual swagger. He's on edge, more than just a little shaken.

"I received a message," he says thickly, proving my suspicion true. With a sigh, he looks up, his expression grave. Anxiously, he wrings his hands together before finally clearing his throat. "A warning, more like. Mischa has already heard this little missive, Donatello, so brace yourself. Our enemies didn't beat around the bush. They've demanded a trade."

"A trade of what?" In an instant, Donatello transforms into the man capable of running a crime syndicate.

"They want the Winthorp woman. Supposedly you've already met her acquaintance."

"Winthorp woman?" Donatello raises an eyebrow, but I can easily picture just who he means.

Briar Winthorp. Ellen's estranged sister.

The same woman we got a bloody introduction to while on a stolen yacht.

"And what if we don't 'trade'?" Donatello snaps.

Fabio sighs again. "They specify they'll take a life if their terms aren't met within twenty-four hours."

"Interesting that they would specify some woman rather than Gregori's own goddamn granddaughter. Mateo's made his priorities clear. So, whose life is on the line this time?"

"They didn't specify," Mischa interjects, and I jump, turning to him. "But it doesn't take much to guess."

I feel a shiver wrack my spine as his gaze flits in my direction.

"It would be bold for them to target her outright," Donatello says, but his tone is less hostile. He's thinking, employing that trademark cunning that always allowed him to zero in on a target. "Not to mention mount an attack in broad daylight. It's stupid, too, knowing the reach of the *mafiya*. It's reckless—"

"I wouldn't call any of this opponent's actions anything other than reckless," Fabio points out.

Donatello shakes his head, still actively bleeding, not that he seems concerned by the constant stream dripping down his chin to the floor. "No, what I mean is, this doesn't exactly square with the patience used to plan an attack on the harbor. Or the hospital."

"There was no tact," Mischa agrees, grudgingly thoughtful. "They're getting desperate."

"Or this isn't the same person," Donatello suggests. "What once was a cohesive operation is splintering. Someone's getting impatient and trying to tie up loose ends, most likely without the input of their other partner who's been helming the plan from the start."

"Infighting?" Fabio says. "We could use that to our advantage while homing in on the leader of this scheme."

"Or," Mischa adds. "This could spur them to be bolder and take more risks. We can't take any more chances."

Donatello nods. "Agreed."

It's astounding how quickly these men can morph from enemy to ally when presented with a larger threat. All three stare pensively into the distance, working through a million different plans and tactics in their heads.

At some point, they must remember the still simmering hostility because they stiffen, training their gazes on each other.

"So, what is our next move?" Donatello asks.

"Our?" Mischa echoes, his tone an octave deeper.

"You can't possibly intend to honor their demands," Donatello surmises. "So, what is your real plan?"

Mischa frowns, mulling over the possibility. Suddenly, his eyes cut in my direction. "We shouldn't discuss this here."

"She's not a child," Donatello says offhandedly. "She deserves to know what's going on as much as anyone else."

"So, you think you can dictate how I raise my own daughter?"

"No." Donatello stands fully upright, rolling his shoulders back. "I'm saying, she can make her own decision without being ordered like a child. Do you forget who saved your wife and son? I haven't."

It's ironic to hear him say this considering he only made that determination for himself within the past twenty-four hours. Still, it serves to shift the mood of the room entirely.

Though, he's only half right. If I'm truly entitled to my own choices, then he shouldn't speak for me either.

Inhaling deeply. I step forward, sensing all eyes turn to me.

"Do you want to stay?" Mischa asks.

My mind is racing with so many opposing thoughts. *Lurk in the shadows. Don't.*

In the end, all I can do is nod.

"That settles it then," Fabio says, stepping forward to coincidentally place himself in between the two men. "Whatever we do, it needs to be quick. I suggest we don't give our enemies any chance to regroup. We strike fast."

"What do you suggest?" Mischa demands.

Fabio begins to pace. "We mount a silent assault. Something deceptively simple, but that will give us the upper hand. We know the docks have been a consistent point of interest for this enemy."

"You want to strike there again?" Donatello asks. "But where? I doubt Mateo Saleri will let us board his boat so graciously this time."

"No. But we know that they have their sights on one area in particular. Your harbor office, Don."

"Yeah, which is now mostly in ashes," he grouses. "So, what should we do? Blow it up our damn selves as a warning?"

"No. I'm thinking something a bit more literal," Fabio says with a devious smile. "If they want it badly enough, we can use that to our advantage. We can't waste time going after every rogue mercenary operation or dead-end lead. We need to cut off the head of this snake."

"So, you offer the territory as a trade instead?" Mischa asks. "I don't see how that presents a better option."

"Not as a trade," Fabio counters. "Donatello offers it for sale at a price too tempting to resist."

"You want me to sell that property for a steal?"

"But that will lure them out," Mischa says, his head thoughtfully inclined. "They won't expect it."

"And they won't be able to resist," Fabio adds, nodding. "If I can trace their accounts, with my various contacts, there is no end to what I could accomplish. Transaction logs. Links to any private airfields or any other purchase. We could use those records to pinpoint their movements and perhaps discover where they might be staying while within the city."

"Then we pay them a visit," Donatello says darkly. "And confront them head-on."

"Won't that take time to arrange?" Mischa sounds skeptical.

"In usual circumstances, weeks," Fabio admits. "But with my contacts, I can arrange to have the property listed within hours. If advertised via the right channels, our mystery buyer will be alerted soon after. I suspect they won't wait long to make a move out of fear that someone else could purchase the property and add a wrinkle to their plans."

"It's sneaky, Fab; I will give you that," Donatello admits. "But, while I'm not a vaunted money man, even I could see that it screams 'trap'."

"Yes," Fabio concedes. "But if they truly need this property—"

"They won't be able to resist. They might try to purchase via a proxy, though."

"Yes," Fabio concedes. "A possibility I'm prepared for. In that respect, the true buyer wouldn't be untraceable, but it would take more time."

"Which we don't have."

"It's better than nothing."

"We need a backup option." Mischa takes the floor now, his brows drawn together in contemplation. "Something to lure them out on two fronts."

"So, you think we should hand over the woman as well? Ruthless, Mischa. I didn't think you would be that cutthroat."

"We don't give them a damn thing. Just *appear* to," Mischa says. "I doubt the ringleader would show his face so easily, but it could leave them unprotected."

"Which could be a decent strategy if we can trace their main location. It would be an attack on two fronts, and they wouldn't see it coming."

"So, we take matters into our own hands," Donatello says. "We set the time and place for the trade within three days. At the same time, the sale goes live, and we wait it out."

"There is one problem with that strategy. It could look like coordination," Mischa says. "Especially if it seems we are in communication."

"Yes." Fabio strokes his chin thoughtfully. "Which could definitely complicate things. However, if the feud between your families appears to be alive and well…"

"They might not second guess either the sale or supposed trade. In fact, they might even feel cocky if both the *mafiya* and Donatello are willing to offer up two vital parts of their strategy."

"So, we need to stage a fight," Donatello says, warily eyeing Mischa. "One that will convincingly show we're not close in the slightest."

"Might I suggest…" Fabio seems to hesitate, his expression dark.

"I think I can guess where you're heading," Donatello says grimly. "It's a dramatic tactic but not entirely implausible."

"Care to enlighten me?" Mischa cuts in.

Fabio and Donatello share a glance before the former says, "A wedding would suffice. One that seems as though it comes at the cost of good relations between both families."

"So, you want to use my daughter as bait?" Mischa's voice is so cold I can't tell what exactly he's thinking.

"Frankly, I was planning on marrying her anyway."

The silence that falls is chilling.

"Mischa…" Ellen steps forward, reasserting her presence. She places a hand on his shoulder, but he gently shrugs her off.

"And you think admitting that now changes a damn thing?"

"It was for security," Donatello says. "Inheritance. So, she could have complete access to my assets should anything happen—"

"Your assets…" Mischa turns to me, his brows drawn.

Of course, Ellen must have told him what the doctor revealed. I wait for him to voice as much.

"An archaic solution, but strategic," Fabio says before he can. "And, to be blunt, it wouldn't be the most egregious part of this situation by far."

"In your opinion," Mischa growls. "But you aren't the grown man with a failed career and no prospects who preyed on the woman who was supposedly like a daughter to him. After, of course, you sold her into slavery and left her to die."

Donatello flinches as if struck, but my cheeks flame. I've never heard him talk like this. Judging from the gleam in his eye, this is only a fraction of what sparked his hostility when it comes to Donatello.

"Not to mention, the rumors," he adds in a dangerous hiss.

"Oh, don't play coy now, Mischa," Donatello counters. "Lay it all out, gossip and all."

"Well, the *gossips* claim that you killed your wife in a blind rage, your son along with her. That you sold your young ward not out of petty revenge, but out of prudence. Those same gossips claim that the girl witnessed your crime, or had knowledge capable of incriminating you. Rather than kill her yourself, you took the coward's way out."

So much for the fragile comradery. The shift in the atmosphere is so palpable the temperature seems to drop. It's degrees colder, but no one moves or reacts. We're all frozen.

Fabio recovers first, clearing his throat. "Given the subject matter—" anxiously, he tugs on his collar, his cheeks reddening. "I don't think this conversation is appropriate to have right now after all—"

"No," Donatello says hoarsely. His expression is stoic, but those eyes betray him, wild and narrowed to slits. "Let's hear his so-called gossip, which sounds far too outlandish and specific to have been thought up on the fly. I wouldn't have pegged you as one to fall prey to rumors, Mischa."

"Not a rumor. Let's call it secondhand information that came directly from a source with firsthand knowledge of at least one of your crimes. They don't have the best reputation, but in this case, they have no reason to lie, either. And paired with your current actions? I'm more inclined to believe them."

"And what does that mean?"

"That I wouldn't put it past you to manipulate a woman who might hold the key to ruining your name for good. Manipulate and seduce her into ignoring the past and keeping her silence. Before, you sold her to gain leverage, but now you use more underhanded tactics. Does that sound too 'outlandish' for you?"

I watch as Donatello processes the accusations one by one. Whether intentionally or not, his expression shifts to visually convey alarm, then disgust. And finally…

Guilt? The tension in his jaw makes my breath catch. Just as quickly, he quashes all traces of the emotion behind an iron mask.

"I shouldn't dignify that bullshit with a response." Real anger breaks through his fracturing composure. "But I will anyway. I would never hurt my wife. Ever. Funnily enough. You have. The scars are visible for anyone to fucking see, and yet you want to insinuate that I'm the monster?"

"Enough," Fabio exclaims, once again scrambling to insert himself between the two men. "All this fighting will do is waste more time, and nothing will be accomplished. Set your differences aside. There will be plenty of time for name-calling later. At present, all that matters is neutralizing this threat and finding out their true aims before more bloodshed is unleashed. Understood? First things first, I believe the wedding plot will be the perfect way to throw off suspicion and potentially lure them out. In fact, we should go a step further. Set the wedding on the same day as this supposed trade. I don't think they'll be able to resist such a tempting arrangement. They could launch an attack, secure the harbor and their target in one go."

"Which means they'll pool most if not all of their resources on that location," Mischa says, switching into the mindset of a tactician with a chilling ease. "Which could also increase the risk. But we could head them off. They won't be expecting the full resources of the *mafiya*."

"But that will all require careful planning," Fabio says. "No room for deviation and no room for mistrust. Whatever the details are, we need them nailed down securely. We won't be able to communicate until the day of to avoid rousing suspicion. We need full transparency and trust."

"I'd be risking my neck while you get to stay safely within your manor walls," Donatello points out, his face still partially bloodied. "It wouldn't be hard for you to turn the tables and join forces with our enemy to take me out for good. I doubt working with an arsonist and crazed murderer would be any different than taking intel from a human trafficker."

Mischa scoffs. "You forget, those bastards tried to kill my son."

"I could say the same when it comes to you."

The tension ratchets up again, until Fabio claps his hands loudly. "Enough! If the threat of carnage and death isn't enough to cease this infighting, then nothing will. So go ahead. Kill each other here and now and save anyone else the trouble. One would think that nothing would trump seeking out an enemy who has managed to catch you both unawares not once, but several times. I understand there are…complications. But for fuck's sake!"

"You're right." Donatello clears his throat. "We will have plenty of time to kill each other later." He laughs, but it doesn't reach his eyes. "In the meantime, we need to settle on logistics and fast—"

He winces, rubbing at the bandages around his shoulder.

"We'll need to leave the property unseen," he grates. "Then we need a base of operations. Somewhere in the city that won't raise alarm."

"No doubt they'll be watching our every move," Fabio says. "But if you *were* to elope in three days, the hotel suite wouldn't be out of the realm of possibility. I've already had your suite surveilled for sniper access, and it's relatively safe from that kind of assault. I could arrange to buy out the nearby suites for your men."

"It's more secure than the house," Donatello admits.

"So that's settled," Fabio says. "Then I'll find a way to make it known that tensions are higher than ever between the two of you and that the impending wedding is a powder keg."

"But won't they question it?" Mischa says. "My daughter is attacked, and I let her go with you without hunting down the attackers?"

"We'll need a way to throw off suspicion," Fabio admits. "A plausible way to explain why you wouldn't join forces."

Donatello clears his throat. "Well… If I thought you had sent them after me, without realizing Willow was nearby, that would explain it."

Mischa nods, his expression thoughtful. "It would give me an opening to contact them seemingly on friendly ground."

"And plenty of opportunity to forge an alliance," Donatello adds. "Not that you would."

"This is a game of wits, gentlemen," Fabio insists. "We must keep ours and remain one step ahead. Now, with that settled, we need to put our plan into action. Soon. I'm sure our enemies are watching this manor and have already noted Donatello's presence. If we delay any longer, their suspicion will be piqued before we can even get a real plan into motion."

"Fine," Donatello grudgingly says. "How to beat a madman at his own game? Where to begin?"

17

DON

I've learned the hard way that there is no benefit to being sentimental. The past is a weight around a man's neck and to dwell on it is to tighten the noose.

Or maybe that's just what I told myself to cushion the blow that I barely remember those bitter days around Liv's death.

I could write off Mischa's accusations as petty jabs. But not her reaction. Not the look in her face as he voiced each one in cruel detail. There wasn't alarm or even horror to be found in her eyes. Just fear.

Terror.

As if she already knew.

To her credit, she's tried confronting me herself with Olivia's letters, and, like a coward, I used that desire as leverage.

I should be grateful to whatever sick motherfucker has me in their sights. They've bought me time to stall, but I can't avoid the truth forever. It gnaws at me, playing on the gaps in my memories and planting festering fears in those spaces. As bullshit as Mischa's little explanation sounded…

It also makes sense. Fuck, it makes *too* much sense—that I'm a worthless monster who killed his own wife and tried to silence the sole witness.

That would explain her pain. Her hate. She sought me out intending to kill me, and I more than deserve that retribution. If I hurt Liv…

I'd deserve death.

Yet, I still can't bring myself to face those accusations directly. Instead, I hide. Not even in our shared suite but the one below it. Under the guise of clearing the premises, I've been in this room overlooking the bay for nearly a fucking hour. It's cowardly, but I can't bring myself to leave. Not until I've gathered the nerve to face the truth, no matter where it may lead.

"Sir?" One of my men calls from the doorway. "Any trouble?"

"No." I turn toward him, heading into the hall. "All clear. You can bring the others in."

"Right away, sir."

Out in the hall, another holdout from Antonio Salvatore's forces stands guard, falling into step behind me as I approach the elevator.

Thank God for Fabio. The man must list God among his many connections because barely two hours after our conversation at Stepanov Manor, he's managed to clear out the necessary rooms in the hotel and arranged to have part of my men meet me here.

All that's left now is to enact stage two of the plan.

"Give me a minute," I tell the guard once we reach the upper floor. He stands at the ready as I withdraw my cell phone. Typical Fabio, he answers on the first try, but I can hear the tension in his voice.

"I take it you're back at the hotel. The rest of your men should be arriving shortly, along with your 'guest'."

Judging from his strained tone, he's referring to Kisa Salvatore.

"I think you'll be pleased to know that a buyer has already expressed interest in your harbor offices. Several, in fact."

It sounds too damn good to be true.

"Any clue on which one might be our mystery man?"

"Not yet," Fabio admits. "Frankly, I think I underestimated the popularity of that particular location. You've gotten far more inquiries than I expected. It shouldn't be hard to weed them out. It's simply a matter of who is willing to pay more."

"So now what?"

"Now we wait," Fabio says simply. "In the meantime, might I suggest you go over the plans for your sham wedding? It needs to be convincing, after all. An event suitable of rubbing Mischa's nose in your dastardly scheme."

"That's one way of describing it," I croak. While I haven't been able to get the bastard's taunts out of my mind, it seems Fabio hasn't either.

"In any regard," he says, "feel free to drain your emergency accounts all in the name of making this event convincing. Financial ruin wouldn't be the worst situation you've put yourself in by far."

"Thanks for the encouragement, Fab," I snap. "What about the church? Think it will work as a suitable trap?"

"I have a team on it now," he says, serious once again. "We won't be able to completely eliminate the risks. I suggest that we take every precaution."

"What? You mean a bulletproof vest?"

"Can't be too safe," Fab says. "But... There is one more thing."

"What?" The change in subject has me gritting my teeth in grim anticipation. "You've sounded off from the second you picked up. What's wrong?"

He sighs. "I take it you haven't heard, then."

"Heard what?"

My guard is up instantly. Has Mischa decided not to play nice after all?

"I honestly don't know if you'll see this as good news or bad, but… This wedding might turn out to be more of a sham than intended, which is a good thing in my estimation."

"What the hell are you getting at?"

"Willow might not be pregnant after all, according to the tests run at her last exam. It's a longshot, but this all might have been a fluke of blood work explainable by other factors."

"A fluke."

Jesus Christ, he wasn't lying. Good or bad doesn't seem like the right characterization of this news either way. To be honest, he could have stabbed me, and I'd process it better.

On the face of it, Willow Stepanova gets her perfect life back and a future without me in it.

On the other hand…

"Don?" Fabio's voice is a fraction louder, as if he's been repeating my name with increasing alarm.

"Yeah… I'm here."

"This is the worst possible time to go, I know—but I think it might be best if we don't communicate regularly for now. Before I hang up, there is one more thing."

"That you think I killed Liv?" I'm only half joking. All things considered, he has every right to suspect me of the worst. His hate would be easier to handle than whatever I feel swelling in my chest.

"No! Vincenzo."

"How is he doing?"

"He's fine," Fabio says. "Itching to leave the hospital, in fact. I've doubled his security detail, and there is no sign that he's been targeted."

"Is this your way of telling me that I can't see him until further notice?" It's hard to keep the irritation from my voice.

"Not at all," Fabio says, surprising me. "In fact, I think you should see him. Perhaps tomorrow. Anyone with the slightest bit of reliable intel would know that if you truly believed Mischa was partly responsible for the attack on your life, nothing short of the Devil himself could keep you from checking on Vin."

"Point taken. It isn't like you to be so accommodating."

"You're right," Fab concedes. "I'm merely hoping you take that juicy carrot and won't complain as much when I bring out the stick. Given how tenuous relations are, and your past history, I believe it would be best if you and Willow settle on a few boundaries."

"You mean that if she isn't pregnant, don't use this timeframe to make it so," I taunt—only my tone isn't even close to joking this time.

"I'll let that gross insinuation slide because even you aren't that sick," he says tiredly. His polished persona slips, revealing the true man beneath. One so damn exhausted he can't even bother to put energy into his voice.

Damn. I've been so selfish I didn't stop to think how hard this might be for him, constantly hearing Liv's name dredged up.

"I'm sorry," I say, not that it matters any. Still, I feel compelled to offer him something, no matter how small. "You know I would never hurt Liv—"

"Of course, I know that," he starts. "Don't even think I would—"

"But to be totally fucking honest with you, Fabio… I don't remember. Everything is in bits and pieces. I don't think I would…"

I eye my free hand, scowling at the divots and marks scarring the palm. A blue patch represents the sole remnants of a sprawled message written in ink. Only one word is still legible—*truth*.

And the truth is…

I have no fucking idea what I could have been capable of. The memories of that time are a jumbled mess with no real clarity to be found. But I do know one thing.

Mischa Stepanov won't be the one to throw whatever truth there is in my face. I'll seek out the answers my damn self, starting with the most obvious.

"You were my rock in those days, Fab," I say hoarsely. "Tell me what you remember, no matter how fucked up it might be."

Hell, I'm even holding my breath.

"No," he snarls. "You need to be focused only on the present. Looking backward won't solve anything. All it will do is just bring up more pain for everyone involved."

"I know where I can get some answers, though," I say, turning in the direction of said answers, and the person wielding them.

"What are you talking about?" Fabio demands.

"Don't worry about it. I'm sorry you ever got dragged into my shit. You're the best, Fabio."

"The best," he echoes faintly. "Don't forget it. I always have your best interest in mind, and that when you forge into these situations alone is when things tend to go wrong. Don't shut me out. What answers are you talking about?"

This affects him too, doesn't it? He deserves to know something.

Swallowing hard, I croak, "You know about Liv's letters?"

His silence is disarming. It isn't like Fabio to be speechless. After a few more seconds, he clears his throat. "I do. And I thought we both agreed that it would be better for everyone if they weren't disturbed. The past should remain in the past."

"Easy for you to say. You aren't the one who could have killed his own damn wife."

"Do you really think I would have stuck by you all of these years if I believed that?"

"Fab…"

To be brutally honest, I don't know why he has stuck around all this damn time. He doesn't owe me anything, and after all of the hell I've put him through.

"Some people might say you should have cut me loose years ago."

"Some people are dumbasses," he counters. "All that matters is getting through this current peril unscathed. To do that, we need total honesty. Where are the letters?"

His reference to them irritates me for some unknown reason. It could be his cautious tone, the same one he might deploy when dealing with an unruly child.

"I'll deal with them, don't worry about it. Take care, Fab. You're right; we shouldn't talk much."

I hang up, sensing in my gut that something is off. Unbalanced. Despite Fabio's insistence to the contrary, the past is alive and well, and I will never outrun it.

The only way to leave it behind for good is to overcome it.

No matter the cost.

Stowing the cell in my pocket, I finally enter the suite, ready for anything.

The entrance hall is empty. The only other occupant lurks in a study overlooking the harbor, her back to me. There are no pretty words to ease into this conversation. No way of avoiding the hard reality, either.

"The letters," I blurt out gruffly. "I'm ready to read them."

She spins to face me, an eyebrow raised. In the space of time since leaving the manor, she's changed into one of her new outfits—a plain black dress with long sleeves. It might only be her proximity to the window that allows the faint daylight to paint the panes of her delicate cheekbones, but she looks older in a heartbeat. Someone who has seen too damn much in her time, aged by pain and trauma.

"I'm ready," I repeat, crossing over to a nearby desk.

I wait for her to leave and retrieve them. Instead, she turns to face me fully, revealing that she already has them pressed to her chest.

I swallow hard as the old handwriting catches the light. My nostrils flare, sensing the faintest hint of sweet perfume. Each breath guts me. For a second, I'm there again. The woman before me morphs into one with a similar build but dark hair, her gaze accusatory.

Did I hurt her? Every fiber of my being tells me no. I never would. Damn Mischa for ever insinuating as much.

But deep down...

Doubt infects that confidence, festering with every passing second.

"Please." I extend my hand, and the specter of Olivia morphs back into Willow Stepanova. She approaches me warily, placing the letters before me one by one. What I at first mistake for a haphazard arrangement soon reveals itself as something more deliberate.

"This is the order you want me to read them in?" I ask, meeting her gaze.

She nods, but her expression isn't gloating or triumphant. If anything, she looks resigned. Like someone lighting a match, intending to set off a bomb—but with no excitement toward the impending boom. Just dread.

Unlike Fabio, she isn't afraid to set things into motion though. Finished with her placement of the crumbled letters, she steps back, turning her gaze to the window.

I stare at her for a dangerous few seconds. Far longer than I should. I'm only stalling from the inevitable, but I stubbornly let my gaze linger, hunting for any signs of hatred or disgust that I might have missed. She should be brimming over with both, to be honest. She should hate me.

And if I truly hurt Olivia and sold her to hide my own guilt...

She should want me dead, and she'd have every fucking right to.

18

EVGENI

For one woman to so thoroughly throw my plans into disarray, chaos must be a talent of hers. Along with destruction and deception.

Unfortunately for her, her luck might have just run out.

They're keeping her on the lowest level of the house—a layer of security that might be unwarranted for someone of her stature. Unless, of course, they want to keep her protected rather than merely keep her prisoner.

It's a thought that won't stop weighing on my mind as I make my way through the labyrinthine halls to reach the old wing where two men stand guard. They nod wordlessly as I approach and let me past.

"I've seen worse forms of captivity," I announce, taking in the spacious room and the sole woman occupying it.

They didn't give her any windows, instead shutting her within an old storeroom lit only by an overhead lamp.

Someone cleaned the cobwebs from the rafters, at least. Fresh sheets drape the lone bed, and she was provided with a table and chairs to sit on.

Regardless, I suspect that Briar Winthorp finds these lodgings far beneath her standards. I've never seen her stare quite this cold. She doesn't even flash a charming grin as I advance. Instead, I can almost see the hair on the back of her neck rankle.

"You seem stressed, Ms. Winthorp," I say, though nowhere near as nastily as I could.

Regardless, her eyes flash, and she's practically on tiptoe. "Damn you. Unless you've come to uphold your goddamn bargain, then get the fuck out."

I feel myself raising an eyebrow. "That's not the usual greeting I've come to expect from you."

"Do you think this is a game?" She gestures wildly to the plain white walls surrounding us. "You think this will hold them off? God damn you fools. I warned you, and now we're all nicely packaged for the slaughter."

"Explain."

My tone startles her into silence. She blinks, raising an eyebrow of her own.

"As if you didn't orchestrate this idiotic excuse for a plan," she snarls. "I'm sure your hand was all over this, but I will warn you now, it won't work. God, I should have left when I had the chance—"

"I don't know what the hell you're talking about," I say over her. "So, I suggest you start talking before you pepper me with insults."

Her lips flatten into a hard line as she inspects me, her head cocked. I can see her suspicion warring with confusion. Finally, she inclines her head further. "Your beloved master aims to use me as bait in a trade. The idiotic fool doesn't seem to realize that he's fallen for a very clever trap. They won't settle for biding their time for a neat handover. They want me dead, and they don't care who gets in their way."

"A trade?"

Her eyes narrow, and once again, I sense her questioning my motives. I wish she had a reason to be so skeptical, but the twisted part is that…

I don't fucking know what the hell she's talking about. After his meeting with Vanici, he and Mischa left the compound, and none of the men left behind seem to know a damn thing. Until he returns, I'm in the dark.

But I know better than to let her know that.

"You don't know, do you?" she surmises. Rather than taunt me over that fact, the line of her mouth grows even tighter. "It seems you still haven't wormed your way back into your master's good graces."

"Then I suggest you drop the act and enlighten me if you hope to have an ally in this mess."

Her eyes widen for a split second before more suspicion displaces the shock. "Is this part of the trap? Feign innocence to get me to reveal what I know?"

"You say that as if you haven't been honest up until now, Ms. Winthorp."

"And perhaps I haven't." She steps up to me, her lips still pressed in a stern line. "I wanted you to help me find my son so I could leave this godforsaken place and never look back."

"You could have left without him," I point out. "And you yourself admitted that you aren't the maternal type. I'm supposed to believe that overnight you had a change of heart?"

"No," she says softly, and something in her gaze shifts, darkening the hue of those blue eyes. "You're supposed to believe that I am prudent and ruthless but not heartless. Have you stopped to think what drove me from them in the first place?"

"You learned something," I say, hazarding a guess.

She nods. "And I'm sure that even a man as literal as you can guess what that was. Think. If you were a man who stood to gain everything, what might you do to anyone or anything you felt might impede your progress?"

"Your son," I say. "He threatened him?"

"Not in so many words." She looks away, and I'm sure it's to hide her expression. She's lying.

I grab her shoulder, wrenching her around to face me. Her expression conveys an emotion alright. Fear.

"Maybe I was stupid enough to be tempted by his lies," she admits, her chin jutting stubbornly. "That I could have my family's wealth and prestige returned with the flick of a pen."

"It sounds too good to be true," I point out.

"Of course, it does," she snaps. "But I don't think you've ever known what it is like to go from having the world at your fingertips to ruin overnight. To having to rely on the very people who ripped your life apart to pick up the pieces."

"I think you should be careful when it comes to insinuating things about me, Ms. Winthorp," I counter.

"The point is, I didn't realize the full extent of their plan."

"But you knew it involved a child, Eli Stepanov, losing his life in the process. You just didn't think you'd have to get your hands dirty to carry out that part of the process when it came to regaining the world at your fingertips."

"I knew he had to be removed from the line of succession," she clarifies coldly, her expression stone. "I didn't think he would have to be killed to achieve that. Use your imagination, Mr. Volkov. Everything isn't so damn literal."

"And the real world doesn't cater to the blind naivety of a penniless socialite desperate to regain her family's fortune, either. So, you joined in with this grand scheme and got cold feet. Then what?"

"Then, I realized that there was never any real choice presented to me, either. If the plan did succeed and Alexander stood in line to rightfully inherit what is his birthright, that bastard had no intention of sharing the wealth any more than Mischa and his brood."

"You would find that both you and your son were the new obstacles needing to be 'removed'."

"Exactly," she hisses.

"But it's more than that, isn't it? A child can be manipulated, but not if his ambitious mother is there to whisper in his ear. No… You found yourself becoming the obstacle. It wasn't the case that you miraculously gained a conscience overnight. It's that you realized sooner or later, you would be next on the chopping block."

"So, what if I did?" She shrugs in defeat, but her gaze is suddenly averted from mine. There's more to this she isn't saying. "It doesn't matter now, does it? I've been here too long, and they've probably suspected the course of action I'd attempt to take next."

"Retrieving your son, you mean?"

She nods, meeting my gaze again. Her eyes blaze with a fierce, vicious energy, but for the first time, I suspect it isn't directed my way. "They won't take any chances now."

"You mean they'll move him?"

She nods. "He's probably out of the country by now."

"He might be," I say. "But I think you're overlooking one key detail."

"What?" Her brows draw together, her irritation palpable. "Don't play games with me, soldier. Just spit it out."

"Unlike you, I'm not partial to shrouding everything I say behind word games and a riddle," I snap. "He bought him here for a reason. What was it?"

From the way her eyes narrow in contemplation, I have my answer. "You don't know. Do you?"

"I assumed he wanted him close out of smugness at his impending victory," she says dryly.

"But it might be for something else. What?"

When she doesn't answer, I grab her wrist. Fear flits across her features, and it takes her longer than normal to recover. I feel her stiffen, every bit of muscle going rigid beneath my grip.

"You think manhandling me will get you the answer?" she asks tersely, still jutting that chin.

"No." I release her and turn toward the door. "I think you don't have any fucking options left but to give me an answer. Or watch me leave knowing that all of your efforts spent manipulating me weren't worth a damn—"

"I know where he might attack next," she says.

Damn her. I stop short, still poised to take another step. "Where?"

Slow, confident footsteps march in my direction. I don't look, but I can easily picture her reassembling that stoic mask piece by piece. When she finally comes to stand before me, I realize I'm right.

"Wouldn't you like to know?" she says with a coy tilt of her head. "But that would require cooperation, Mr. Volkov. Frankly, my patience is running out trying to get that through your thick head."

"It also requires honesty," I say. "Something you seem to be reluctant to give. No more. Either you tell me the truth, or I leave. Better yet, I'll convince Mischa to go along with the trade, no backup in mind. Then I'll see firsthand just what your old master has in store for you."

Her eyes widen, her lips pursed. I've struck a nerve, it seems.

"The harbor was just the beginning," she says. "A distraction. He's laid the groundwork to take over the city quickly, but now he needs to put it to good use. If you were a man intent on running the world, what might you deem necessary to enact your devious plan?"

It's another fucking riddle, but at least this one has a more obvious answer.

"I'd disable my enemies," I say cautiously. "Then position myself to replace them at a rapid pace. Make it impossible for anyone else to compete."

"And if you were using the Saleris as your cover, what business might you be interested in?"

I mull it over, feeling my eyes narrow as I home in on the most likely target. "Trafficking. I'd trick the Saleris into thinking I wanted to help them broaden their reach and clientele. Then I'd bring in my own resources on top of their head. By the time they realized what was happening, I would have already parasitized their network for my own."

"Exactly." Is that grim approval I catch in her tone? "But even more ruthless than that. To take over an existing network, you need allies, but you also need resources. Such as…"

"Manpower," I say, not liking where this is headed. "I would feel confident if I knew I had other allies hidden in the background, waiting to advance and push the previous partners out. He's aiming to bring them in."

"And soon," she says. "My suspicions tell me they must exist outside of the country, but with access routes via water that should be easier than ever to utilize given the precious destruction."

"And you don't know any names? Any organizations?"

Though a few come to mind already—none of them reassuring.

"Now you see the reason for my urgency?" she says. "Once he gets those reinforcements in place, it will be a numbers game, and I can assure you that the math isn't on our side."

"Shit." She could have mentioned this all sooner, not that it makes a damn bit of difference without knowing any of the specifics.

"What if there was a way to alert the Saleris? Get them to turn if only in their own self-preservation?"

"I don't see how," she says. "They seemed pretty convinced. I don't know what he's told them, but it must be enticing enough to ignore the many red flags. They won't see the betrayal coming."

"But they might if it comes from the right person," I say, warily. "I think I know someone who could fit the bill. We don't need them on our side. We just merely need them to withdraw their support or at least try to circumvent their destruction. It could buy us more time."

"All this use of 'ours' and 'we'," the woman says, her smirk returning in full. "It's very heartwarming, soldier."

"I don't mean you," I snarl, ignoring how her face falls. "Mischa. You can still serve your purpose as bait."

Her upper lip pulls back from her teeth, her hands in fists. I half-expect her to lunge at me, given her fierce expression. Instead, she scoffs.

"Still playing the role of a thick brute, I see."

"Bait, for appearances purposes," I say. "While I do your dirty work and gather intel. Isn't that what you wanted all along?"

She frowns, startled by the shift in subject. Her eyes tell all as she wrestles with the idea of trusting me or not. In the end, she seems to settle on the only solution available to her. She doesn't have a choice.

"Give me locations to check and anything else you remember. I'll need to do reconnaissance on the Saleris while also trying to discover who the other ally might be."

"While I get to sit here and look pretty?"

"Don't tell me you'd prefer to be out there getting your hands dirty?" I toss back.

"Fine. I will tell you what I know," she says, but I can sense the caveat coming a mile away. "In return, you add one more task to that little list of yours."

"And what is that?"

"You find where my son is, and you get him back."

"He's the key to this whole masterplan, isn't he?" I ask. "Without him and the promise of a Winthorp fortune to pay off his debts, your old master can't fund his devious little plans. That might leave him in a bind with a lot of dangerous enemies."

"Rationalize it how you'd like," she says without revealing a shred of emotion either way. "Just promise me you'll do that."

"I don't make promises." I turn to the door and knock once. Meeting her gaze from over my shoulder, I add, "Especially not to someone like you."

"To a 'threat' you mean?" she counters.

"No. A dangerous liability."

WILLOW

*I*t's wrong. But I thought I would get a sick sense of satisfaction from watching him relive the past, finally. As he does, I witness the same realizations dawn over him in the exact order they must have affected me the first time I read them.

Shock. Confusion. Then utter despair as he fully surrenders to the throes of agony, having to face the consequences of his own actions.

And yet, this isn't the same as holding him to account for his betrayal. What happened between him and Olivia was more personal. Intimate. Something that I know in the pit of my soul I have no right to see unfurl.

I'm not entitled to the kind of pain that contorts his body the more he reads. It started in his face, with his brows drawn tightly in concentration and his lips pursed. Then disbelief. His jaw went slack, his eyes widening. I thought he'd drop the letter entirely, but he didn't, finishing the page before woodenly grabbing another.

Then another.

The most terrifying thing to witness in him is the grudging acceptance. It steels into his expression, hardening every line. Before my eyes, he's stone, impossible to discern anything from.

I don't know how long he stares at that final page, crinkling the paper beneath trembling fingertips. It feels like an eternity before he finally lowers it, cradling his face in his hands.

Once, I prayed to witness the destruction of Donatello Vanici with my own eyes. I craved to see his despair. Weep. I wanted to gloat over the bastard at his lowest point and be the one to have driven the knife in deep.

Faced with that very sight, I don't feel the triumph I thought I would.

It's cruel. It's harrowing.

It's pain.

"Is this what you wanted?" His voice is so deep I can barely make out the individual words among the mass of grated syllables. "For me to know that my wife was unfaithful. That my son... That he wasn't mine. Is this what you wanted me to see?"

He looks up, but the anger I expect to find is absent from those worn features. He just seems old. Exhausted. A man at his limit, unwilling to carry on a step further.

And my heart aches, bruised and swollen with guilt I shouldn't feel.

"I deserve this," he admits with a weary sigh. He smooths his hands over the letters as if grasping for any trace of the figure who wrote them. In the end, his trembling fingers come up empty. "Every fucking bit… But—"

He breaks off, gritting his teeth, his gaze on the window. Watching him is like viewing the ravages of time on a man in mere seconds. He ages, hunching over as if life is draining from him.

"I didn't know. Or I didn't fucking remember. Fuck." He rakes a hand over his jaw, drawing notice to the dark stubble growing there. It's been days since he's shaved. His eyes seem darker in contrast, haunted by the horrors he's survived until now. "How could I not remember?"

It's something I've been dwelling on since he first made that assertion. How? It seems improbable that something that's shaped my entire life could conveniently leave his memory.

But now I see the truth. He hasn't let himself remember. He's blocked off that space of time, building mental walls around the pain and drowning his present thoughts in whatever vice he could to dull the pain.

"I loved her." He stands, gripping the desk. There's a harshness in his movements that wasn't there before, as if every step—

every breath—takes all his effort. He sways unsteadily as he crosses to the window, and he braces both hands over the glass as if it's the only thing in the world capable of holding him up.

That uncomfortable feeling in my chest throbs the more I watch him. Sympathy? Or remorse?

This seems…wrong. All wrong. Like I'm seeing only a small piece of a larger, more complex puzzle—and it's jagged, liable to cut anyone foolish enough to handle it without knowing the fuller context.

"God, I loved her," Donatello says, scowling down at the city he once claimed for himself. "Can I even blame her if she felt alone? Neglected? I loved her, but I can't deny that she came second. There was always something else in the way."

Another bastion of control to take. Another bit of power to snatch. Another piece of the world to conquer.

"I knew what it was doing to her," he adds. "What it did to all of you."

He turns, meeting my gaze, and I stiffen at what I find lurking behind those dark irises. Agony. His eyes glisten, threatening an inevitable outcome.

And yet, I don't believe it when the first few tears fall, painting a sparkling trail down his cheek.

I have to inch forward and touch one for myself, catching a fat bead of moisture. It's so warm and wet, bursting open over the pad of my thumb.

He doesn't cringe from me or attempt to hide the aftermath. At the same time, the sight doesn't reduce him any. A crying Donatello is every bit as fearsome as the smirking man, wielding a knife, painted with blood.

"You think I did it?" he asks me gruffly. "That I killed her? I couldn't blame you if you did. Hell…" He shrugs me off, turning back to the window. His fingers flex against the glass as he repositions them, and he looks less in need of stability and more…

Assertive. As if any minute, he intends to barge right through the barrier and plunge himself into the world waiting below.

Fear bites through me, shocking in its intensity. I think he's capable of it. In fact, he's liable to do far worse. No man should look like this. As though the entire world is a weapon at his disposal, and he wants nothing more than to use it.

But not against any perceived enemies. Just himself.

I reach for his shoulder before my brain even processes the motion. In shock, I register the hard plane of muscle rippling beneath my fingertips. At times, he seems so strong. Untouchable.

Laws of nature don't apply to him. He can embody two sides of the same twisted coin. Like being both repulsive and irresistible. It's wrong to step closer to him the way I am now. To let my guard down even a fraction wherever he is concerned.

I can't help it.

I know pain. Even so, I can admit that whatever he's feeling is beyond my comprehension. It goes deeper than a physical wound, or betrayal. It guts him.

Despair hollows out those usually fiery brown eyes, and he's an empty shell gazing blankly at the outside world. Sympathy should be the last thing I feel toward him, but it infects me regardless.

In this moment, I identify the source of the pain in my chest. It's compassion. Before I know it, I'm even closer, bracing my body against his.

He lets me linger by his side for longer than I should. This form of nearness is dangerous. Addictive, comparable to a child sticking their finger in an electrical socket out of curiosity about what it might feel like.

Electric is the answer. A potentially lethal mixture of shock and alarm that darts down my spine as if someone traced it with the tip of a knife. He must feel it too, because he abruptly shifts beyond my reach, putting a hairsbreadth of distance between us.

And yet, it feels as wide as the gulf between the sea and sky.

"You don't have any more?" he grates, referring to the letters.

I shake my head, feeling the same desperation that has him groaning out loud.

"So, what the hell do I do now?" he demands from the darkening sky. "Turn myself in? God, if I hurt my wife…"

He breaks off, but it's only when I feel a shudder run along my palm that I realize why. I've touched him again without meaning to. It's like some part of me is driven to comfort him, and I feel my cheeks flame when I contemplate why that might be.

He's right. We're linked together whether we like it or not, and the past no longer feels as looming as it once did. The future is far more terrifying to face.

"You should go." He shrugs me off a second time, only to sink to his knees, pressing his forehead against the window. He looks like a man due to be executed, eagerly awaiting the feel of the blade slicing into the back of his neck. So intent on suffering, he doesn't even react when I crouch beside him.

"I know," he says with a grimace.

My pulse stutters at the soft accusatory note in his voice, but he doesn't seem angry. If anything, the sound he chokes out next could be a broken imitation of a laugh.

"I know that you might not be pregnant. So go home. I won't hold it against you, and we can find some other way of luring out the attacker."

Perhaps it's morbid curiosity keeping me here now. What my brain chooses to interpret as sympathy is really a twisted sense of satisfaction. I must enjoy this.

"You're right," Donatello says with a dry laugh. I stiffen. Has he read my mind for real this time? "If anyone deserves to stay, it's you. You deserve to see me burn in hell for what I did to you. This is merely the start. So, take it in. Maybe your father has more evidence than he led on. That I killed Liv. Why I did what I did..."

He trails off, lifting his head enough to eye his hands. They're both bruised and battered from recent events. I keep replaying those scenes in my head. How he threw himself in front of me without a second thought. Rather than grateful, I'm annoyed. It seems more desperate than selfless. Even Fabio insinuated that the man has a death wish. That could be all there is to it.

But I don't believe it.

He's too calculating for that. He did what he did because, in that instant, his sole intention was to save my life, no matter the cost.

I'm too lost in thought to notice him moving at first.

He lurches as if intending to stand, but he staggers. Alarmed, I reach out to stabilize him, and before I realize it, he's on his knees. Then on his side and his head lands...

On my lap.

We both go rigid. I'm holding my breath, my hands held awkwardly at my sides. From this angle, I have a close-up view of him that drives home just how close to perfection he is—even beaten down and worn to the bone. His timeless features are reminiscent of a statue's, apparent even after the decades have taken their toll.

Misery suits him unfairly well. The grief enhances the stern line of his jaw and the moisture glistening on his cheeks just seems like delicate touches of natural highlight.

I hate the curiosity he rouses in me. It distracts from the hate, displacing it before I'm ready. If I don't loathe him as much, it's far easier to trail a fingertip along a wayward strand of dark brown hair. He hasn't brushed it in days, but it still feels so damn soft. Silk that easily parts as I smooth all five fingers through it.

He stiffens, and I freeze. Once again, we're nearing those dangerous boundaries we both know so well. I can tell he doesn't want to cross them, not now. He tenses as if he means to stand and shrug me off. Then he sighs.

"I wanted to erase you."

Barely a whisper, his voice still resonates beneath my skin down to the bone.

"I thought if I could relegate you to nothing, you'd cease to have a hold over me. You *shouldn't* have a hold over me," he adds. "It's my own damn fault, but still… I thought if I could break you down, I wouldn't have to look back and face what I've done."

He's said this line before in so many words, but this time feels more real. Final. This is part of the disjointed thought process swirling around his mind. But this isn't for my benefit. No.

There is no polish, no softening of the harsh reality. He's speaking to himself.

"It didn't work," he admits.

I feel his jaw flex against my upper thigh. The heat of his breath easily scorches through the fabric of my dress, warming the skin beneath. I draw in a ragged breath. Even with our past interactions considered, this nearness feels the most dangerous. The most unnerving.

"You found a way to worm inside my head regardless. Do you want to know what the worst part of this all is?"

He gestures aimlessly with his hand as the weight of him settles more firmly in my lap, as if he let his body relax without meaning to.

"I'm not a monster. I know what this looks like. I know you don't even have a clue as to the hell I've set you up for. No idea. You might think you do, but you don't. I know that. It's wrong. I deserve hell for what I've done. But pushing you away… Shouldering the blame or acting like the noble asshole for taking responsibility, that just makes it easier on me. The hard part would be to let you take the lead. To give you control. I'm too damn old. You're too damn young. But I can't act like I have all the fucking answers, because I don't. Not now. Not ever."

It's hard for him to admit that out loud, and shock forces the air from my lungs in a single exhale.

"It wouldn't be fair of me to act like I do." His eyes are magnetic in this moment, piercing and electric. "I don't have the right to push you away. I can't ask for anything from you. I can't tell you a damn thing as to how to think or feel."

He reaches up hesitantly, giving me plenty of time to anticipate what he intends. I'm riveted as his fingers waver near my cheek, inching closer before pulling away. Finally, he bridges the gap, stroking along my jawline.

I feel that touch in every inch of my body down to my toes. It's gentle enough—but the texture of his calloused flesh awakens a million dangerous sensations and bothersome thoughts. My heart feels heavier, and when I remember how to breathe, the air scrapes down my throat as if laced with glass.

"I'm not a moral authority," he admits. "All I can do is be honest with you. So, believe me when I tell you that I will never love you the way you deserve to be loved."

He frowns, disappointed by the admission leaving his own mouth.

"I won't. I will never be able to care for you. I will never be able to return any affection you might have for me. I will only bring you pain. I can't expect you to understand what that means, not now anyway—" He breaks off with a grimace. "Fuck. I'm doing it again. Playing the higher authority. The point is. I'll let you make your own choices, but I can never make you happy."

He says that like it's some great revelation I should be thankful for. He's finally admitted his role as the villain in this story, good for him. Donatello Vanici is every bit the heartless, selfish criminal I always believed him to be.

But this is yet another cop-out. Another way to skirt any real responsibility. Another way to undermine his own claim to surrender control to me.

I don't want him to martyr himself.

I want him to try. I deserve that. I want him to fight against the doom and gloom he's prophesized because I know that would be harder for him. I want him to want me even though he shouldn't. He deserves nothing less than hating himself every damn second of every day because he's happier chasing a fantasy than living a lie.

It's the same fate he's damned me to for almost a decade. A living hell of playing pretend, all while knowing that the one person you crave is the very monster responsible for ruining your fragile peace in the first place.

I want him to chase chaos for the rest of his life and never again resign himself to the role of victim.

Just stop.

Reacting on impulse, I flatten my palm against his chin, sensing the unruly stubble beneath. His face is so expressive that even a frown takes a concerto of muscle and tissue to achieve. I feel each one straining in harmony as he inclines his head, letting what little light there is illuminate his features.

God, I hate this man. It's unfair how beautiful he is. How ugly he makes me feel.

More than anything, I hate what he's made of me. After everything we've been through, I shouldn't be this spiteful. But I am. I relish the way he flinches as I capture the other side of his face with my opposite hand.

Alarm dances across those dark irises before a grudging resignation settles over both. I can see myself reflected in his gaze. Angry and vengeful, like an angel from hell with golden hair.

Tears still fall from his eyes, painting a silent trail that doesn't diminish him any. If anything, the vulnerable display of emotion just makes him seem stronger. Invincible.

Some petty part of me wants to test that theory. When I lean down and drag my mouth over his, he shouldn't budge an inch.

But he does.

A groan rips from his throat that I can taste on the tip of my tongue. His flavor is a rich, dangerous spice that clearly conveys just what he's feeling—pain. He wants to pull away, but only sheer force of will keeps him here. Keeps him with me.

Good.

I don't take mercy on him. Instead, I continue my exploration, dragging my fingers along the rugged panes of flesh and bone that make up the stern expressions of Donatello Vanici. With every inch of him I trace, his brows draw further together. Like black holes, his eyes seem darker, and his mouth is so rigid that it doesn't give, as the tip of my pinky smooths over it.

When I draw back, he sighs.

"You always were so damn stubborn." His voice resonates with the grim finality of a man on his death bed. He knows he's doomed; there's no use in fighting it.

So, he doesn't even try.

A flutter of alarm runs through my belly, but some part of me is driven to ignore it.

So, I prove him right and *stubbornly* probe his mouth again.

The second time our lips meet, he hisses, coming alive in a burst of movement. His fingers latch onto my skull, fisting through my hair. My heart hammers as I wait for him to tug me away, but he doesn't. The contact seems intended to reinforce his presence more than anything. He's still desperate to maintain control at any cost.

But he restrains himself, though it must kill him to.

Frozen at this awkward angle, we coexist in a strange sort of limbo. Our breaths mingle, our bodies contorted. My hair falls forward, creating a cocoon that shields us both. In this shadowy sliver of the universe, previous rules and boundaries mean nothing.

But he's the one leaning forward this time, bridging the gap. I don't know what drives me to do it—seize a corner of his lip between my teeth and bear down.

He grunts, bringing his other hand to my chin. His fingers twitch as if it's taking all of his strength not to push me away. Instead, his thumb slips out, stroking along my jaw, and shock makes me release him.

But I don't pull back, and neither does he.

I wouldn't call this a kiss. It's too sloppy for that. Too hesitant. In a sense, it's just another form of exploration. I get to poke and prod at Donatello Vanici in this aspect, and he can't bring himself to stop me. Lust isn't what I sense from him, either. Just resignation.

He promised me power, and this is how I choose to claim it.

By tasting him. By deepening the kiss. By making him endure every probing jab from my tongue. I can feel the tension ripping through him, coiling in every muscle.

And somewhere amid it all, he turns the tables.

We collide in a mass of twisted limbs, and I'm in the air. In his arms, pressed to his chest, my legs around his waist...

A heartbeat later, I'm blinking up at the ceiling, feeling the mattress conform to my spine. All I can do is stare as he comes into view, moving to settle over me. My heart flutters, and for a second, something bubbles up within my chest that might be fear.

Until I see the look in his eye, tortured and broken. He brings his face near mine, but his breaths are labored. He doesn't touch me, bracing his hands on either side of my body instead.

For what feels like an eternity, we just coexist, sharing the same thinning air.

I don't know what it is in my expression that makes him finally raise one hand, stroking it along my chin. Maybe it's that I don't push him off. Or how my lips part, remembering his taste.

When his fingers ghost the side of my throat, I can't stop my spine from twisting toward his touch. It's as if he is magnetic, calling to some twisted force within me.

The nearer he is, the more it burns. Ignites. Explodes.

I'm shaking, my teeth chattering, though I'm far from cold. If anything, I'm overwhelmed by his heat, dizzy and breathless.

Slowly, he rears back, bracing his weight on his thighs instead. I can feel him settle over my hips, and the unfamiliar weight draws my attention to the space between my legs. I'd almost forgotten what this feels like.

Dangerous intimacy. Foreign fire and an uncomfortable pressure that aches. My thighs twitch, desperate to rub together. Soothe it somehow…

But my memories taunt me with the only force capable of providing relief—the last time, at least. His fingers. His touch. The pressure only he can apply…

The images flood my skull one after the other as my eyes drift shut, robbing me of my view of him—but I can still hear. It's as if in the absence of one sense, the others grow stronger. I can perceive every raspy inhale he takes. Every ragged exhale.

And I can feel the way his fingers shake as he brings them to my thigh, snatching fistfuls of my skirt, lifting it. An inch at first. Then higher. Higher…

It should make me feel weak as he bares me to him, removing my dress altogether. Weak and pathetic.

But the way his breath catches makes me shiver in return. When his calloused fingertips trace my inner thigh next, I don't clamp my knees together against the intrusion.

I spread them, letting him coax my quivering knees further apart.

I marvel at the power he has over me as he fingers the hem of my panties.

With a single touch, he has me holding my breath, shuddering in time with the shifting mattress. I hear the rasp of fabric over skin before the texture of his shirt vanishes, replaced by bare skin. The purr of a zipper next warns that another piece of his clothing has met the same fate.

But it's a testament to the enigmatic pull he has that I'm not afraid.

I'm ready as he pushes inside me with a single thrust. We both go still as my body stretches around him, forced to accept every inch—desperate to.

I open my eyes again and feel my breath catch at the sight of him pressed against me, every inch of him on display. Almost as if taunting me, the scarlet letters etched into his chest gleam.

I run my fingers over them one by one, feeling a tremor run through him.

S. A. F...

And with every letter I trace, his groans deepen, becoming guttural. Broken. Growls.

Until he loses control completely. Desperate, his hips rock against mine in a fierce rhythm that takes my breath away.

Our gazes lock, his swollen with an emotion I can't decipher right away.

But it's dangerous.

A promise.

And a warning.

We're bound together more deeply than even this act.

Whether we like it or not.

2 0

DON

I'm going to hell. Admittedly, my descent began years ago, so why resist the fall now? The only thing left to do is brace for the inevitable fiery ending.

If only it didn't feel so damn good. Hellfire burns sweeter than expected. There are no hordes of demons to torment me with searing flames—just one angel.

She lords her goodness over me, daring me to corrupt it. Take it. Claim it.

But I already have. Is it really a sin if I touch her again, raking my fingers through her hair to draw her closer? Is it wrong to slip my tongue between her lips, stealing the startled breath she intakes?

In short? Yes.

I'm going to hell.

Every second I extend this moment just increases the amount of damnation attached to my soul. The sick part? I'm not the least bit repentant. Hell feels far better than that torturous road toward forgiveness.

But I don't make excuses. Even as I further the kiss, I don't explain away the wrongness of it all. I don't make it easier by drowning this under the guise of being out of my mind. I make myself feel it.

All of it.

There is plenty of time to burn later.

And plenty more sins to commit before then.

❦

By the time I leave the suite, it's noon, and I'm alone, forced to face this next test of my sanity with no one to hide behind.

Will I tell him the truth?

I don't know. The hospital doors feel like a portal, transporting me back into what my life *should* be. A clinical maze of neutral colors and blank sterility with Vincenzo at the center. No distractions.

No secrets.

No lies.

He's sitting up in bed when I enter his room, and the sight stops me in my tracks. "Vinny…"

A few weeks, and he's damn near back to his usual self. The only glaring reminder of what he's been through is a bandage still wrapped around his skull.

"They say I might be able to leave in a few days," he says by way of greeting. His tone is accusatory rather than triumphant. "You haven't been here pushing for that to happen soon," he adds, the apparent source of his suspicion. "So why not? It isn't like you. Unless you don't want me out."

"What?" I force a smile he doesn't return. "Don't tell me you're sick of the free food, constant supervision, and having a pretty nurse at your beck and call already."

Shit. His mouth flattens into an even sterner line. Of course, he sees right through my bullshit.

"I'm not an idiot, Donatello," he scolds in a tone reminiscent of Fabio's. "I know you. If you think I'm safer in here with a thermometer shoved up my ass every six hours, then it's because you're more afraid of whatever is out there—" He jerks his chin toward a window displaying the concrete jungle that is Hell's Gambit. "You told me that everything between you and Mischa was settled. So, what did you leave out?"

I can't even look at him. *Fuck.* I cross over to the window he indicated and glower at the stormy horizon. If everything Fabio put into motion is to be believed, then in just a few days, this war will come to a head. Afterward, Vincenzo will be home free and on his way back to his studies.

In a perfect world.

That's the fantasy I'm clinging to, regardless. It doesn't include the possibility of him finding out about a maybe-future Vanici who will rival his place as my sole heir. Vincenzo isn't that petty, though. The only thing about the addition of a new family member he'd take offense to is who the father is.

And the mother.

I could tell myself the same bullshit I have been all along. That she is an adult, and so am I. Our relationship, however twisted it may be, is our business. No one else's.

Until last night, that is. Besides, no excuse erases one glaring fact. I know how Vin will react. I know my boy. I know…

He'll hate me for this. He'd have every right to.

"Do you think I'm an idiot, Don?"

I look over at him, taking in the subtle details I missed before. They've let him wear his own clothing, and he has a book open on his lap, displaying a dedication to his studies that no Vanici before him ever possessed.

"I've had full access to the internet as well as the news channel while I've been here," he adds, crossing his arms, the book forgotten. "Everything going on in the city right now could be written off as typical chaos, but I don't believe in coincidence. What aren't you telling me?"

His tone alone sets me on edge. I know to tread carefully.

"What do you mean?"

He frowns and adjusts his glasses over the ridge of his nose. The beeping of medical machinery creates a chillingly mellow backdrop—though this conversation is shaping up to be anything but.

"It wasn't as hard as you might think to bribe one of the men on my security detail to tell me the latest gossip. One of my night nurses let me use the internet on her computer to verify. It's not on the mainstream news broadcasts, of course, but the local forums catch everything."

Oh fuck. Does he know? I fight to keep the panic from my expression, praying to God my voice sounds steady. "Like what?"

"Like a wedding," he says without any inflection.

His frown is skeptical, but the boy is as sharp as ever, and like a dog with a bone, he won't stop until he satisfies any curiosity. After all, that's exactly how I taught him to think.

"*Your* wedding, Don. Which would be strange, since last time I checked, you didn't even have a girlfriend, let alone a fiancée—"

"The amount of money Fab and I pay these bastards to guard you, and they spend their time gossiping?" I make a show of faked indignation, forcing a laugh. "Sounds like I need to visit you more often if you're that damn bored."

"Don't coddle me." He's never spoken to me like this. For a heartbeat, I swear I see something flit across his gaze before vanishing. Hurt.

"You're right," I concede. "I shouldn't coddle you—but I should protect you. Whatever's going on out there—" I jerk my chin toward the window. "That's out there. All you need to focus on is what is in here—getting better so that you can return to that fancy school and earn enough money to take care of me for the rest of my fucking life. Got it?"

I know my tone is convincing enough. I've told him lesser lies with twice the ease before. But this time…

He smiles as he typically would, but it doesn't reach his eyes. "Whatever you say, Uncle Don. Maybe you do have a point—because you would never lie to me, would you? About anything, no matter how trivial or how big. You would never lie to me."

But I have. We both know it. Whether I could justify it at the time as in his better interest, it doesn't fucking matter. Still, I force a chuckle and lie to him again.

"You're damn right; I wouldn't. Now, are we done with the third degree? Why don't you tell me more about that night nurse of yours? It's about damn time you notice something other than those stuffy medical texts."

He doesn't even blush. Instead, he shifts to sit on the edge of the bed. When he looks up, none of the piercing intensity has left his gaze. Not one damn bit. If anything, he seems more determined to probe whatever issue has him so unsettled.

"Willow," he says softly. "She didn't come with you?"

I flinch, knowing damn well that he can read that slip-up for what it was. I turn away, choking out what I hope passes for another laugh.

"Invite a woman whose presence might hamper my ability to tease the shit out of you? Hell no. I can have her come later, if you want," I add.

"I do want her here," Vin says. "We're a family, aren't we? Or at least... We were."

Shit. Not now. I don't have the right to beg for more time—and stave off the inevitable—but I don't have a choice. Where he's leading is a road we both aren't equipped to travel.

As much as it dings my pride to admit, I wish Fabio were here.

"You never told me what happened," Vin adds. His voice wavers, and I look over my shoulder to find him attempting to stand.

"Don't." I scan the room for an alarm button. "Let me call a nurse—"

"I can stand on my own," he snaps, proceeding to do just that. "The doctor's ordered me to take laps around the wing every couple of hours. You'd know that if you were here more often. If you weren't so busy."

I wince. He could have punched me, and it would hurt less than the pain in his voice. "Vin…"

"I'm not a child, Don." He sounds less angry, just exasperated. Against my suggestion, he unhooks himself from whatever devices he's connected to and stands fully upright with a steadiness that leaves me dumbstruck.

He's right. I haven't been here often enough. I missed the subtle signs of him regaining his strength. He moves easily, and perhaps he isn't wrong to question why I haven't inquired about his discharge.

"Look at me."

He's by my side within seconds, and I do a double take. He looks so much like his mother. Though Donella would never give a damn whether or not I kept her in the loop. She'd have her own ways of finding whatever information she sought. A true Vanici, she trusted no one.

If only Vin could have inherited that trait from her.

"I am not a child," he repeats. "You don't have to protect me anymore. Gone are the days when I'll blindly accept that people die without a funeral, or wonder in silence why I couldn't outwardly mourn the person I loved like a sister. You have your secrets; I understand that. But where my life is concerned? No more. I am done standing in the dark because you think I can't handle the truth."

"It's not that," I admit hoarsely. "Come here."

Before he can resist, I throw my arm around him, drawing him close. Despite his bravado, he's not as strong as he wants me to believe. He sways, easily knocked off balance, too weak to pull away.

"I know you can handle it," I tell him. "But I can't. I can't lose you too. I won't. So, if that makes me a fucking coward, then I'm sorry, Vin. Just give me time."

"You want to know the only way you'll lose me, Don?" He pulls back, meeting my gaze directly. "If you lie to me. I have my own ways of finding out the truth. Please don't make me do that. I want to hear it from you."

Now he does sound like his mother. Could he possibly know the truth already? Even the prospect makes my blood run cold, and I shake my head to clear it. *No*, he couldn't. Even a gossipy soldier wouldn't be able to tell him, because supposedly no one outside of Mischa and his immediate family knows. And Fab.

I couldn't see him telling Vin, either. Though hell, my perception of everyone has been so shit lately; who knows what secrets he could be hiding?

"Don?" Vin sounds further away as if he returned to the bed. Sure enough, he's seated there when I finally face him.

"You can tell me anything," he says. "I know that sometimes you aren't the best decision maker in the world, but you always have the best intentions in mind."

Do I? I think one woman, in particular, might take offense to that characterization. Two, perhaps.

"Enough of this gloomy talk," I say with a smile. "You're right. It's about time that we find out when you can get the hell out of here. How about we call that doctor over and discuss it, huh?"

Like me, Vin is good at disguising his emotions. Even so, I still identify what sentiment causes his mouth to turn downward—disappointment.

"Yeah," he says softly, no longer looking my way. "Whatever you say, Don."

We both continue to sport our fake grins, but I know in my gut that I've horribly mis-stepped.

If only I knew how.

By the time I finally leave Vin, I've convinced myself that everything is fine. Whatever I sensed before was just paranoia. Considering how he was laughing as I departed, whatever plagued Vincenzo's mind has been put at ease.

So why the hell am I so edgy, glancing over my shoulder as I exit the hospital? It could be common sense warning me to be on guard as Fabio sets his plan into motion. There is a wedding to organize, after all.

But I can't shake the feeling that something's off. The dread haunts me every inch of the drive back to the hotel, and I nearly race up to the suite. The first person I find inside is Willow, apparently unharmed—but she isn't alone.

"You," I blurt, frozen in the doorway.

"Hello, Mr. Vanici," the visitor replies. There is no mistaking those blue eyes, and while I know they aren't related—with her daughter beside her—it strikes me just how similarly they carry themselves. That stony confidence must be a trademark of the Stepanovs.

"Mrs. Stepanova," I say, stiffly returning the introduction. My gaze darts to Willow, but she doesn't attempt to make eye contact. Doubt creeps into my thoughts. Did last night snap some sense into her? Or is there another explanation… I have to wonder if Fabio is behind this.

Whatever the reason, Ellen Stepanova doesn't seem to be in a hurry to reveal it.

"I've been meaning to talk with you," she says, her tone cold but still cordial. Even without her husband in view, she cuts a striking figure, commanding respect. Apart from the slight paleness to her skin lingering even now, no one would be able to guess the ordeal she went through just a few weeks ago. She's steady on her feet, her hands folded neatly over her waist. But those eyes blaze, removing any doubt that this is a friendly visit.

"You're welcome here," I say thickly. "Please, have a seat."

She nods and claims one half of a chaise. In silence, Willow joins her, and that sense of dread continues to build. Looking at her face alone, I can't tell what she might be feeling—a warning sign if there ever was one. As the seconds pass, her eyes remain averted from me, her gaze distant.

"My husband doesn't know I'm here," her mother says to preface her speech. "So, I come to you entirely of my own accord, if only to make one request."

I fight to keep my tone as polite as possible. "And what request is that?"

"I want you to leave."

I wait for the threat that must surely accompany that statement—but either she's shrewd enough to think she doesn't need one, or just simply that confident in her family's power.

"This isn't a threat," she adds, though her tone isn't any softer. "It's merely me speaking as one mother to a father."

Though I doubt this newest child is whom she refers to. Either her husband's kept her out of the loop when it comes to his gossip mongering, or she has far more tact than he does.

"I'm listening," I say, but my focus is on the woman beside her. Her lips purse, flattening into a thin line. I assume whatever her mother intends to say has already been discussed between the two.

"I'm not telling you this out of a maternal sense of protection, or even because of the morality. I'm telling you this from the viewpoint of a woman who knows what it is like to have a child with a man of power. A beautiful blessing—but also a sentence to a life of pain for everyone involved, especially the child in question."

"I take it you're not referring to your current husband," I say dryly.

"No," she admits. "There was another man before him, and there isn't a day that I don't regret letting him control me the way he did. My only solace is my oldest son. I wouldn't trade him for the world. But I hate that his life will always be burdened by the sins of his father. There is no erasing those ties."

"And you think my child is doomed to the same fate?" Gone is the politeness. I can't keep the anger from my voice, hearing it leech into every word. The worst part? The rage isn't directed at her.

She's regurgitating what I already know.

I can't stop myself from glancing at the woman in question. Maybe I expect to find agreement on her face? Not... annoyance. Her teeth capture her bottom lip, though she stares straight ahead.

Her reaction tempers some of my anger—but not all of it. "I would caution you to remember that, despite your past relationship, your current husband is no saint," I point out, returning my focus to Mrs. Stepanova.

That draws a rise out of her—not Mischa's wife, but *her*. Willow. She's looking at me now, her gaze like a razor blade slicing through my brittle resolve. God, I want more than anything to banish this stranger from the room and draw out the thoughts on her mind. Still, I have enough sense to know that she wants me to hear this spiel, whatever it might reveal.

She wants to see how I'll react to it.

"Mischa is many things," his wife admits. "But he is selfless when it comes to his children. He knows when to protect them and when to let them go—" She looks at her daughter briefly, but I can tell from her tortured expression that she might not cleave to that same principle. "He knows when to let them make their own mistakes, and he isn't afraid to show his love. But do you want to know what truly sets him apart from my previous husband? I chose him. Despite the circumstances and the chaotic backdrop against which we met, I still had a choice. I wasn't threatened or coerced. There was no fear. No imbalance of power."

"With all due respect, Mrs. Stepanova," I say, clinging to what little civility I have left. "I've heard the rumors, and your love story with your husband isn't half the fairy tale you want me to believe it is. I know that he kidnapped you. Tortured you. Scarred you. God knows what else he did. In your capacity to forgive him, I'm sure you can imagine that other women might be able to do the same for less."

"You are entitled to your opinion," she concedes with a graceful nod. "And I am entitled to mine. I think if you truly care about Willow, the best thing to do would be to leave. To allow her to cut you off completely and move on."

"And this is your *expert* opinion?"

Both women flinch. My tone came out too harsh.

"This is my biased opinion," Ellen admits. "But one honed sharp after years of dealing with men like you. I know how your world works, Mr. Vanici."

Everything from her tone, to how she carries herself reveals a glimpse of the woman rumored to equally rule Mischa's empire. She's good at playing calm and meek; I'll give her that. But she's right. No woman could survive in a shithole like Hell's Gambit without sporting a few claws of her own.

How sharp are Ellen Stepanova's? I suspect I'm about to find out.

"I'll speak to you plainly, Mr. Vanici," she continues, her pink lips turning downward. "You know your actions have been wrong, predatory even. And yet you continue to play these games and manipulate those in your orbit."

Picturing last night, I might not be the only predator in this equation. My gaze flits to her again, and my stomach tightens. Faint color paints her cheeks, and I know I'm not the only one reliving that shift in our dynamic.

"I think you should speak to your daughter." I start to stand.

"Wait." It isn't the commanding note in her voice that stops me. It's the rage blazing in those light blue eyes. She's disguised it well until now, but it's there, every bit as violent as her husband's temper.

Maybe guilt is what makes me stop and listen.

"I love my daughter, and you've hurt her more than you will ever know. By staying in her life, you will only continue to hurt her, and I refuse to sit by and watch it happen—"

Glass shatters, and the woman falls silent out of shock. I'm already on my heels, my eyes on the window in case of a sniper. Belatedly I register the absence of a gunshot. Then, my gaze settles over the apparent source of the commotion —a broken glass lying on the floor inches away.

There's another glass and a pitcher of water on the coffee table—presumably, the women had both been drinking from it before I came in. Considering the whole cup is positioned closer to Ellen, the person nearest the broken glass might be responsible for it falling.

When I turn to her, she finally faces me, her cheeks red, those brown eyes ablaze with that chilling, quiet intensity. She's angrier than ever, but it isn't directed at the woman beside her.

Just me. Always me.

"Willow?" Ellen Stepanova clears her throat. "I'm sorry. I know you don't like being spoken over—"

"She doesn't like being treated like a child," I interject without thinking. "Which she isn't. Therein lies the flaw of your argument toward me. Whether I stay or leave, it isn't my choice to make. The door is there. Both of you are free to go if you want. And to stay."

Ellen frowns, but Willow…

She seems to sigh, exhaling a sharp breath. The rage leaves her gaze, revealing the confusion left behind. The same way she looked as I kissed her last night. As if she was unsure what in the hell possessed her to kiss me back.

"I'm sorry, Mrs. Stepanova. I do appreciate you coming here, but there are other pressing issues to deal with at the moment. There will be plenty of time for familial drama later."

"There is another reason why I'm here," the woman admits, clearing her throat. "One more tactical. Mischa couldn't take the risk of coming here himself. There is information you should know."

"Such as?"

"How close are you to the Saleris?"

I raise an eyebrow. Switching from the topic of my predatory nature to the Saleris is a subject change I didn't see coming. "'Close' being the operative word, not very," I admit.

"Could you still arrange a meeting with them? Or at least draw their attention?"

The gears in my mind shift from anger to calculation. "For what purpose?"

"We have reason to believe their distribution network is being used in a larger scheme. One they might not even be aware of. We need a way of testing that theory without alerting them to the bigger plan."

"Did you stop to consider that Mateo might have been the bastard who arranged that little hit the other day?"

I grit my teeth at the thought. My eyes return to Willow. She could have been killed, and it would have been my fucking fault for letting my guard down for even a second.

Guilt isn't what I find on her face, however. She's watching me in return, the gears in her mind turning. I think she's come to the same conclusion I have regarding her mother's suggestion.

"Playing detective by arranging to meet with the son of a bitch doesn't seem like the smartest plan," I say, voicing it out loud.

"I didn't say it had to be a friendly meeting," Ellen says tacitly. "In fact, it might be better to goad him into making a mistake and exposing his role in this scheme."

Even I can admit that she has a point. But what might goad Mateo into making yet another reckless move? One plan comes to mind.

"I think I have an idea," I say grimly. "It might be a little unorthodox, though it's a good thing for you that you seem to enjoy the company of children."

She raises an eyebrow in confusion.

"Gregori Saleri has a granddaughter who happened to fall under my care."

After I killed her father—a fact that I'm sure she's aware of because her eyes widen in horror before she manages to school her expression again.

"I could always make an overture to him under the guise of arranging a trade to return her to her family. But I would need backup as well as intel of where Mateo is holed up. *And*," I add, feeling bold, "I want assurances from Mischa that he'll be ready to hold off another attack."

"Using young girls as leverage in your twisted power struggles. That must be a preferred tactic of yours."

I wince at that, glancing at Willow once again. Despite myself, I'm also impressed. While Mischa may be more physically direct in his attack strategy, his wife, it seems, prefers words as her weapon.

Ironically, much like her daughter.

"It isn't like that," I reply.

But it is. Isn't it?

One of said pieces of leverage is watching me again, her expression impossible to read. I don't even have to run the plan by her to know she doesn't approve.

I compose my reply carefully and direct it toward her more than anyone else. "Using Kisa is the best method we have of drawing out Mateo Saleri without alerting him as to our other motives. I don't intend to ever put her in any real danger. She'll be safe."

Does she believe that? I can't tell. Damn, I almost feel blind. Though, at second glance, her nostrils flare with a resigned exhale. She understands.

"Fine," Ellen says expressionlessly, of the same opinion. "I'll make the arrangements with my husband and have one of our guards contact you."

I can guess who that might be; the same bastard who always seems to turn up in the nick of time comes to mind. Evgeni. Without naming him, Mrs. Stepanova stands, smoothing her hands down the front of her skirt.

"I have one other request of you," she says. "Though, if you do want to prove that you don't assert your influence in a predatory way, then you'll allow my daughter to leave with me, right now. Do I have your word on that?"

"If she agrees," I hiss through clenched teeth. It takes everything I have in me to keep from glancing in the direction of the person in question.

Because that's exactly what this woman expects me to do. It's ironic. From an angle, the faint scars marring her cheek are visible—clear evidence that her husband is no better than I am. Yet, she thinks he is without a doubt. In a world of monsters, I'm no better than the devil to her.

"Fine." She turns to her daughter, extending her hand. "You can come home with me," she says.

I don't witness the exchange that transpires in silence. I only know that when Ellen Stepanova does finally leave the suite, head held high, she's alone.

I look back. The woman behind me doesn't acknowledge my presence, but her shoulders slump, robbed of that tense posture. I think she's relieved.

So am I.

"I meant it," I croak, regardless. "Whether you stay or go, it's your choice."

She inclines her head, turning that impassive stare my way. I might imagine the slight nod she gives me. Either way, she doesn't make a move for the door, and I have my answer.

Ellen Stepanova and me aside, she made her own decision.

But with her own aims in mind. For all I know, those reasons might have nothing to do with me.

EVGENI

ollowing a plan devised by Donatello Vanici is as laughable as it is foolish. But said plan, once relayed by his accountant Bocelli, seems…

Well, it might be just crazy enough to work. Or at least, draw Mateo and his puppet master out of hiding. Either way, it's better than nothing.

In the meantime, I have my own task to undertake, however reckless it may be. Ironically, it might help benefit Vanici's scheme in the long run—and prove if Briar Winthorp is worth trusting yet again.

To spare my last shred of patience, I didn't bring her along on this detour. Instead, I work alone, using the cover of nightfall to my benefit to infiltrate a home just beyond the city boundaries.

In theory, the mission is simple—get intel on the Saleri mansion myself and determine if Briar's son could be here after all. While I'm at it, any information on the distribution network would be a plus.

That's assuming I don't get shot to death in the process.

This mansion in the hills overlooking Hell's Gambit seems unremarkable at a glance—opulence aside. It's as gaudy as any other property connected to the Saleris, with a towering three-story home atop an expansive stretch of land. For once, the excess plays to my advantage as the ornate gardens, complete with towering shrubs and bushes, provide plenty of places to hide once I breach the outer gates.

The only thing standing between me and the main house is at least twenty guards patrolling the grounds, each one armed to the teeth.

It's odd. Given the current tragedy befalling the family, I'd expect to find the mansion draped in black crepe and flowers, signifying mourning.

Not assault rifles and armored vehicles.

A parade of dark vans streams through the property gates in an almost constant caravan. They circle around to the back of the house and enter a multi-car garage—only to drive off minutes later, heading toward the city.

A strange occurrence, even if Mateo wasn't under suspicion for sending an assassin after Vanici and killing his own father in cold blood.

For hours, this process has been underway. I've counted at least five such departures by the time I finally decide to leave my hiding place near a row of shrubs for a better look.

Slowly, I creep up to the house, avoiding the steady stream of patrols.

Mateo Saleri, for all his pomp, is still a smart bastard at heart. His father's death hasn't shocked him into skimping on security. In fact, it looks as though he's tripled their usual detail. Either the man prefers to be overly prepared, or…

He's afraid of something. Which only brings up the plausible possibility that Briar hasn't told me everything. Am I surprised? No.

Gritting my teeth, I shirk the tree cover for a row of hedges, my eyes on the garage. It's reckless to risk being seen, but I can't shake this impulse driving me to get closer.

Gravel crunches beneath the wheels of an oncoming truck, and I look up, spying yet another vehicle turning through the gates. I take the chance to follow it, keeping to the shadows cast by more overgrown hedges lining the central driveway.

Up ahead, a guard marches past, a weapon displayed openly across his back. Even Mischa's guards aren't this alert. As soon as the man's back is turned, I take my chance, lunging closer to the garage just as another guard storms into view.

I slip around the back and through an open door, right before the van continues its approach, pulling into one of the few empty parking spaces. The entire garage is filled to the brim with boxes stacked one on top of the other. Overall, the space is lit only by a strip of overhead lights that barely provides enough illumination to see by.

A benefit to the clutter is that I easily find a hiding place behind a row of crates near the back of the building.

On the other hand, it doesn't look like long-term storage—but a temporary makeshift depot meant to hold items in a pinch.

Or in preparation for something.

Briar's warning itches at the back of my skull, and while I haven't searched the main house, I feel in my gut that a child isn't on this property. At least not now.

These men are guarding something else, ready to shoot anyone who comes too close.

Eager to find out what, I turn my attention to the van and crane my neck for a better look. One of the guards opens the van's trunk, revealing a glimpse of what lurks within the back—at least two more crates, made of the same black material as the rest.

A pair of guards lowers one to the floor, ripping off the top.

And I now have a better idea of just what Mateo is hiding.

Weapons.

A shit ton of them.

"You lied to me." I don't aim for coy. My voice reverberates around the room, and the only other occupant shrinks, pressing herself against the wall. Just as quickly, her mask is reassembled, her head thrown back at a haughty angle.

"Did, I now? Are you truly surprised?"

"No," I say, trespassing further into the room she's claimed as her own. "I just feel pity for you that your worried mother act was a lie. Even a stray dog has a stronger maternal instinct than a dishonored heiress, as it turns out. There isn't a child on the Saleri estate. I can tell you that for a fact."

Her eyelids flutter—a rare glimpse of confusion. Another act? Of course, it is. "Care to enlighten me as to what exactly I've been lying about?" she asks.

I scoff, turning on my heel. I can't even look at her. "There wasn't any sign of a child on the Saleri compound," I reiterate coldly. "I doubt a mouse could get in there with the amount of security. Is that what you wanted me to see? Or were you far more tactless and wanted me dead."

"I think *you* are the one who is lying." Her voice loses that polished exterior quickly, deepening into a hiss. Head held high, she braces both hands on her hips, jutting her chin defiantly. "Either you aren't as good at reconnaissance as you think, or you took too damn long, and they've moved him by now—"

"I'm telling you, there was no hint of a child ever having been there. It's like a fortress. They're planning for war."

Rather than accept defeat, caught in her lie, she…

Looks panicked. Her eyes widen as she shakes her head. "No. Then he is somewhere else."

I frown at the hoarseness in her voice. It could be yet another disingenuous ruse—but… She seems driven more to tears and hysterics to get her point across. That was unwarranted. I've caught her by surprise, and she's genuinely thrown off.

The look on her face furthers that assessment. She's glaring, fighting to keep her confident mask intact.

"I should have known that a murderer ought to be the last person on earth sent to rescue a child. You could have taken me with you, at least. I would have known what to look for. Thanks to your bullheaded actions, I can't even find him myself, and we are running out of time!"

Her voice rises in pitch, a convincing display. I must fall for the ruse, because I find myself asking, "Where else might he be?"

She stammers. "I-I don't—"

"If he isn't with the Saleris, and you truly believe he is here, then where?"

Her eyes flit around the room. Then, suddenly, they widen. A laugh trickles from her throat next, and I steel myself for a quip or a joke at my expense.

Instead, she slaps her own forehead. "Damn him! I am such an idiot for not seeing it before."

"Seeing what?"

She whirls on me, an eyebrow raised. "Where would you go if you were desperate to assert your ties to a family that refused to acknowledge your existence?"

An answer comes to me, but it isn't relevant to this scenario —a modest, crumbling farm that is probably wrecked by now. But then, I approach that same question from the viewpoint of a spurned bastard, and it clicks.

"Winthorp Manor."

Briar nods. "I've heard it's in ruins, but that could be where his main base is."

"Or a trap," I add. "Someone as clever as you portray this man to be might assume we'd head there first."

And I'm sure that either Mischa, or Vanici has kept tabs on the property. They would know if it were overrun in the recent weeks. Right?

"I heard the place has been burned to the ground," Briar says dryly. "Perhaps, he's found a way to infest whatever is left behind without drawing notice?"

It could be worth the risk to take a closer look. Or just another line spun in her twisted little web, meant to ensnare me further.

"You should take me with you," she says. "If I'm wrong, you can throttle me in person—"

"Or you could throttle me." I'm sure the idea has crossed her mind more than once. To her credit, she disguises any murderous intent well behind a harsh laugh.

"If I wanted to kill you, there have been plenty of opportunities before now, you must admit. And if I wanted to lead you into a trap, why would I help you circumvent what could have been a very nasty assassination attempt on your precious ward? Believe me or not, but hear this—I'm going there, one way or another."

"Fine," I relent. "But we do this my way. That means on my terms and via my rules. Tonight, is too risky," I add, thinking up a plan on the fly. "We go in the morning and not without backup."

"You soldiers and your goddamn protocol." She rolls her eyes. "I wouldn't expect anything less. Don't forget to get permission for our little adventure from your master as well."

"I won't," I warn. "Because we aren't going alone."

Alarm flashes across her gaze. She doesn't like that idea, but to my shock, she doesn't argue. Instead, she merely points her chin in my direction, an eyebrow raised.

"Well, let's not waste any more time, then. Why can't we go now?"

"Tomorrow," I insist, thinking through the logistics. "Better to minimize the risks of an ambush."

"Of course," she says, nodding. "And to make sure that you adhere to the stereotypical rules of a dutiful soldier. No risk. No ingenuity."

"And little chance for you to escape," I add. "I'll indulge your little hunch one more time, but I'm warning you. If it doesn't pay off, you won't see the chance to attempt a third."

"I'm so scared," she says softly. "I best be on my most perfect behavior, then."

WILLOW

I am young. If I hear that phrase again, I might scream. I want to rail against the constraints that being nineteen seems to place on me. I hate having what feels like the entire world walking on eggshells to ignore the obvious.

I am young, but so were they once. Mischa, Ellen, Donatello, Olivia…

They made their mistakes, and they can't shame me for doing the same. We all have our weaknesses and our vices.

Why can't mine be him?

I want to know more, and that terrifies me. I want more of this world I've only gotten a glimpse of. If I'm going to be condemned for it, I deserve to experience it all.

Not out of rebellion or hate. Perhaps it's plain masochism. He warned me what a future with him on the periphery would be—but it's no different than how it's always been.

Having him at a distance, brooding over a past that neither of us has any control over.

The thought emboldens me as I reach the door he's hidden behind. Slowly, I push it open, unprepared for what I find on the other end.

I exhale, feeling my fingers tremble over the doorknob. He's sprawled over the bed, still wearing his dress pants, and rumpled white shirt, the tie partially undone and askew, with his collar open beneath.

A sliver of his chest is visible, coated with a thatch of dark hair, as well as a strip of white near his shoulder, alluding to his bandages. His eyes are on the ceiling, his mouth pulled into a twisted grimace of concentration. At a glance, I doubt he's slept. Whatever Ellen told him must weigh heavily on his mind—not to mention the revelations Olivia's letters revealed.

He's so lost in thought; he doesn't hear me come in at first. I make it all the way to the foot of the bed before he finally notices. His nostrils flare with my scent first before he cocks his head, lifting it from the pillows to aim that scowl firmly in my direction.

"Is something wrong?" He starts to sit up, but I shake my head before perching myself on the end of the mattress.

With my back to him, it's easier to ignore the glaring reality in which we exist. He's a man. I'm a woman.

And yet, there is so much between us that sets those simple facts at odds. We're enslaved to the past. The truth is that, outside of that box, I have no idea who I really am anymore. The role of Willow Stepanova feels as distant to me now as Safiya Mangenello. Both were shells of a scared little girl forced to find her place in a drastically different world from what she previously knew.

But now…

The world seems more or less the same, but I've changed in too many ways to name. I'm not braver, or more mature. If anything, I've regressed in those aspects, becoming more selfish. Curious. Rebellious. Questioning.

Spiteful.

It doesn't bother me one damn bit that when Donatello releases another heavy sigh, I can hear the dread in it. He doesn't want me here.

But I'm through letting him dictate our dynamic.

Because as much as it stings to admit, I feel closer to whoever I'm meant to be near him. Someone angry and vengeful, unwilling to be restrained. With his scent in my lungs, every breath feels sharper, and I sense my pulse quicken as if my heart is eager to send that tainted air to every inch of my body. We melt together into a twisted musk that lingers in my nostrils, potent enough to taste on the tip of my tongue. Like fire and smoke. Something spicy and dangerous but warming at the same time. A thin layer of sweat slicks my skin in the aftermath, relieving any chill I may have felt.

"You're not here for any particular reason," Donatello declares suddenly. It's as if he's driven to narrate my thoughts out loud, so confident in his abilities to read them. "You couldn't sleep either."

He isn't wrong. I tossed and turned in the other room, unable to quiet my racing thoughts. The present danger wasn't what taunted me, though. Just him. His face as Ellen spoke. The weight of his head on my lap. His pain. His anger. His taste.

I can still remember the heat of his mouth and the way his hands felt running over my skin. That quiet moment in the dark plagues me still. Maybe because I can't decipher it. Was it a trick on his part—a subtle manipulation meant to unnerve and confuse me? Or was it merely a lack of control.

The sick part is I almost prefer that scenario; that he compromised those lofty morals for me. In many ways, I'm no different than him, just as sadistic.

And just as cruel.

"There is a lot to set into motion," Donatello says, a subtle hint that dealing with me isn't on that list. "We need to deal with the Saleris, and plan the diversion—" I notice that he doesn't say "wedding." Already, he's craving the outcome that this was nothing more than a lab glitch. A mistake. "Not to mention dealing with Fabio and his many requirements to pull this off. We should probably get a move on soon."

He breaks off, and my heart stammers as I realize why—I've shifted toward him fully.

That elusive tension returns, robbing him of whatever he meant to say and stealing my senses. I inch closer despite every cell in my body warning me not to. I can't help it. He is magnetic, but the pull to him is a painful mixture of anger and…

Curiosity. I'm reaching out without permission from my brain, swiping my fingers across his jaw.

"What are we doing?" he croaks, but I sense it's a genuine question.

His eyes are puzzled, his lips twisting into that trademark frown. I ghost my fingers along his mouth until those lips part instead. I drag myself closer, trying to decipher for the umpteenth time why he inspires these emotions in me.

My throat feels tight, my tongue damp. Every breath I take feels heavy. He disrupts my body in the most intimate way, and I hate him for it. At the same time, some sick part of me must be addicted to his nearness.

I keep advancing, rising onto my knees.

He lets his head fall back against the pillows, almost as if in surrender. His hands fan out over the sheets until I come within his reach.

I shiver as his palm captures my waist, dragging me closer. One look at his eyes tells me this isn't aggressive on his part.

It's a dare. He wants to see if I'll pull away, perhaps to satisfy his own curiosity.

But I don't move. Instead, I lean into the movement, inching even closer. My thigh brushes his, my fingers contacting his arm. I inhale, and the rise of his chest warns he's doing the same. His gaze seeks out mine, his eyes narrowed in a way I can't interpret. Thoughtful and yet calculating. Dark circles betray just how tired he really is.

Last night aside, he hasn't slept well in days.

Wordlessly, he watches as I settle in even closer. My cheeks flame, bitten by the impropriety that's been driven into my skull by him and everyone else. It's wrong to be this close to him. To seek him out. To let my body contort into what feels like the most natural position to watch him in.

From above.

He grunts as if biting back a refusal. For whatever reason, he doesn't voice it. Instead, his hands shift to support my weight as I straddle him, bracing my hands over his chest.

His pulse hammers like a song. Despite hours of study of musical notes and composition, this is one tune I can't decipher easily.

His breaths scrape at the air, heavy and yet steady. "You can stand to be this close to me?"

I blink, caught off guard by the line of questioning. He could be referring to so many different topics. Then I remember the most recent revelation that might be weighing on his mind.

Olivia and her letters.

"What does that make you?" he wonders, his tone dangerously soft. "If I'm the monster. Are you the prey, or something worse?"

I don't think he expects me to answer. Communicating with him like this is a game of roulette. I never know which way the dice will fall.

Still, I feel compelled to answer him in the only way I can. I reach for his right hand, and he curls the fingers into a fist.

"Prey," he says, naming the option that hand signifies.

My throat tightens as I make my choice, entwining my fingers with his—but the ones on his other hand.

"Something worse," he declares in defeat. "Either way, I'm responsible for whatever you've become."

He can't resist asserting control, even under the guise of taking the blame.

"Why do you want to stay here with me?"

His tone deepens into a throaty rasp. Suddenly, the air feels thick between us.

"I know why." He untangles his fingers from mine, bringing that hand to my cheek. "To punish me," he says, laying out one option. "To hurt me."

There is no in between in his mind. Every motive must contain him at the center. The reality, however, is far simpler.

I shake my head, and with another tortured sigh, he lets his hand fall.

He inclines his head, eyeing me more skeptically. Something in the intensity of his gaze sends a shiver through me. Sometimes it's alarmingly easy to tell what he's thinking.

This time, his gaze contains a single dare that sends another tendril of unease down my spine.

It's a lot like the look I presume a wolf might give a prospective rabbit caught in its path. To bite, or to let it hop in blissful innocence a little while longer?

But what this wolf doesn't know is that the rabbit isn't prey. It's an equally dangerous hunter.

"I think you should leave," he murmurs, close enough that his lips brush my jaw with every movement.

When I don't, he pulls me beneath him, looming above.

I swallow hard, aware of his strength. His thighs dent the mattress on either side of me, forming a prison from his body heat.

I choke down the apprehension and run my hands down his chest, feeling his heartbeat. My fingers find the edge of his shirt to touch the skin beneath. He feels so hot—like a live wire.

His lids grow heavy as he looks down, tracking every movement of my trembling fingertips.

I go lower. Lower. Too low.

He sucks in a breath snatching at my wrist. Then something flits across his eyes, and he returns my hand to its position.

"You want to play with fire? Then play."

I take him up on the dare. I can barely manipulate the zipper, but when I finally get the latch freed, he inhales, every muscle rigid.

I tug the material down inch by inch and let myself view what lies beneath.

The first time is so vivid in my mind, but even those images barely do him justice. Beautiful is the only term to come to mind. Beautiful and dangerous.

Until he takes it upon himself to turn the tables, palming my hips.

My body burns in ways I'm not familiar with. His heat becomes a weapon, igniting parts of me I've barely explored. He teases me above the fabric, almost daring my hips to shift against his palms in a silent invitation.

He takes his time winding the thin material between his fingers, dragging it up...up... Then he removes the thin barrier beneath, until his eyes are on the part of me that makes my cheeks flame.

"You are so beautiful," he breathes out as if the confession is too dangerous to voice too loudly. "So damn beautiful."

But he doesn't touch me, only utilizing his eyes to rake over every exposed inch.

I take it upon myself to touch him first, and he groans, his head shooting back. His fingers latch onto my wrist again, restraining where I can wander. Only the faint light gives me a glimpse of him, and I trace the shape.

"Slow," he grates, his eyes wide.

I strain his grasp instead, shivering as his heat burns even hotter. In this arena, he's held the lion's share of control, I can admit. Partly due to my own ignorance, and maybe a little fear as well.

Sometimes, he can seem so damn untouchable. Like there isn't a hint of softness to be found beneath his skin. I run my fingers over the ridge of his collar bone, and that belief is instantly proven false.

The man is more dangerous than a solid, unmoving mass. He has the ability to melt like molten steel, molding to my body perfectly. When I brace my hands under his chest and shove, he falls back easily, those dark eyes glinting with confusion.

My heart quivers against my ribcage as I follow him, using my body to pin his this time.

With a low groan, he lets his head fall back, his hands by his sides. I'm forced to mount him unassisted, navigating the planes of muscle alone. His shirt is a hindrance, and I reach for the buttons.

His throat cords as I undo one. I can see a refusal playing on the tip of his tongue. It's unnatural for him to cede control like this without a fight.

Still, he lets me undo the rest and drag the material from his shoulders.

Now, there is nothing to stop me from exploring him in full, tracing the divots along his ribcage before finding the jagged, raised line of his tattoo.

I'm too lost in exploration that I don't realize he's continued his own investigation of me. Not until the pad of his thumb grazes my nipple over the fabric of my dress, freezing the air in my lungs.

"You are so beautiful." He doesn't put effort into his voice. The growled, gruff syllables betray who he is at his core. Someone who eyes my body hungrily with an intensity that doesn't match the gentleness with which he finds my belly, pressing his palm flat against it.

He looks up, hiding nothing. Regret should be what I find there. Not…

Desire. And hope. And a desperation that seems impossible for one man to harbor toward another being. A warning sensation pricks the back of my eyes. My eyelids flutter as it takes more effort to breathe. Think.

To counter the wave of emotion, I feel driven to a reckless action I don't have time to think through. I reach down, finding that dangerous part of him that throbs greedily against my fingertips.

His nostrils flare, his eyes narrowing as that hope gives way to another emotion. One a part of me hesitates to name—but I do so anyway.

Lust.

"Slow," he reminds me, his words barely audible.

Instinct takes over instead, driving me to curl my hand around him completely. Stroke, sensing him harden.

I can't imagine how he fit within me the first time. Or the second...

Until he eases a finger inside me now and my body has to make room.

Our eyes meet as he fills me, hissing at the feeling.

It's different than before. Less a rush of sensation and more concentrated.

We move together in a way that feels too natural for words. Like I was born for this. For him.

And he was made for me.

DON

It's wrong to savor this. Her heat. This moment. The snatches of sleep we've managed to steal despite everything looming beyond this room. Lulled by the soft sound of her breathing in my ear, it's too easy to ignore it all.

I haven't felt this way since… Not since Olivia and the days when sleeping in was a rare treat considering our growing household. This isn't quite the same. The woman beside me is smaller, her presence quieter than Liv's playful chuckles. Her scent is lighter, the air poisoned with it. One inhale, and I'm under her influence, drunker than a million bottles of alcohol could ever achieve.

This form of intoxication isn't a crippling blanket, meant to blind me to the state of my life. Instead, everything feels enhanced to a painful degree. Magnified. What once looked dark and grim, now holds a hint of color I never noticed before. There might even be some beauty lurking within all that grime.

Like that of the woman beside me. She rests on her side, inspecting me with those watchful eyes. Only a thin sheet covers us both, but she has her end tucked beneath her arms, wrapped tightly around her torso with a modesty that reinforces just how new this is for her.

Intimacy.

A good man would ease her into this. Instead, I cross the sliver of space between us, brushing the flat of my palm across her belly. She shivers, her eyes meeting mine, but I ignore the eye contact, for now, watching the thin material shift with every breath she takes.

Another life could be growing right beneath my hand, and it strikes me that I haven't stopped to consider what that might mean—beyond the negative connotations anyway.

It means a potential person with eyes like hers or a nose like mine.

I feel my lips quirk at the mental image of him or her. I'm tempted to lie here for as long as possible and embrace this new outlook, putting off whatever waits beyond this bedroom door.

As always, fate seems to have other plans.

Muffled noise comes from the front of the suite, like that of a door opening. Then a voice, "Donatello?"

That familiar baritone penetrates this warm cocoon, shattering the peace instantly.

"Shit!" I bolt upright, sensing my companion startle beside me. There isn't time to do anything more than bark, "Stay here," and lurch to my feet. Cursing, I snatch my pants from the dresser, pulling them on while stumbling into the hall.

And I nearly run into Fabio, who pivots in time to avoid me.

"You're late," he says as his eyes skim over me with disapproval.

I barely manage to slam the door in his face, praying to God he didn't see inside.

His exasperated sigh doesn't relieve that fear one bit. "Not even dressed yet at this hour?"

"This hour…" I spy a glass clock hanging on the wall of the room behind him and hiss through my teeth. It's almost noon.

Hours spent in bed listening to someone breathe— something I haven't done since…

Too damn long. I'd forgotten what it feels like to sleep— truly sleep. My head feels clearer, my movements easier. It could be that sobriety is finally kicking in. I'll blame that, nothing else.

"In case you've forgotten, we have maybe a few trivial things to take care of today," Fabio says, gearing up to scold. "Such as, oh I don't know, finding the person who made an attempt on your life, more than twice now. I'm sorry if you don't find that issue pressing enough to get out of bed for!"

"I'm sorry," I say. There's no arguing with him when he's like this. He's more composed than yesterday, but the bags under his eyes are darker than mine.

"Don't be," he says softly. Then he cocks his head, his eyes narrowing. "You look different. Better, I think. Maybe it's not such a bad thing you've set us behind schedule if you aren't scowling at me. Now come on, let's get you dressed properly."

He reaches past me for the door.

"W-Wait!" I surge down the hall toward the main room, sensing him on my heels. Thank God. I fight to keep my voice steady, fishing for any change in subject. "Remind me again. What's the game plan?"

"I don't understand you, Donatello," Fabio snaps, shaking his head. "Did you just happen to forget the bullet wound on your arm?"

The funny thing is I have. The pain sears like an afterthought, easily drowned out by the remnants of another's body heat.

"Don?"

"You're right, Fab. Which is why you should jump at the chance to talk logistics."

"I've made the arrangements for the sham wedding," he states, his disgust evident. "But it's up to you to put your plan for the Saleris into play. Mischa's man found something strange at one of their estates."

I hazard a guess. "The answer to our mystery man and what he's after?"

"Not quite. Only a weapon's cache with enough firepower to supply a small army," Fabio says deadpanned.

I nearly choke. "Shit—"

"Exactly," Fabio says, grimacing. "Which is why I think it's best if we accelerate our timeline and lure out our enemies into a trap as soon as possible. Mischa told me that you have a way to rile Mateo? It's a risk to provoke him, but if we can get a lead on their accounts, we can track them down more accurately."

Which brings up another point. "Any news on the real estate front?"

Fabio sighs. "Not yet. Still too many interested parties to home in on one for sure, but I'm winnowing the list as we speak. If you can goad Mateo into making a more blatant offer, perhaps? That could give me the clue I need."

"Done," I say. "Firepower or not, I can handle Mateo Saleri."

"Let's hope so," Fabio says softly. "Now… Where is Willow? Still sleeping? Usually, she's up well before this hour. Anyway, let's get her sorted. I have an idea how to further our ruse while keeping her safe—"

He heads down the hall at a pace I have to sprint to keep up with.

"Wait!"

He's at the door to her room before I can stop him, pushing it open. "She isn't here," he says, and a hint of alarm tinges his tone.

Shit.

"I… Maybe she went into the study—"

"Oh," Fabio says, inclining his head. "She must be in the bathroom."

Sure enough, I hear the sound at the same time he does—a rush of running water alluding to the shower being run.

"Well, let's get things into motion," Fabio says, clapping his hands, his expression stern. "You deal with the Saleris, and I'll handle Willow. And, you won't like it, but I think coordinating with Mischa can be worth the risk, if done carefully. We should stay on guard."

"Fine. I'll let you handle that as well."

"And one other thing…" He sighs, leveling me with a look that instantly sends my guard up. "You read the letters by now, I'm sure," he says carefully. "You're taking things well."

There's no mistaking the wary expression on his face for anything other than dread.

"You knew," I rasp, so thrown off that I stagger back. It's not just the shock of having that dredged up again with nothing to distract from it—Olivia was unfaithful to me. But it's the knowing, pained expression on Fabio's face that hits like a punch. "You knew Nico wasn't… That he might not have been mine."

"Don…" His eyes glisten, even as he tightens his jaw. "There is no use in tainting the past with lies and half-truths we can't verify," he says tightly. "I don't want you to let this tarnish your view of Olivia. She loved you. So damn much—"

"Do you think I killed her?"

"What?" He frowns, his brows drawn together. "Of course not! Don't be foolish."

"But someone did," I say. "I thought it was Gino for so damn long, but maybe the bastard wasn't that sick."

But I was.

"Don't do this to yourself," Fabio insists, placing his hand on my shoulder. "You have enough to focus on in the present. Now, let's get a move on."

I relent to him, letting him steer me down the hall. "Whatever you say, Fab."

But something feels off, though I can't put my finger on it. It's a lack of anger on his part—like he knows far more than just the fact that Liv was fucking Gino. Could he know for certain who killed her?

I shrug off the thought. Fab is many things, but a liar isn't one of them. Whatever he knows, if anything, he's hiding for a good damn reason.

So, as hard as it is, I push it out of my mind. For now.

"There's something else," I add, turning my attention to yet another little dilemma. "Considering you haven't led off with this little detail, I assume that you weren't given a heads-up. Mischa's wife came here yesterday. Alone."

Shock isn't a strong enough word to describe Fabio's expression. He stops in his tracks, releasing me. The color drains from his face, and he glances around as if expecting to find the woman's dead body.

"What did she want? God damn it, Donatello. Tell me you exercised some decorum—"

"I didn't beat the shit out of her, if that's what you mean," I snap. "Though if she were a man, I might have."

Color returns to Fabio's expression in the form of his cheeks turning bright red. "I take it she didn't come bearing gifts?"

"Depends on your definition. She's the one I told about my plan to see Mateo."

His eyes widen. "I didn't think to ask for specifics before, but maybe I should have. Just how do you intend to provoke him?"

I shrug. "I do have his niece."

"The girl?" Fabio lowers his voice as if afraid the girl in question might hear him, one floor below. "You really think it's a prudent move to dangle the life of a child as leverage?"

"I'm not heartless," I say. "She's merely the excuse necessary to get me an audience with Mateo. Nothing more."

"Be careful," Fabio warns. "I've had my men dig more into Gregori's death. The short story is that it seems he had a heart attack. The long story is that said heart attack was brought on by a knife, apparently. The severe nature of his wounds leads me to suspect he didn't expire entirely of natural causes."

"So, he was murdered. It isn't that shocking if you know Mateo," I say, picturing the ambitious bastard. "He's been itching to take over the reins for a while now. I guess he got tired of waiting."

"Which just makes him more dangerous," Fabio warns. "Stay on your guard."

I grimace in a way that might pass for a smile. "Don't I always?"

"In the meantime, I will make sure that Willow is protected while still furthering our ruse."

"How so?"

"You'll see," he says grimly. "Let's call it a surprise."

That doesn't sound very reassuring. If anything, this "surprise" sounds more like a punishment.

One designed with me in mind.

WILLOW

*H*e haunts me. I feel his presence long after he's gone, distracting from everything else.

I barely even notice what's happening around me until I sense the caress of fabric over my skin as a gentle voice brushes my ear. "What do you think of this color, Miss?"

It's white. A blinding shade of ivory that clashes with my skin tone, making my eyes look darker and larger. Like black holes.

I blink, and the rest of my surroundings come into focus—the hotel suite, though with the main room transformed into a makeshift fitting area.

It was Fabio's idea—further enhance this fake wedding with a fake wedding gown. In reality, I think this is his way of driving home just what he thinks of this entire farce.

A dangerous play during which I shouldn't forget my role. To pretend.

"What do you think?" the seamstress prods. I can't even imagine how Fabio found her on such short notice, but she's a pretty woman just a few years older than me with brown hair and a kind smile.

Following her gaze to a full-length mirror placed before the windows, I *think* this sham looks more obvious than ever. I resemble an actress more than a prospective bride-to-be, draped in the shell of a pretty, white wedding dress.

Paired with what happened last night, I'm more confused than ever by this entire ordeal. Trying to contextualize my relationship with Donatello Vanici feels a lot like trying to nail smoke to a wall. Impossible.

And yet, I can't escape the irrational impulse to capture it by any means rather than watch it dissipate.

I hate the uncertainty being around him inspires within me. It's maddening. One minute it's like he's seeing through me, and the next, I'm the only creature in his view.

In this dress, I doubt he'd notice me at all, though. He might prefer that. Then I'd merely fit the image of the virginal martyr he wants me to be, if only because that version of me is easier for him to ignore.

But he can't overlook the reality lurking beyond his self-pitying image. He isn't a victim, and neither am I. We're opponents in a war I refuse to let him surrender. Not now.

"Miss?" The seamstress smiles awkwardly. "Should we try another style?" She inclines her head toward a nearby rack she brought with her, overflowing with fabric samples.

Viewing them in the mid-afternoon sunlight instills an inexplicable sense of dread in me. They all look pretty and artificial, perfectly befitting the sham that this wedding is purported to be. Clothed in any one of these fabrics, Donatello will be able to have his sacrifice and further cling to his tortured role as the unwilling savior in this fairy tale.

He won't look at me as he did last night.

Like I'm worth craving.

Like wanting me wasn't a mistake.

"Why don't we take a quick break," the woman suggests while removing the strips of cloth from me. "I'll see if there are other pieces of fabric you might like in my car."

She leaves, and I use her absence to pace, inspecting the various materials she left behind.

Fabio must have given her a vague idea to go off of. Something beautiful if serviceable, able to be composed quickly. Ironically, if I had to picture some nameless woman walking down the aisle to meet this current iteration of Donatello Vanici, she wouldn't be wearing something so beautiful.

Her dress would sport bloodstains and tears within the pretty lace. Her hair would stream down her shoulders as she stalked to meet him.

Though it wouldn't have always unfolded quite like that. I'm sure Olivia wore a beautiful gown with a flowing veil, her beauty exquisitely showcased. She would resemble an angel on earth, paired with his image of the devil.

Of course, Fabio must have imagined something much of the same, but the fabric I feel drawn to is of a richer hue. Scarlet. Black. I finger a bolt of crimson fabric and picture a dress garish in design that wouldn't quite fit within Fabio's careful planning.

Or Donatello's pitying game of self-destruction.

"Oh? Would you like to try a different color?" The seamstress returns, carting a rack of even more pristine fabrics. "That choice would be unconventional," she adds, coming to stand beside me, "but it's a lovely hue."

Sometimes I feel at a loss as to how to make my desires known without a voice. This time all I do is nod and know my point has been made perfectly.

If this is to be a costume, then why not make it fit my vision?

Not Fabio's, or Donatello's, or anyone else's.

EVGENI

The old Winthorp estate remains on the outskirts of Hell's Gambit, a sprawling hellscape of crumbling architecture and overgrown weeds. But all isn't quite as it appears—though someone has definitely gone out of their way to make it seem unremarkable.

"I had a reconnaissance team give me some background on this property," I tell the woman beside me.

I've commandeered another unmarked van from the Stepanov arsenal. Parked on a ridge overlooking the estate's west end, we have a partial view of the charred husk that once was the grand Winthorp mansion.

"Your sister inherited the property initially, but later donated it to the city. Since then, it's fallen into disrepair and quietly passed hands through a few different entities, eventually winding up in the possession of an organization that at first seems dedicated to preserving the city's unique architecture. In reality, it doesn't exist. It must be a shell company used by this brother of yours to cover his tracks."

"Clever," Briar says softly. A hint of genuine admiration taints her voice, displacing some of the usual haughtiness. It might help that she's opted for a black shirt and jeans rather than a prim ensemble, and her hair—save for a curl pinned behind her ear—is loose, draped over her shoulders like a cape. She could almost be mistaken for a normal woman and not a cunning disgraced heiress on the run.

"Very clever. I suppose you've gleaned more than that? A thorough soldier such as yourself."

I grunt in grudging acknowledgment and let the taunt slide. "It seems that, though no one has moved in to claim the property, the facilities remain powered with electricity and fresh water. A strange expense for an abandoned property."

"Very strange," she agrees with a laugh. "So, what now? We continue to gawk from the safety of this comfy vehicle?"

"The area could be booby trapped to alert its owner of any trespassers. We should be careful. Gather reconnaissance before making any definitive moves."

"You make it sound so serious."

She's smiling, and I'm more uneasy than if she were nervous.

"If you're aiming to reassure me that this isn't a trap, it isn't working the way you hope."

She pats my shoulder playfully. "I only aim to inspire utter confidence, soldier. I wouldn't dream of betraying you now." Her teeth gleam in the overcast daylight.

"Then prove it. If you believe they're here, and you know this place so well, then where? Where could they be hiding?"

"Nowhere on the upper floors," she says, inspecting the remnants of the once-grand estate.

I can easily picture her waltzing along these grounds in their heyday, her head thrown back, every bit of arrogance on display. Ironically, she seems much like the property—ravaged by the passages of time, clinging to her once-grand veneer, desperate to hold onto whatever glory remains.

"I bet the rain would have worn the roof away, and any repairs would have been noticed. No... The core of the house seems intact, but the safest bet would be in one of the underground passages. My father had a fondness for service tunnels. They made for an efficient way to move both servants and supplies throughout the estate as well as a convenient stash for enemies."

Her smile is wistful, as though the thought brings back warming childhood memories.

"My brother was particularly fond of those caverns," she says softly. "Always using them to squirrel away his toys."

"That doesn't sound like the typical playhouse," I say.

She blinks as if she forgot I was even here. "Oh, it wasn't. We had what might be deemed an unconventional childhood, though, isn't everyone's? Yours, for instance. I take it you didn't spend your time with puppies and playhouses."

"Not quite," I admit. "Now, where do these so-called catacombs begin and end?"

She uses her finger to trace a path from one end of the massive house to a few yards beyond it. "They were pretty expansive. Even after years of disuse, I'm sure they might still be secure enough to use as a temporary base, at least. There were a few entries, but I think the old service passage might be the most accessible. It has an entrance near the garden shed."

I inspect the dilapidated shack she gestures to with a nod of her head. It's on the furthest end of the property, and would definitely make for a fitting hideout.

"Useful to know. For now, we watch and wait. If anyone is here, they need to move at some point. After nightfall, we move in."

"We *wait*," she echoes nastily. "Knowing you personally, I find it hard to believe you're the same man whispered about in all those rumors."

"And I think you're exactly who I've heard you are."

"Oh?" If I didn't know any better, I'd assume she takes offense to that. "The truth is, you don't know a damn thing about me."

"Oh, I don't?"

"No," her voice deepens in a way that sets off an internal alarm. *Danger.* "Because you wouldn't have denied me if you did."

I lick my lips before replying, weighing the response on the tip of my tongue. An insult would serve to put her in her place. Instead, I toy with her, still eyeing her old family home. "And why wouldn't I?"

"Because…"

I hear her shift and whip around to face her, instantly on guard. Her hand is raised, but harmlessly lands over my chest. Slowly she bridges the gap between us, settling her weight onto my lap.

"What are you doing?" My voice lacks the anger it should have. Try as I might, I don't feel any, either. Almost amused, I watch her climb out of her seat, and I don't raise a hand to stop her.

She's surprisingly light, easily fitting in between my body and the steering wheel. Her scent lacks the hint of perfume I've become accustomed to. Instead, she smells…

Rich. Like shampoo and fresh air and a tinge of something I can't place.

"I'm bored," she declares, her sweet breath hitting me full in the face. "Can you think of a way to pass the time?"

I should push her off. Instead, I cock my head, meeting her gaze head-on. "Like what?"

"This."

Her hand hooks around my neck. A heartbeat later, her lips find mine, and I don't resist, letting her ease my mouth open with the tip of her tongue. It's as conflictingly sensual and unsettling as her last kiss.

Only this time, she uses her hands to aid her assault, running them through my hair. Down my chest. Lower.

I stiffen, hissing through my teeth as her fingers find the front of my pants, wrenching on the zipper. I grip one of her wrists. A refusal is on the tip of my tongue.

Only I never voice it.

She feels so damn good, and some selfish part of me can't deny that. As if sensing the lack of fight, she wrenches open the fly and eagerly slips her hand within the resulting gap.

In return, I snatch at her waist, feeling fabric give beneath my fingertips. Her own jeans are slightly too big on her, borrowed most likely. It's easy to tug the waistband from her hips.

But she's eager to assist, using her free hand to wrench them down.

Shit. An instinctive need to feel her takes over. The bare skin of her hips. Her thighs. Between them...

She wastes no time palming my cock in her fist, applying friction that has me hissing through clenched teeth.

Common sense can't break the lust that seems to come from nowhere. Though maybe I've been repressing it all along.

The need to kiss her recklessly. Wildly. Bite.

I can't think. I can't seem to clear my head at all until I feel her warmth swallow me like a glove.

Fucking her isn't a beautiful, perfect moment of passion.

It's messy. Brutal. I have to arch my hips and bend her over the steering wheel, taking her in a senseless rhythm she somehow manages to match.

Together, we're selfish, each greedy for our own pleasure.

And yet, when my head rears back, throat cording around a groan, I hear her mewl in return.

Her nails dig into my lower back, my teeth cinching her lip.

We're both panting when it's over, the windows fogged, the skyline slightly darker. And even as she shimmies off my lap and back into her own seat…

I don't feel an ounce of regret.

Judging from her dazed, resigned expression, she doesn't either. Her hair is a mess, tousled and ragged. Sensing my gaze, she tiredly runs a hand along the blond curls.

Glinting in the space between us, I spy a small object that I grab, inspecting it warily—a gold hairpin that seems out of place given her modest ensemble, and yet a perfect encapsulation of who she is at her core. A walking contradiction.

"Here." I reach over without permission, returning the pin to a mass of curls.

Her lips twitch in a pale imitation of her usual grin. "Only a soldier would care about order and neatness at a time like this."

I don't argue with that assessment.

I just stare forward, eyeing the darkening sky while questioning what the hell I've just done.

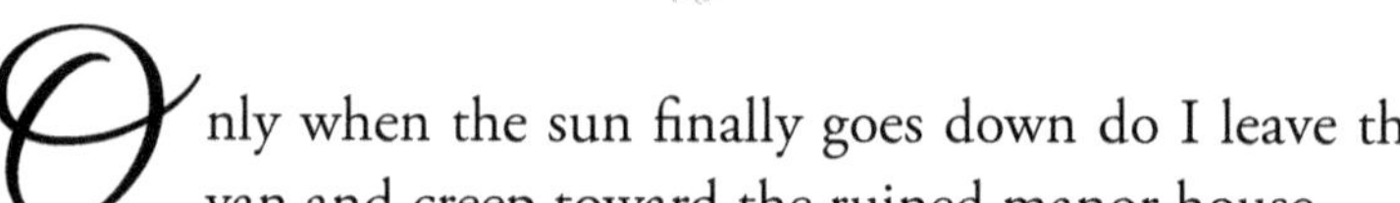

*O*nly when the sun finally goes down do I leave the van and creep toward the ruined manor house.

Supposedly, she'll wait like a good girl until I give the all clear—and even if she doesn't, I have the only set of keys with me.

Still, I can't shake this itch bitching at my concentration, irritating me as I trek through overgrown weeds to the garden shed.

I can't tell if it's my intuition warning me that I've been played—it's a trap.

Or if simply….

Something's wrong.

As I finally reach the decrepit shack, one fact becomes clear, though. Given the amount of debris and rotten wood piled in the center of the building, no one could access the tunnel entrance, let alone form a hideout here.

That uneasy feeling blossoms into full-blown paranoia. Once again, I have to question if Briar Winthorp had another aim in mind for bringing me here.

Unsurprisingly, when I return to the van, she's gone.

DON

This isn't the first time I've gone toe to toe with the Saleris—but it feels different. Maybe because there isn't a woman on my arm, her quiet presence unmistakable? Either way, an uncomfortable tension fills the air as I mount the rounded stairs leading to the entrance of the mansion.

Formed of white marble and tasteless architecture, Mateo Saleri, and his brother-in-law Antonio had one thing in common—their lack of class. Still, I'm surprised I've made it this far unchallenged.

Apart from watching me with their weapons in view, his guards haven't stopped me, nor has Mateo himself appeared to put a bullet through my skull yet—which only means one thing.

He isn't caught off guard. The motherfucker's been anticipating this—expecting me.

So much for Fabio's grand plan of action, and yet the closer

I come to the heart of the estate, the easier it is to sense the prevailing unease lurking beneath the façade.

Something's off. Despite the show of force, the men lining the main driveway seem stretched thin—nowhere near the numbers Evgeni reported. It's as though only a fraction of them are actually here, leaving gaping holes in their coverage. In normal times, it wouldn't stick out, but now…

Where the hell are those extra reinforcements?

They don't seem to be inside the mansion, either. Instead, mingled among the Saleris' opulence are even fewer guards, all armed to the teeth and jumpy as hell.

"You have some damn nerve," Mateo declares as I enter the spacious room he's holding court from. It overlooks the back of the estate, where a bubbling fountain spits water from the mouth of two snarling lions. "To dangle my niece's life over my head. I didn't think you still had it in you."

I match his tone, ire for ire. "I didn't think you still had the capacity to give a damn about anything beyond money. People change, it seems. Or maybe your father's death has humbled you."

He flinches, tugging at the front of his suit jacket with a trembling hand. He's gone for a white suit today, and the color appears modest compared to his usual ensembles. It seems he's been preoccupied, too distracted to focus on his typical fashion.

"Where is Kisa?" he snaps. "You were brave to come here alone to make your demands. Though I have to wonder if you even have it in you."

"To sell her?" I counter coldly. "You've heard the rumors, Mateo. I've done it before."

"And what do you want?" he scoffs. "Money? Brave man to come here on your hands and knees alone."

"I'm no fool," I warn. "It may look like I'm alone, but I'm not. You can shoot me now and see what consequences lie in store. Though, I think you've already made a recent attempt on my life, haven't you?"

His eyes flit away from me as he continues to tug at his collar. So, he was behind the hit—but considering I'm still alive, his plans have changed. Why?

Rather than dwell on the unease, I incline my head and extend a hand. "Why don't we put our differences aside in the name of the greater good?"

He spits at my feet. "Enough talk. What is your price?"

"I desire a mere conversation. I'm looking to sell my harbor. Have you heard about that?"

He has. His eyes narrow into slits, betraying his interest. "You mean the ashes? I might accept it if you're giving it away for free."

"Not quite," I say with a cold smile. "It seems I've gotten many interested buyers. I can't imagine why."

Again, his mask slips. His nostrils flare, and he grips the armrests of his chair. *Bingo.*

"Double your offer, and you can have your niece safely returned," I say.

"Oh, but when will you find the time?" Mateo snarls. "Shouldn't you be busy with your wedding preparations?"

I fight to keep my expression blank. At least now I have confirmation that Fabio's trap drew his notice as intended.

"I'm never too busy for business, Mateo," I counter. "You should know that better than anyone."

"I'll tell you what I *do* know Vanici, I'm not in the mood for a visit after all." He stands, his gaze ice. "Get out."

He doesn't have to tell me twice. Aware of a pair of armed guards watching from the shadows, I turn on my heel and start to leave.

"My offer still stands, Mateo. But keep in mind that I plan on picking a buyer by tonight. Double your offer."

I don't know if I'm relieved to make it to my car unscathed or further unsettled. I've barely made it through the gates before I have Fabio on the other line.

"Watch your accounts. I think any minute, you should be getting a signal from Mateo Saleri's accountant. Hopefully, that can lead you to the puppet master pulling his strings."

"I can't believe you met with him alone," Fabio scolds. "You should have waited for the Stepanov guards for backup."

"I bought us an hour at least," I say. The truth is that being beholden to Mischa seems just as appealing as taking a Saleri bullet to the brain. Still, I appreciate that the man kept his word. "With *mafiya* reinforcements, we can stand a chance against whatever they're planning. But we need their headquarters."

"I'm on it," Fabio says. "This could be it, Donatello. If you're right, tomorrow could serve as a defining moment. They aim to catch you off guard as expected."

"Which explains why Mateo let me walk out of his home alive," I say dryly. "Is everything else in place?"

"Yes," Fabio says. "Let's hope this works."

"It has to," I counter. "There isn't any other option."

"Well, there is one," he points out. "You could always walk away from this mess entirely and sail off into the sunset as the world falls apart."

"Nice try." I choke out a laugh. "Maybe. If I wasn't still so damn sober."

"Make sure you stay that way. You need to be in the right state of mind for your wedding, after all. It is tomorrow."

I wince at the reminder. "Fake wedding."

"That doesn't mean that the overarching situation has changed. There are plenty of issues still waiting to be resolved after this. You know that."

"I do. But frankly, Fabio, I'm just trying to stay alive."

And forget the woman who haunts my every waking moment.

I arrive at the hotel before sundown. I've barely stepped from the elevator when someone comes to block my path. Instinctively, I reach for my weapon before I even register my "attacker's" face.

Recognition stops me from drawing my gun. "Luciano—"

"Is it true?" he demands, his hands in fists. His face red, his eyes cut to slits. These past few days, I've barely interacted with the ex-Salvatore soldier—let alone enough to enrage him. In fact, him sticking around as long as he has is more of a testament to his loyalty to the lone remaining Salvatore rather than to me.

"Is what true?" I say.

"That you used Kisa as your fucking bargaining chip? What the hell is wrong with you?"

"I used her name as my way in to speak with Mateo Saleri," I clarify, pushing past him. "She won't be going anywhere. Besides, even Mateo isn't stupid enough to believe that I seriously meant to trade. The bastard was stalling. He wants me alive to bait the wedding trap we've already set. I think he and his cohort believe to catch not only me, but the *mafiya* off guard."

Which means the bastard was entertaining a meeting with his own means in mind—a thought I push to the back of my mind for now.

"What are you planning for her, anyway?"

"And what are you planning for Kisa?" I toss back. "Considering that you're her biological father."

It's a suspicion I couldn't confirm.

Until now, when he blinks as if struck, his face reddening further. "You don't know what the hell you're talking about."

"You can't look at that child the way you do and not have a tie to her. A blind man could see the truth for what it is. Why deny that?" Anger I wasn't aware of leeches into my voice, raising it. "Instead, you let her live with that bastard Antonio. He's dead. You should be eager to claim her. If nothing else, then to keep her away from the fucking Saleris—"

"You mean like you?" he counters softly.

I feel my irritation deflate, replaced by guilt. "No. Not like me. Though to my credit, the people I've failed haven't been my child by blood."

"So, what if I am her father?" Lowering his voice, he casts a wary glance at the suite up ahead. "You think I can provide for her better than Tony? He was a twisted son of a bitch, but he could give her a life I never could."

"And now he's dead," I point out. "But you don't have to worry about Kisa when it comes to me. You have my word on that. Now, where is she?"

Her location isn't a mystery for long. As I continue down the hall, I'm assaulted by a wave of childish laughter that stops me dead in my tracks just outside of the door to the suite.

All I can do is push the door open wide enough to watch and listen.

"This is how you play," Kisa explains while sitting cross-legged on the floor.

Across from her is a figure only slightly larger. Before both is an array of glass marbles.

"Like this." Kisa flicks a larger marble with her thumb and forefinger, sending it colliding into a mass of smaller ones. "Then you try to knock out more from the circle—" She breaks off, her large blue eyes moving in my direction.

Shock is to be expected. Not the fear that sends her mouth slack and has her scrambling back.

Confused, Willow turns in my direction.

"It's okay." Luciano moves forward, crouching down beside her. "Let's go back to—"

"No. Don't," I say thickly. "Just... Just let her play."

A request that seems impossible. Wide with fear, her eyes remain glued to me; she doesn't move.

Not until Willow picks up the larger marble first, using it to knock out three more. Warily, Kisa returns to the circle, her eyes darting in my direction.

I don't know how long it takes before she begins to relax, laughing openly—but I can't describe what it feels like to hear that sound again. Laughter, infectious and childish.

The sound only drives home the last time I remember seeing Willow Stepanova as carefree—juxtaposed with the last time I saw her when that joy turned to fear.

And hate.

WILLOW

I creep into the empty room that's been designated as mine though I have yet to spend a single night in here. Even as I sit on the edge of the mattress, I doubt I'll be able to get much sleep. When the door opens a second later, I know for sure that I won't.

"We've been dancing around the issue," Donatello says, his voice low.

He doesn't bother to turn on the light. Instead, he blends into the shadows, moving to stand across from me, with his back to the wall.

The windows display a pristine view of the city, speckled with neon lighting. As loud as the colors are, Hell's Gambit itself seems to fall away, becoming more distant with every second we spend occupying this space, close enough to touch.

"After tomorrow… I need to know for sure," he says, and at first, I'm not sure what he's referring to.

Oh. Then it clicks.

"Please. If you are… If you aren't," he adds thickly. "I need to know either way."

It should be a scary prospect, finding out the truth. I think I've been avoiding it, refusing an exam even after what happened at the restaurant.

A part of me doesn't want to know, not really.

Mainly out of fear. Fear for what that answer means for my future, as well as his.

And fear that no matter what the answer might be…

He'll leave me either way.

"There is one other thing…"

I jump as his lips brush my ear. While I was lost in thought, he didn't leave. He's closer, stroking down the length of my arm before entwining my fingers with his—but that isn't all. Something firm slips in between my palm and his, shockingly familiar.

"You'll need this," he says before pulling away, leaving that object in my grasp. "Just in case."

I look down at the small blade, still sharp despite everything it's been through. My heart pangs as I run my finger over the cutting edge, recalling the last time I held it.

"Don't think about that," Donatello warns, intruding upon my thoughts once again. "It can keep you safe if I can't.

Focus on that. Here—" He lumbers into the hallway, returning seconds later with an object he must have taken from his room. It's slender, catching what little light penetrates the windows—a black tie.

Crouching, he reaches for my thigh, and I stiffen, biting my lip. He barely touches me, instead looping the tie just above my right knee, securing the blade there in a way that keeps the edge from my skin.

"Keep this on you from now on."

I nod, staring down as he looks up. From this angle, he looks different. Less ravaged and worn—but not like the man I remember, either. He is a stranger I must get used to with no prior preconceptions to rely on.

A man I have to trust entirely of my own accord.

For better or for worse.

I t's surreal standing before this church again. At the back of my mind, I know that this occasion is little more than an elaborate scheme. An act in an overarching play.

And yet, I feel oddly at peace with this role as I approach the steps with my head held high, and a knife strapped to my thigh—ready and willing to face my opponent on even ground. He can't make the rules here. We both hold sway with a power to end this sham before it even begins and expose it for what it was all along. Just a sick, twisted lie.

I'm ready. I can sense everyone around me, but their expressions don't penetrate this iron wall I've built around myself. No one can touch me, and when I reach the mouth of the aisle, I feel invincible.

Until I see him standing near the altar, his back to me. His posture alone betrays the true purpose of this moment. Not a heartfelt ceremony, but a battle in which he's willing to sacrifice everything to win. When he inclines his head, it's with the swiftness of a soldier sensing the approach of an opponent.

And as he spins to face me fully, I stop short. My breath catches, and I sense my palms growing damp with sweat. The air feels thicker, and the looming walls and cavernous ceiling close in, threatening to crush me in their midst.

His eyes are the only anchor I have to latch onto. Their steady, steely gaze draws me forward when my steps start to falter. There is something in the daring tilt of his chin that issues a challenge I can't resist even now.

You're here—but do you trust me?

Alarm nips at my fragile reserve of composure. When I draw close to him, he brings his mouth inches from my ear.

"Change of plans," he says. "There's a detour we need to take first. Will you come with me?"

I don't even hesitate before nodding. Then I cut my gaze to the rest of the assembled audience for our sham wedding—just a few guards dressed in plain clothes. After all, it's meant to be a secret elopement.

"It will be quick. What Fabio doesn't know won't kill him," Donatello says. "He isn't here yet. Our nuptials aren't officially scheduled for a few more hours, at least. Besides, I think this might serve us better in the long run."

I eye him warily, but when he reaches for my hand, I take it.

"Trust me," Donatello warns as his destination comes into view.

Once he parks his car, that request seems easier said than done as my entire body goes cold. I shiver, feeling my teeth chatter, but the temperature of the outside air isn't the cause of this chill.

Just horrifying memories.

I'm in a skirt and a sweater while Donatello wears his suit. Ironically, our clothing serves as an unnerving callback to the very first time I came to this property.

I've never been able to forget it.

The gray structure looks unremarkable from the outside. More like a warehouse than the opulent lair of a human trafficker.

My mind goes back to that day, seven years ago, when Donatello dragged me here out of the blue, shortly after Olivia's death. Trust is the furthest thing from my mind. Though, I had plenty of it back then...

Along with hope and unwavering faith in the man beside me.

Why on earth would he bring me here now?

"Willow?"

I jump as he snatches my hand, gripping the fingers tight enough that I have no choice but to look at him. He holds my gaze with an intensity that takes my breath away.

"Trust me. I think it's time we both got answers, don't you?"

Answers? From Nikolai himself.

My stomach turns as I eye our combined fingers. A few days ago, I would've run—before those nights in his bed and everything that's happened since. But now?

Finally, I let him guide me from the car toward the lone structure that somehow looks the same now as it did all those years ago.

The only difference is that the old man isn't waiting for us at the front of his compound.

Donatello has to knock on the front gates, loud enough that I'm sure he can be heard by anyone within a ten-mile radius.

"I know you can see me, you son of a bitch," he snarls, glaring in the direction of a square device affixed to the front of the barrier that must be a security camera. "Let us in."

"Donatello Vanici…" The voice comes from a speaker, laced with static. "To what do I owe this visit?"

Donatello eyes me sharply before hissing, "You *know* what."

Suddenly, the gates part, presumably operated by an unseen mechanism.

Still holding my hand, Donatello advances toward the main building.

But I sink inside myself with every step. The pain I feel strikes without warning. My eyes burn, and even as I try to blink back the threat of tears, they fall anyway.

He can see them, his jaw clenched.

I feel so damn pathetic, and a million insecurities swarm my mind at once. He's lying. For all I know, he intends to sell me again. I was a fool to trust him…

Far too soon, we enter through a tattered metal door that opens onto a darkened space with concrete flooring. A few cars are parked within white squares made of chalk, but the area is primarily empty.

The only potential link to what it actually contains is a lone elevator shaft that sputters open the second we approach.

There is only one level to press, and when the doors finally part—revealing the entryway of the underground den where Nikolai holds court—it's like a noose has been placed around my throat.

The smell worms into my lungs, conjuring a million terrifying images. I must stop short because suddenly Donatello is in front of me, smoothing his hands along my cheeks.

I flinch and start to shove him off, but he doesn't budge.

"Listen to me," he insists, his voice gruff. The dim lighting casts his face half in shadow, and he's a living embodiment of the creature Donatello Vanici is at his core—part darkness, part something else.

"I'm done hiding from the truth." His voice breaks. He means it. "We can face it together, whatever the hell it reveals—"

"Touching." The voice comes from behind him where a man stands, clapping sardonically. I feel my eyes widen, taken aback by how different he is to the figure from my nightmares.

This man sports a brown robe, left open to reveal the gray shirt and jeans he's wearing beneath it. He seems to favor one leg, and an ornate walking stick propped against the wall behind him takes on greater significance.

All in all, seven years haven't been kind to Nikolai or his business, it seems. The once rich burgundy wallpaper is faded, torn in places, and the emerald carpet has seen better days. And yet, the man carries himself with all of the cold, ruthless indifference I remember.

"Donatello Vanici," he says in a thickly accented voice. "To what do I owe this visit? Though, you're a little too late to the party—" He points to his left eye where a mottled patch of skin alludes to what once would have been a gruesome bruise. "I've already divulged the sad tale to someone else."

"Mischa Stepanov?" Donatello asks.

Nikolai laughs, but it's a brutal arrangement of syllables. "Who else? And I hate to cut this little reunion short, but I'm on a time crunch, and you aren't invited."

"Then repeat your little story and be quick about it," Donatello demands. "What do you remember about the time I came to you, seven years ago?"

"Ah. I was wondering when you would darken my doorstep again." Nikolai hobbles to his cane and begins to pace, slamming the wooden device against the floor in an eerie staccato. "Of course, I remember it," he says with a low chuckle. "It's rare for a man to deposit just one piece of merchandise with me and nothing else."

"If you don't want another black eye, I suggest you watch your words," Donatello snarls, taking a step.

"Of course." Nikolai waves him off with a dismissive swipe of his free hand. "Perhaps I should have kept that one." He turns his gaze to me. "She grew up pretty enough. Could have fetched far more than what I sold her for—"

"What do you remember about that day?" Donatello demands.

"You came to me with a girl and asked for a price," Nikolai says with a chilling smile. "That's it. No sordid backstory. No theatrics. Just a simple transaction between two men—"

"No." Donatello takes another menacing step forward, his fingers curling into a fist. "There must be more than that."

"I never said there wasn't, did I? You overlook one detail. A transaction between two men. I never said the other man was you, did I?"

"What?" Donatello staggers as if struck. "But I... I had to negotiate a price," he points out. "What the fuck does that even mean?"

"You said a lot of shit when you came here," Nikolai counters, inspecting him with a graying eyebrow raised. "None of it mattered. Our terms were already decided. When you came to me, you brought the girl. Someone else, however, arranged the transaction. It's conceivable that you didn't understand the nature of my business model."

Donatello shakes his head, seemingly more confused than I am. "No, that doesn't make fucking sense—"

"Then I suggest you speak to your accomplice. I've kept his secret for too damn long, even to my own detriment." Once again, he gestures to his face. "But a deal is a deal. Tell your friend our bargain is null and void from here on out. Now I hate to cut this conversation short..."

A man I didn't notice before steps forward, a gun brandished on his hip.

Donatello doesn't move. I'm sure he'll rage. Demand more answers. Attack these men as he has so many times before.

Instead, he inclines his head to me and offers his hand. "Let's go."

I don't even recognize the sound of his voice. Still, I follow him out, shaken as the daylight erases the darkness and stench of Nikolai's den.

When we return to the car, Donatello sighs. "He's lying. What the hell did he mean? I don't…"

He breaks off.

"Fabio."

At first, I assume the man must be calling him. Then his expression falls, and it hits me.

Nikolai meant that Donatello didn't arrange the transaction but that another man did.

Someone cunning enough to forge such a connection and yet smart enough to keep his hands clean.

I don't believe it at first. I'm wrong. It can't be him.

But the more I turn the concept over in my mind, the more only one name seems to fit.

Fabio.

EVGENI

Vanici's accountant isn't much in person, but he's smart. When he staggers into Mischa's study toting a stack of documents, he pauses to spit out a single location.

"I've scoured Saleri's accounts and any connected to them. There is only one place they could be," he says to preface the revelation. "Where else but hiding in plain sight?"

And I feel like a fucking fool. While Mischa heads to confront Mateo Saleri, I take a smaller contingent of men to hopefully track down this puppet master once and for all.

His location isn't as much of a shock as it is a cruel, mocking twist of fate.

Winthorp manor.

The bastard was here all along—and I led Briar Winthorp straight to him.

When I approach the remains of Winthorp manor, this time in broad daylight, I'm convinced that Vanici's accountant was wrong after all. The place looks more than deserted. Cursed—a barren landscape of silence and decay.

On the other hand, it would make for the perfect hiding place.

"You go around the back," I tell one of the four men Mischa sent with me. "I'll go in alone."

It's a stupid move, but I can't get the woman's words out of my head. I'm sure she's been here all this time, laughing with her so-called brother, gleefully planning how to lead us into another trap.

Damn her.

Preferably, she's watching now, hidden in her secret lair, convinced I won't find her. Well, she thought wrong.

Anger clouds my vision, and I go in blind, heading straight toward the main house.

I don't obey any of the tactics I cautioned Briar Winthorp to. I go in loudly, heedless of any booby traps or hidden snipers.

When I make it to a rotting back door, coated in vines, I'm sure that either no one is here, or this clever mastermind forfeited any heightened security measures.

Or…

The bastard never expected to be found.

Gun drawn, I prowl a darkened hall that reeks of mildew, imagining how it must have once appeared. Pretentious. Grand.

Nothing like the home I grew up in.

And yet, Briar spoke almost fondly of this place and the caverns she claimed lurked beneath it.

They made for an efficient way to move both servants and supplies throughout the estate…

Assuming this is a servant's wing, there should be an entrance to the lower level from here. Sure enough—past what might have once been a kitchen—I find a series of steps leading down.

Common sense warns me to make a note of this route and return with backup.

Anger, however? It spitefully drives me forward, utilizing every skill this "soldier" possesses to remain silent in the darkness. A task that seems damn near impossible as every step echoes the second I reach the lowest level.

It's dank, the air thick. There seems to be no sign of anyone who might have traversed here in recent days, perhaps years.

Until I hear it…

The noise is faint at first, driving me further down a nearly-pitch black space. It's every bit as cavernous as Briar described—until I round a corner and spy a sliver of light piercing what should be utter darkness.

Cautiously, I adjust my grip on my weapon while grabbing my cell phone with my opposite hand. With the press of a button, I alert the rest of the men, along with my location.

Then I brace my back to the wall and shift my weight enough to peer around a round doorway.

It must have been a storeroom at one point, though now a makeshift dwelling.

But instead of Mateo Saleri or his elusive puppet master.

Or even Briar Winthorp…

The only figure I find is a boy with blond hair, his blue eyes fixed on a book open on the filthy concrete floor beneath him.

I don't know what shocks me more. The fact that he seems to be alone or that with one look, there isn't any doubt in my mind who he is.

His face solves that mystery instantly.

He looks just like his mother.

My shock lasts for a heartbeat before caution overrides it. According to Briar, this boy was the keystone of her so-called brother's master plan—manipulate the Saleris, and God knows who else, with the promise of the Winthorp fortune.

And yet, for someone seemingly so important to that scheme…

This boy is alone.

I strain my hearing for a sign of anyone else nearby and come up empty. Another glance at the room he's in doesn't reveal a guard, or criminal mastermind lording over him.

Fuck it. Warily, I pocket my weapon and round the doorway, both hands raised.

He looks up, his eyes widening. It's strange witnessing those familiar features display fear so openly in comparison to his mother.

I soften my voice in response, crouching on one knee. "Are you alone? Is anyone here with you?"

Viewing him up close, I'm sure there was at one point. He's clean and neatly dressed, his blond curls combed. Though, apart from the little cot behind him and a handful of toys, this room doesn't seem designed to hold anyone else. I assume whoever's been caring for him, does so on a schedule. It's clever.

No wonder my initial search here turned up so damn little.

I stand and inspect every inch of the space, hunting for a booby trap or security measure. It isn't long before I find one, crudely affixed to the wall above the boy's makeshift bed.

A camera.

"Would you like to leave?" I ask, turning to find the boy watching me. It takes more effort than I would have thought to speak gently, absence of the irritation his mother inspires.

He shakes his head. *Shit.*

I take a step toward him, but—time crunch or not—traumatizing a child isn't an appealing option. So, I improvise.

"Your mother," I say cautiously, watching the boy's eyes widen, his head cocked. "I know where she is. Would you like to see her?"

He doesn't speak, holding my gaze for what feels like an eternity. Finally…

He extends a tiny hand.

I take it, lifting him into my arms, and I retrace my steps back to the upper level of the house. My backup is already there waiting for me, but as I scan our surroundings, I'm again struck by how deserted the place seems.

And a paranoid suspicion growing in my gut blooms in full.

This was too easy.

Too damn easy.

"He went to a party."

The tiny voice seems to come from nowhere. Alarmed, I spin in a circle, scanning the property before realizing that the speaker is in my arms. One of his tiny hands clutches my collar, and he tugs at the material as if fascinated.

"A party?" I say softly. "Who is at a party?"

"The man," he replies without taking his focus from my jacket. "He said if someone came to tell them hi. And that…" He frowns as if struggling to remember his assigned lines.

"What?" I prod.

"Oh!" The boy looks up, meeting my gaze directly. "That he'll see you soon."

DON

We return to the church and find Fabio waiting near the front of the cathedral. Rather than confront him, guns blazing, I hang back.

Dread is an unexpected reaction, all things considered. I should be ready to rip the bastard apart—especially if he had a hand in what happened.

But Fabio is the same man who held me together when I reached my lowest. Anger isn't the only emotion coursing through me. It's something beyond betrayal, beyond petty hurt.

A few weeks ago, I would be driven to drink in a desperate bid to drown it out. Now? I embrace every agonizing second. Eyeing the woman beside me, I know it's only a fraction of what she must have felt all those years ago.

A wound so deep I can't imagine how it could ever heal.

"You should go change," I tell her hoarsely. "Let me handle him."

Whatever we wear to this sham wedding no longer matters —implying as much is merely a ploy to send her away.

Her knowing glance tells me she's aware of that. And yet, she leaves without resisting, and the gratitude I feel guts me. The grim truth is that my wanting to face Fabio alone isn't brave. It's cowardly.

I can't let her see me like this, accepting that the one man I've trusted with my life could have been the very person to destroy it. Even the pain in my shoulder can't compare, and I grit my teeth, squaring my jaw with determination.

"Fabio…" Finally, I step forward, drawing the man's attention.

He seeks me out instantly. "Don!"

Rather than scold me for leaving, he approaches me in a rush. "Change of plans," he blurts, his eyes wide with excitement. "Mischa and his men have surrounded Mateo Saleri. He'll be bringing him back to the estate. We should head there now—"

"What?" It's too much whiplash to handle—to go from knowing he might have brokered the sale of a child years ago, to our present dilemma.

"That's not all," Fabio continues, oblivious. "It seems Evgeni has a lead on our mystery puppet master… Are you okay, Donatello?"

I'm not.

Standing here, it all sinks in.

Selling a girl under my protection of my own accord would be one thing. Monstrous. Sick. Unforgivable.

But having someone else do my dirty work? I can't understand it.

And Fabio…

He never mentioned his role in that scheme. He didn't want to speak of Olivia, either. He even let me think Nico was mine all this fucking time.

Why?

My skull throbs with the pressure of those conflicting truths. Groaning, I rub my temples, and I miss the moment that draws everyone's notice to the front of the room.

"Oh," Fabio says simply. His tone is too soft to be alarm at an ambush.

"What?" When I turn as well, my mind goes blank.

Willow Stepanova took my suggestion to heart, changing into the gown I assume Fabio gave her to wear for this occasion.

Only this is no average wedding dress. She's wearing red, the furthest thing from a virginal sacrament, and I can't help the broken laugh that rips from my throat.

She's so damn beautiful it hurts to face her head-on. The rest of the world looks gray in comparison, and my overwhelmed brain can't help but come to another bittersweet conclusion.

This isn't anything like the day I married Olivia. More than that. This moment feels like an unofficial severing of my ties to that past. For us both.

Safiya is gone forever, and I have no choice but to acknowledge the woman standing in her place.

And I will protect her.

No matter what.

"They have him," Fabio says, appearing by my side. His stern frown shatters the nostalgia, and the present danger returns in full force.

Absently, I choke out, "Who?"

"*Him,*" he insists. He's holding his cell phone, eyeing the screen in disbelief. "It seems our little scheme worked after all. They're at the manor. We should go now."

He still hasn't sensed anything wrong between us. Fuck it, let him linger in that ignorance for a while longer. Addressing the past can wait. For now, it's time to do what I failed to accomplish seven years ago.

Protect my family.

"Don?" Fabio prods. "Time is of the essence. We should tell Willow—"

"I'll see what she wants to do." I move before he has the chance to reply, approaching her ironically near the altar. I can't resist the impulse driving me to run my finger along the scarlet neckline of her makeshift gown. It's formed of delicate lace, shrouding the peaks of her breasts in a subtle nod to her newfound maturity.

"Clever," I say thickly.

All in all, I approve. White wouldn't suit her. Just this. An angry hue, reminiscent of rage. And passion.

And violence.

"We might have a lead on the puppet master," I say, meeting her gaze. "They're at the Stepanov Manor. You can come with me or not. It's your choice."

Something in her expression wavers. For a second, I'm sure I fucked up. Another misstep by saying the wrong thing. Then, her eyes dart to Fabio, and it dawns on me just what has her so affected.

I'm not the only one willing to put off the inevitable, it seems.

Slowly she shakes her head, and I have a suspicion that returning home now amid this chaos—and the potential revelation regarding Fabio—may be the last thing on her mind. Fair enough.

I'd leave too if I could, if only to parse through these thoughts together.

Instead, I come up with another plan. "You should return to the hotel," I suggest. "You can have time to think things over."

She nods, and I savor this rare victory.

Transitioning our relationship won't be easy, but now more than ever, it seems…

Possible.

That's all I can ask for.

Mischa is a twisted son of a bitch—but he is damn good when it comes to what he does best—strategize a virtual war.

His men found more than Mateo. It seems they discovered his puppet master with him, ready to pull his strings as they plotted an attack on the church. On *me*, when they thought to find me isolated.

The tactician in me can grudgingly admit that it was a clever scheme—take advantage of an apparent rift and pool their resources to snuff out who they see as a primary threat in the moment. Me. Presumably, afterward, they'd transition to taking out the *mafiya*.

As it turns out, the joke's on them.

They have him tied to a chair in the lowest level of the manor, and he's far from the smug figure I first met on the

Saleris' private yacht. His tan suit is speckled with fresh crimson liquid, blood trickles down the corner of his mouth, and his glasses sit askew on the bridge of his nose. Still, he grins, flitting his gaze from me, to Fabio, to Mischa, and finally Evgeni.

"The happy family," he says in that unnerving tone.

"Who are you?" Mischa demands. "What the hell do you want?"

"Recognition," Evgeni says, stepping forward. "He's a Winthorp bastard desperate for his daddy's acknowledgment from the grave."

"And you believed that witch?" The man turns his soulless gaze on Evgeni, his lips parted into a sly smile. "Lies."

"I thought so too," Evgeni admits while I struggle to keep up with the conversation.

Are they referring to the Briar woman?

"Thanks to her, I've found your only leverage."

"A boy was discovered in the Winthorp ruins," Mischa explains, cutting his eyes to me. "Presumably, he's the son of Briar Winthorp, which makes him an heir in the line of succession."

Which explains why Mischa's eldest son was targeted in the first place.

But what about me?

"So, you wanted a fortune," I say as my first guess while approaching the man, my hands empty at my sides. "Why attack me?"

An attempt on my life was made long before the shit with Mischa began, stemming from a sniper attack the night of Willow's debutant ball.

"You?" The man laughs brokenly, spraying blood down the front of his crisp shirt. When he smiles again, scarlet liquid coats the front of his teeth. "Only a fool would rely on one bit of leverage. You asked what I wanted? I want the city, of course. All of it. And you will hand it to me on a silver platter. That is…" His lifeless eyes flit to Mischa. "If you want your daughter alive."

"She's at the hotel," I say, turning to Fabio. "Right?"

He inclines his head, reaching into his pocket. "I'll check with my contacts." He leaves the room as the man continues to chuckle.

Not even a minute later, Fabio rushes back inside. "She never made it to the hotel," he says, his eyes wide.

"No." Fear is a white-hot lance shooting through me—laced with poisonous suspicion. Fabio saw her leave. Could he have arranged to have her taken unnoticed?

I look at him, and my vision goes red.

But another man beats me to the punch—literally. In a blur of motion, Mischa lunges, a fist brandished, and the blond man doubles over, choking on presumably more blood.

Tied as he is, the entire chair rocks with the force of the blow, dangerously close to tipping over.

"Where is she, you son of a bitch?" Without even giving him the time to answer, Mischa rears back for another blow, but the bound man smirks, though his glasses now rest on the floor, feet away. In pieces.

"I have no idea what you're talking about—"

His words end in a spray of blood as Mischa's fist collides with his jaw. "Where the hell is my daughter?"

"Your daughter." The man's monotone voice turns every word into a joke. "Shouldn't you know the answer to that question?"

"You piece of shit—"

"You can waste time brutalizing me," the blond man says, still unnaturally calm. "But I'll warn you that there isn't much time before the city is treated to another explosive bit of redevelopment. You may find that your daughter could be caught in the blast, should you fail to reach her in time."

The threat lands with all the impact I'm sure the man expects—the room falls dead silent.

"Willow..." Mischa's jaw goes slack as horror threatens his stoic expression. "What the hell are you talking about? You son of a bitch—"

"Insults won't get us anywhere," Evgeni says, standing to block his employer's next move. "Where is she?"

"Might I suggest we get down to business?" the man says. Apart from his swollen bottom lip and reddening jaw, he seems unfazed. His expression could even be deemed a smile as his tongue traces his bloodied lips, cleaning them.

"You knew," I say, taking in his apparent calm. "You wanted us to find you."

And rather than aim to attack the church, he had his men waiting to take Willow instead. It's a level of intelligence I can't underestimate. In fact, the only man capable of rivaling it may be the figure standing beside me who disguised his own hand in a treacherous scheme for seven years.

"This was your plan all along," I say, meeting the man's stare directly. "What do you want?"

He makes an amused grunt in his throat. "I want control of the *mafiya* territory, of course. As well as the harbor office. Have your men stand down, make the necessary arrangements, and your daughter will be returned safe and sound. As a bonus, you can even have the traitorous little Winthorp whore, free of charge."

"You took her," Evgeni says with a harsh laugh.

"I am a fan of tying up loose ends," the bastard says, still smirking.

"What's stopping me from killing you?" Mischa demands. Judging from his stance, he seems more than eager to do just that.

I'm the last person in the world keen to stop him, but I approach him anyway. "Let's try and get him to talk," I suggest, flexing my fingers. "By any means—"

"There isn't time for torture," the man explains in that eerie monotone. "Kill me, and your daughter dies. I shouldn't have to state that so bluntly. If my associates do not hear from me by midnight, our discussion will be moot, regardless."

"A few hours is plenty of time to make you talk," Mischa says murderously.

"Wait." Fabio stands near the doorway, cell phone in hand. "There might be another way." He inclines his head, beckoning me into the hall.

I only hesitate a second before following him, aware of Mischa begrudgingly on my heels.

"He wants us to panic and fight," Fabio explains, his gaze still on his cell phone screen. "But I've decided to retrace his steps instead. He mentioned the explosion. My gut tells me I might know where he's keeping Willow."

I can't help the suspicion that rises within me, hardening my voice. "And you want us to trust you?"

Fabio blinks. "Have I ever given you a reason not to?"

I grit my teeth rather than answer that question, not that he seems to expect a response.

"If you can trust me, I think I can give us a rough location to search. The downside is there are several potential properties. If I lead you in the wrong direction, there might not be time to salvage that mistake."

"We don't have any other options," I admit. "Where?"

"A clever hiding spot, if correct," Fabio says with a hint of grudging admiration. "I probably would have picked a similar locale myself were I a psychopath."

"Which is?" Mischa interjects.

"The site of his last crime, of course," Fabio replies. "Now hurry. There isn't much time."

I don't need to be told twice.

"I'll drive," Evgeni calls from the doorway. He must have overheard the entire conversation because he surges into the hall, racing ahead of me.

"I'll see if I can get more information from him," Mischa says ominously. "You go."

Even with everything hanging in the balance, I hesitate. Trusting Fabio again could be the biggest fucking mistake of my life.

But I can't even think of what will happen if he's wrong.

He can't be.

WILLOW

The first coherent realization my mind can form is that I taste blood, and my head is throbbing.

But why? Pain sears through my head when I try to recall anything else. The last thing I remember is leaving the church…

Then nothing. I don't know where I am, or even how long I've been here.

One thing I am sure of is that I'm not alone. I can hear someone else's heavy breathing, along with a quiet, persistent ticking noise. A clock?

"I suggest you don't resist," a woman says dryly. Her voice comes from nearby, echoing throughout what must be a cavernous space. "I've tried. They've gotten smart and used a thicker rope. We'd need a knife to cut it."

What? I recognize her voice though my skull aches as I try to place it with a name. Someone like Ellen but colder, speaking with none of her gentle cadence. *Briar?*

I can't see if I'm right. My eyelids flutter, but it's pitch dark wherever we are. Not only that, but the air smells like rust and wet metal. Not the church, I suspect. Somewhere more confined.

"I assume we're underground," the woman says as if reading my mind. "And I'm sure you hear that infernal sound. What is that?"

A hint of fear taints her otherwise toneless speech.

"I suggest we find a way of getting free, first. Hello? Do you understand anything I've said? Though… That's right, you're the mute one, aren't you? Serves me right. Jonathan is quite the sadist. Even if I told you everything and you did escape, you wouldn't be able to tell anyone, would you?"

Irritation flares as that statement plays on a million different insecurities—the same ones Donatello aggravated before he finally acknowledged that I am not a child. I'm so sick of being underestimated. By him, and by this stranger—but I ignore her in favor of getting my bearings.

I'm seated upright with my hands bound behind me and my feet on a firm surface that must be the floor. My mouth is free, and I don't feel a blindfold shrouding my vision— which means the darkness is a side effect of wherever we are.

Underground, the woman said.

It's cold. I can hear the faint drip of running water, and the only place that comes to mind is a sewer system of some kind. Or perhaps the harbor. Could that be where we are?

"I won't sugar coat it," the woman continues with a heavy sigh. "Unless we can find some way of breaking these binds, we might both wind up dead."

She lamented not having a knife. But I do. I can still feel its weight against my right thigh, securely tied with a strip of silk—not that it does me any good with my hands bound. I test the binds, unnerved to find that Briar was right in her assessment. They're strong.

But if living with Donatello Vanici has taught me anything, it's that strength is relative. There is always a weak point. In this case, at least, my legs are free.

I kick out my heels against what feels like a solid, gritty floor. Whatever I'm tied to doesn't budge, however. It feels too firm, like a ledge, not a chair. Still, I can feel the mass on my thigh shift with the movement. When I lift my leg and slam it down, the knife slides just an inch.

"Are you stomping in morse code?" the woman asks. "Pay me no mind. Carry on."

I do, repeatedly slamming my heel against the floor until the tie begins to loosen. Looser…

Sweat drips down my neck with the effort, my knee burning with exertion. Then, finally, the blade falls free with a clatter.

Now to find a way to grab it.

I strain my binds again, finding them just as immovable as before. Then an idea strikes me. Force won't help.

It didn't serve me against Donatello. No…

Instead, I utilize patience, turning my focus to extracting just one wrist. Slowly I can feel the tension give way, tightening over my left wrist, but allowing just enough give for me to wrench on the right. Slowly. Slowly…

My shoulder screams with pain at the unnatural angle, but I keep going until finally, I tug my hand free.

My heart races as I lean forward and feel along what seems like damp concrete until my fingertips brush over a familiar leather handle. I grab it and contort myself to attack the ropes, still restricting my left hand.

They give way, and I stand, staggering to find my balance in the dark.

"What's happening?" the woman demands. "Are you freed?"

I follow the sound of her voice, feeling out until my fingers strike a warm, flesh-like surface.

"Is that you?" I feel the woman flinch out of my reach, only to cautiously place herself within my range again. "Help get me free!"

I brush over what I'm sure is her arm and work the blade through the mass of ropes coiled at her wrist.

"Finally!"

Clattering noises echo wildly, forming a deafening clatter. Footsteps? The woman's, I assume, because I suddenly feel warm breath on my shoulder.

"Now, to find a way out..."

Her disjointed footsteps continue, coming to an abrupt stop.

"There's something here," she says. "A box… Damn. I think this is where that noise is coming from."

Her fear is so visceral I feel a cold sweat instantly slick the back of my neck.

Tick. Tick. Tick. That soft metronome seems louder by the second. There aren't many objects I know of capable of making such a noise.

"This must be a bomb. Get back," Briar warns, and I sway as she slams into me in her rush to move. "I was partly joking before—" Her voice shakes. "But I might not have been wrong after all. If we can't get out of here, we're dead. We need to find an exit. Now! Try getting on your hands and knees so that you don't trip over any more explosives."

I obey the suggestion, wincing as my hands and bare knees come in contact with the ice-cold floor. It's slightly damp, and several potential explanations come to mind—none of them reassuring. Choking back the disgust, I move cautiously, feeling out for any nearby structures.

It isn't long before my arm brushes a solid, metallic area that rings hollow as I tap my knuckles against it. A pipe? It's several feet tall, and its contours feel familiar to the surface I woke up tethered to. Behind it, my fingers strike what feels like concrete. A wall?

Inching back, I discover a few yards of empty space before I finally contact another firm barrier.

"We're in a room of some kind," Briar remarks, sounding close by. "There are pipes, and—wait! I think this is a door. But… Damn! It's locked."

I hear a thud against a metallic surface, and I pivot, crawling toward it.

"It's made of bars… Like a jail cell door. I can't get it to budge. I think it's chained." She howls in frustration. "There is a padlock here on the outside. Can you feel that?"

I reach between the metal bars and immediately strike a bumpy mass of what could be chains. They must be looped around the outside of the door, secured by the padlock. Sure enough, I strain my wrist further through the bars and brush against a dangling, round object.

"We need to find a way to open it," Briar says. "Give me your knife."

Warm fingers swipe blindly at my forearm, but I hesitate, gripping the handle of the knife tighter. I've been clutching it all this time, and relinquishing it to a woman I barely know isn't appealing.

"Come on," she snaps. "We have to try something. Or would you prefer to blow up?"

Sure enough, that quiet, steady ticking noise relentlessly counts down the seconds.

"Please."

Finally, I hand the blade over, but a second later, the woman scoffs and shoves it toward me. "It's too big. I need something smaller. Damn. Do you have a hairpin? No... I think I have something," she says. "Thank God for macho soldiers."

Rather than explain, she falls silent, and the ever-present sound fills the void, as if counting the seconds down.

Tick.

Tick.

"Fuck, this is harder than it looks," Briar hisses.

Tick.

"Damn it!"

Impatient, I reach out until I find her shoulder.

"What?" she snaps. "You want to try? Wait... Here—" she shifts, urging me closer. "See if you can help me. Hold it steady."

I don't follow the logic, but I let her snatch a lock of my hair and use it to guide me closer to the bars. They feel ice-cold, with barely enough space to fit a hand between them. The lock faces away from us, making it hard to reach easily. I manage to grip its scratchy, presumably rusted, surface as the woman once again attempts to open it.

"Come on… Come on!"

Tick.

Tick.

"Shit. I… I think I've got it!"

Suddenly, the lock gives way, and I paw at the chains, freeing them. When we push on the bars, the door itself easily gives way with an eerie creak.

"I think this might be a way out," the woman says as we enter a passageway and feel a wave of fresh air rush past, displacing some of the suffocating stillness. "We don't have a choice but to try. Let's go," she says, feeling for my hand. "Who knows how long we have?"

DON

Fabio managed to pinpoint one location, though it doesn't look promising when we arrive.

As he stated, it's a spot near where the initial explosion rocketed through the city, but there's nothing in view, certainly not somewhere large enough to hold two women.

"This can't be it," I say to Evgeni. "Fuck, we need to check the next property—"

"Wait. Look!"

He points to a spot in the distance that seems little more than a shifting bit of debris strewn over the earth.

Until a human-shaped figure crawls from beneath them.

I don't think before taking off, reaching the area in an instant.

By the time I reach them, it's clearer to make out the shape of a woman's body, small and lithe. Someone else scrambles from the wreckage behind her, her face streaked with grime.

"I suggest we get out of here," she says in between pants. "There's a bomb down there. We need to go! Now!"

I grab the woman nearest me while Evgeni rushes forward to take the other.

Then we run blindly for the car. As the quiet murmur of the city hums in the background, our frantic scramble toward the van must appear comical to anyone watching.

Until a monstrous sound rattles the silence. It's like something slams into my back, pushing me forward. Only by sheer force of will do I remain on my feet, steadying Willow against me.

When we finally reach the vehicle, it's a mad rush to climb inside while Evgeni takes the wheel.

"We need to regroup," he shouts, slamming on the gas, propelling the vehicle into reverse before quickly changing direction. "Here—" he tosses a cell phone onto my lap. "Call Mischa."

I reluctantly dial the number he rattles off, unsurprised as a gruff voice answers.

"You found them?"

"Yes," I reply. "But barely. Apparently, he wasn't kidding about an explosion."

"I haven't gotten much out of him," Mischa admits coldly. "But what I have learned, I'll relay when you bring my daughter home."

I don't argue. Given that Evgeni has the wheel, I couldn't change our course if I wanted to. Still, I put all thoughts of Mischa and anyone else from my mind and turn to the only person who matters in this moment.

She's beside me, her hair matted and streaked with mud. A foul smell clings to her, emanating from the muck coating her extremities.

I grab one hand, scanning the rest of her pale limbs for any hint of an injury. "Are you alright?"

She meets my gaze and nods, but one look at her face contradicts that assurance.

"You're hurt." I swipe at a cut on her forehead with the pad of my thumb. It's bleeding, though it isn't deep. Thank God.

Still, when she doesn't flinch at the contact, I use the pretext of searching for more injuries to touch her, feeling along that delicate jawline.

A wave of guilt washes over me, rousing a dread I can't shake. How the hell can I expect to protect her, let alone anyone else? She'll never be safe with me.

I've barely let the thought fester when I feel a faint touch ghost across my cheek as if to argue against that thought.

Confused, I look down at the pale fingers pressing there, and I sigh.

"You're safe now," I say thickly, capturing her hand in one of mine. "You're safe."

*f I go the rest of my life without seeing the inside of Stepanov Manor again, it will be too soon. This time, though, Mischa isn't the figure waiting to greet me.

I turn back to Willow, willing to stave off the inevitable for a little while longer. My fingers are still in her hair, smoothing the strands from her face.

Fabio can wait. As we exit the van, I pull her against me, tempted to return to the hotel and avoid facing Mischa as well.

But if I'm reluctant to have this conversation, so is she. I can see the confusion in her eyes as her gaze flits in Fabio's direction.

Unwilling to be ignored, he takes the initiative to approach us, his hands clasped behind his back.

"Thank God, you're okay," he says with genuine relief. Once again, I'm reminded of just how unassuming he can seem.

Until he has a knife pointed at your back in a way you never saw coming. Deep down, am I truly surprised? His calculating nature was always an asset to Fabio, but I'm only starting to understand that I was always in his crosshairs. While he gleefully used his manipulation tactics to help advance my interests, he also used them on me all this fucking time.

To make sure I didn't remember. That I blamed myself and wallowed in pain so deep, I would have done anything to end it. Anything.

The sad part is I don't even know if I have the right to be angry with him. After all, I made his job ten times easier by running from the truth myself.

"They should go to the hospital," Evgeni says, coming up behind me, his arm slung around a woman. She's so alarmingly pale that, at first, I don't recognize her.

Then she eyes me, her chin haughtily in the air. "I didn't know you had it in you to be so civil, soldier," she says hoarsely. Despite the audible weakness in her voice, her mocking tone is unmistakable.

"I'll put a team together as an escort," Evgeni says.

By my side, I sense Willow stiffen, but he's right.

"I'll meet you there," I tell her, easing my arm from around her waist. "Then I'll tell you everything."

She wants to argue; I can see it in her eyes. For whatever reason, she doesn't, relenting to follow Evgeni back to the van.

As I watch her go, it hits me—she trusted me at my word.

"Is something wrong?" Fabio questions as I turn back to him.

There isn't a pretty way to broach this topic. Even his fancy words can't soften the blow.

"You knew," I tell him coldly.

He stops short, his eyes widen.

"About Olivia. About her affair—but it's more than that." I add, not caring who can hear as my voice echoes loudly. "You've always known from the fucking start."

He can't even face me. He turns, eyeing a ridge of trees in the distance. "Don…"

"You knew about Liv." I sound like a child, repeating it so tonelessly, but I can't seem to find a better way to put it. "You knew she was fucking Gino—"

"Of course, I knew," Fabio croaks as the color drains from his face. "I was the one she told when she was planning to leave you for him."

I flinch. A million different memories come flooding back. *Olivia…*

"Did you kill her?"

Rather than gloat, he groans. "How can you even ask that? Of course, I didn't kill my sister!"

"But you know what happened, don't you? I went to have a little chat with my old friend Nikolai—"

If possible, he turns even paler.

"Our friend, as it turns out—because you were the one who arranged the sale. Didn't you? Tell me!"

In all the time I've known Fabio Botelli, I've never seen him break. It's the only word to describe it. He visibly deflates, and only sheer force of will seems to keep him standing. "Yes," he rasps. "I'm the reason you sold Safiya. I arranged it. I had you take her there. I even named the price."

A pain I've never known claws through my chest, ripping apart whatever sliver of my heart remained intact after all these years. Amid the destruction, all I can croak is one word. "Why?"

"Because I hated you."

He lets that statement hang, as tears flood his eyes. "For what happened to Olivia. God, I hated you. For so long… I couldn't see past it. God, I hated you and anyone connected to you, who I held responsible. Even a child."

I've never heard him talk like this. Gone is the trademark calm and poise. His voice wavers, his cheeks wet with shed tears. The sight awakens a possibility I would have never considered until now. The Fabio I knew was incapable of violence. But this stranger?

"Did you kill her?" I ask again, curling my hands into fists. "Olivia. Did you kill her?"

"No," he croaks. "But I felt responsible anyway. So damn responsible. She was there that day because of *me*. I'm the one who told her to stay with you. To end that stupid affair for good and pray to God that you never discovered it. Olivia was a lovesick fool, but I knew you were a better option than that bastard Gino, who couldn't even love his firstborn. You would protect her. Or so I thought."

"Then who did?"

"I spent years trying to figure it out before I settled on the only logical answer. Gino Mangenello preyed on my sister. He never loved her. He used her as bait to lure you out. It's not poetic, but there it is."

"Why didn't you tell me?"

He shrugs. "That I hated you enough to use a child as a tool in my revenge? How could I face you and admit that? And looking back… You were a dead man walking. I believe you don't remember." His eyes glisten, and he sways, bracing his hand against the wall. "I could have told you to jump off a bridge, and you would have. I don't know when I realized that you weren't responsible. Maybe I always knew, deep down," he admits, looking down. "But it was too late. I learned that Safiya had already been sold, and I… How could I come clean about what I'd done? I tried to make amends in my own way, first through Vincenzo, by protecting him. I know he isn't my son through blood, but he might as well be. I did everything in my power to keep him safe, and even at your darkest moment, you did the same. That's when I realized… Don, it took me years to see that, but you have to believe me. You and Vincenzo, you are my family. You're all I have left."

"I don't have a choice," I croak. "You've been there for me when no one else was. But," I add, "I want you to tell Mischa the truth. And Willow."

He winces, but nods. "Of course, I will."

"And…" I draw in a ragged breath and force myself to meet his gaze. "If you were able to stand by my actions for nearly a decade, I should be able to return the favor."

Forgiveness won't be easy, but nothing in my life has been. Whether I like it or not, Fabio earned his place in my family.

And it's only with his help that I can salvage what little of it remains.

EVGENI

Willow's safety is my paramount concern. Once she's safely ensconced within a hospital room, however, by her side isn't where I find myself heading.

Ironically, my destination is the next private room down, where two figures sit on a narrow hospital bed. The smaller of the duo is asleep, his small body curled on his side, his head near his mother's lap.

I thought he would look like her. Blond with piercing blue eyes and cherub cheeks.

If anything, he's her in her truest form, untainted or jaded by the Winthorp legacy. His hair is a little more golden, his eyes slightly darker. When viewed together, she almost looks normal in comparison.

"Thank you." It hurts her to say those two words, but she does anyway. "Considering that I'm not in chains... I think you have something to do with that."

"Something," I say gruffly. "Your little friend won't be so lucky."

Though sympathy is the last thing I feel. Still, his fate will be fitting enough.

"Mischa hasn't killed him," I add. "But I've heard him mention the name of a prominent human trafficker, so who knows where he might end up."

"Is that a threat?" she asks, an eyebrow raised, but I shake my head.

The truth is that I believe the Stepanovs are too busy dealing with their changing reality to give a damn as to Briar Winthorp.

"I'm only here, to learn where you'll go now."

Not that it matters. She's just as dangerous as Mateo Saleri and anyone associated with him. A smart man would put her in chains, rather than risk letting her go.

But I doubt even captivity would hold her for long.

"Where?" She laughs, but the sound isn't as mocking as I expect. Paired with the wary glance she casts the room, I think it might even be a sign of genuine confusion. "Where is there to go?"

Her nose wrinkles, and she smooths her hand along the sleeping boy's head, seemingly out of instinct. "Ellen… I thought she'd gloat," she says with a scoff. "But no. Always the bleeding heart, she had to prove she's the better woman. The better sister. The better mother—"

"What did she say?"

She frowns. "She offered me the manor. My home… The Winthorp house." She clears her throat and shrugs. "A pity offering, of course."

"And yet, it's a place to go," I point out. "So stay, and stop running from your past. Face it and demand a future here. You're bold enough."

She purses her lips, withdrawing her hand from her son. "A future alone?"

I don't answer. Whatever happened between us should smartly be written off as a mistake, never to happen again. I know that.

But I don't leave, either.

WILLOW

Despite the ordeal at the harbor, I feel fine. Physically at least. If anything, I submit to an examination at the hospital if only to buy myself some privacy. A chance to breathe.

Instead, Mischa and Ellen arrived soon after, and I nearly had to force them to leave.

"We won't be far," Mischa warned, stroking his fingers through my hair. "We will always be here."

At his shoulder, Ellen flashed a worn smile. "Of course, we will. For now, we'll let you rest, but we'll be back soon. Perhaps with some of that jam, you like?"

I watch them go, feeling oddly relieved. And confused. After everything that's happened, no one could blame them for wanting to wash their hands of me for good.

The fact that they haven't sends a pang through my chest, and I'm more grateful to them both than ever.

Yet, even as they leave, one figure remains, lurking beyond the room until finally given clearance to enter.

"Are you alright?" he asks.

I know he must have gotten a report already from one of my doctors or a nurse, but still, he demands an answer from me.

I nod, but something pangs in my chest as if to contradict that.

I'm not okay.

The superficial bruises and scrapes barely register against another exam running in tandem.

Does he know the results of that test?

Looking at his face, I can't tell.

He chooses not to say as much, either way. Instead, he takes a seat near the window and faces me. "There is something you should know," he says grimly.

a narrow hospital bathroom should be the last place I hope to seek refuge in. Still, I stand before a wide mirror and watch the woman starring back.

It terrifies me to realize that I don't recognize her. Not those dark, hollow eyes or the grime smeared over my skin.

It could be shock. Hearing the truth from Donatello doesn't provide the relief I thought it would. There is no closure to be found in the layers of conflicting emotions washing over me.

Fabio knew of Olivia's affair. He convinced her to stay, but she wound up dead regardless.

And, suspecting Donatello, he used me as a pawn in his revenge.

I should hate him—seethe in rage and fury. In all honesty, I think I feel more exhausted instead. After seven years, the truth doesn't tie up everything with a neat bow and a happy ending.

It's confusing and complicated.

Do I blame Fabio?

Yes. But even Donatello seemed to harbor some tiny semblance of forgiveness toward him. Could I find the space in my soul for the same?

Rather than come to a conclusion now, I spy a shower and eagerly strip my clothing, turning the water as hot as I can stand it. Methodically, I erase all traces of that underground prison, scrubbing until my skin is red in the aftermath.

When I emerge and face the mirror again, I wipe away a swath of steam and find a shadow of myself beneath it. The same Willow, just slightly older. It's unreal how much someone can change in just a few short weeks.

And depending on the results determined by a doctor, I may stand to undergo even more drastic changes. Am I even ready for that?

I look down, inspecting my stomach, running my fingers over the ridge of flesh. It feels the same it always has. I can't imagine the prospect of another life potentially growing beneath the pale flesh.

I don't know how long I stand here—long enough that most of the steam has dissipated, and someone feels driven to come find me. They knock first, easing the door open when I don't reply.

"Willow?" He breaks off with a sharp intake of air.

I'm still naked, freezing to the point my teeth chatter. When I look back, he's gone, only to return with a towel taken from the room. He comes up behind me, easing the material around my shoulders.

The picture we make is an odd one, I can admit that. He towers over me, and the artificial light enhances the shadows etched into his features, and the dark circles beneath his eyes. Somehow, I know without him having to say it out loud that he's learned the definitive answer to the question looming between us.

Still, he takes his time drying me off, securing the towel with a knot that rests against my collar bone. Then he grips the edge of the sink on either side of me, bringing his mouth to my ear.

"It would have been easier for you if that test was negative," Donatello says softly, and the pain in his voice… I don't deny for a second that it's genuine. "You could have moved on with your life without me. You still can."

He's as single-minded as ever, but it doesn't irritate me this time. He's right.

And I feel driven to respond to his unspoken question the only way I can.

My finger shakes as I raise it, finding one of the few remaining patches of steam. Slowly and carefully, I form a series of letters, every bit as jagged as the ones etched onto his chest.

As he reads over my shoulder, I feel my cheeks flame.

But he doesn't laugh. He eyes those words in a way that makes my heart ache. Suddenly, his weight feels heavier, as if he's using my body to stabilize his.

I could move on with my life, but hopefully, these words resonate within him more loudly than if I spoke them aloud.

I choose you.

At least this time, it's my choice. The truth is, I haven't had a life without him, not only because of the trauma he caused. I'm broken in that I've always mourned him in some way. Always.

But ignoring him or leaving won't change a damn thing.

This isn't about us anymore.

"Fine. You've made your choice," he says thickly, even as he stands to his full height. His breaths echo, unsteady and broken. Finally, I feel his hands palm my hips, barely touching. "I have no choice but to honor it. I'll be here. No more relying on Fabio. No more lying to Vin."

I still don't know if I can trust him, but therein lies the reality I have no choice but to face.

I can't rely on the past. I only have his present actions and words to go off of.

It won't be easy or perfect, but it's a future I can imagine, imperfect and beautiful.

EPILOGUE

DON

$\mathcal{A}$ baby changes nothing.

It shouldn't anyway. A new life can't heal two broken people on opposing ends. Such healing can only begin internally; the effort of so much fucking hard work, it seems impossible at times.

No way can there be a light at the end of this dark, winding tunnel.

But then you see it. A light that comes in the form of a smiling face, conveying such innocence it doesn't seem possible to exist.

It's a second chance.

This house, far from the shadow of Hell's Gambit, is merely a symbol of that fresh start. Or so I hope.

"You going to just stare, or are you going to help, old man?" someone remarks from behind me.

I feel my lips quirk into a grin as I turn to find Vin, a cardboard box in his arms. Looking at him, no one would guess that just over a year ago, he had a brush with death.

Of course, he wasn't surprised when he learned the truth—like his mother, he'd already discovered it for himself. He only needed to hear it from me.

And much like with Fab…

It seems that the ties that bind family go deeper than even an apparent betrayal.

As long as I promised from here on out—no more lies.

It's been strange watching him, and Willow connect again, in very different roles. At their core, they're the same as they've always been. And yet…

Vin's changed as much as she has, throwing himself into his studies. The rare times he pulls himself away is when I see a hint of his old self again. Carefree, he scampers up the front steps, nudging open the front door with his hip.

"Wait for me!" A blur of black and pink brushes past me, scampering after him.

"Don't go far, Kisa," Luciano warns, carrying a box of his own.

"Don't worry, Daddy! I'll be with Vin." Her cheerful tone marks a world of difference from the scared girl who used to cower at the sight of me.

Having her real father in her life might have helped in that aspect.

"You should watch that one," I feel compelled to say to Luciano. "In a few years, she may make a run at being my daughter-in-law."

"Funny," Luciano says without an ounce of humor. "Remind me why I decided to stick around your ass again?"

Because I'm rebuilding my own empire, but this time I'm making another crack at doing things on the straight and narrow. Mostly.

"For the pay, of course," I tell him.

With an amused grunt, he continues toward the house. "I'll expect a raise."

"Get a move on, Don," Vin calls back, sticking his head through the doorway. "Or we won't be done before you start sprouting more gray hairs."

"Laugh all you want," I call after him. "Once you graduate from that fancy doctor school, I'm sure your hair will be gray soon enough."

He doesn't reply, presumably deeper inside.

Only slightly larger, and made of brick, this cottage doesn't resemble Havienna in the slightest. There is none of the wild harm that old house held. This home is different, nestled on the outskirts of Stepanov Manor—as close as a compromise with Mischa that we could come to.

I still wake up every damn morning not believing that she married me—in that red dress with Mischa's grudging approval.

Months later, I'm still getting used to it.

And every day tests that part of my soul I swore couldn't care for anyone beyond a select few again. I once told Willow exactly that—I could never love her the way she deserves.

Maybe I still can't. She deserves far more than me, and always will.

But I can't deny that the battered, neglected shell of a heart in my chest beats stronger as I sense two figures come up beside me. One is slender, her blond hair loose, her youth more apparent than ever. In this instance, it's a strength, boding that she'll be more than able to keep up with the figure in her arms, nestled within a blanket.

If I imagined how our child would look, no image would come close to the reality.

A perfect creature with dark eyes and hair like spun gold.

She's every bit as beautiful as her mother, and I know in my soul I don't deserve them. My *tigre* and a little cub with an equally probing stare... Adelina, meaning royalty in our native tongue, a fitting name for a princess.

But I'll protect them both until the day I die. That, I can promise.

You have finished book one of Donatello and Willow's story. Do you want to see where it all began? Check out the War of Roses Trilogy!

XV: Fifteen: War of Roses Trilogy Book One

Kidnapped, Ellen must do whatever it takes to survive her cruel mafia captor, Mischa. Will he break her— or will she outsmart him?

WHEN HATE BECOMES OBSESSION…

Mistaken for her beautiful half-sister, Ellen Winthorp is taken captive by a madman who declares that she will be his "fifteen": the fifteenth victim of a vicious mafia blood feud. Armed with only her instincts, Ellen must resist her captor for as long as she can—which is easier said than done the more she's exposed to the complex man beneath the beast.

Because Mischa Stepanov isn't a mindless monster—he's a wolf, and she's the unwitting doe caught in his midst.

Unraveling the torment of his past may be her only hope of salvation...

Or the secrets uncovered may destroy them both.

Noise…
Chaos…
Briar…

The first thing I'm aware of is that I'm blindfolded—a fact that could be a blessing in disguise as my thoughts blur and jumble together. Only one coherent question escapes the fray: *Where am I?*

No answer comes to me immediately. My straining ears can make out only a few words muttered nearby in unfamiliar voices. Deep, *masculine* voices.

Various smells irritate my nostrils as well: sweat, body odor, male. *All* male. God, *where am I?*

I try flexing my shoulders only to wince. My hands are impossible to move, tied behind my back with something rough. Rope?

Oh, God.

Familiar terror gnaws at my belly as moisture gathers in my armpits and sweeps across my palms. At least, now, I have an inkling of my fate. I'm trapped in another one of his games. My nostrils flare with renewed purpose: seeking out *his* scent.

He must have hired lackeys this time; foreign body odor drowns out the stench of his cologne. I can't smell him.

But you can survive this. I fall back on the mantra that has gotten me through every day for sixteen years. *You can survive, Ellen. Focus, Ellen. Breathe, Ellen.*

Ten hours—that's how long I endured last time. My resolve had nearly splintered by the end. I'd almost given in. Almost.

But even psychological wounds eventually heal and leave tougher scar tissue behind. I can last another ten hours with Robert. My brain makes that distinction as the barrage of scents dissipates, revealing one that overpowers the rest: a man's. I taste the nuances in his stench rather than smell them—he's *that* potent, composed of a multitude of different things.

Cigar smoke.

Vodka.

One scent in particular makes my heart stop. Salty and sweet, it's almost as familiar as the flowery perfume wafting from my skin now. *Blood?*

Robert never smokes. He doesn't drink. Whenever he hurts me, he always washes his hands before and after. It is our routine, and he is nothing if not predictable.

No. This is someone new. Someone taller, whose shadow completely blots out what little detail plays across my blindfold. His footsteps are steady. Heavy.

"This her?"

I sense the outline of his fingers before the callused edge of one grazes my forehead.

"You made sure?"

His voice is deep. Almost *too* deep to be intelligible: a series of grated, rumbling notes. There's an accent tucked among them—something thick. Eastern European? Briar had a maid from there once. Sonja.

Sonja liked to read Jane Eyre. She liked scribbling love notes to Robert Sr.'s men before fucking them in the broom closet late at night when she thought no one was looking. Sonja liked a lot of things before Robert took a liking to her.

But another figure from my memory possessed this accent as well. Even though his words were hissed in a whisper, I still remember. *Breathe!*

"Bring her."

Those two words snap me back to the present. Unfamiliar hands grab my shoulders, cinching the soft silk of my blouse. *Briar's* blouse. She dressed me in it lovingly, remarking on how the color complemented my eyes. Our eyes, the same shade of light blue.

"Move!"

A tug on my shoulders hauls me upright and unseen hands shove me forward. Every sound echoes. Four footsteps, including mine. The biggest man takes the lead, I suspect, his gait rhythmic against creaking floorboards.

In contrast, the men holding me dig their nails into my skin and scurry toward an unknown destination. A rusty squeal seconds later conjures the image of an old door opening, and the footsteps trail off.

"Move!"

Something rams into my side and I stagger for balance until my cheek strikes a hard surface. It's warm. *Human.*

"Get her on the bed."

Those harsh hands return to my shoulders to fulfill the command.

"Sit her on the edge…like that. Cut her hands free."

A metallic hiss sends a shiver down my spine—then *pain!* Fire courses through my fingertips as circulation returns to them. I long to flex each one, but I know better. Instead, I keep them close, settling them onto my lap.

These men kept my skirt on, at least. Her skirt. The hem comes down past my knees, and I've never been so grateful for four inches of satin. It will buy me more time.

Ten hours. I've already lasted ten minutes. *You can do this,* the courageous part of my soul whispers. But then that voice dies in the wake of two more words uttered in that guttural cadence.

"Leave us."

The two smaller men scatter in the direction we entered—but it's all wrong. No. No. I don't smell Robert, and he'd never leave me alone with another man. Not his lackey. Not even his own father.

Most alarming of all, this man certainly is no Winthorp. His voice isn't familiar and this house doesn't smell like any property on the familial grounds.

They took me from the motorcade…

Fire sears through my skull as memories return in snatches. The clearest one is of her face. *Briar.* So beautiful, dominated by that pure, sweet smile. "I want you there," she insisted. "We're sisters, after all."

Sisters. I cherished how that word sounded in her soft cadence, tucking that moment inside myself like one of the trinkets hidden in my secret cache. Love was more precious than a button or rock I'd stolen away. Those four words meant everything. *I want you there.*

But the memory of that moment serves as a weak antidote to the terror paralyzing me now. More bits and pieces come back.

I was in the car—the beautiful limousine for once, instead of one of the servant vans that took up the rear. For part of the way, I was even sitting beside her while she braided my hair. "We look alike now," she wistfully remarked, beaming at our reflections in the polished windows.

We look alike. The phrase haunts me. As if I could ever look like Briar, with her lighter ringlets and her creamy skin. The only feature we truly share is our eyes. Our mother's eyes. Large, round, and blue. In every other respect, she takes after her father, with a beautiful aristocratic nose and a graceful neck. Every Winthorp possesses the same subtle characteristics—markings of the blood, they like to claim. Good blood. Blue blood.

I take after my father, whoever he is.

Briar loves to tout our tentative resemblance anyway—especially to her benefit. *I* am the one the maid saw sneaking out back two summers ago. *I* am the one who scurried out of the room of that visiting businessman one winter.

And now…

We look alike.

"Take off the blindfold." That voice…

I swallow hard, uneasy. Robert has found a new monster to play with. Someone who shares his flair for the dramatic. *But where is he?* My tormentor always relishes this part of the game. How he enjoys savoring my fear as I try to piece together where I am. Admittedly, it wasn't this hard before; he never strays too far from the property.

His favorite lairs are the boathouse, or the deserted crypt, or the east wing. I could always hear the bluebirds chirping throughout the grounds, no matter which corner of the estate he deemed my chosen cell.

My ears strain, searching for that faint, familiar song. This time of year, they're nearly deafening, able to be heard in even the farthest reaches of Winthorp Manor.

Two seconds. Three.

I hear nothing.

"Take off the blindfold."

The harsh rasp of syllables steals my breath away. I know anger on Robert. On Robert Sr. Even on Briar. They stutter. They shout. They scream.

None of them ever exude their impatience to the point where I can sense it in the air. Or taste it: copper on my tongue. This man isn't a Winthorp.

The realization coaxes my body into action. My sore fingers finally contort, trembling after what must have been hours of captivity. Whoever tied my blindfold snagged bits of my hair in the process and every tug on the knot at the base of my neck rips tiny strands loose from my scalp—comparable to my pathetic hopes being ripped from underneath me one by one.

I don't hear the bluebirds.

I can't smell Robert's favorite cologne.

When I finally get the knot loosened enough to uncover my eyes…

I see hell.

Mother used to say it was beautiful, forsaking the teachings of the local priest. "Hell is a rose," she used to murmur, her gaze turned inward, wistful and distant. "A flawless one, with all the life sucked out of it. The thorns have become knives. Its leaves have swallowed up the stalk. It's grotesque. It's deadly. But never forget that, underneath the violence, it's still beautiful."

He is beautiful. Or he was once. Blond hair draws my attention first—a sun-kissed gold in places, darkened with age in others. It's been clawed back from his face into a ponytail longer than mine was before Briar trimmed it. His eyes are that dangerous color between blood and brown. Like a flame, they catch the light filtering in through a sloppily boarded-up window beside him. His face is angular. Chiseled. Stone. Every feature is sculpted to convey just one emotion: determination. The way an owl might watch the mice scurrying underfoot in the stables. Or the way Robert used to look at me.

The way the devil looks, I presume, as if he has all the time in the world. More than ten hours.

An eternity to torture me.

~ Continue Reading XV ~

A WORD FROM THE AUTHOR

Hey there!

Thank you so much for reading! If you enjoyed the story, please leave a review and recommend the book to any friend you think would love this twisted world. You'd have my eternal gratitude. Even a short sentence goes a long way!

Then, come join the rest of us dark romance lovers in my Facebook Group where you can get snippets, sneak peeks of upcoming books and even help vote on aspects of future novels.

Come to the dark side:
https://www.facebook.com/groups/lanasbeautifulmonsters/

WANT MORE STUFF TO READ?
Join my newsletter and get a **free book**! Plus, you get to stay updated with any new releases, random giveaways and exclusive sneak peeks!
https://www.lanaskybooks.com/newsletter

ABOUT THE AUTHOR

Lana Sky is a reclusive writer in the United States who spends most of her time daydreaming about complex male characters and parenting her Cockapoo Joey. She writes dark, twisted romance across several genres. Her titles include everything from mafia romance to vampires.

For more titles by Lana Sky, please visit:

https://www.lanaskybooks.com